PRAISE FOR HELENA HUNTING

KISS MY CUPCAKE

"An absolute delight from start to finish, this delicious enemies-to-lovers romance sees an independent and driven heroine and an equally ambitious hero take a journey to love that is unpredictable and filled with hilarity, a dash of sweetness, and a touch of steam."
                                    —*Library Journal*, starred review

"Light and fluffy with the perfect balance of sweetness and spice, this is a winning confection."

                    —*Publishers Weekly*, starred review

"The hero and heroine's attraction is front and center, the emotional layers are real and earnestly felt, and the hilarious, awkward moments always land with a laugh."   —*Kirkus*

"A feel-good, humorous, easy, and will-make-you-swoon rom-com...an absolute fantastic ride of a story."

                                    —The Nerd Daily

"Helena Hunting's *Kiss My Cupcake* is another delicious romance from a writer who is a master of the genre."

—Popsugar

MEET CUTE

"Perfect for fans of Helen Hoang's *The Kiss Quotient*. A fun and steamy love story with high stakes and plenty of emotion."

—*Kirkus*

"[A] smartly plotted and perfectly executed rom-com with a spot-on sense of snarky wit and a generous helping of smoldering sexual chemistry."

—*Booklist*

"*Meet Cute* is a novel where you will laugh and cry—sometimes on the same page. It is a story of kindness and affection, sassiness and tenderness, where joy and sorrow are intermingled."

—Frolic

THE GOOD LUCK CHARM

"Fabulously fun! Lilah and Ethan's second-chance romance charmed me from the first page to the swoon-worthy end."

—Jill Shalvis, *New York Times* bestselling author

A LOVE CATASTROPHE

HELENA HUNTING

FOREVER

New York Boston

Forever
Hachette Book Group
1290 Avenue of the Americas, New York, NY 10104
read-forever.com
twitter.com/readforeverpub

First Edition: June 2023

Forever is an imprint of Grand Central Publishing. The Forever name and logo are trademarks of Hachette Book Group, Inc.

The publisher is not responsible for websites (or their content) that are not owned by the publisher.

The Hachette Speakers Bureau provides a wide range of authors for speaking events. To find out more, go to hachettespeakersbureau.com or email HachetteSpeakers@hbgusa.com.

Forever books may be purchased in bulk for business, educational, or promotional use. For information, please contact your local bookseller or the Hachette Book Group Special Markets Department at special.markets@hbgusa.com.

Library of Congress Cataloging-in-Publication Data

Names: Hunting, Helena, author.
Title: A love catastrophe / Helena Hunting.
Description: First Edition. | New York ; Boston : Forever, 2023.
Identifiers: LCCN 2022057905 | ISBN 9781538720066 (trade pbk.) | ISBN 9781538720073 (ebook)
Subjects: LCGFT: Novels. | Romance fiction.
Classification: LCC PS3608.U594966 L68 2023 | DDC 813/.6--dc23/eng/20221208
LC record available at https://lccn.loc.gov/2022057905

ISBNs: 9781538720066 (trade pbk.), 9781538720073 (ebook)

Printed in the United States of America

LSC-C

Printing 1, 2023

For kidlet. You inspire me every day with your wonderful creative brain and your endless empathy.

A LOVE CATASTROPHE

chapter one

THE KITTY WHISPERER

Miles

"I can't believe this is real." I stare in mild disbelief at the top trending advertisement on my computer screen for several seconds before I move my cursor to hover over the website name. I'm afraid that what's being advertised and what will pop up when I click the link are two very different things. I squeeze one eye shut and narrow the other, already expecting the worst.

A knock on my office door has me accidentally clicking the link instead of closing the window.

"The Kitty Whisperer?" Thankfully it's not my boss. It's my best friend and colleague, Josh Halpern.

I spin around, eyes wide. "Wanna say that a little louder? I don't think Tom at the end of the hall heard you."

He steps into my office and closes the door, one eyebrow raised as he surveys the space.

It's a small office, but it has a window. The view is of the side of the building next door, but it opens, so that's nice.

And it's better than my last job, where I worked in what we affectionately called the dungeon. Three other guys and I had cubicles in the basement. It was next to the laundry room, and noisy, and sometimes it smelled a bit funky, unless the laundry was on the dryer cycle. Then it was hot, but at least it smelled like dryer sheets.

"Uh, dude, unless you're actively looking to get your ass fired during your first month, you probably shouldn't be checking those sites at work."

"It's a cat-sitting service, not one of *those* sites. And to be clear, I would not willfully use the company server for that kind of browsing."

Josh is the reason I have this job, and I don't want to do anything to make him look bad. Or get myself fired before I even have a chance to prove I'm an asset to the team. We're heading into the regular NHL season, and my role as a data analyst is to run player stats and help inform management when to use players to maximize performance.

"You just gotta be careful, man," he warns. "You're new, and any non-work-related browsing should be limited to nonwork hours. Management is pretty strict about that."

I motion toward the cup of ramen noodles in front of me. "It's my lunch break, so I figured it would be okay."

"Oh. Well, you don't have to eat lunch at your desk."

"I know. I just needed to get this situation managed, so I was killing two birds with one stone."

"What situation is that?" He steps up beside me and leans in closer to get a better look at my screen, his face scrunching in confusion. "Is this for real?"

"It certainly seems that way, yes." The website has an overwhelming number of cat videos. And there's a meowing soundtrack in the background that takes all of five seconds to become grating. I turn down the volume.

"Why are you on this site?" He raises a hand in front of his face as a space cat gif cycles every five seconds. It's a lot. "Dude, can you do something, like click to another screen? I'm getting a headache from all the flashing."

I click on one of the social media icons, navigating away from the website.

"Kitty Hart? A hundred thousand followers? That can't be her real name," Josh mutters. "It must be a gimmick." He steals the mouse from me and clicks on the individual images, apparently no longer concerned about the inappropriate use of my work computer. It's understandable, since this is an alluring albeit strange rabbit hole to fall into. The first picture is a closeup of "Kitty" holding a . . . surprise, surprise . . . kitty. A tiny one with a smooshed-in face.

Kitty—the human—smiles widely at the camera, apparently unconcerned about the awkward angle of the selfie, so we're essentially looking right into the black holes of her nostrils. Regardless, the image has seven thousand likes and nearly four hundred comments, most of which are positive with lots of heart eyes and people telling her they love her.

"Why are you creeping on this woman?"

"I'm not creeping. I need to find a cat sitter."

"But you have a dog," he reminds me, as if I'm unaware that my four-legged friend isn't the psychopathic variety.

"It's my mom's. She's in the hospital, and we're heading to Montreal tomorrow night, so I need to find someone to look after the little gremlin while we're gone." My mother has been relentlessly asking the hospital staff about Prince Francis and messages me almost hourly for updates.

"She's still there?" Josh drops down into the chair across from me. "I thought she'd be out by now and that they were just checking her over. Is everything okay?"

Josh and I have been friends since middle school, and he's very aware of my family history. "I figured she'd be out in a couple of days, but the doctors are running some tests and think there's more going on and that she wasn't sleepwalking or whatever." I rub my temple, feeling the pressure there. Three days ago, the police picked up my mom after she was found wandering around in her pajamas and a pair of slippers in the middle of the night. When she couldn't tell them where she lived, they brought her to the hospital, thinking maybe she'd been on some kind of drug or something.

"Why didn't you tell me this until now? Can I do anything to help?"

I normally see my mom on birthdays and major holidays. Any other time I ever tried to stop by for a visit, she would cancel, or forget, or reschedule and forget again.

I message her regularly and call, but she has a habit of making me feel like crap for not calling more. Doesn't matter if it's weekly or monthly or every other day; she would make it seem like I hadn't reached out in an eternity. Over the past year, my text messages and calls would often go unanswered for days, or sometimes longer. But now I'm starting to see that maybe it wasn't her being passive-aggressive.

And since she's been in the hospital, I'm fielding countless messages and several calls a day from her. "I talked to a doctor a couple of hours ago. They want to keep her for more tests. I'm still getting my head around it."

In addition to the stress of my mother's hospital stay, we had a team meeting this morning where the general manager announced that I would be traveling with them to some of the games. Which is great, because it means I'll have more opportunities to prove the value of my role. But it's unexpected, an added layer of complication, since it means I can't be here to deal with my mother, and I need a dog sitter. The owner of the team is old-school and is on the fence about having me on board. Josh is the one who pushed for them to give me a chance, so I want to make sure I don't let him down, or the team.

It's a lot. I can't afford to take time off to deal with my mom, not at this point in the season, anyway.

"Right. Yeah. Does your mom have any friends you can ask to help with the cat?" He taps on the arm of the chair.

I flip a pen between my fingers. "There are a couple of neighbors, but the only one who might be capable of helping is on some six-week cruise, so that's out. And I'm sure as hell not bringing the thing back to my place." I can only imagine the stress it would cause my dog, Wilfred. He's a Dane, but he seems to think he's a teacup poodle with the way he's always trying to sit in my lap. Plus, based on how much my mother's cat doesn't like people, I don't think I'm going out on a limb in assuming he's not great with other animals.

"Yeah, I don't know how Wilfred would react to a cat. They can be territorial. So a sitter it is, then." Josh glances at the computer screen again.

"Apparently this woman is top rated on all the websites in the area as the best kitty whisperer out there." Whatever the hell a kitty whisperer is.

"Say that again."

"Say what again?"

He tips his chin up and smirks. "You know what."

I roll my eyes but smile. I can deal with stupid jokes a lot better than I can deal with what's going on with my mother and her cat situation.

"She has to know how that sounds. I mean, how can she not?" Josh says.

"Well, I'm about to call her to find out if she's legit." I pick up my cell and unlock the screen.

Josh rolls his chair closer, pushing me over a couple of feet so he can scroll her feed while I dial her number, set my phone to speaker, and listen to it ring.

She picks up on the second one. "Kitty Hart, the Kitty

Whisperer. Please hold!" Her voice somehow manages to be sultry and upbeat at the same time.

"I just—"

"You are the handsomest man in the universe! Are you going to show me your belly? Oh yes, you are!"

She sounds like she should be a jazz lounge singer with the slight rasp and the somewhat singsongy tone she uses. I look at Josh, but her voice doesn't seem to affect him in the same way, considering he's silently laughing so hard he's about to fall off his chair, so I focus my attention elsewhere.

"Who's my favorite boy? Do you want a treat?" Something jingles on the other end of the line.

"Uh, miss?" I have no idea what's happening right now.

"Just one second, please!" she calls out. "You need to ask for it nicely."

I can't decide if she's intentionally trying to sound seductive or what. A muffled meow follows and the sounds of a digital voice, but I can't make out what it's saying.

The woman's voice drops a couple of octaves. "Such a good boy. Oh! Listen to that motor run!"

Josh makes a cut motion across his throat and reaches for my phone.

"Okay! Sorry about that! I was in the middle of a training session. How can I help you?"

I swat his hand away and accidentally knock my phone off the desk in the process.

"Hello?" she calls from under my desk.

"Fuck," I mutter as I try to reach it.

"If you're just going to swear at me and breathe into the phone, I'm hanging up on you."

"I wonder how often that happens," Josh mutters.

I punch him in the back of the calf and manage to nab my phone. Just because I thought the same thing doesn't mean I can afford to lose this potential contact. "No! Please don't hang up!" I try to back out from under my desk and smack my head on the keyboard tray. "Ow! Shit. Sorry. I dropped my phone and now it's covered in dust bunnies and I bashed my head on the edge of my desk trying to reach it. Don't hang up, please."

"Oh no! Are you okay?" She sounds genuinely concerned.

"I'm fine." I manage to get myself out from under the desk, no thanks to Josh, who's busy massaging the back of his leg while also grinning.

"That's good. Dust bunnies aren't nearly as cute as the real thing, are they, sweet little Misery? And wouldn't you just love to chase one? Yes, you would! But you're an indoor kitty, aren't you?" She coos some more and then makes a sound that could be a sneeze, but I can't be sure. "How can I help you, Mister . . . " It takes me a moment to realize she's not talking to the cat anymore, but to me.

"Is that cat's name Misery?"

"It is, and his brother's name is Company. Misery loves Company. And it's very true. Misery loves to hump poor Company any chance he gets. Don't you, you frisky boy?" It's followed by more cooing and Josh cough-laughing into his sleeve.

I silently threaten him with violence, and he manages to get himself under control again. Not that my threat has any real impact. Josh is built like a freight train, and I'm built more like...a more muscular upgraded version of Gumby.

"Hello? Are you still there?"

"Yeah. Yup. Still here."

"I don't think I got your name." There she goes again with the sultry tone.

"Miles." I clear my throat. "Miles Thorn."

"Hi, Miles Thorn. I'm Kitty Hart, the Kitty Whisperer. I'm here to help with all your feline needs and questions. What can I do for you today?"

There is no way a human being can be this upbeat. I glance at the computer screen where Kitty Hart smiles back at me while dressed in a leopard-print cardigan, matching glasses, and a shirt that reads I'M A CAT PERSON. Or maybe it is possible.

"I uh, I need someone to watch my mother's cat while I'm away."

"Would you require the overnight service, or just the daily drop-in, feeding, and kitty love package?"

Josh makes a lewd gesture, and I spin around in my chair so I can't see his face. "The kitty love—I mean the second option. Just drop-ins and feedings. I don't know about the love part." I scrub a hand over my face, take the phone off speaker and bringing it to my ear. Josh's muffled laughter in the background isn't helpful. This is the weirdest conversation I've ever had in my life, and that's saying something, because over the past few days I've had some pretty freaking weird conversations with my mother.

"All kitties need love, isn't that right, Misery? Yes, it is!"

"This one is...not the friendliest." And I'm starting to question what exactly I'm signing on for. But the team leaves tomorrow evening, and with this job being so new, I can't ask for time off to take care of a freaking cat. I could try a kennel, or whatever the cat version of that is, but I'd have to be able to catch Prince Francis, and so far all my attempts have left me are a bunch of scratches. The last thing I need is tetanus to round out my super-shitty week.

"Hmm. Well, I'll just have to meet him or her and find out if that's true, won't I? Where are you and your kitty located? What dates will you need care for your feline friend?" she asks.

"Just west of Toronto, in Terra Cotta, and I'll be away from Thursday to Sunday."

"Oh! That's a lovely location, and within my service area. Let me check my schedule." It sounds like she hits the wrong button a couple of times.

I glance over my shoulder at Josh, who is now sitting in front of my desk, clicking on pictures of the Kitty Whisperer and scrolling through the comments.

"Okay! It looks like you're in luck. I can definitely help. Would you be free this evening at six so I can meet the feline and get a sense of what they're going to need while you're away with your mother? Which, by the way, is very sweet."

"Uh, that's, uh..." I don't know what to say, so I stumble over my words and avoid correcting her. "I can meet you at six."

"Excellent. Why don't you text me the address? Oh, and what's the kitty's name?"

"It's Prince Francis," I half mumble.

"How regal! I look forward to meeting Prince Francis tonight then! Have a wonderful afternoon, Miles. Meow for now!" And with that she hangs up.

chapter two

ROYALLY HISSED

Kitty

Don't do it! Don't you do it, Mr. Munchies!" I'm on the other side of the room, with a good twelve feet separating us. I can't move fast enough to grab him before he knocks the vase of fresh flowers off the mantel, but I have other ways to deal with mischievous kitties.

His white-and-orange paw is raised in the air, little toe beans twitching. My hand is in my pocket, finger on the trigger. I need to be quicker on the draw than he is on the paw. I pull the baby-blue squirt gun free from my pocket, grateful that it doesn't get caught on the inside of my cardigan this time. His eyes round and he rears back slightly as I close one eye and take aim and hit him directly in the face with the stream of cold water.

He yowls angrily and leaps off the mantel, knocking over a picture frame in the process, his tail swatting the vase, which teeters precariously for several terrifying seconds before it stills. I exhale a relieved breath and then groan at the sound of something crashing to the floor in the other room.

Most of the time I love my job, but dealing with cats who behave like wild teenagers is not my favorite. Although they're often the same level of herdable.

I rush through the living room to the kitchen and suck in a horrified breath as I spot Hogwarts on the floor, pieces scattered all over the place. One of Mr. Munchies's humans, Jeff, is a huge Lego fan. When he's had a particularly difficult day, he comes home and unwinds by building something. Over the past several weeks he's been working on Hogwarts. It's quite detailed, with several buildings. The entire kitchen table is occupied by the project. Except now Hufflepuff's dorm is no more.

I spot Mr. Munchies on the other side of the room, hiding behind the garbage can. I take aim, but he's too fast, rushing off down the hall in a bid to escape the stream of water I've just shot at him. It misses, hitting the wall instead.

I sigh and slip the water gun back in my pocket, then check the time. I have half an hour to clean up this mess and drive across town to meet my potential new kitty and his human caretaker.

As I bend and start pushing the scattered Legos into a pile, my knee hits the floor, and a tiny plastic piece bites into the skin. Three more times I accidentally step on the camouflaged pieces and yelp in pain. I'm used to being scratched, and even bitten on occasion, but stepping on Legos is its own brand of torture.

Mr. Munchies makes another appearance, and when he's sure I'm not going to spray him again, he rubs himself on my legs, meowing his apology for knocking over the Lego creation and causing me pain with all the Lego shrapnel. He steps on a piece, too, then does a donkey kick to unstick it from his paw. Once it's free, he drops down on his butt, flops onto his side, splays his toe beans, gives them a lick, and then goes to work on his privates.

"Mr. Munchies, your manners are the worst." I poke him in the side, and he lifts his head long enough to give me a disgruntled look, as if it's my fault I'm cleaning up Legos while he's in the middle of washing his furry nuts.

It's hard to stay mad at him, though. This is his way of telling me he wants attention and that he doesn't like being left alone. I get it. Loneliness and boredom are two emotions I'm not fond of either. Although, with cats like Mr. Munchies to take care of, I'm rarely bored. Lonely is different, because we can be surrounded by people or pets we love and still experience that hollow ache sometimes.

Once the Lego pieces are back on the table, I email Jeff to tell him about the mishap and that I hope I got all the pieces. I leave two small spray bottles on the edge of the kitchen table to deter Mr. Munchies from jumping back up, give him a few extra pets, and feed him dinner. But I forgo the treats because of his naughty behavior and then lock up behind me.

I've only been caring for Mr. Munchies for a few weeks, so he's a work in progress. He's getting better, but it's a slow process.

The neighborhood he lives in is upscale, with big houses and driveways with interlocking stone and manicured gardens tended by landscapers. A couple of the neighborhood kids are riding by on their bikes. They both raise their hands in a quick wave as they head toward the park. The woman who lives next door to Mr. Munchies pulls into her driveway. I suppress an eye roll as she gets out of her Mercedes SUV. She's always dressed like she's going to a funeral, and her mood seems to match.

She opens the back door as Rufus, her black Lab, jumps out. He bounds through her garden and across Mr. Munchies's driveway, tongue lolling, tail wagging, barking excitedly as he approaches me.

"Rufus! Come back here! Rufus! Come back!" his human screeches.

Rufus doesn't heed her command. This isn't new. But before he can jump up on me, I hold out a hand. "No jumping, Rufus!"

He comes to a halt, but stands up on his hind legs, then bounces three times, like he's doing his best Tigger impersonation.

"Sit, Rufus," I command.

And he does. I fight to suppress my grin, because I'm aware that my ability to get this dog to listen to me drives his human up the wall.

I might be a cat person, but I love all four-legged creatures. Except the ones who look at me like I'm a decent meal.

"Good boy, Rufus. Good boy." I scratch behind his ear while his tail thumps against the ground. "Who's a happy boy?" I ask him.

His human stalks down her driveway, heels clipping angrily as she traverses the sidewalk and continues to strut toward me and Rufus. "I don't know why he never listens to me." She grabs Rufus by the collar. "Come on, let's get inside."

I could tell her why, but the last time I offered her advice she nearly bit my head off, so I smile and shrug.

She yanks once, twice, a third time, but Rufus's butt stays firmly planted on the driveway.

"Come on, Rufus!" Her face is turning red.

I take a step back to give her and Rufus some space, and of course he follows me. Likely because he can smell the treats in my pocket. Eventually she gets him to leave, but he's reluctant. He stops and plants his butt on the sidewalk three times before she successfully moves him from the driveway I'm standing in to hers. And he barks the entire way.

When I get to my SUV, I punch the new address into my GPS and check the time. It's a twenty-two-minute drive, which means I'll arrive shortly after six. I hate being late, especially for an introductory meeting with a potential new client. It sets a bad precedent.

I send Mr. Thorn a quick message to let him know and go on my way. Luck and the lights are on my side, and I manage to make it to the new house at six on the dot. Not early, but not late either. The neighborhood is older and more established, with modest houses. The streets are lined with mature trees, the sidewalks cracked in places. The yards vary: some have lovely gardens, and others are dominated by weeds. One house has fake lawn turf instead of real grass. I would hazard a guess that an elderly person lives there.

I pull up in front of an older, slightly run-down backsplit. The shutters look as though they once were dark blue, but they have faded to a murky blue-gray. The white siding is slightly yellowed. The front gardens need a good weeding, and the driveway is cracked and pitted in places. A gold Buick that's at least a decade old is parked in the driveway.

It makes me curious about the person who lives here, and whether this Miles person researched my rates before he called. I'm competitively priced, but talking about money is one of my least favorite parts of this job. Not because I don't think what I do is valuable, but some people don't understand how I can earn a living taking care of other people's cats. Often those people are dog people. They can defend dog walkers, but they can't comprehend that cats need just as much human companionship as their more dependent four-legged counterparts.

A sleek black car passes me and pulls into the driveway. It's a nice car. Probably expensive. I glance at my reflection in the rearview mirror, checking to make sure my hair isn't a complete wreck since I was driving with the windows down.

I grab the lint roller from the seat beside me, give my cardigan and chest a quick roll, cut the engine, take a deep breath, and give myself a pep talk. "You can people today, Kitty. Humans and cats aren't that different. Smile, be friendly, and don't bite." I roll my eyes at myself. I'm much better with animals than I am with humans. Animals don't have conversational expectations the way humans do. But I can deal with people in small doses. And I'm successfully running my own business where I converse with clients regularly, so clearly I'm not *that* terrible with the whole social thing.

I round the hood of my SUV as a man opens the driver's side door. His foot hits the paved driveway. The first thing I notice are his black polished shoes. The second are the socks covered in a bone and paw print. *Dog person?* Then the black dress pants. I allow my gaze to climb as he steps out of the car, rising with his lean frame.

His attention is on the phone in his hand, which gives me the opportunity to do a thorough visual assessment. And I embrace that opportunity with enthusiasm.

He's wearing a pale blue button-down and a tie with what looks like a binary code pattern on it. His jaw is angular, his lips full, his nose straight. He's wearing black-rimmed glasses, his dark hair is parted at the side and styled with purpose. My mouth goes dry as I put together the individual components and create a whole picture.

Miles Thorn is exceptionally good-looking. The kind of good-looking that makes me think of Hallmark movies, or bumping into someone and accidentally on purpose dropping everything in my hands just to have an excuse to stage an introduction.

"Hi! You must be—"

He doesn't even spare me a glance as he cuts me off by raising a single finger. Then he turns away so his back is mostly to me and raises his phone to his mouth. "I'm meeting with a cat sitter right now. I'll message when I'm done. Shouldn't be long."

I'm so busy being disappointed that he's ruined his attractiveness by being horribly rude that I don't pay attention to where my feet are going. My toe catches on the curb, and I stumble forward.

I lose the battle with gravity and go sprawling across the driveway. My purse flies out of my hand, and because I never zip it up, the contents scatter.

"Shit. Are you okay?" Polished black shoes appear beside me, and then two strong hands slide under my arms, lifting me back to my feet.

And now I'm back to finding him attractive. "I'm fine. Thank you. Embarrassed, but fine." Heat climbs my neck and settles in my cheeks.

"What the hell happened?" He glances around as if he's expecting someone to have been responsible for my clumsiness.

"I didn't see the curb." I touch my temple and realize my glasses are no longer on my face. Without them my vision isn't the best. Not so bad that I can't see someone standing in front of me, but bad enough that I can't read road signs. "I lost my glasses."

"I see them." He sidesteps me and bends to pick them up.

Instead of handing them over, though, he brings them up as though he's going to place them on my face like my eye doctor used to do when I was a kid. I startle and he ends up poking me in the cheek with one of the arms.

"I don't know why I did that. Here." He shakes his head and thrusts them at me.

Our fingertips graze with the handoff. It's innocent contact, fraught with my embarrassment and his, but even with how mortified I am, warmth, not from mortification this time, spreads through my limbs and settles awkwardly in the pit of my stomach.

Do not get butterflies over a cute guy with questionable manners, Kitty.

I manage to get my glasses back on without poking out my own eyeball or bursting into flames, which I'm considering a win. There are new scratches on the right lens, but a bit of buffing should take care of it.

He checks his phone again, while asking, "You're not going to sue me or anything, are you?"

"I'm sorry, what?"

He shoves his phone in his pocket. His cheeks, which are high and sharp, are tinged pink. "Nothing. Sorry. It's been a day. You're okay?"

"Fairly embarrassed and feeling like this is an introduction I wish I could erase and try again, but otherwise fine." I extend a hand, wishing my mouth knew when to take a break with the awkward words and hoping we can start fresh with a handshake. "I'm Kitty Hart, owner of the Kitty Whisperer, cat care and training services. You must be Miles Thorn."

He stares at my hand for a few seconds before he wraps his around mine. He has long fingers with neatly filed nails. There's a mark of pen on his thumb. "You can just call me Miles."

But it's the strange hum that seems to run up my arm and then ping its way through the rest of my body that makes my brain cells turn off for a moment and my hormones fire up like a furnace on full blast. It's also the reason my voice gets all husky when I say, "Hi, Miles."

He smirks, like maybe he realizes he's having this effect on me, and says, in the same husky tone, "Hi, Kitty."

I let go of his hand and put some space between us. "I should pick up all this stuff and then meet Prince Francis." I crouch and start gathering the items my purse vomited all over the driveway, like a drunk college kid after a night out on the town.

Miles stands there for a few seconds, watching, before he shoves his glasses up his nose and mutters, "Let me help."

I can't tell if he's equally as awkward as me, or rude, or just…socially inept. I've always been what people call quirky, which is basically a nice way of saying I'm weird. I'm aware that driving around in an SUV that looks like a cat with the Kitty Whisperer advertised on the side is atypical. And I embrace that side of my personality. Why be beige when you can be a calico?

I shift and nab the tampons before Miles has a chance to.

"Wow, you have a lot of pens." He gathers an entire handful. "And lip balms."

"Your lips can never be too soft!" I say, then immediately wish I could drop those words down the closest sewer grate.

He gives me that smirky grin again, while tipping his head to the side, as if the smile weighs his head down. "Hmm." He flips the lip balm between his fingers and holds it up. It advertises a book by one of my favorite authors. "I've never seen lip balm like this before. Is it man flavored?"

I snatch it from him and jam it back in my purse, feeling my face heat again. I can't tell if he's poking fun or not. "It's swag from a book convention I went to."

"They give out lip balms with half-naked dudes on them at book conventions?"

"The romance ones, yes." I push my glasses up the bridge of my nose and grab the packet of tissues that fell out, and a used one I need to toss in the garbage.

"There are book conventions specifically for romance?"

"There are. Thousands of people attend them." And now I sound defensive.

"Huh. I had no idea." He passes over the mitt full of pens, most of which are also from the author convention I attended a few months ago with my sister, Hattie.

Once the driveway is clear and my purse is full again, I fall into step beside Miles as we head for the front door.

The porch is small, with a single rocking chair and a tiny bistro table. A wilted plant sits on top of it, looking like it's in need of a serious drink.

Miles unlocks the door, but pauses before he opens it. "Just so you're aware, my mom is a bit of a hoarder, and I haven't had a chance to tidy up."

"Don't worry." I smile in what I hope is reassurance. "I take care of cats for all types of humans."

He nods and turns the knob, carefully opening the door. He steps inside first, flips on the hall light, then motions me inside.

"You can keep your shoes on," he tells me when I start to toe off my Bobs.

"I don't mind."

"It's safer. My mother's cat is a destructive little shit." His tone does not imply affection.

"I see." I try not to judge him for the derogatory way he

refers to the cat. They're only badly behaved when they're in need of attention. I'm surprised when he doesn't announce our arrival. "Will I be meeting your mother today as well as our feline friend?"

He moves away from the door, making more room for me to step inside the hall. The front entryway is narrow, and a small closet to the right is stuffed full of jackets and shoes. To the left is a narrow sideboard piled high with mail, magazines, and newspapers that have spilled over onto the floor. The name on the envelope reads Tabitha Thorn, who I'm assuming is his mother.

Miles shakes his head. "She's in the hospital."

"Oh my gosh. I'm so sorry." I reach out and put a hand on his forearm, then retract it immediately, because I don't know him well enough to randomly touch him. "I didn't realize."

"I didn't say anything over the phone because there was no good way to phrase it, so I just left it out. And she's okay, but there's a solid chance she might need more care than she can get living here." He waves in the direction of the living room.

And now I feel awful for bringing it up. Maybe he's being nice by saying it's okay. Maybe it's the opposite of okay, and now I'm making things more uncomfortable. Maybe this explains why he's been so rude. "That must be difficult." I try to think of something else to say, but my brain seems to have lost the ability to form thoughts and put them into words of comfort.

He clears his throat. "It's life. I'll get it sorted out. Why don't I introduce you to the resident demon so we can get this wrapped up? I've got a game to watch tonight."

Or maybe he's a completely heartless jerk. His mom is in the hospital, and he's more worried about catching some game than he is anything else. And that's the second time he's referred to Prince Francis with disdain. It's clearly not meant as a term of endearment. I'm trying to be understanding, but his impatience and tone aren't particularly reassuring.

I follow him down the narrow hall, past a set of stairs leading up to what I assume are the bedrooms—they too are half covered in magazines and small boxes. We make a right, and I suck in a gasp as I take in the living room.

"As you can see, I wasn't lying about the hoarding." Miles tips his chin toward the very busy living room and stuffs his hand in his pants pocket.

I take in the room, my gaze skipping over the sideboard to the right. It's full of those porcelain-headed dolls from the early nineteenth century, and their eyes follow me wherever I go. I suppress a shudder as I take a small step forward and absorb the rest of the room. There are two huge floor-to-ceiling shelving units on the other side of the room. They're filled with knickknacks and framed photos. Between them is a gas fireplace. The mantel houses a plethora of gnomes, spanning every holiday. There are Christmas and Easter gnomes, spring and summer gnomes, one whose hat is decorated in a Canadian flag pattern. There's even a Halloween gnome.

And then I spot him. The non-gnome amid the gaggle of stuffed, bearded men.

I reach out and grab Miles's arm. I don't know why, apart

from the fact that I'm irrationally excited over the discovery I've made. This is like finding a poster of your favorite band at a garage sale.

In my excitement, I squeeze his forearm and am pleasantly surprised by the firmness. I must enjoy it a few seconds too long, because his gaze shifts to where I'm kneading his arm. I hastily release him. "You didn't tell me Prince Francis is a sphynx."

"Huh?" Miles seems confused.

"Prince Francis is a sphynx cat. Hairless."

"Oh, yeah." Miles rubs his forearm absently and sniffs.

I tentatively take a step toward Prince Francis, who regards me warily from his perch on top of the mantel. His forehead wrinkles and his nose twitches. "Hello, handsome, aren't you just as majestic as your name implies," I croon.

"He looks like a shaved ball sack with eyes," Miles mutters.

My head whips around. "What a terrible thing to say! He's beautiful."

He gives me a disbelieving look. "He's the cat equivalent of one of those house elf things from Harry Potter."

Oh, Miles is definitely one of *those* humans. The animal lover who can only appreciate the furry friend who believes the sun rises and sets on him. I tamp down the urge to give the man a piece of my mind. His mother is in the hospital. People deal with that kind of stress differently. But it doesn't negate the fact that all animals need love.

When we hear a low thud, we simultaneously look toward the mantel and watch the sunflower gnome tumble to the floor.

Prince Francis licks his paw and yawns loudly.

I give the kitty an unimpressed look. "Prince Francis, that's not nice." I take another step forward and notice the floor around the shelving units is littered with casualties. Not all of them have survived their swan dive in one piece.

Prince Francis tips his head and makes a noise, somewhere between a meow and a squeak. I tip my head as well and slip my hand in my pocket. The water gun is still in there.

"Stay very still," I warn.

"Are you talking to me or the gremlin?" Miles asks.

I frown. I'm losing count of all the insults Miles has lobbed at Prince Francis since we set foot in this house. He's not a cat person. At all.

"I'm talking to you."

Prince Francis raises a paw and bats at the gnome next to him. A tap. A test.

"Prince Francis," I warn.

When he raises his paw again, I withdraw the water gun.

"What the hell?"

Before I can take aim, I'm tackled to the floor.

chapter three

DON'T ATTACK THE KITTY WHISPERER

Miles

Before I consider my actions, I launch myself at Kitty and take her to the ground. It's been a hell of a week already and it's only Tuesday. The last thing I want to explain to my mother—whose mind seems to be failing her at a rate that's difficult to fathom—is that her precious Prince Francis is no more because the cat lady I hired to babysit him shot him. For knocking a gnome off the fireplace mantel.

"What's wrong with you? You can't shoot the fucking gremlin!" I shout.

I end up on the floor with Kitty, my body covering her much smaller, softer one. Her thick, wavy auburn hair is in my mouth. Her body is under mine.

She raises the hand holding the weapon, and I nab it from her while she sputters from under her hair and me. "What the heck! It's a water gun."

Realization dawns and horror slowly seeps in as I fully process the fact that I've tackled a woman to the ground.

I roll off her and pop back to my feet, glancing down at the baby-blue water gun in my hand. It's leaking on the floor, the stopper having popped free. I'm missing the net, as far as first impressions go. It could also be considered assault.

As I'm about to speak, the cat yowls loudly. He launches himself off the mantel, lands on the coffee table, skids across several magazines, hits the floor, and rushes down the hall.

This introduction is not going great. "How was I supposed to know it was a water gun?" I replace the stopper and toss it on the couch before I turn back to her and belatedly extend a hand.

She glares at me and ignores my offer of help, using the edge of the coffee table to get to her feet instead. "It's baby blue!"

"Handguns can be baby blue. My great-aunt Gerdie won one at a fair when I was kid." It's not the best color for a handgun. A little too enticing for kids, as far as I'm concerned, but Great-Aunt Gerdie thought it was very fashionable.

"A baby-blue handgun? That's…" Kitty looks appropriately appalled by this revelation, but she bites back whatever opinion she might have. "Why in the world would you think I'd bring an actual gun to a kitty care introduction? How in the meow would I be able to run a successful business if I went around pulling firearms out of my pocket every time a cat misbehaved?"

I can't decide if I heard that incorrectly or not. "I don't know. The whole pulling any kind of gun was unexpected." I run a hand through my hair and notice that she's once again missing her glasses. And my horror is compounded when I notice that aside from the pink hue to her cheeks, she also has rug burn on the right one. I couldn't make a worse impression if I tried. And I really need to get home so I can watch the game and take notes because Coach Davis is concerned about Parker, our rookie player, and we're playing against Ottawa next week.

Parker O'Toole started with the team only this season, but he's already showing a lot of promise. He grew up not far from where my family used to spend the summers on the lake. He's a small-town transplant, and the big-city life is a whole lot of culture shock. We've already bonded over our mutual love of the butter tart shop in his hometown and ATV trailblazing in the summer and snowmobiling in the winter.

But Parker's game performance needs to take a back seat, because I can't afford to lose this cat sitter. I don't have time to find another one. She's still staring at me with something between disbelief and irritation. Her eyes are huge and wide and a deep, rich, forest green. Her hair, which was already wavy and voluminous, is now a wild mess, thanks to me attacking her.

Her top lip is thin and bowed, her bottom one full and pouty. Her nose is small and cute, her chin narrow. Her face is almost heart shaped. She's curvy and soft, and I should not be noticing any of these things right now, because I just tackled her. Checking her out makes me creepy on top of being a grade-A jerk.

"Look at me!" She motions to her rumpled shirt with THE

KITTY WHISPERER written across her chest and her leopard-print cardigan. "I love cats! Why in the world would you think I'd *shoot* one?"

She makes a good point, not that I'm willing to admit it aloud. "Well, you *were* actually planning to shoot him."

"With freaking water!" She points to the still-leaking water gun sitting on the couch. It's very much a glaring beacon for my idiocy in all its baby-blue glory.

"I'm still not wrong." I don't know why I'm so committed to being a giant d-bag, other than I don't want to be here and I don't have time for this or my mother's pain-in-the-ass cat.

She makes a noise that sounds somewhere between incredulity and frustration. Then drops to her knees again, searching under the table for her glasses. Which I knocked off her face. When I tackled her to the floor.

"Sorry," I mutter belatedly.

She grunts and almost bangs her head on the table, nearly knocking over one of the many otter figurines covering the surface, but they teeter back into place. Unfortunately.

Kitty stands and replaces her glasses, adjusting them so they sit straight, and touches her hair before smoothing out her top.

This intro could've gone a whole lot smoother. "I shouldn't have tackled you."

"Next time I'll issue a water gun warning." She rubs her elbow.

I knead the back of my neck, trying to figure out a way back to her good side. Maybe honesty will do the trick. "I have a dog. I don't really get cats."

She purses her lips, but slowly arranges her mouth into a stiff smile. "I figured you were a dog person. Cats are different."

"They're furry little psychopaths—or in this case, a naked one." I'm awarded with a raised eyebrow.

I should probably shut the hell up. I stuff my hands in my pockets, unsure what to do with them. Josh would be laughing his ass off if he could see me now. I'm notoriously not smooth with the ladies. See me tackling this one for details.

"They're independent, not psychopaths. And they pick up on negative energy, which would explain why he's hiding from you. Should I assume he's generally skittish when you're around?"

I blow out a breath, working to find some patience, and maybe a side of manners. "I haven't had enough contact to be able to answer that." I've only just met this woman, and I need her to take care of this furless nightmare. Telling her I haven't seen my mother since I dropped flowers off on Mother's Day probably isn't going to win me any points. In fact, it only adds to my d-bag status.

She nods, not pressing further. "Do you know where your mother keeps Prince Francis's treats? It might help if we can entice him with something he loves rather than continue to insult him."

"Probably in the kitchen." I found his food in the pantry, so I'm hoping the treats are close by.

I lead her through the living room, motioning to the broken trinkets as we skirt around them. "I didn't have time to stop in yesterday, so I'm thinking he was pretty mad about that."

"How long has your mom been in the hospital?" Kitty's voice is soft and raspy, as though she needs to clear her throat.

"A few days. The doctors think she might have early-onset dementia." Which is something they told me a couple of hours ago when I stopped at the hospital before coming here. It reframes a lot of our conversations over the past year. Now I'm beginning to realize she honestly didn't remember the calls or the visits. And that makes me feel even shittier. "I don't know how long she's going to be there, to be honest, and I live in the city, so driving back and forth all the time isn't always reasonable, and sometimes I travel for work." And so far, all my interactions with Prince Francis have been less than pleasant, so covering more than the basics hasn't been high on my priority list.

"Right. You said you have a trip coming up."

I nod. This is better. If I can stick to facts maybe I can also be less of a jerk. "I'm only gone for a couple of days, but trying to juggle work and my mother in the hospital and her cat is a lot. Which is why I called you."

She's lost a bit of that stiff edge, and her expression turns sympathetic. "That's a lot of stress."

All I've done so far is dump a container of cat food into the bowl when I stop by, clean up whatever crap Prince Francis has tossed on the floor, and then drive home. And I've only done that twice. This being the second time.

Based on her website and social media, Kitty seems to be dedicated to taking care of other people's cats, so hopefully she's better at managing Prince Francis than I am.

I open the pantry door and turn my head away, raising my arm so I can sneeze into my elbow. "Freakin' allergies."

"Bless you," Kitty mutters.

I drop my arm and cringe at the sheer volume of food my mother keeps on hand. She lives alone, so there's absolutely no reason for her to have six boxes of cornflakes or ten jars of peanut butter, half of which are probably expired. Until a couple hours ago, I believed it was because of her compulsive sale shopping, but maybe she doesn't remember what she has in the pantry, so she overstocks. This place needs a deep clean, that's for sure. I don't know when I'm going to have the time to do that. And being in this house isn't exactly pleasant. The memories I have of living here aren't great.

"Ahh, here we go." Kitty brushes by me, the brief contact pulling me out of my head and my unwanted trip down memory lane. She picks up a package of dry treats and two different cans of cat food. "Do we know which one is Prince Francis's favorite flavor?"

I shrug. "Isn't it all the same stinky shit?"

She rolls her eyes. "No. It's not all the same stinky shit. Just like some people prefer beef over chicken or seafood, so do cats. You could try asking your mother."

"Yeah, sure. I can do that." She seems to remember she has a cat without a problem, but I have no idea if she'll be able to identify his favorite kind of food.

"We'll give this one a try and see how he responds." She returns one of the cans to the shelf and brushes by me, the smell of her perfume or body wash lingering as she passes. I close the pantry door and follow her back to the kitchen. I learned the hard way that when the door is open, Prince Francis has access to anything that's in a paper bag. He chewed a hole through the dry food and gorged until he puked the other day. There were barely chewed kitty kibble puke snakes all over the kitchen floor.

Kitty shakes the container of treats, and a few seconds later Prince Francis's bald head appears. Kitty tosses a couple treats in Prince Francis's direction and makes a tutting sound. Slowly, over the course of a few minutes, Prince Francis makes his way across the kitchen toward her.

I check my phone for new messages. The game has already started, and the GM is blowing up my phone with messages about strategy and pulling numbers for tomorrow. "Be careful," I warn absently. "He's not the friendliest."

"He probably senses your dislike for him." She keeps her attention on the cat as he prowls closer.

I don't argue, because she's undoubtedly right. Instead, I message the GM and tell him I'm not home but I'm recording the game and I'll message as soon as I'm free.

When I finally glance up from my phone Prince Francis is stretched out on the floor beside Kitty with his head half in her lap, kneading the air.

"Oh, look at you, what a handsome boy you are! What a beautiful pink belly you have!" she exclaims.

I lean against the doorjamb and watch this grown woman cooing at the ugliest cat in the history of the world, telling him how handsome he is and how much he must miss his human. She's an odd one, that's for sure. She's also pretty in an unconventional way. Not that it matters what she looks like. Prince Francis just wants food at regular intervals.

Eventually she gives him half a can of food, which he devours in less than two minutes, and then he climbs into her lap and puts his paws on her shoulders. She stands, holding Prince Francis like a baby. He purrs contentedly and rubs his head against her chin, then tries to stuff his head down the front of her shirt.

"Prince Francis, dude, that's harassment. You can't do that if you want Kitty to come back." I'm not sure I have a right to scold him since I tackled her like a football player, but I really do need her help. He clearly has no intention of listening to me, because it looks like he's trying to climb right inside her shirt. "Do you want me to shoot him with the water gun?" I think it's still in the living room.

That earns me another eye roll. "No, you don't need to shoot him." She shoves her own hand down the front of her shirt and a few seconds later produces a kitty treat. "Ah, there we go." She lets Prince Francis eat it out of her hand. "Hazard of the job."

This is so weird. "I, uh, need to clean up the mess he's made. It's probably better if I do that while he's occupied." Also, I feel like me talking less is better.

"Go ahead. I'll just get some snuggle time in with the little Prince. We definitely don't want all those broken trinkets on the floor, where they can cut his toe beans."

"Toe beans?"

"The pads of his feet." She crosses over to the lounger, which has been around since I was a kid, and she sinks down. Literally. It seems like the springs have gone in the seat cushion. She doesn't complain, though. Just lets Prince Francis knead her legs until they're tenderized enough that he can curl up in a ball in her lap.

I quickly sweep up broken knickknacks, sneezing, occasionally checking on the game and my messages from the GM between trips to the garbage can. I toss a bunch of the stuff on the side tables into a box to prevent more issues in the future. I need a weekend to go through the place, but that's not going to happen until I'm back from my trip. Hopefully with Kitty around to help, there will be less tossing stuff off shelves.

By the time I'm done, Prince Francis has wrapped himself around her neck like a hideous stole while Kitty leafs through a very ancient copy of *Woman's Day* magazine.

"I'm all set."

She looks up from the magazine. "I'll feed him one last time then." She sets the dog-eared magazine on the stack of others just like it and leans forward. Prince Francis stands up on her shoulders, back arched and mouth open in a wide yawn before he hops onto the arm of the chair and then onto the floor, trotting toward the kitchen like he already knows the drill.

"Why isn't he destroying things?" I don't mean for it to come out sounding like an accusation, but based on her arched brow, it does.

"Because he's getting what he wants—love and attention." She dumps the balance of the stinky food onto a plate. "Should I assume you don't know what his feeding schedule is like?"

"I can ask my mom, but I can't be sure she'll know." Every time I admit this, I feel like an even bigger bag of shit for not seeing how bad things have gotten. Her house wasn't nearly this cluttered the last time I was in it. Or maybe I just didn't notice. Or chose not to.

She sighs, and some of her haughty irritation wanes. "Why don't I start by coming by twice a day? I can adjust depending on his behavior. He's knocking stuff off the tables because he's not getting the love he's used to, and it's the only way he can tell you how he's feeling."

"Kind of like how my dog will chew my shoes if I'm too late coming home," I mutter. That's only happened once. Wilfred is a great dog.

"Yes, but usually it's on a smaller scale. And when they do it in front of you, like Prince Francis did when we first walked in, it's a good sign that he's not happy and he wants you to know. He misses his human—your mom, I mean."

"I think they're pretty much attached at the hip, or the lap." At least that's how it seems with the frequency of messages about him.

She nods and makes another little noise. "There's a good chance. Consistent affection will help. You said you'll be away for a few days? Does that mean you'll only need me to stop by while you're traveling?"

"If I could get on your regular schedule starting Thursday for a while, that would be good. It'll probably be temporary, a few weeks at most? But food twice a day seems normal?" I'm crossing my fingers the doctors will give her the all-clear soon, but that might be wishful thinking.

"I should be able to fit Prince Francis into my twice-daily route. I'm used to everything from short-term care to daily check-ins. I have a pair of doctors who are both on shift work this week who live close by, so I stop in and feed Mr. Munchies at least once a day, sometimes twice, and then I'll head over here."

"Mr. Munchies?" I don't know why I keep asking questions.

"He's a rescue who was owned by a family who habitually overfed him people food." She deftly transfers Prince Francis to one arm and holds him like he's a football. He doesn't seem to mind in the least. She pulls her phone out of her pocket and shows me a picture of Mr. Munchies. He looks like a giant orange and white fluffball. Sort of like an inflated furry cat balloon.

"Wow. He's—"

"Squishy? We have him on a diet and exercise routine. It's slow going because he's only motivated by food." She smiles fondly at the picture.

"I hope he's an indoor cat, otherwise he might get mistaken for a giant, furry Kong."

Kitty's top lip curls. "What a terrible thing to say!"

"But also not untrue." My foot-in-mouth-syndrome is only getting worse, it seems.

She sets him on the floor. "I'll put Prince Francis on temporary rotation with Mr. Munchies."

"Okay, thanks. I uh . . . know my mom would appreciate this."

"No kitty wants to be alone all the time." Again with the slightly stiff smile. "I'll just need a key, and I'll send you a list of questions for you to ask your mom right now." She punches a bunch of keys with one hand and my phone dings in my pocket.

Prince Francis rubs himself on her leg, and she bends to give him an affectionate scratch under his chin. "It was really great to meet you." She addresses the cat, then turns her attention to me, her smile dropping. "I look forward to working with Prince Francis and seeing if we can't get a handle on his behavior."

I walk her out and stifle another sneeze.

"Bless mew," Kitty murmurs, or maybe she said "bless you" and I misheard her.

"Thanks. Sorry about tackling you earlier." I don't know why I can't leave that embarrassing moment in the past instead of dragging it forward with us.

"You're a dog person. I should've warned you." She adjusts her glasses. "It's better than being tackled by a four-legged furball who wants to lick your face with the same tongue it licks its privates with." Her expression pinches. "I'm going to go now. I think my conversation skills have been tested enough today. Don't forget to email me back with as much information as you can get from your mother." She nearly falls down the front steps in her rush to get to her car.

I go back inside so I don't embarrass either of us any further and find Prince Francis sitting on the windowsill. He yowls forlornly as Kitty approaches her SUV. The Kitty Whisperer is written on the side in fancy cursive. The *i*'s in *kitty* and *whisperer* are dotted with heart-shaped cat heads, the grill has whiskers, and the front of the SUV has a decal wrap that makes it look like a cat face.

When Kitty disappears inside the car, Prince Francis looks up at me accusingly and meows loudly.

"Don't worry, ball sack." I stifle another sneeze. "She'll be back."

He meows again.

"And hopefully you'll get your regular human back soon, too."

chapter four

THE ROUTINES WE LOVE

Kitty

On the way home from meeting Miles the grump and Prince Francis the adorable and regal sphynx, I stop at Kat's Cat Café. Kat and I have been friends since ninth grade. We met on the first day of school in our English class. We compared schedules and realized we had all but one class together, and since then we've basically been inseparable.

Two years after she graduated from college, she opened Kat's Cat Café, which is exactly what it sounds like. A café full of adorable rescue cats, most of which are available for adoption. You can grab a coffee or icy beverage (in a covered cup, because there is an incredible amount of fur in the air) and hang out with cats.

I have a desk in her office in the back where I take care of paperwork for my business and help Kat manage inventory and order supplies for the café.

I park, pop the trunk on my SUV, and retrieve the bag of old towels I picked up over the last week from clients, as well as a bag of new promotional items. It's part of what I do in exchange for the office space. Towels are one item they can never get enough of, along with scrap pieces of carpet they can use to refurbish scratching posts.

I find Kat sitting at one of the tables, her laptop propped in front of her, and a tabby curled up in her lap. Another cat sits on her hand, under which I'm assuming is a mouse—the kind you use for a computer, not a toy or real one.

On the other side of the café are Meryl and Louie, an elderly couple who live in the retirement apartments a few blocks over. They're not able to have a cat of their own anymore, so they come here almost every evening for tea and a snuggle with a kitty. I murmur hello to a few of the other regulars scattered around the café as I make my way to Kat. She waves with the hand that isn't under a cat butt. "Hey! I wasn't sure if you'd be in today. How'd that meeting go with the Matt guy? Is the cat a cutie?"

I slide into the seat across from her and set the bag of towels on the floor. Paws, Horace, and Tux, three of the cats who live at the café full time, check out the contents by trying to climb inside the bag. "His name is Miles. The cat is an adorable sphynx, and mischievous. The human is a dog person." I say it like it's a bad word and glance around, making sure no one is within earshot, and lower my voice. "He compared the cat to a shaved ball sack."

Kat's mouth drops open. "He did not!"

"He insulted the poor baby so many times. I mean, read the freaking room, dude. I'm clearly a cat lover." I motion to my shirt.

Kat gives me a knowing look. "Why are so many dog people anti-cat?" Her reaction makes me feel better about my own to his constant disdain for poor Prince Francis.

"I don't know. They're equally loveable, just for different reasons." Maybe I'm extra defensive about Prince Francis because I know what it feels like to be judged solely by my appearance. I've learned to embrace my quirkiness, but I don't have a Teflon coating, and not all the barbs aimed at me slide off with no impact.

Kat rolls her eyes. "He sounds like a real jerk."

"His mother is in the hospital, so that could be part of the reason he was so crusty."

"Oh, maybe. But still, that sounds like an awful first impression." She tucks a few wayward strands of hair behind her ear, then shakes out her hand and blows out two quick breaths, sending a fluff of cat hairs floating to the ground. It's a hazard of the job. Kat is petite, with dark hair and eyes to match. She grew up in the Philippines, but her family moved to the States when she was ten. Her mother is a doctor, and her father is an engineer. They were a bit confused when she decided to open a cat café, but eventually they embraced her chosen career.

"Yeah, it definitely wasn't the best, but the cat is a cutie, and he's the one I'll be dealing with the most, so I'm not too worried." Yet, anyway. Besides, this is a short-term care situation.

"Mm, the human variable is always the thing, isn't it?" Kat gives me a sympathetic smile.

We spend the next half hour making a list of her inventory. Because of my robust social media following, I have a few sponsors who provide free pet supplies in exchange for product placement in videos. It's helpful for keeping costs down, and I pass on the perks to Kat, with the approval of the sponsors, of course.

I take a few videos while we test out the promotional items. I'll edit them later, at home, and then upload them to our social media accounts later in the week. "We need to find a night to go out for dinner or something non–work-related," I say once we're finished with the filming and the inventory order.

"Agreed. Maybe we can plan something next week?"

"We should probably schedule it if we want it to happen, since we've been saying this exact same thing every time we see each other for the past month." I flip over to my calendar in my phone.

"Good call." Kat does the same, and Tux headbutts the device, clearly wanting her attention.

"What about Thursday? I'm done at five."

Kat's eyes light up. "I actually have a date."

"What? Since when? Why is this the first I'm hearing of it?"

"It just happened today. He works at the pet store a few blocks over. I've told you about him before. His name is Brad. I had to grab some emergency cat treats because we ran out."

"Oh, I remember. Who asked who out?" Kat has been crushing on him for a while. Enough that she stops there to buy slightly overpriced cat treats on a semi-regular basis, hoping to run into him.

"He asked me."

Her blush makes me grin. "Well, we definitely need a lunch

or dinner or coffee date after your actual date so I can get all the details."

We make a tentative plan to have lunch or coffee, depending on time constraints. Both of our schedules are pretty full, but a date is exciting.

I gather my things, and Kat pulls me into a hug, transferring tabby fur onto my shirt and cardigan. It's the reason we both carry lint rollers in our purses at all times.

It's closing in on eight by the time I get home from the café. Both my mom's and my sister's cars are already in the driveway, which isn't a surprise. My mom doesn't usually go anywhere in the evenings, and my sister, Hattie, is in her final year of college. She's typically home at this time of night, unless she has an evening class or a study group. I'm too busy running my business to have much of a social life. It helps that Kat is also in the cat business; otherwise, we wouldn't see each other nearly as much.

I open the front door and call out, "Hello! I'm home!"

"Hi, Kitty Kat! I'm watching *Two and a Half Men*, and Hattie's in her room working on an essay, I think," my mom calls out.

I toe off my shoes, leave my purse by the stairs, and follow her voice to the living room.

I find my mom sitting where she always is at this time of day: in my dad's old lounger. It's beat up and threadbare, and the footrest sometimes gets stuck in the up position, but it's full of memories, so we keep it. I can't imagine what this room would look like without it.

Every night after dinner the routine is the same. We wash

dishes and clean up the kitchen. If I have paperwork or social media posts to manage, I'll join my mom in the living room, while she watches reruns of Dad's favorite TV shows. It's been like this ever since he died a decade ago. And before that, when he was alive, I would bring my homework to the living room, set up a TV tray, and work on it while he watched TV and my mom worked on the word games in the newspaper.

She pauses the show, stopping it in the middle of a laugh track. "Have you had dinner yet? I made lasagna. There are leftovers in the fridge."

"Thanks. I'll heat up a piece."

"There's some salad too. It's Caesar, so hopefully it's not too wilted. It's been a couple of hours, though." She frowns for a moment before her mouth tips up into a smile. "How about you bring it in here, and we can catch up on your day during the commercial breaks?"

The shows are recorded and still include all the commercials. They're a throwback to my teenage years and the time before our lives were changed by loss.

"I'm a bit fuzzy, so I'll jump in the shower and then come join you." Eventually I plan to get my own place, but for now there's comfort in the predictability of routine.

"Perfect." She returns her attention to the TV.

I mouth the joke I've heard a million times as I make my way upstairs, a smile on my face. I hear low music coming from my sister's room as I pass, so I knock.

"Come in!" she calls out.

I peek my head in the door. Her room is decorated much like one would expect from a college student. One wall is covered in movie and band posters, another has a whiteboard-corkboard combination affixed to it. Over her desk are four peelable wall calendars, her assignments color-coded for each class and marked by due date. Her double bed sits in the corner, piled with throw pillows that complement the dark blue comforter. The only remnant of her childhood is her stuffed cat, Pumpkin, which was a birthday present from our dad, given to her the year before he died.

Hattie's long hair is the same as mine, thick and wavy, but it's a dark chestnut brown instead of auburn. And like me, she often wears it up in a ponytail. But that's where our similarities end. While I'm softer, like our mom, Hattie is tall and lean, with striking features. Somehow she always manages to look put together, even in a pair of ratty sweatpants.

She spins around in her computer chair and stretches her arms out and over her head, yawning widely. She slaps a hand over her mouth. "Yeesh. Sorry about that." She glances at the clock on her nightstand. "You're getting in late." Her eyes light up. "Did you have a hot date?"

I roll my eyes and motion to my outfit. "Does this look like date-appropriate attire?"

She shrugs. "Not really, but you never know. Leopard print is all the rage. Working late then?"

I lean against her doorjamb. "I had to meet a new cat and his human."

She makes a disappointed face and motions to her desk, which is stacked with books. "One of us needs a social life, and I'm too busy with school for dating, which means you need to step up to the plate."

This is a frequent conversation that doesn't change. I'm busy running a business, and she's busy with classes. I cross over and sit down on the edge of her bed, picking up Pumpkin. I run my fingers over the satin on the inside of his ear, worn with time and love. "The last couple of guys I've dated haven't exactly made me want to jump back into the dating pool."

"Are you taking about Microdick Mick or the basement gamer?"

"Both." I grimace. "And let's never say Mick's name aloud again."

We went out on a handful of dates about six months ago. He was nice to look at, and I'm embarrassed to admit that I suffered through a few extra dates hoping that the conversation would improve. I'm even more embarrassed to admit that I ended up back at his house hoping that the chemistry was better than the conversation. Unfortunately, he had the finesse of a horny teenage boy, and, well...it didn't get better from there. Needless to say, that was the end of Mick.

"Sorry, I shouldn't have brought him up. I know that whole situation was pretty traumatic."

"Hence the reason I'm not all that keen to get back on the horse and ride." I point a finger at her. "I mean that figuratively and metaphorically. Also, you're the one in college, which, if you were unaware, is full of single people looking for a date."

"Guys in college are immature." She flips a pen between her fingers. "And going to a keg party is not my idea of a date. I'm hoping that once I'm out in the real world I'll meet someone with an actual job and life goals that extend beyond leveling up in *Genshun Impact.*"

"I don't know how much that changes after college."

The guy I dated after He Who Shall Not Be Named was a prime example of that. When I arrived at his house to pick him up for our second date, his mother answered the door and basically begged me to never dump her son. Then she took me down to his apartment in the basement. It smelled like feet and cheese, looked like it hadn't been cleaned in...ever, and he'd been sitting on his futon, game controller in one hand, the other tucked down the front of his pants, looking like he hadn't showered or shaved in several days, yelling agitatedly at the screen and then his mother for interrupting.

I turned around and walked right back up those stairs. I later found out that his mother was the one who set up and monitored his profile. And that he spent ninety percent of his time playing video games and the other ten percent sleeping.

It was the last time I used an online dating app.

I nod to Hattie's computer screen. "What are you working on?"

"An essay for one of my classes. It's on the dry side, but if you don't mind looking it over later and giving it the red pen treatment, I would be super grateful. This professor is a stickler for grammar and annotations, so I want to make sure it's in good shape."

"I can absolutely have a look. Just tell me when you're ready, and I'll get out my trusty red pen for you."

"Is Mom watching TV?" Hattie's expression shifts, and for a moment she looks sad.

"Yup. I'm going to shower and then join her, but I can work on your essay while she and I hang out."

"I don't know how you can handle watching the same shows all the time."

I push up off the bed. "It's background noise."

She sighs. "I guess, but you'd think at some point she'd want some variety. I feel like we're all kind of stuck in this loop on repeat."

I squeeze Hattie's shoulder, aware that we feel differently about this. I make a joke to defuse her sadness. "Maybe when Blu-ray players are obsolete."

She rolls her eyes. "I can just see her scouring eBay for all the old ones and hoarding them."

"I'm cat sitting for a semi-hoarder now." I change the subject because this conversation about our mom always makes me uneasy.

"What do you mean semi-hoarder? I didn't realize there was an in-between."

"It's more...a lot of clutter. Or collections of things. You know those porcelain dolls Grandma Hart used to collect?"

Hattie makes a face and shudders. "The dresser in the spare room was always full of them. It felt like they were watching me sleep."

"You always ended up in bed with me when we had to stay there." I smile fondly at the memory.

"And you made us sleep foot to head." Her tone is laced with accusation.

"So you wouldn't breathe in my face. It was a twin bed. There wasn't much room, and you move around a lot. A foot in the face is better than you breathing directly up my nose." Hattie is also a cuddler, so she was always basically pressed against me.

"Whatever. So, more about this semi-hoarder." She makes a go-on motion.

"The house is full of knickknacks, and the cat likes to knock them on the floor. It makes the clutter that much more cluttery."

"So kind of like the inside of your purse?" Hattie arches a brow.

Considering the number of pens and lip balms that ended up on Miles's mom's driveway, it's hard to argue, but I defend myself anyway. "Worse than my purse by a long shot."

She narrows one eye at me. "You're blushing. Why? What happened?"

"Nothing." I bite my lips together.

"Something happened. Was it the new cat and their human?" Her eyes light up. "Is the human a guy? A cute guy?"

"It doesn't matter if he's cute. He's a jerk, and our introduction was the kind of embarrassment you don't really recover from." Especially when my tripping was followed by him insulting his mother's cat and tackling me to the floor.

"Embarrassing how?" She grabs my hand and pushes me back toward the bed. "You need to spill it. Your face tells me there's a story."

I blow out a breath, aware she'll barricade me in her room until I spill the beans. "Remember your first day of high school, when I tripped up the steps in front of the entire football team between first and second period?"

Hattie's eyes go wide and her cheeks tint with secondhand embarrassment. As it is, the memory makes me want to crawl under a blanket forever. "Please tell me this cat's human wasn't one of those football players."

I hug Pumpkin to my chest. "No. Thank catness." I never lived down that moment. Not for the rest of my high school career. Every time I saw one of those guys in the hall, my face would burst into flames. Thankfully, my long hair was able to act as a shield and a veil, but it didn't stop me from hearing their snickers and little jabs. "But I did trip over the curb and fall flat on my face."

"Oh no. I'm so sorry. Did it get better after that? Was he at least nice about it? Did he help you up?"

"Eventually. Sort of. But then he ruined it all by being a dog person." I purse my lips; his disdain for Prince Francis is grating on me. "And then he tackled me, so the whole helping me up was kind of wiped out by that."

"Why in the world would he tackle you?"

I give her the abridged version. "You see what I mean, though? He's definitely not a cat person. You know how different dogs are than cats. Dogs want your approval; cats want your submission."

Hattie chuckles. "That is the truth. Too bad about the cutie human being a jerk. Maybe he was just having an off day?"

"Maybe, but he was lobbing an awful lot of nasty names at the poor cat." Not that it matters. I won't have to deal with the cat hater for long.

I leave Hattie to finish her essay while I wash away a day of cats, then heat up some dinner. The salad is wilted, but not so bad that it's inedible. I grab a glass of water and head to the living room, where a TV tray has already been set up for me on the couch next to the chair.

"Perfect timing—the commercials just came on. Tell me all about your day." Mom lowers the volume, and I have her un-divided attention for two full minutes before the show resumes. I give her the CliffsNotes version of my day, omitting Miles, because any time I mention a man who might be in my age range, Mom automatically assumes he's dateable. And Miles, while nice to look at, does not have the personality to match.

She hmms and says *that's nice* in all the right places, then we go back to watching *Two and a Half Men* as soon as the commercials end. My heart aches when one of my dad's favorite cheesy jokes comes through the TV, my mom reciting the punch line along with the character, and we both chuckle along with the laugh track.

I eat my dinner, waiting for the next commercial break before I ask about her day. At ten we switch to news, and I work on edit-ing Hattie's essay while the newscasters impart today's tragedies. By the time I'm done giving the essay the red pen treatment, it's after eleven.

I have an early start tomorrow, so I get ready for bed. I wait until

I'm snuggled under my covers before I check for new messages. My comforter is a quilt with a cat print on it, obviously.

I'm surprised to find several from Miles.

> *Miles:* *Hi Kitty. Sorry this is so late, and I'm sorry again about tackling you. I'm honestly not in the habit of knocking over women with water guns. Real ones maybe. Situationally dependent.*
> *Miles:* *[Cringe face gif]*
> *Miles:* *[football tackle gif]*
> *Miles:* *Maybe too soon for the tackle gif? I can't unsend that.*
> *Miles:* *I've emailed info about PF's schedule. My mother wasn't in the mood to discuss his needs, but I've cobbled together what I know, which is not much. I'll be in touch later this week, and you can always reach me at this number. I hope PF is on his best behavior, but I'm unsure what that looks like, or if tossing trinkets off shelves is his jam. Signing off before this becomes an actual novel. ~ Miles*

I lie in bed, frowning as I read the text messages through twice more. The thing about text messages is that I can't read the tone. He could be apologizing only because he needs my help. I have a rug burn on my cheek.

I'm also irritated by the slightly endearing quality of his messages. But I'm probably reading too much into the apology. If he was a grandpa who tackled me, would I have taken the job? I'm even more irritated by the fact that the answer to that is probably no. I let his pretty veneer influence my decision. And he's a dog person who doesn't like cats to boot. We might as well be from different planets.

I move on to my email and read over the one he sent me. He wasn't kidding about the information being scant. Most of the questions I sent him have the "I don't know" emoji attached to them. I do not want to find that cute.

What he does know is that Prince Francis loves bacon and cereal marshmallows—so odd—hanging out on a lap, and wet food over dry, and when he's really mad, apparently he'll poop in shoes. It's good information, even if there isn't a lot of it. I'll be able to figure out the rest as I go.

I barely resist the urge to send him a cute cat gif in response, which he probably won't appreciate anyway, and instead go with:

Kitty: *Usually when I get tackled, it's by my neighbor's giant Saint Bernard. On the upside, at least you didn't lick my face.*

I set my phone on the nightstand and close my eyes. I roll to my right side, then cringe at how sore my elbow is. From being tackled. Ugh, stupid, pretty cat-hating dog lover.

chapter five

KITTY MAGIC

Kitty

Thursday morning I wake up from an incredibly weird dream. In it, I'm dressed in football gear, complete with helmet, and I'm apparently playing defense. I don't really watch much in the way of sports, apart from the occasional hockey game on TV with my dad when he was still here. What horrifies me is that the football has the face of a cat. And the quarterback for the other team happens to be Miles.

When he tries to throw the cat-ball, I tackle him to the ground. The gratification quickly morphs to mortification because when we hit the ground, we're both naked. Apart from the helmet. He's still wearing that. I shake off the dream and get ready for my day.

Hattie's already in the kitchen, slathering butter on toast. She slaps on some avocado and tomato slices, covers it with another slice of toast, and wraps a paper towel around it. She kisses me on the cheek, gives Mom a hug from behind, and rushes to the door. "I'll be home for dinner. Text me if you need me to pick anything up. Love you both. Bye!"

"Have a good day and drive safe!" Mom sips her coffee and flips to the obituary section of the newspaper. It's a morbid way to start the morning, but it's part of her routine.

"Egg and cheese on an English muffin?" I ask as I pour myself a cup of coffee. We take turns making breakfast for each other.

"I'm easy. Whatever works for you." Mom smiles, but her focus is on the paper.

It only takes a few minutes to get breakfast ready and bring it to the table. The chair that my dad used to sit in is always set with a placemat, and his favorite mug sits empty in the center. Sometimes I wonder if it's become such an ingrained part of her routine that she doesn't even realize she still does it.

"Do you have a busy day?" she asks conversationally, setting the paper aside so she can eat.

"Just my usual rounds, plus that new client I picked up, but I'll be home early enough to help with dinner. I need to do an inventory check later, so I can make space in the garage." It's where I keep most of my cat-sitting supplies. It's also where all the sponsorship overflow items are stored. At this point I've filled the entire garage and part of the basement.

"Space?" Mom perks up.

"I have a new order coming in."

"Oh." She deflates. "Will you need help with that? Do we need more shelves in there?"

"I should rent a storage unit." When I started the Kitty

Whisperer four years ago, I assumed it would be my side hustle, not my full-time job. And for a while it was a part-time thing. I also worked in an office, organizing schedules. It was not riveting work. When it seemed like I was going to have to either step into one role or the other, I made the decision to go out on my own. And now here I am, running my own business. I never expected to make an actual living. Or to basically take over part of my mom's house, and that's with my office space being at Kat's.

Mom waves a hand around in the air. "You don't need to do that. We have the space."

"It'd be nice if you could park your car in the garage in the winter, though." Especially when there are three vehicles to push snow off and move around when there's a storm. The garage was supposed to be a temporary home for my business supplies.

"Eh, I've survived this long. What's a couple more years?" She pats my hand and takes another bite of her sandwich. "This is great, by the way."

"I'm glad you like it." I focus on my own sandwich for a moment, mulling over that last comment about a couple more years. I shouldn't read into that. I'm in my midtwenties. I don't intend to live at home forever, but it seems like I'm being given a timeline. Two years isn't unreasonable, so I'm not sure why her comment unsettles me.

We finish breakfast, and I load the dishwasher while she washes the pans. And then I'm off to see my first four-legged furball of the day.

Bumbles is a striped tabby with a scrunched-up face and a

slightly surly demeanor. He's the cat version of Miles. His owner is an elderly man who has severe cataracts and only partial vision, so I stop by on a regular basis to help tend to Bumbles's needs.

I ring the doorbell and wait for Mr. O'Toole to open the door. It often takes a few minutes for that to happen. I check my messages and find I have a new one from Miles.

I don't love the silly fluttery feeling in my stomach. As a result, I hold off on checking it. I'm about to ring the doorbell a second time, worried about the possibility that Mr. O'Toole has lost his hearing aids again, or worse. He's ninety.

The tough part about working with a lot of elderly people is that they occasionally have accidents. I've yet to be the one to find a client in a serious state, thankfully, but I've been on the receiving end of a few sad phone calls. Those are always hard to handle. While I spend the most time with their pets, I still get to know their owners and we share a special bond because of our cat love.

Thankfully, the front door swings open. "I couldn't find my pants!" Mr. O'Toole shouts. "Or my right hearing aid!"

Even though I try to keep my gaze fixed on the bald spot on top of his head, my gaze dips. The screen door separates us, creating a haze and semi-barrier between me and Mr. O'Toole, but I can very clearly see that the pants situation is still a problem. He's wearing a long gray button-down that was probably once white but got mixed in with something dark and a tweed jacket, as is customary for Mr. O'Toole. His boxer shorts are navy. One of his white socks stops just under his knee, and the other one slouches around his ankle. He's wearing gray slippers.

"Shall I help you find them?" This isn't a first.

"That would be great, Miss Kitty. One second they were in my hand, and the next they were gone. It's like a ghost up and stole them." He throws his hands in the air, his bushy eyebrows shooting up and then pulling together, resembling two caterpillars dancing on his forehead.

He opens the screen door and shuffles back a few steps to let me in. The house smells like a combination of mothballs, cat litter, and cooked onions. Not the most appealing, but it certainly could be worse.

Bumbles, his striped tabby, comes lumbering through the kitchen, meowing loudly. Much like his owner, he's ancient, and also not a fast mover. But he tries his hardest to run, despite being almost as round as he is tall. I've tried to explain to Mr. O'Toole that he shouldn't feed Bumbles people food, but he says it's one of the only good things left in life, so why should either of them suffer.

He has a point.

"How is my favorite striped tabby?" I crouch and hold out a hand. Bumbles rubs his face on my hand, gives me a little nip—that's his surly side coming out—then bumps against my knee and headbutts my thigh on his way to my pocket. He does an about-face and rush-bumbles back to the kitchen. A digital British accent calls out "Treat" several times in a row.

To help Mr. O'Toole, I've been teaching Bumbles to use communication buttons. So far we have *treats*, *outside*, and *pets*. The treat button is unsurprisingly his favorite.

"Good boy, Bumbles!" I call out.

He trots back to where we're still standing in the front hall, meowing with zeal. I pluck a treat from my pocket, and he gobbles it up, then heads for the kitchen again.

"We'll figure out the pants situation before we deal with Bumbles, shall we?"

"He's been hitting buttons all morning. I ran right out of treats," Mr. O'Toole grumbles.

It doesn't take me long to find his pants. They're slung over the railing on the staircase.

Mr. O'Toole disappears down the hall to his bedroom to finish getting dressed, and I feed Bumbles and clean his litter box.

When I return, I find Mr. O'Toole in the kitchen with his pants on. One of his shirttails hangs out from the back, and his fly is down, but it's an upgrade from being pantsless.

I agree to a cup of tea, although I won't be drinking it, since Mr. O'Toole is a frugal man and reuses the same tea bag at least four or five times before he throws it out. Regardless, I sit with him on the front porch, and we chat while I brush Bumbles to help cut down on his hairball problem.

"What about a boyfriend, Miss Kitty? Any young men looking to court you?"

I smile at his phrasing. Mr. O'Toole grew up during the Second World War and married his high school sweetheart. She passed away a decade ago, and just last year he started "courting" one of the other ladies in the neighborhood, who he calls a "spring chicken" compared to him. She's eighty-two.

"No boyfriend. Work keeps me busy."

"You're too young to be working this hard. Have I mentioned that I have a great-grandson in the NHL? He's a bit young for you yet, but give him a few years to catch up."

"You have mentioned your great-grandson. He just graduated from high school last year, didn't he?" Mr. O'Toole tells me about his great-grandson every time I visit.

"That he did. Got snapped up by the league just like that." He snaps his fingers and startles Bumbles. "He's sowing his oats right now, but eventually he'll be ready to settle down with a nice girl like you. But by the time that happens you'll probably have found yourself a husband."

"Only time will tell, I suppose." I chuckle and change the subject. "Oh! I took on a new client this week. Prince Francis is a sphynx cat."

"A sphynx cat, you say. Those are the naked ones, aren't they?"

I chuckle. "That's right, he's hairless."

"Can't say I'd love wandering around in my birthday suit all the time, but I guess he's a lot less likely to be coughing up hairballs." He slurps his tea noisily.

We chat for a while longer, until I've managed to comb out enough fur to make a whole flock of birds comfortable nests, and then I tell Mr. O'Toole that I have to go visit with my next client.

I take my teacup to the kitchen and dump it down the drain, then remind him that he can turn off the Treats button if Bumbles is using it too much. And then I'm off to see Prince Francis.

When I get to the house, I realize I don't have a key. I'm about to message Miles, but I find he's beaten me to it.

Miles: *key is under the dying plant and tuna might be PF's fave food.*

I compose a thank-you message three times before finally erasing the entire thing and sending a thumbs-up emoji instead.

I open the door cautiously, in case Prince Francis is waiting close by with the intention of bolting. But apart from the stack of unopened mail on the floor, the hallway is empty. "Hello, Prince Francis, it's Kitty! I've come to love you!"

Silence follows as I flick on the light and close the door. The first thing I notice is that the horrible porcelain dolls are no longer staring at the entryway because they're lying on top of each other. One of them is on the floor, facedown.

"Uh-oh, Prince Francis, have you been up to no good?" I cross over and pick the doll up, unsure if I'm relieved that the face isn't shattered. I set it back on the sideboard and continue to the living room.

It's as if Miles hadn't swept up the floor debris at all yesterday. Below the two shelving units flanking the fireplace are new piles of fallen items. I scan them, and the fireplace mantel, which is now missing several gnomes, but I don't spot Prince Francis anywhere.

I check behind the couch, since it's a go-to hiding spot for badly behaved kitties.

But I notice the curtains shift across the room. I also note, for the first time, that they're not in the best shape. There are pulls along the bottom, a sure sign that Prince Francis has been using them as a scratching post or a ladder. I follow the line of the curtain all the way to the rod that stops about a foot from the ceiling.

And there he is, perched like an angry, adorable gargoyle on top of the rod, staring down at me.

"Hello, Prince Francis! Did I scare you?"

He stares back at me, still as a statue.

"Would you like to come down and have a treat?" I pull the small baggie I carry with me from my pocket—in case of emergency or cuteness overload—and shake it.

His right paw and eye twitch, but still nothing.

It's a standoff. Well, a one-sided one, anyway.

And the best way to end it is to ignore the culprit. I take a seat in the lounger, and a minute later he jumps onto the table and paws at the bag of treats sitting there.

I set one by his paw and give him a scratch behind the ear as he gobbles it up. "We need to get a handle on this destructive behavior, Prince Francis. Your mom would not be impressed if she knew what kind of shenanigans you were getting up to while she's away."

He purrs and makes a squeaky sound, like a dog toy being chewed. Eventually he climbs into my lap, and we spend a good while sitting there, me petting him, him purring. It's clear he's used to lots of affection, and with his human away, he's feeling abandoned.

It's a symbiotic exchange of love and comfort. And while in some ways it's conditional because he knows there's food attached to me and my warm lap and my affection, it's not the kind of conditional love that humans are guilty of, the kind that can break a heart. Cat love is different. You know you belong to them when they choose you, not the other way around. It's a special kind of bond.

And in some ways, I can understand why certain people have an inclination toward dogs instead of cats. They're forever children who require love and attention. But when a cat needs your love, you know you've become theirs.

I snap a quick picture and send it to Miles along with a short message:

Prince Francis is soaking up the love.

I want to show him that Prince Francis isn't a naughty gremlin. That he has love to give if a person is willing to give a little themself.

I have a feeling that if I let him, Prince Francis would spend all day in my lap, but I have other furry friends to attend to, so eventually I encourage him to get up so I can feed him properly and take care of the litter situation, another thing I forgot to ask Miles about.

Once I've fed Prince Francis—he has special plates of his own—I go in search of the litter box. I don't find it anywhere on the main floor, so I go upstairs. The ascent brings with it a spike of anxiety, along with old, painful memories I try not to let float to the surface. Not entirely rational, but I take a deep breath and remind myself that this house is empty apart from me and Prince Francis. All I find are a few knocked-over items in what appears to be the master bedroom.

I head back to the main floor, stumped, until I spot the cat door leading to the basement. Once I open it, I can smell that I've hit the jackpot. And not in a good way. I use my cardigan as a barrier between me and the horrible odor that grows progressively worse the closer I get to the bottom of the stairs.

"Well, this might explain some of the destruction," I mutter, then gag, because I'm breathing in not just the smell of ammonia, but also a lot of cat doody. Prince Francis has taken a stand, his irritation with his inadequate bathroom facilities dotting the floor in little piles.

He appears beside me and plunks his butt down on my foot with a squeak.

"It's pretty gross down here, isn't it?" I ask.

He licks his paw.

I cringe, because I'm standing on litter.

I take a photo of the situation and send it to Miles, irked once again that he didn't take care of this before he left. I'm not entirely confident I'll know where to find the extra litter, and I can't see any through the tears, my eyes are watering so badly.

It's neglectful to leave it like this, but I'm also at risk of passing out from the fumes, so I climb the stairs and head for the back porch, gulping down fresh air.

I'm so busy trying to breathe and shake the stinging in my nose that I accidentally send a picture of my nostrils to Miles.

chapter six

A LITTLE BIT FASCINATED

Miles

I'm sitting next to Josh, eating breakfast with the team, when my phone pings. It's in my bag beside my foot, and every time I get a new message it sends a buzz up my legs.

Another buzz.

"Is that your phone?" Josh asks and then shovels a forkful of scrambled eggs into his mouth.

"Yeah. Kitty is supposed to check on my mother's cat this morning." I reach into my bag to see if it's her texting me. I hope that happens soon, because the messages from my mom have been relentless, and apparently she requires photographic evidence of PF's well-being before she's satisfied. I get it, sort of. My neighbors who are watching Wilfred while I'm away have already sent a whole slew of photos, and I can't say I don't appreciate it.

"I still have a hard time believing that her company is called the

Kitty Whisperer and her name is also actually Kitty. I still think it's a gimmick," Josh says.

I shrug. "If it is, it's a pretty good one."

Parker, who's sitting across the table, leans in. "Are you guys talking about that woman who trains cats? She's got a solid social media following. Kitty the Kitty Whisperer?"

"Yeah, that's the one. What do you know about her?" Josh answers for me.

"She takes care of my great-grandad's cat. He's got real bad vision, and even with cataract surgery, it's not getting any better. But he loves that freaking cat, so I hired her a few months back to help him out, and now she's trained Bumbles to talk." He shoves an entire strip of bacon into his mouth, accordion style.

"Wait. What? Do you mean he meows and sounds like he's saying *I love you* or whatever?" I ask.

Parker shakes his head and holds up a finger, swallowing the bacon before he continues. "There's this dog on social media who uses all kinds of buttons to communicate. I know this because my sister follows animal accounts and sends me the reels all the time. Anyway, I guess this Kitty woman figured she could apply the same principle to cats, and now Bumbles has three." He grabs his phone and pulls up a video of a very round cat hitting a button that says "treat" repeatedly in a digital voice. "Here's the video she posted last week. She's pretty cool. Kinda hot, too."

"Have you met her?" I don't know why that idea irks me. Maybe because Parker is a walking hormone, and the fame of making the

NHL, coupled with the attention on social media—particularly from women—is inflating his ego a little too quickly.

Parker sets his phone back on the table and shakes his head. "Nah, but I watch her videos sometimes. Have you?" His brow quirks up.

"Yeah, yesterday. She's watching my mother's cat while I'm away." I cringe as the image of tackling her to the floor pops into my head. I really wish I could undo that event. I also wish my body would stop having inappropriate reactions to that memory. It's very conflicting to have a semi over tackling an odd but attractive woman to the floor. Over a water gun.

"Oh man, you're all uncomfortable. You got a thing for her, don't you?" Parker grins and nods knowingly, as if he's reading my mind.

I wipe my damp palms on my pants under the table. "I met her once, and she's taking care of my mother's cat." As if that has any bearing on her level of attractiveness.

"Yeah, but admit it, she's got that sexy librarian vibe going on."

"Sexy librarian? Really?" Josh grabs his own phone and punches at the screen with his finger.

"You were browsing her IG account when I called her," I point out.

"Yeah, but I wasn't paying attention to what she looks like." He flips through photos until he reaches one with Kitty's entire face in the shot, then cocks a knowing brow at me. "Oh yeah, Parker's right about the sexy librarian thing."

I brush off their comments. There's no way I'm admitting I

find her attractive. Or that her disgruntledness with me when I was a d-bag is also hot. "What she looks like has no bearing on her ability to take care of a cat."

Parker scoffs loudly and makes a lewd comment, and suddenly everyone is on my ass about the Kitty Whisperer.

I ignore their juvenile behavior and check my messages.

I have two from my dad and a voice mail. I haven't told him Mom is in the hospital yet. Or that the doctors think she has early-onset dementia. My parents started a family later in life, but even still, she's only in her mid-sixties. Their relationship has been tricky since they divorced. So much so that my dad moved back to British Columbia, where he grew up. He needed to escape the memories, and he has siblings out there. I don't blame him. The end of their relationship came as a result of too much loss. I don't know how he's going to feel about the news, and with this new job and all my own baggage, I just don't have the bandwidth to take on his, too.

I leave my dad's messages unanswered and scroll to the next ones, which are from Kitty. Thank God. Because under hers are ones from my mom.

Kitty: *Did you know about this litter situation?!?*
Kitty: *I didn't mean to send that picture of my nostrils.*
Kitty: *I was trying to escape the smell from the previous picture and sent it by accident. [puking emoji]*
Kitty: *Do you have any idea where your mother keeps the fresh litter? Prince Francis is taking a stand against his current bathroom conditions and it needs to be managed.*

I can't read the tone of her messages, but I imagine she's pissed based on the punctuation at the end of the first message. Great. Just what I need, another strike against me.

I scroll up to the picture that's basically a closeup of her nose and a bit of chin, and continue to the previous image. It's a litter box, one that needs to be changed, like a week ago, if I had to guess.

Dogs always do their business outside. I didn't even consider there might be a litter box that would need to be changed. And now I've left Kitty to deal with that disgusting task. I wonder if she'll charge me more for that. Probably. I would if I were her.

I send her a bunch of emojis, including the cringey face one and the shrugging shoulders.

In the background the guys are still talking about Kitty and her hotness level. It's an astoundingly juvenile conversation.

A new gif appears—she seems to be a fan of these—and it annoys me an irrational amount that it's a cute cat talking on a phone. A message follows:

Kitty: *Can I call you?*
Miles: *sure.*

A phone conversation is probably easier than texting, and I'll be able to gauge how annoyed she is with me and whether I'll need to find another kitty whisperer when I'm back in Toronto. Two seconds later my phone rings. Which, for whatever reason, I don't expect, even though she just asked if she could. I hop up from the table and knock my chair over in the process. It clatters to the floor with a bang and draws even more attention, making my hasty exit impossible.

And because Parker is young, and apparently a jerk, he yells, "Who you talking to? Is that Kitty? Ask her if she has a boyfriend and if it's serious. And if she's interested in hot hockey players with excellent stamina."

I right my chair and shoot a glare his way, then bust my ass away from the table. "Hey. Hi. Hello." My conversation skills and my coordination are clearly suffering this morning.

"It sounds like you might be busy." Her voice is raspy. She clears her throat and sniffs once.

"It's fine. I'm out with the team."

"The team?" she echoes.

"Yeah. I'm a data analyst for Toronto's NHL team. We're out for breakfast."

"Oh. Wow. That's . . . you work for the NHL?"

"Yeah, behind the scenes, though, not a player." Not that she needed the clarification. I'm not built like hockey players. Where they have legs like century-old tree trunks, mine are more like slightly mature saplings.

"So you work with numbers and hockey players?" Her voice sounds far away, or quiet.

"In a nutshell, yes." It's a bit more involved, but only people who do stats can appreciate the art.

"That sounds . . . interesting."

I can't tell if she's mocking me. I don't even know why I care. She's my cat sitter, not someone I should be trying to impress.

Even though for some reason that seems to be what I'm doing. "Yeah. Anyway, I don't think I'm going to be much help with the litter situation, since I didn't even realize it would be an issue."

"Clearly, considering the state of the litter box. My olfactory senses are decimated thanks to that."

She doesn't laugh, so I'm guessing that's not a joke. Maybe she's being overdramatic about it. "It can't be that bad."

She huffs; it's an annoyed sound. "If it wasn't neglectful, I'd leave the mess so you know exactly how disgusting it is when you're forced to clean it up. Have you ever been to a summer music festival?"

"I don't get what this has to do with the cat litter situation." Man, she's seriously ramped up right now.

"Have you ever had to use one of those portable toilets at a concert?"

"Sure. Yeah."

"Think about how disgusting they are by the end of the concert. Especially with all the drunk assholes who pee all over the seat and leave it for the next person. Now multiply that by about a thousand, and you might have a chance at understanding how disgusting Prince Francis's bathroom situation is."

"Come on, Kitty. You're exaggerating." I grimace at my condescending tone and my foot-in-mouth response.

"You would say that." More huffing on her end. "In the interest of making sure this doesn't happen again, I'd like to set Prince Francis up with an automatic scooper. I get a promotional discount, which I'll pass on to you."

"What does something like that cost?" I'd ask what in the world an automatic scooper is, but she sounds frustrated with me as it as.

"I think you should ask what it will *save* you. Which is me quitting on you. The really high-quality ones run about six or seven hundred."

"Dollars? That's ridiculous. Does it clean itself or something?"

"It removes waste so Prince Francis doesn't have to step around his own poop. If that's too expensive, we can go with a basic one, which are about a hundred and fifty dollars and work well enough."

"For a litter box? Yeesh. This is just more proof that dogs are better pets. Their poop bags cost all of five bucks for a roll of a hundred."

"Why am I not surprised to hear those words coming out of your mouth? If I didn't care about Prince Francis and his welfare I would quit right now. And I'll need to pick up the litter to go with it. And that will be another hundred and twenty, but it'll give you at least two months' worth of litter and it works out to about ten dollars a week."

"Ten bucks a week for litter? That seems inflated. I've seen those huge bags at the pet store for the same price."

"The non-clumping litter is cheap. This is not that. Would you buy one-ply toilet paper for your bathroom?"

"He's a freaking cat. He licks his own damn balls and his asshole."

"Well, it would be a lot nicer for Prince Francis if he didn't have to also lick stray litter out from between his toe beans."

I can practically see her with her hand on her hip, glaring angrily at me. *Why in the world does that jack me up?*

"A few hundred dollars to upgrade Prince Francis's bathroom situation and curb his destructive tendencies seems like a pretty reasonable price to pay, don't you think?"

"Man, cats are hella high maintenance."

She makes a noise that sounds a lot like a growl. "Hopefully once this issue is taken care of, he won't be as hard on your mother's drapes or her trinkets."

I nod my agreement, then realize she can't see me.

Parker pokes his head out into the foyer. We're in the hotel's buffet restaurant, and I'm standing in the lobby. "You still talking to Kitty Whisperer?"

I put my hand over the receiver. "Can you fuck the hell off?"

"Excuse me? I'm trying to be helpful here! Keep it up and I'll report you for improper animal care!" Kitty sounds rightfully indignant.

"Shit. Sorry. Don't report me. That wasn't directed at you. One of the players is giving me the gears. Hold on a sec." I don't bother to cover the receiver this time. "Parker, you're not even nineteen yet. You're barely legal to vote, you can't buy alcohol here or anywhere in Canada except for Quebec, you still think making fart noises with your armpit is funny, and you only need to shave your face once a week. I'm not going to ask Kitty if she's interested in dating you, because I'm pretty sure I already know the answer."

Parker gives me a look. "I shave twice a week."

Kitty chuckles. It's the first time I've heard her make that sound. For some reason it reminds me of adorable birds from a princess movie twittering in the background. Oddly, I think Parker managed to defuse the escalating situation between me and the Kitty Whisperer.

"She's laughing."

"Don't tell him that! You'll hurt his feelings," Kitty chastises.

"He makes three million dollars a year as a rookie and flirts like a fiend. He'll be fine."

"Why you doing me dirty like that? Ask her if she's seen Great-Grandad O'Toole lately."

I'm annoyed that Parker is out here, making it impossible for me to finish this conversation with Kitty.

"Oh! He's Mr. O'Toole's great-grandson? Tell him I just saw him this morning, and he couldn't find his pants. I think he needs to get his eyes checked again. Or maybe some new glasses."

And now I'm annoyed that she's already friendlier with Parker than she is with me. Granted, I have been a dick.

"I'll pass the message on." I wave Parker away. "By the way, you always tip to the right when you're about to take a shot on net. That's why the opposition steals the puck from you just before you take the shot."

His jaw drops and he runs a hand through his hair. "Fuck."

"Now let me finish my conversation in peace, or I won't tell you how to fix the problem."

Parker disappears back into the restaurant. "Sorry about that." I sigh. It's not just data that I analyze. It's assessing the plays, too, and figuring out what works and what doesn't. It's my absolute dream job, but sometimes the ego and the player antics can be a lot to handle. "Kitty? You still there?"

"Yeah. Yes. Here." She exhales softly. "Did you just give advice to an NHL player?"

"Sort of. My role is to look at the numbers and watch players so I can help the coach build on their strengths and understand their weaknesses as individuals, and as part of their line. Like who works best together. That sort of thing." I rub the back of my neck.

"I've never seen a hockey game live, but I used to watch it on TV with my dad sometimes. He was a big fan. If he couldn't watch it, he would listen to the games on the radio." She makes a humming sound. "Funny that of all the things my dad loved, my mom never actually sat down and watched it with him."

I realize she's talking about her dad in the past tense, and it makes me want to ask questions. But I don't have the chance.

She clears her throat, and her voice takes on that sharp edge I've grown accustomed to. "Anyway. I need to get Prince Francis's litter situation handled, and I'll try to keep the costs down."

"Should I send you money up front for that?" I don't even know how often she bills yet. But from the rates on her site, it seems like cat sitting is a lucrative job.

"I have a couple of litter boxes on hand, so it's not out of pocket."

"If that changes, let me know." I should stop griping about money so she can be less annoyed with me.

"Of course. Well, I need to handle this litter box before Prince Francis decides to leave another poop bomb on the floor. Tell Parker I said good luck!"

"You too!" I say, like an idiot.

"I have cats on my side. I don't need luck."

She ends the call, and I stand there for a moment, trying to figure out what exactly it is about Kitty that makes me want her to hate me less. Maybe because I've already made a terrible first and second impression with her? Or because our crappy intro is an echo of the rest of my life? Who knows?

But apparently I suck with people.

And cats.

And Kitty.

chapter seven

THAT ESCALATED QUICKLY

Kitty

After five days of caring for Prince Francis, I can conclude that a clean litter box doesn't make a lick of difference where his destructive behaviors are concerned. Which means I was right about the real issue being the lack of snuggle time and missing his human.

Miles is back from his trip, and I'm meeting him at his mother's house so we can go over a plan of care for Prince Francis. I'm also hoping to get a bit more information on how long I'll be making double daily visits. Constant cat care can be costly, and currently I'm giving him my short-term fee, but if I'll be checking in on Prince Francis for an extended period, I'll adjust to my long-term rates.

Money conversations always make me nervous. I love what I do, so much so that I would do it for free. But that's not savvy business practice, and I can't earn a living on smiles and love. Plus, I help my mom with the household expenses, and I'm trying to squirrel money away so one day, apparently in the next two years, I can buy a place of my own.

I turn down Pebble Street and park in front of Prince Francis's house. Miles's car is already in the driveway. I take a deep breath and tamp down the surge of irritation that makes the hairs on the back of my neck stand on end. I've texted Miles with updates on Prince Francis while he's been away, as I generally do with all my clients, sending daily photo updates—upon his request, which surprised me. At least until I learned they were for his mother. I keep my messages brief and to the point. Especially since I've had that stupid football dream basically every night. The most annoying part is that every time I have it, the outfits I start out in become increasingly outlandish. Last night I was wearing skimpy lace lingerie and a helmet, and that was it. I will admit, Dream Me rocked that lingerie.

I've never been physically attracted to someone I strongly dislike before, and I find it extra conflicting. My body doesn't seem to care that he's a dog-loving, cat-hating jerk. It seems to think all that matters is ticking my physical attraction boxes.

"You can do this. You can handle dealing with an attractive jerk. Pretend he's Mr. Potato Head if you need to. Remember, he's probably the kind of guy who toots and blames it on his dog. Also, do not draw your water gun without warning this time. And if he tackles you again, it's probably a sign that you should stop caring for his mother's cat, no matter how much you like him. The cat, obviously." My recurring dream comes back in annoying flashes. "Or maybe it means he wants to make out with you." I frown at my reflection in the rearview mirror. "This whole opposites–attract fantasy stops here, Kitty."

I leave the safety of my car and avoid tripping on the curb on the way to the front door. Today I knock, because Miles is here. I hear a shout from inside the house to let myself in, so I do.

I find Miles in the living room standing in front of the fireplace, several boxes at his feet. He's wearing yellow rubber kitchen gloves, which seems odd, until he picks up a gnome and a head pops up between a Christmas gnome and an Easter one. Prince Francis hisses, then swats Miles's hand. He grabs the gnome with two clawed paws and bites its butt. I bite my lip to stifle a laugh.

"Seriously man, you need to chill out." Miles releases the gnome.

Prince Francis takes the opportunity to wrap his entire body around the little gnome and rolls onto his back, doing some bicycle kicks, which in turn knocks three gnomes off the mantel. Prince Francis nearly falls off the ledge himself, but catches his balance before he joins the gnomes on the floor.

"Some cat is in a frisky mood," I observe. I'm talking to Prince Francis, not Miles, but he must not realize that.

"Every time I try to put something in a box, he attacks me or the object. I tried to corral him into one of the bedrooms, but he's about as herdable as a squirrel. It's making this whole packing shit pretty damn difficult." He starts to run a hand through his hair, but stops when he remembers he's wearing rubber gloves.

Packing indicates moving, which means the situation with his mom might be more serious than I realized. "Is your mother okay?"

"It's looking a lot like she'll need full-time care. The doctors are saying her dementia is far too advanced for her to keep living alone." His shoulders curl forward, and he strips one glove off his hand and wipes it on his jeans, then pinches the bridge of his nose. "Sorry, my mother's mental state isn't your problem."

As frustrating as dealing with Miles has been, I do have a heart, and based on his expression, his seems bruised over all of this. I set aside my feelings and try to put myself in his shoes. Taking care of his mother's cat while she's in the hospital, not knowing what the situation is going to look like when she's released. Maybe his disdain for Prince Francis has more to do with the situation than it does the actual cat. "That can't be an easy thing to deal with."

He flips the gnome over in his hands. "I didn't realize that someone her age could decline this quickly. I thought maybe she could have a personal support worker stop by a few times a week, but the doctors are telling me she's likely to wander off again. She's lucky the police found her and something more serious didn't happen." He drops the gnome in the box. "Anyway, I started looking at homes yesterday, but there's a lot to take into consideration. And I can't have this freaking cat knocking crap off the shelves all the time. He's bound to step on broken glass, and that's another expensive problem to fix."

My heart was getting melty until that last statement.

He blows out a breath. "I realize that I sound like a d-bag when I say things like that. And you should probably consider raising your rates since I'm using you like a freaking therapist, but I went to the hospital this afternoon and they gave me the news, and then I came here and found this mess."

And I'm back to being melty. If I were in the same predicament as Miles, I don't know that I'd present the best version of myself either. So I set aside my negative feelings and press my empathy button. "The therapy session is on the house. This time, anyway."

He gives me a sidelong glance and smirks a little.

Prince Francis does a butt wiggle and prance, then launches himself onto the arm of the couch and bounces to the floor, weaving between my feet with a purr.

Miles gives Prince Francis the stink-eye. "Oh I see how it is. A pretty lady shows up, and you're all romance and seduction."

I choke back a laugh and make a squeaky sound instead. *Do not get all swoony over an offhand compliment, Kitty.* "He associates me with food and pets, and he associates you with change," I explain. "It has nothing to do with romance and everything to do with food."

"Maybe I should start bringing him snacks, so our mutual loathing comes down a few notches." Miles sneezes into the crook of his arm.

I hold out a baggie full of treats. "It couldn't hurt. Why don't you give him some of these, and I can find some of his toys to distract him while you pack?"

His eyes flare, like he's surprised by the offer. "Are you sure you don't mind?"

He takes the baggie, and I tuck my hand back into the pocket of my cardigan. "I was planning to hang with Prince Francis anyway." Besides, I'm not doing this for any reason other than Prince Francis's well-being. At least that's what I'm telling myself.

Prince Francis jumps up on his hind legs, claws digging into my jeans, until he realizes I'm no longer the holder of the treats. He redirects his affection, rubbing up against Miles's leg and meowing loudly.

Miles opens the bag and makes a face, probably because the treats don't smell all that great. Although dog food doesn't smell any better. He crouches and holds out a treat in his palm, but leans away from Prince Francis, as if he's expecting an attack.

Prince Francis paws at the treat a couple of times before he decides it's safe, swats it to the floor, and gobbles it up. Then he meows and rubs himself on Miles's leg again. "If I'd known it was this easy to win him over, I would have fed him treats from day one."

"It might have made your life easier. Can I use one of these?" I motion to an empty box.

"Knock yourself out." He makes a face. "Not literally, though."

"That seems to be your strong suit, not mine." I tamp down the memory of the dreams I've been having, where I'm the one doing the tackling, not Miles.

While I try to keep my mind from wandering to inappropriate places, Miles feeds Prince Francis another treat, and I check under the furniture for his toys.

I poke a few holes in the side of the box and use some twine to create swinging toys for Prince Francis to play with. I also add catnip mice that I brought along today to give Prince Francis something to get excited about.

Once the cat play station is set up, I toss a couple of extra treats inside to entice Prince Francis. It does the trick, and a minute later he's lying on his back, chewing on the catnip toy, meowing happily.

"They're kind of like temperamental, slightly psychopathic dogs, aren't they?" Miles stands with his hands on his hips, poking at his full bottom lip with his tongue. I really wish he were less attractive and also less cat intolerant. It would make being in his presence less frustrating.

"They're not psychopaths. They're independent." I take a step toward the kitchen. "I should put out fresh food and change the litter box."

"I already handled the litter. I was on the fence with how expensive that contraption is, but it's way more convenient than managing it manually."

"So you don't think I'm trying to rip you off anymore?" I need to curb my catty comebacks. "The convenience factor is hard to beat, and it counts the number of times Prince Francis uses the litter, so you'll know when it's time to change it." I motion to the shelves and soften my surly. "This looks like a big job to tackle on your own. Do you want some help?"

"It's all right, I can handle it." Miles bites the inside of his cheek, gaze darting from the box in front of me to the shelves.

"Mostly I'm offering because it would be safer for Prince

Francis if he's not at risk of stepping on broken pieces." So much for dropping my surly.

Miles rubs the back of his neck. "Right. Yeah. That makes sense."

I grab an empty box and get started on the shelf to the right of the fireplace, full of dusty knickknacks. The awkward silence is making me uneasy, so I fill it with questions. "How was your trip? Did it go well?" I stifle a sneeze.

"Bless you. It was good. Our team won both games. It helps that one of Montreal's key players is out with an injury, and that our center is self-aware and I had a chance to sit down with him and really go over his weak areas."

"How did you end up as a data analyst for an NHL team? I didn't even know that was a thing." This is good. Maybe I'm better at small talk than I thought.

"Baseball has been doing it for a while, but the NHL is beginning to see the value in it. Sort of. I'm on a trial contract. I worked in the finance department for the Ontario Hockey League, and a perk is free tickets, so I'd go to all the games. I started seeing the patterns in the plays. Well, *started* isn't quite accurate. When I played rec hockey, I picked up on the same things, and we'd always sit down after games and talk through how we could improve." He waves a hand around in the air. "Anyway, long story short, my best friend is Toronto's general manager's assistant, and he suggested they bring me on this season to see if I could provide insight, so here I am. I just need to prove to the team that I'm worth keeping."

I set a smiling otter in the box. "Wow. That's a lot of pressure."

He lifts a shoulder and lets it fall. "But if I help the team increase their overall scoring record, we get better ratings. That can sometimes help morale, and I get to keep doing this. I knew I wasn't ever going to be able to play professionally, since I'm not really built for the sport." He motions to his long, lean frame. "This way I get to work in the field I love and help the players reach their maximum potential."

I can appreciate his enthusiasm for his job, because that's how I feel about mine. And we both work in atypical roles. "What kind of credentials do you need for something like that?"

He sneezes and excuses himself before responding. "I have a degree in sports management and statistics. I geek out pretty hard over numbers. And occasionally I'll get to travel with the team, like this past weekend, which is also cool. The rookie players are always exciting, because there's so much room for upward trajectory." He waves around a hand. "Anyway, I'm blathering on about this, and you're probably just nodding and smiling to be nice." He coughs into the crook of his elbow, following it with a double sneeze. "I took an antihistamine before I came here, but I think all the packing is probably disturbing a lot of dust and dander and making my allergies act up."

"You're allergic to cats?" That could easily explain his open disdain for the independent four-legged fluffballs.

"Every time I come here, I'm sneezing and coughing and my eyes end up red and watery." He motions to his face and sniffles once. His eyes are a little red.

"Hmm. Usually sphynx cats are better for people with allergies, but everyone is different."

"We never had cats growing up. But I have a Great Dane, and I've never had a reaction to him."

"Oh wow. Danes are huge." I like dogs well enough, but I'm a bit more partial to the smaller ones that can't knock me over. "We only ever had cats in my house."

"Wilfred is a big dog, but he's a total marshmallow and would like to think he's a lap dog. This taking care of a cat is a first for me." He motions to Prince Francis, who is happily rolling around on the floor. "Anyway, tell me more about how you ended up as a cat whisperer. How does one realize that's their calling?"

"It just sort of happened, I guess." I lift a shoulder and let it fall. This is such a different side of Miles, and I wonder if we just got off on the wrong foot. Well, I know I sure did. "A friend was going away for a couple of weeks, and he asked if I would mind checking on his cat while he was gone. He actually asked me if I would house-sit, and he lived in a nice place downtown, close to a café my friend owns. I thought it would be kind of fun. Like a staycation. While they were gone, I taught their cat, Mario, how to use the toilet instead of the litter box."

His eyebrows lift. "You can do that?"

"Sure. Despite popular belief, cats are trainable. With patience and the right motivation, you can teach them how to do almost anything. And these people lived on the twenty-second floor of a high rise, so getting rid of litter is a job, and it's smelly in small spaces. Having a potty-trained cat eliminates that problem."

"Do you think you could do that with this guy?" He points to Prince Francis, who is currently drooling all over the cat-nip mouse.

"Maybe. He just needs a motivator. I could see about starting that next week if you're still going to need my help." If his mom is moving into an assisted living facility, I might not be needed for much longer.

"Oh yeah, I guess we should talk about that. I don't know how long it's going to take to find the right place for my mom, and they're already talking about moving her to a temporary facility." He drops another gnome into the box.

"How do you mean?" Maybe I've been irrationally hard on this guy. He just started a new job, his mom is in the hospital, and now he has to find her a place to live. That's a lot of stress. And he's allergic to cats. If I was in the same boat, I might not find them quite so endearing either.

"They need the bed in the hospital ward, so if I don't have a place for her, they'll give her a room in a facility that has the right level of care until I can. Basically, she's at the mercy of the system, and so am I." He plucks another gnome from the mantel and a tumbleweed of dusty debris floats to the floor. He sneezes twice into his elbow. "Excuse me. So yeah, I'll need your help."

"Is it just you and your mom?" I can't imagine what it would have been like to have lost my dad and not have my sister around for support. Even though she was only fourteen, at least I had her on my side, and I didn't have to try to manage my brokenhearted mother alone.

"It's just me, and my parents split up when I was thirteen. They don't really speak, so it's up to me to handle this."

The more I learn about Miles, the more certain I am that I've misjudged him. "That makes it even more challenging, doesn't it? Do you think your dad would help you if he knew how much work this all is?"

Miles sneezes into the crook of his arm again. "Excuse me." He sneezes twice more, peels off a rubber glove, then pulls a perforated pill packet out of his shirt pocket and frees a tablet, swallowing it without water. "I'm not convinced it would be better to have his help on this. Not because he wouldn't be willing to offer it, it's just...complicated. When my parents split it was...tough. I ended up living with my dad because it was closer to the school I wanted to attend, and they had a great hockey program. But that hurt my mom, and she's always been big on doing things herself and not asking for help, so it added another layer of difficulty. Anyway, all that is to say, it's probably better for me to handle this rather than dredge up old hurts."

He's so alone in all of this. It reframes all our previous interactions and reminds me not to judge a book by its cover. "That's a lot of responsibility to shoulder."

He gives me a small smile and clears his throat. "I'll get it sorted out. And it doesn't hurt for you to have some background since you're helping manage this guy." He motions to Prince Francis, who is a drooly, happy mess on the floor.

"I'm happy to help in whatever way I can."

"I appreciate that." He coughs again, and this time it sounds

more like a wheeze. He tugs at the collar of his shirt, sucking in a
breath that sounds painful.

"Are you okay?" I take a step closer, tipping my head back
as I move into his personal space. He's quite tall. I'm not short,
but he's long and lean, and I'm pretty much average in terms of
height. "Do you have asthma? Do you have a puffer?"

"Not asthma." He clears his throat again, sucking in another
wheezing breath. "I think." *Wheeze.* "I'm having." *Wheeze-wheeze.*
"An allergic reaction." *Gasp.* "Can't breathe."

"Oh! Oh my God. Do you have an EpiPen?" I had a friend in
high school with a peanut allergy, and we had to stab her more
than once. It was terrifying.

He shakes his head.

"How can you have an allergic reaction to something that
causes you to not be able to breathe and not have an EpiPen!" I
belatedly realize that now is probably not the best time to scold
him. "We need to get you to the hospital. Right now." I shimmy
up next to him and duck under his shoulder, wrapping my arm
around his waist. His muscles flex under my fingers.

He stumbles, and I weave our way to the door.

When we get outside, he tries to suck in a deep breath, but
again, it sounds like an elderly person trying to suck a thick
milkshake through a too-small straw. At first we start toward my
SUV, but then I think better of it. If he's reacting to Prince
Francis, putting him in a car loaded with cat dander and cat fur is
a bad idea.

"We should probably take your car." We stop in front of his

black Tesla. I tip my head up. "I've never been in an accident before. I promise I'm a safe driver, and I will take care of your steel baby, but I'd really like it if you survived today." Especially since it seems my original disdain for him wasn't quite so necessary. "Where are your keys?"

He inhales another labored breath and sags against me. I shift so he's leaning on his car and pat his hip, over his pocket. I can feel the outline of his keys. I don't ask permission, and jam my hand in there.

I find my face mashed into his side and my boob pressed against his ribs as I feel around for the key ring. I briefly graze something squishy and he grunts, but I manage to hook the keys with my pinkie. "Got em!" I shout into his side, then yank my hand free.

"Don't." *Gasp.* "Need." *Wheeze.* "Them." He opens the passenger door.

Well, that would have been good to know before I touched the head of his penis through the pocket of his pants. I'm not going to address the penis–elephant, though.

Ever.

I help him into the passenger seat, close the door, rush around the hood, and launch myself into the driver's side. I'm very grateful that Miles backed in, so all I have to do is buckle up, push a button, and put the car in drive.

It only takes seven minutes to get to the hospital, although I did run a lot of stale yellows to make it happen. I pull into the emergency parking and get him inside. His wheezing has lessened slightly since we left the house, which I'm taking as a good sign, but his eyes are red and puffy, and so are his lips. They're usually quite full, but right now they look like they've been stung by a hive of bees.

I don't want to leave him alone in the emergency room, but the nurse assures me they're taking care of him, and I have to park the car so it doesn't end up getting towed. I return a few minutes later, but he's no longer sitting in intake. I rush up to the nurse's station, frantic all over again. Flashes of memory from my teen years flicker through my mind and I shove them down. This isn't the same. But still, they come, and I can't help the question that never seems to go away, no matter how much time passes. *If I'd found my dad sooner, would we have gotten him to the hospital in time?* Maybe he would still be here and there wouldn't be a huge hole in our family that belongs to him.

"Miss? Can I help you?"

I shake my head, pulling myself out of the memories and back into the present. "Oh. Yes. There was a man. Miles Thorn. I brought him in. He was in that wheelchair and now he's not." I point to the empty chair, then wring my hands.

She clicks on her keyboard for a few seconds that feel more like hours. "Oh yes, let me take you to him." She rolls back her chair.

"Is he okay?"

"The doctors are with him now."

I notice she doesn't answer the question directly, and my panic ratchets up a notch or two.

I don't really know Miles, not well, apart from the messages we've exchanged over the past week. But the conversation today was a lot less hostile on both sides, and I would like to have another one of those with him. I'm beginning to think he's someone I might like to know. And the possibility that he may not be okay freaks me out. Logically, I'm aware that I'm in fatalist mode, and that I'm probably blowing this out of proportion, but until I see he's okay, I don't think I'm going to be able to calm myself down.

"You did the right thing by bringing Miles to the emergency room," the nurse reassures me. She pulls back a curtain and there lies Miles, lips swollen, face blotchy, hooked up to machines, a needle in the back of his hand.

One of the doctors injects something into the drip bag. "You'll be sleepy after this. We'll monitor you for a few hours to make sure you're okay before we give you the all-clear."

"Okay," Miles rasps, his gaze darting to me. "Hey."

"Hey yourself." I give him a small smile, then turn my attention back to the doctor. "Is Miles okay?"

"We'll need to set up some blood tests to determine exactly how severe the allergy is, and we'll prescribe an EpiPen in the meantime, but he had a serious allergic reaction. We want to make sure we know the exact cause so he can avoid future contact."

"We were packing up some boxes in his mother's house. She has a sphynx cat. I thought they were usually better for people with cat allergies, but maybe we disturbed all the dander in the carpet and that's what he's reacting to?"

"It's possible." The doctor nods. "But this is a severe reaction, so we'll do some tests to confirm the allergy."

Once the doctor is confident the reaction is under control, and Miles's breathing is back to normal, he leaves to tend to other patients.

The nurse pats Miles on the shoulder. "The antihistamine is a strong one. It'll probably knock you out." She looks at me. "You're welcome to stay and keep your boyfriend company, but you might want to grab a book or a magazine."

"Oh, I'm not his girlfriend. I'm just..." *His mother's cat sitter* doesn't seem like the right thing to say after what we've just gone through. "A friend."

She glances between us and smiles. "Okay, well, I'll let you two figure things out."

She pulls the curtain closed behind her. I stand at the end of the bed. He's so long his feet poke out of the bottom. He's still wearing his socks, which have little bones on them again.

"You don't have to stick around. I've already taken up more than enough of your time tonight." He clears his throat and sniffles once.

"I don't mind staying if you'd like some company." And I won't feel very good about myself if I leave him here on his own. "No charge, obviously," I tack on with a cheeky smile.

His lips turn up in a slow smile. "My eyeballs already feel like there are weights attached to them." He heavy blinks a couple of times. "I'll probably pass out on you."

"That's okay. Unless you'd like me to go. Maybe I'm

exacerbating your allergy?" I'd say I don't know why I'm so insistent about staying, but I do. I want to make sure he's okay, and the only way to accomplish that is to hang around until he's released. I glance down at my outfit. I'm wearing one of my Kitty Whisperer T-shirts, a long cardigan with a cat and ball of yarn pattern, and a pair of jeans. They're relatively free of cat hair, but that doesn't mean anything considering.

He's silent for a few beats before he says, "I'd like it if you stayed."

chapter eight

I KIND OF LIKE YOU

Miles

I should probably let her go home. There's something endearing about the nervous way she keeps fidgeting with the buttons on her cardigan, sizing up the chair beside my bed. Or maybe it's the drugs. Regardless, the whole airways closing deal is unnerving, so I wouldn't mind some company apart from passing medical staff.

I reach for the plastic cup of water on the bedside table and prop myself up enough so I can take a sip, but I end up dribbling the contents all over my shirt.

"Oh! Let me help."

She takes the water from my hand as I try to dab at my mouth, which feels . . . odd.

She pulls several tissues from the box on the bedside table and moves my hand away from my face. "You're a little swollen still; it probably makes things awkward."

"How swollen?"

She dabs at my mouth with the tissues, and then my chest.

The contact sends a welcome shot of warmth through my arm.

"Um, sort of like you hired the wrong plastic surgeon and they went overboard on the collagen injections."

I grimace. "That does not sound good at all."

"The swelling has started to go down, so soon you'll be back to your handsome self."

"You think I'm handsome?"

She arches a brow. "The compliment has already been given; no need to fish for more."

I settle back against the pillow, my eyes already feeling heavy. "Well, I think you're pretty." The words are thick in my mouth.

"You're also on drugs."

I pry my lids back open. "You were pretty before the drugs."

She smiles faintly and our gazes meet. Her cheeks flush and her eyes shift away. "Thank you."

"Thank you," I repeat.

Once she's finished patting me dry, she brings the straw back to my lips. This time I manage to get a mouthful without it dribbling down my chin. I let my head fall back against the pillow. At this point it feels like it's made of lead.

"Who's taking care of your dog? Do you need to call someone?" she asks.

I'm not sure if I imagine it, but I swear I feel her fingers in my hair. Opening my eyes is getting harder.

"I should call my neighbors. Joe and Mark take care of Wilfred when I'm away."

"I can do it for you if you'd like."

"Just need my phone." I slap around at my waist, feeling for it.

"It's right here." She holds it up in front of my face, which unlocks it.

She even helps me bring up the contact list, but when I try to jab the screen I miss.

"I can take it from here. You just rest."

I nod once and close my eyes. I can hear her talking, but she sounds far away. I reach out, I'm not sure what for, but fingers close around mine and then I'm sinking into darkness.

The next time I open my eyes it's to the sound of whispered voices. I crack a lid.

"The swelling has gone down, and he's breathing normally," the nurse says quietly. "We'll give him an EpiPen just in case, and I can show you how to use it as well, so you can administer it in an emergency."

"Oh, uh—"

I clear my throat, and both of them startle. "Oh!" Kitty flits around the side of the bed, hands fluttering in the air. "You're awake! That's great! How are you feeling?" For a moment I think she's going to touch my face or run her fingers through my hair, either of which would be unexpected, but also not unwelcome. She drops her hands before she makes contact, though, which is slightly disappointing.

"I'm okay. What time is it?"

"Just after ten," the nurse supplies, gaze moving to his clipboard and then back to me.

"Ten? I've been out for hours." I don't know how many, but it must be several, since it was around dinnertime when Kitty first arrived at my mother's.

"The antihistamines were strong." Kitty awkwardly pats my shoulder, then clasps her hands together again.

"Thanks for staying." My voice is hoarse with sleep, but my throat no longer feels like it's trying to close, so that's great. It's one thing to sleep with someone beside you who is also sleeping. It's another thing to be out cold on drugs while someone I don't know all that well, who isn't very fond of me, sits by my bedside and watches over me because I had an allergic reaction. Possibly to my mother's cat.

"It was more for my peace of mind than anything," she mutters.

I don't know what that means, and there's a nurse in the room, whose gaze keeps flipping between us, as if he's trying to figure out the dynamic. I know I am.

The nurse takes my vitals and gives me the all-clear, but tells Kitty that I shouldn't drive for at least another eight to twelve hours and that it would be best if I wasn't on my own, in case I have another attack.

"Shit. How am I going to get home?"

After a few seconds, Kitty says, "I can drive you."

"I live in the city, though. And then how will you get home? I'll call an Uber."

"But the doctor said you shouldn't be left alone." She clasps her hands behind her back. "Unless you have a roommate or a girlfriend who lives with you?" Her cheeks flush.

That's an interesting reaction. "No roommate or girlfriend, just my dog. Crap. He's been alone all day."

"I talked to your neighbors, remember? Or maybe you don't. But they took him for a walk and brought him back to their place. I told them you'd call when you were being released."

"Right. Okay. That's good." I vaguely remember her offering to call them. It feels like days ago, not hours.

"I think it's best for me to drive you home and stay to make sure you don't have another reaction," she says decisively.

"My neighbors are right across the hall."

"If your throat closes and you pass out from lack of oxygen, it's going to be hard to call them," she argues. "And I'd say you could stay at my place, but I live with my mom and sister."

"And I'm sure you have at least two cats." I clear my throat; just saying the word makes my windpipes feel like they're constricting.

"No cats, just embarrassing family members."

"You don't have a cat?" That's a surprise.

"Not since I was a teenager." She drops her head, and her expression grows pinched.

I feel like there's a story there. How can someone who adores cats not own one? That seems...preposterous. But I leave it alone, not wanting to add to the weird tension. "Are you sure you're okay to take me home?"

"I'm sure. Besides"—she gives me a cheeky smile—"your car is fun to drive."

"Ah, there it is, the real reason behind the offer." I throw my legs over the side of the bed and look down at my hospital gown–covered torso. "I need some clothes."

"They're right here." Kitty passes me the pile, which was sitting on the small table beside the bed.

I cross to the bathroom. After I'm dressed I sign the release papers and nod and agree with the doctor about allergy tests that have been set up for me, not being alone for the next twelve or so hours, and not getting behind the wheel of a car.

Once I've been discharged, we start for the exit, but I remember I was supposed to see my mother tonight so I could prepare her for the trip to visit a retirement village later this week, and she happens to be in this very hospital. Visiting hours are long over, but I want to check in with the nurse to see how she's doing before we leave.

"Hey, Miles, you're here late." Stephanie, the night nurse, who I've met on several occasions since I mostly stop in after work, tips her head to the side. Her gaze shifts to Kitty and then back to me.

I motion to my face. "I had a bit of a thing."

At the furrow in her brow, Kitty pipes up. "He had an allergic reaction. Possibly to a cat. At least I'm hoping it's the cat he's allergic to and not me." She laughs, like she's surprised that those words came out of her mouth, and her cheeks turn pink.

"I don't think it's you," I tell her and turn my attention back to Stephanie, who looks amused. "Anyway, I just wanted to check in and see how my mother's day was. I'd planned to visit, but obviously that didn't happen."

"She had a few lucid moments. She asked about you, actually. She remembered you were supposed to stop by."

I nod and rap on the counter once before I jam my hand in my pocket. "I'm sorry if that caused you any issues, my not showing up."

"Nothing we couldn't handle. Should I let her know that you'll be by tomorrow if she asks?"

"That'd be great, thanks."

On the way to the car, I call Joe and Mark to let them know I'm on my way home. I reassure them I'm okay and that I can manage Wilfred tonight. I fold myself into the passenger seat of my Tesla and press Home on the GPS. "I'm sorry I monopolized your entire night."

"I would have watched reruns of *Two and a Half Men* if I'd been at home, and I can pretty much recite every single line down to the laugh track, so you saved me from lip-syncing to an old TV show." She pulls out of the spot and heads toward the exit.

"Why reruns?"

"My mom likes to watch it. It was my dad's favorite show."

"Was? What happened to your dad?" This isn't the first time she's referred to him in past tense.

She keeps her eyes on the road and her grip on the steering wheel tightens briefly. "My dad passed away when I was a teenager."

That familiar pang makes my heart sore for a second. "Oh man. I'm so sorry. Was it unexpected?"

"He had a massive heart attack. We didn't get him to the hospital fast enough," she says softly.

"That must have been hard." And explains why she was so intent on getting me to the hospital as quickly as possible, and staying the entire time, and driving me home. Another reminder that I've been a jerk to her, and here she is, taking care of me anyway.

"It was. Sometimes it still is." She glances at me for a second. "Losing someone you're close to is . . . like having a piece of your soul go missing that you can't ever get back."

"That's an astonishingly accurate way to describe loss." I rub at my chest, the ache making me want to . . . do something. Like hug her. Soothe us both, maybe.

She hums her agreement. "I imagine it's equally difficult to have a parent with dementia. It would feel like a loss, but the person is still there, they just can't access their memories anymore. It would be both frustrating and painful. They look like the same person, but they're not really there anymore."

This time I'm the one who makes a sound, and I give voice to the worries that have been plaguing me since my mom went into the hospital. "Lately my mom has been talking to me like I'm still a kid. It's like her brain is stuck in the past. Maybe if I'd tried harder with her, it wouldn't be this bad."

Kitty reaches over and squeezes my hand before quickly withdrawing. "Don't do that to yourself, Miles. You can't hold the blame for her memory failing her."

I wonder if she'd say that if she knew the entire truth. "Sometimes it's hard not to play the what-if game, you know?"

"I do." She smiles faintly, but she keeps her eyes fixed on the road.

"Anyway, if I keep up with this introspection, you really are going to have to up your rates and charge me like a therapist."

Kitty chuckles. "This is why other people's pets are great. You can tell them all your woes, and as long as you give them pets and treats, they'll listen. Not great with the actual advice, but cathartic nonetheless."

"Mmm. That's a good point."

"Tabbies are particularly good listeners and exceptionally cuddly," Kitty says.

"What about dogs? Do they count?"

"Oh yes, definitely. Pugs and bullies are the best. A little snorty and drooly, but the snuggles make it worth it."

"I hope I wasn't snorty and drooly when I was all hopped up on those antihistamines." This conversation I like better. Not me going down a rabbit hole of guilt I can't get out of.

That earns me a chuckle, and I find I like that sound, a lot. "You don't snore, but you do talk in your sleep."

I let the headrest do its job and close my eyes. "I hope I didn't say anything incriminating."

"It sounds like you were giving a player a pep talk." The repetitive *tick, tick, tick* tells me that she's signaling to turn or change lanes.

I crack a lid and note that we're getting on the freeway. At least it won't be too busy at this time of night. "I do that a lot, dream about plays."

"I dream about talking to cats."

I laugh and then yawn.

The next time I open my eyes it's because we've arrived, and Kitty is waking me up. I'm groggy on the elevator ride up to the apartment.

"You're cool with dogs, right?" I ask when we reach my floor.

"I'm more used to medium-size ones, but yes, I'm cool with dogs."

"Wilfred is big but very friendly." Except sometimes when he's on a leash and he sees a bird. For whatever reason, birds get him ramped up. And kids on skateboards. "He's more likely to lick you to death than anything else."

"Death by licking?" Her eyebrows rise, and her gaze goes to my mouth for a second before she looks away and her face flushes.

And suddenly I have a very lurid image in my head that has absolutely nothing to do with my dog.

Kitty chews on her bottom lip while her entire face turns bright red. I keep my mouth shut and open the door, shuffling her behind me as Wilfred comes bounding down the hall. As soon as he reaches me, he shoves his nose into my crotch. "Dude, no thanks."

He backs up and plunks his butt on the floor, tail wagging so hard it's almost a blur.

"Wilfred, meet Kitty."

His tail thumps on the ground and he looks from me to her and back again, like he's waiting for permission to say a proper hello.

She holds out a hand and steps up beside me. Wilfred gives her a cursory sniff, then nudges her hand, looking for pets. "He is so sweet."

"Until he tries to sit in your lap or steal your dinner off your plate," I say.

She scratches behind his ear, but her gaze moves to me. "You should probably lie down."

"I should feed Wilfred first."

"I'll take care of Wilfred. You're slow blinking and using the wall to prop yourself up. If you pass out, I might be able to soften your fall, but I'd prefer if we don't add sprained body parts, yours or mine, to the list of things that have gone wrong today."

"That's a very good point. I'll show you the spare room?"

"Sure. That sounds good."

Wilfred trots along beside me as I guide Kitty down the hall. The spare room gets used occasionally when friends come to town or my dad visits. He's usually here once in the summer and during the holidays. Now that I'm working for the NHL, there might be opportunities for me to go out his way more often, even if the visits are brief.

"I'm just down there." I point to the door at the end of the hall, then the one across from us. "And the bathroom is just there. I'll leave you a toothbrush. But you don't have to stay. If you'd rather grab an Uber, I would totally understand and reimburse you. I don't want this to be awkward for you."

"I'll feel better knowing that if anything happens, I'm here to help. Unless you'd prefer I go home." She chews her bottom lip nervously.

I'm guessing this need to make sure I'm okay has something to do with what happened to her dad. "I trust you, Kitty."

"Okay. That's good." She gives me a shy smile.

"Wilfred sleeps in my room, so you don't have to worry about him bugging you." He's leaning against my leg, tail wagging, whining quietly. He has a dog bed in my room, but half the time I wake up with his head on the pillow beside me. I shouldn't let him get away with it as much as I do, but when he gives me his puppy-dog eyes, it's hard to say no. Also, I don't have a girlfriend, so there really isn't a reason to kick him out of bed, apart from his having bad breath, anyway.

"I'm sure he always wants to be where you are. And dogs can sense when there's something up with their owners. Cats are the same." Her smile wavers, and she looks down at her hands and twists the ring on her middle finger, then nods toward the other end of the hall. "Anyway, enough of my nattering, off to bed for you."

"'Night, Kitty."

"'Night, Miles."

The exhaustion sweeps over me again as I step into my bedroom. I manage to get my dress shirt and my pants off, but I don't bother brushing my teeth before I climb into bed, oddly reassured that Kitty is down the hall.

chapter nine

ALL THE EMBARRASSING MOMENTS

Miles

Iwake up to a wet nose against my cheek and terrible breath. My eyes pop open, and Wilfred's concerned face comes into focus. "Hey, buddy. Is it time for breakfast already?" I scratch behind his ear and roll over onto my back, glancing at the clock on the nightstand.

My alarm is set to go off in two minutes.

It's typical for me to wake up a couple of minutes before my alarm, mostly because Wilfred functions like a dog alarm. His tail thumps on the floor, clearly excited that it's morning and his bowl will be full as soon as I get my ass out of bed.

I close my eyes again, positive I could fall back to sleep and stay that way for several more hours. But his whimper and another nose nudge remind me that if I stay where I am, I'm going to get a face bath. With a tongue that's likely licked a set of balls recently. Seems like maybe cats and dogs aren't all that different after all.

I throw my covers off and trudge to the bathroom. A nagging feeling that I'm forgetting something important tickles the back of my mind, but I'm still groggy and only half awake. Wilfred follows along and plunks himself down in the middle of the bathroom, tail wagging, panting happily as he watches me angle my semi down and relieve myself. I check my reflection in the mirror as I wash my hands.

The allergic reaction. My face is back to normal, no more puffy lips or hives. I'd like to find out sooner rather than later what exactly I'm allergic to so I can avoid a subsequent reaction. If this is what happens every time I try to fill a box, cleaning out my mother's house is going to be a serious hazard to my health.

I leave my worries in the bathroom and head down the hall, Wilfred's nails clipping along on the floor as he trots after me. When I reach the kitchen I'm surprised—but probably shouldn't be, as memories of last night filter through—to find Kitty sitting at my kitchen table with a coffee cup in her hand and yesterday's paper in front of her.

"Hey." I run a hand through my hair.

She startles and coffee nearly sloshes over the rim of her cup. She recovers, though, and her gaze lifts from the paper to me, standing in the middle of the open-concept living room. Her eyes flare and move over me, cheeks bursting with color. "Oh! Hi!" Her voice is high pitched, and her gaze darts to the side, then bounces back to my waist, and away again. Her face grows redder by the millisecond.

Which is when I realize I'm only wearing boxer briefs and a white T-shirt, and I'm still sporting my morning semi.

I drop a hand in front of my crotch. "Shit. Sorry. I forgot you were here. I'll be right back!" I spin around and rush down the hall to my bedroom.

Wilfred barks once and follows me halfway down the hall before stopping, probably confused.

I make sure he's not on my heels before I slam my door shut and berate myself for being an idiot and not putting on pants before I left my bedroom. But in my defense, my brain is slow and sluggish, probably from all the drugs they gave me last night.

When I return to the kitchen, Kitty is no longer sitting at the table. For a second I think she's left, or maybe she's hiding in the spare room. But I find her on the other side of the kitchen, next to Wilfred's bowl, where she's pouring kibble into the dish. He waits impatiently, tail wagging so vigorously that his entire butt is swaying back and forth. She murmurs to him, words I don't catch because her voice is too low.

He waits until she gives him the go-ahead before he shoves his face in the bowl, tail expressing his delight. She gives him a quick pat on the back before she turns around. "Oh!" Her gaze darts from my face down to my waist and back up again before shifting to the side. "Hey. Hi. I made coffee. I hope that's okay."

I'm thankful we're going to ignore the semi flashing. "Oh yeah, I'm glad you made yourself at home. Did you sleep okay? Thanks again for last night. I know it probably wasn't how you expected your evening to go." Neither of us seems to be able to hold eye contact for more than a millisecond.

This feels a lot like the awkward aftermath of a one-night stand, but without the sex.

And suddenly an image of Kitty, naked, in my bed, wearing her leopard-framed glasses, pops into my head. Which is a ludicrous fantasy, considering all I've managed to be for her so far is a giant pain in the butt. I blink twice and try to focus on other things. Like the enthusiastic sound of Wilfred snort-eating his food.

A knock at my door prevents Kitty from responding.

I glance at the clock on the stove. It's just after seven. "I'll be right back."

Sometimes my neighbor down the hall borrows cream or sugar. I throw open the door and find not my neighbor, but Josh, ready to use the spare key to let himself in.

"Hey, man, why aren't you dressed? We gotta be at the rink in an hour, and I want to stop at the bakery first. I have a hankering for a cinnamon roll." He brushes past me, and I don't have a chance to warn him that we're not alone before he reaches the living room and comes to an abrupt halt. "Oh. Hey. Hi there. Why didn't you tell me you had company?" He glances from Kitty to me, one eyebrow raised.

She's still dressed in yesterday's outfit, but it's significantly more rumpled. Which means she probably had to sleep in it. I should have given her a shirt or something. *Then it would smell like her perfume.*

I inwardly cringe at how creepy that sounds in my head. And I realize, belatedly, how this must look to him.

"I had an allergic reaction," I explain.

His eyebrows try to touch each other over the bridge of his nose.

"I drove Miles to the hospital. And then home. And the doctors said he shouldn't be alone, so I stayed to make sure he wouldn't blow up like a balloon again. I'm Kitty." She steps around the counter and wipes her hand on her pants before extending it.

Josh takes her much smaller, delicate hand in his. For reasons that mystify me, it makes me want to punch him in the face.

"Hi, Kitty. It's nice to meet you." He gives her his customary smirk. "I'm Josh. Miles and I work together. I've heard a lot about you."

And now I have different, less territorial reasons for wanting to punch him.

"Oh?" Her gaze slides my way, her tone dripping sarcasm. "All good things, I'm sure."

Josh either misses the sarcasm or decides to ignore it. "Only the best. You're kind of internet famous, aren't you?"

She giggles and waves a hand around in the air. "I'm not famous."

"You've got a pretty huge following on social media and some real dedicated fans."

Bless her sweet, innocent heart, Kitty's eyes light up, as though she's found a kindred spirit in Josh. "Are you a cat lover?"

Before he can say something highly inappropriate, I interrupt. Unlike me, Josh is a ladies' man, and for whatever reason, that smirk he has should be patented as a panty remover. And I do not want him trying to remove Kitty's panties. Ever. Or flirting with her. That's a realization I'm not sure what I should do with.

"Hey, uh, not that this isn't a welcome surprise." I hope he catches the hint of derision. "But what are you doing here?"

He gives me a look. "We gotta be at the rink in—" He glances at the clock on the stove. "Fifty-four minutes."

That's right. He said that when he first arrived. "Shit." I glance at Kitty, standing a few feet away, looking beautiful despite her rumpled clothes.

"I can take the train home," she says. "I wanted to make sure that you were feeling okay before I left, and you definitely are." Her gaze dips to my waist, and her cheeks flush for what seems like the millionth time this morning.

Stupid body, being a jerk and embarrassing us both.

"Why don't you take my car?" I blurt without thinking about what I'm offering and who I'm offering it in front of.

Josh's head whips around. I don't make eye contact, though, or even glance in his direction. Instead, I stay completely focused on Kitty.

She, however, does glance in Josh's direction. "Oh, uh, that's not necessary. It's been a while since I've taken the train. It'll be an adventure."

"I'm heading your way to see my mother later this afternoon. And I'm totally used to the train. At this time of day it'll take a while, and then you'll still have to get from the station back to your car. And you've been more than generous with your time." I grab the keys from the counter and hold them out to her. This is the perfect way to get myself off her shit list, show my appreciation, and get her away from Josh. "Seriously. I insist. You're a great driver. I trust you with my baby."

Her uncertain expression says it all.

I step closer and take her hand in mine, flip it palm up, and drop the keys into the center, then fold her fingers around them. I should let her hand go and stop trying to force my car on her. But there's new energy in the air. All our previous bickering and negative tension has been wrapped in her kindness. My previous frustration with my situation has shifted. The contact is completely innocent and should not in any way invoke the desire to lean in and kiss her, and yet I find my eyes darting to her lips. Which she licks.

"Okay?" She sounds more confused than anything.

"I owe you for last night." I lift my gaze and get lost in her forest-green eyes for several seconds. At least until Josh clears his throat.

I reluctantly drop her hand and glance his way. It appears as though he's trying to telepathically communicate his thoughts through his eyebrows.

"I'll grab my purse and be on my way. Unless you need any-thing else?" Kitty crosses the room and picks up her oversized bag with a cat face on it.

"Nope! All good. I'll touch base later." I can't tell if I'm making things better or worse.

"Sure." She slips her feet into her cat-print flats. "I wanted to discuss me potentially staying the night at your mother's place. I think part of the reason Prince Francis has been so destructive is because he's not used to being alone so much. It might help to have someone in the house with him at night, and since that's not safe for you, I'd be willing to give it a shot. Maybe we can talk that through later."

"Yeah, absolutely." I rush ahead down the hall ahead of her so I can unlock the door for her. "Thanks again for all your help. With everything. Especially the whole getting me to the hospital. Dying in my mother's house in a pile of old trinkets is not the way I want to go." *Way to go, Miles. Ruin a perfectly good thank-you by talking about your potential death.*

"I'm really glad I was there." She adjusts her purse and gives me a small, uncertain smile. "Timing really is everything."

"It is. Who knows what would have happened if you hadn't arrived when you did." I need to stop thinking about the what-ifs. It's freaking me out. "And thanks again for spending the night."

The sound of a cat meowing out a song comes from her purse. She digs her phone out of her purse and brings it to her ear. "Hello?" She makes a range of facial expressions as the voice coming through the phone rises in volume. "Oh, that's not good at all. Have you tried the salmon treats? Those are his favorite." She makes a kiss face for a moment and then taps her lip. I almost lean in, until I realize this is her thinking face.

"Hmm. Okay. I can be there in less than an hour. Just use your calm voice and try to relax. We'll get him out." She reassures whoever she's talking to twice more before she ends the call.

"Is everything okay?" Clearly it's not, based on the side of the conversation I heard, but I still feel compelled to ask for whatever reason.

"Bumbles is stuck in the wall."

"The wall?" I echo. "How does a cat get stuck in a wall?"

"I'm not sure. But Mr. O'Toole has cataracts and hearing aids, so it's very possible Bumbles isn't stuck in a wall at all, and he's just managed to climb into one of the cupboards again and can't get himself out." She readjusts her glasses again.

"That's not good."

"Not for Bumbles, no. I'm going to head there now. And thank you again for letting me take your car. I promise I'll drive with the utmost caution." She takes a step toward me and for reasons I don't understand, I think it means she's coming in for a hug. So I open my arms.

Her eyes flare. And in that moment, I realize she wasn't coming in for a hug, she was just trying to get around me because I'm standing in front of the door. But I'm committed to seeing this through, even when she makes a surprised, squeaky sound.

As I wrap my arms around her, I manage to slam my elbow into the wall. I suck back the groan, because I don't want to look like I can't handle a little pain, but man, hitting your funny bone hurts like hell. For a couple of seconds, she's frozen, but eventually her arms come around my waist, and she pats me on the back. Her nose bumps my pec before she turns her head. I wonder if she can feel or hear how fast my heart is beating. I glance down the hall and spot Josh peeking around the corner. Again, his eyebrows shoot up.

Kitty gives me a brief squeeze and as she steps back, her eyes are extra wide, and her cheeks are once again pink. "I'm glad your face is back to normal today. Your lips were already kissable; you really didn't need them to be any fuller than they are in the first place." Her own lips go thin, and it looks like she's biting them together. "I have to go! Have a good day! Stay safe and keep breathing!"

I hold the door for her while she steps into the hall. "Have a good day, Kitty! Thanks again!" She glances over her shoulder and waves, then disappears around the corner, where the elevators are.

Josh is standing in the living room, one of his manicured eyebrows popping. Literally, it's bouncing up and down like a car with hydraulics. I have no idea how he does it.

"Dude. You have some explaining to do, but after you get dressed, because I want a cinnamon roll."

"I need to take Wilfred out to use the bathroom before we leave," I tell him.

"I can take him while you get ready." Josh grabs the leash from the hook on the wall. "Come on, buddy, let's go pee on a fire hydrant."

Wilfred hustles over, tongue lolling and tail wagging.

"Okay. Thanks. I'll be right back." I take a two-minute shower, throw on a fresh suit, and meet Josh in the hall ten minutes later. I grab my messenger bag from the counter, give Wilfred a pat on the head, assure him I'll be home at a reasonable time tonight, and that Mark and Joe will be by soon to take him and Herman for their daily trip to the dog park, then I leave my apartment with Josh.

As soon as we're in Josh's sports car, he starts firing questions at me. "Are you doing the dirty with the Kitty Whisperer?"

I give him a look. "No."

"She slept at your house last night, and you're telling me nothing happened?"

"I had an allergic reaction. A bad one. I wasn't in any condition to do anything but be thankful I can breathe."

"Okay, back this up and start from the beginning." He makes a rewind motion with his finger.

So I tell him the whole story.

He chuckles. "Well, there's a special brand of irony right there."

I frown. I'm still spacey from the antihistamines, I think. "What are you talking about?"

"You're basically allergic to your girlfriend."

"She's not my girlfriend."

"She stayed the night at your house."

"In my spare room. Because I almost died."

"So you'd be cool with it if I ask her out on a date, then?"

"Over my dead fucking body."

Josh smiles. "That's what I thought."

chapter ten

A LITTLE HAUNTED?

Kitty

Turns out I was right about Bumbles. He was stuck in the cupboard, rather than the wall. He chewed through a bag of food and ate a good portion of it, then dropped a deuce in a basket of potatoes now destined for the garbage.

With Bumbles managed, I drive to Miles's mother's place to switch out our cars—I don't know why I don't just refer to her as Tabitha in my head since I've seen her name on her mail. Maybe because I've never met her? Prince Francis is displeased with my short visit, but I promise I'll be back later to hang out. My next stop is home so I can shower and change into fresh clothes.

While I'm in the shower I play over the parting hug with Miles. It was clumsy, mostly because I didn't expect it. It's possible it was a gratitude hug, or a reflexive one. Regardless, I enjoyed it. Everything was easier when I believed he was a hot cat-hating jerk. Now our interactions are steeped in awkwardness.

By the time I'm done in the shower it's noon. Mom is dressed for work at the bakery. Two plates sit on the counter, one empty, one with a BLT sandwich. She pushes it toward me. "That's for you."

"Thanks, Mom." I kiss her on the cheek and pick up one of the triangles, taking a bite. All I've had today so far is coffee. "When does your shift start?"

She checks the clock on the stove. "Not until two, but I'm only there until six, so it's a short one."

I swallow my bite of sandwich. "I'm sitting overnight for a client, so it's only you and Hattie for dinner. Speaking of, where is Hattie?"

"She went to the library for a study group this morning, and she has a night class, so she won't be home for dinner either."

"Oh, that's right. I could pop by and have dinner with you so you're not alone, if you want," I offer.

"You don't need to do that. Marie invited me over tonight, so I think I'll accept, since I'm going to be the only one here." She drums on the counter.

I try to hide my shock, but I think it comes through in my pitch. "That's a great idea! How is Marie these days?" Marie has a son around my sister's age. Last I heard he was on scholarship at a university out of province.

"She's good. Trying to keep busy now that the house is empty. She's taking a flower-arranging course because she's convinced there are wedding bells in her son's future."

"He's only Hattie's age."

Mom smiles and shrugs. "I think it's probably more about trying something new than anything else. She asked me if I wanted to join her, and I think I will. It's only one night a week. It'll be fun. Besides, you and Hattie are just so busy these days."

"I'm glad you'll have company." It's good that Mom is making plans with friends instead of spending the night in front of the TV watching old shows.

Mom leaves for work, and I pack an overnight bag. I stop at Kat's to manage some paperwork. It isn't my favorite part of the job, but at least I can hang out with Kat for a bit and fill her in on the excitement of the last few days. She sits in the office with me while I fill out invoices, and a new, adorable kitten named Smush climbs all over her. He's a Persian with a congenital birth defect that makes his face asymmetrical. He has the sweetest disposition.

"That must have been scary." Kat's eyes are wide as I explain my unexpected trip to the emergency room. "Anaphylactic reactions are no joke."

"It was a harrowing fifteen minutes, that's for sure. And now I'm nervous about him coming to the house. It's weird, though, because he's been coming there for nearly two weeks, and it's the first time he's had any kind of reaction. But he's going for tests, so hopefully he'll get some answers soon, and I don't have to be anxious about it anymore."

Kat arches a brow. "Sounds like you've changed your tune about the cat-hating jerk."

"I think maybe we got off on the wrong foot." I shrug. Since I've gotten to know him a bit better, my impression is shifting.

"Now tell me about your date with Brad. I need all the details."
We haven't been able to make our schedules align recently, so
this is the first chance we've had to really sit down and chat since
they went out.

Kat fills me in on her date, which ended with a toe-curling kiss
and a request for a second date. After I'm finished with invoices,
we spend half an hour taking videos with Smush and include a
few of the kitten products for our sponsors, and then I'm off to
love some kitties.

Later in the evening I make another stop to see Prince Francis.
The second I slide the key in the lock, he meows from the other
side of the door. I carefully push it open, and he rushes onto the
front porch, weaves between my ankles, then promptly throws
himself down at my feet and stretches out, little paws curling as
he kneads the air.

"How's my favorite naked kitty? Were you a good boy today?"
He rolls to his feet and scales my leg. I pick him up, and he
immediately rubs his face against mine, licks my cheek a couple
of times, and then burrows through my hair, his whiskers tickling
the back of my neck. He stretches himself around my shoulders
and hangs around the back of my neck like a living stole.

The living room is in its usual chaotic state with boxes over-
turned, and the remaining mantel gnomes litter the floor.

His ear twitches against my cheek as I sigh. "Oh, Prince
Francis, what am I going to do with you?"

He nudges me with his wet nose and licks the edge of my
jaw. Then he tries to bite my earlobe before he starts purring.

Ironically, or depressingly, depending on how one looks at it, this is the most action I've gotten in a long time. Apart from the unexpected hug and the accidental key-retrieval peen graze. I wish my interactions with Miles were slightly lower on the embarrassment scale.

"We're having a sleepover tonight. Does that sound good to you?" I rub his whiskery cheek.

He meows and starts purring, as though he understands.

I feed Prince Francis, hunt down the vacuum, and suck up the catnip toy that's now a shredded mess, before I tackle the fallen gnomes.

I've just finished cleaning up when I get a message from Miles, indicating he's stopping by in a few minutes.

My heart rate kicks up a few notches, and of course, because my brain does what it wants, an image of him from this morning pops into my head. His hair was a sexy mess, eyes still heavy with sleep, lips back to their normal, full, luscious condition. His long, lean limbs were wrapped in a rumpled white T-shirt that hugged his chest and showed off the hint of a six-pack. Or maybe a four-pack, but I've never seen him shirtless, so I'm totally guessing.

But the real showstopper happened to be hiding in the pouch of his boxer shorts. He'd been rocking some serious morning wood. And the light blue boxer shorts covered in a hockey puck print didn't do much to mask the problem.

Now that his jerk status has been shelved, and I'm no longer irritated by my attraction to him, I'm finding it a challenge *not* to think about what he might look like minus the boxers and the shirt. Thanks to my overactive imagination, I'm nervous about seeing Miles this evening. I'm also concerned about his allergies. So worried, in fact, that I meet him outside on the front porch.

He's wearing a pair of black dress pants, free of animal hair, and a light blue button-down—which happens to be the same color as his boxers this morning. I quickly try to corral my excited imagination, but his tie is hockey themed too, so the image pops back up like an untamable gopher.

He's not wearing a suit jacket, but as my gaze lifts to his face I feel my eyebrows rise. A blue surgical mask, the kind doctors wear, is looped around his ears and hangs under his chin like a fabric beard.

"Hey." He raises a hand as he walks up the steps to the front porch.

"Hi. How was your day?" I make a general motion to his face.

This was a lot easier when his jerkiness interfered with his attractiveness. Now when I look at him, all I see is the hot guy I took care of last night who's going through a tough time.

"Not bad. Just a bit tired. You'd never know I almost had a brush with death yesterday."

"It's a bit surreal, I imagine."

"Yeah, kinda." He pulls his hand from his pocket and starts to rub his chin, but the mask is in the way. "I did some on-line research, and one suggestion was to wear a mask so I'm not breathing in the dander. If that's the problem, anyway. But a mask is a barrier between me and whatever is causing the allergy. The internet gurus also suggested goggles, but the only kind I have access to are swimming ones, and I draw the line at wearing those outside of the ocean." He holds up a pair of blue surgical gloves. "But I also have these."

"It looks like you raided the nurse's station at a hospital." If he was wearing a pair of scrubs he'd look like a doctor.

"I haven't been there yet today, but that would have been a lot cheaper." He rolls up on the balls of his feet, then drops back to his heels.

"Do you want to come in, or..." I let it hang, unsure how to proceed and nervous he's going to have another allergic reaction. One brush with death in twenty-four hours is more than enough.

"I've been inside my mother's house a lot over the past couple of weeks, and yesterday was the only time I had a reaction like that. I'm sort of hoping it's a one-time thing." The way his voice lifts at the end makes it sound like a question.

"Do you have your EpiPen with you?"

"Yup." He pulls it out of his shirt pocket.

I nod and blow out a breath. "This feels a lot like I'm sending you into a burning building."

"I'm sure everything will be fine." He runs his hands over his thighs and pulls the mask up to cover his nose and his luscious, full lips. It's almost a relief that I don't have to look at them anymore.

I step back and allow him to open the door.

I don't know what I expect to happen. Maybe for him to blow up and turn blue like the girl in *Charlie and the Chocolate Factory* when she eats the gum that tastes like a four-course meal with blueberry something or other at the end.

But he crosses the threshold and doesn't immediately start gasping for air. He leaves his shoes on, a habit I've gotten into as well, thanks to Prince Francis and his twitchy paws.

When he reaches the living room he stops, toes an inch away from the carpeted floor. His eyebrows lift and his head turns my way. "Was this place clean when you got here?"

"I tidied up," I admit.

Now his eyebrows pull together. "You didn't have to do that."

"I was here early, and it only took a few minutes to put everything away." Or toss it in the garbage.

He nods once, like that makes sense. "You mentioned staying overnight to monitor Prince Francis. Do you think you still need to do that?"

"It depends on how much longer he's on his own. You said you had an appointment at a home?" I keep waiting for him to make a comment that's going to throw him back into jerk territory, but so far so good.

He nods and glances at the smartwatch decorating his wrist. "I wanted to stop by here and check in with you first."

"Are you taking your mother with you?" I don't know why I'm so inclined to ask personal questions, but I guess it's better than bringing up what happened this morning.

"I'm not sure how she's going to react, so I figured it was better for me to check it out before I take her on a tour." He adjusts his mask and tucks a hand in his pocket. "I'll show you the spare room before I go, so you can get settled in. Kinda weird that I'm doing this two days in a row, although I don't remember much about last night, so maybe you found the spare room on your own?"

"You showed me. You were a gracious, albeit groggy, host," I assure him.

"That's good to know." He leads me up the short staircase to the second floor. There are five doors up here. One is a bathroom; another is a linen closet with fresh sheets and towels. "That's my mother's bedroom. It basically looks the same as it did when I was a kid." Miles motions to the bed with an old quilt that reminds me of the early two thousands.

He moves to the door across the hall. The hinges creak as he pushes it open. "I don't think this room has been updated since I was a teenager." He flicks on the light.

"This was your bedroom?" I soak up the space, trying to imagine a teenage version of the man standing in front of me lying on that double bed.

"It was. After my parents separated, I stayed here every other weekend through my teen years. I don't think anyone else has ever slept in here."

The comforter is hockey-player inspired. The pillows have the same pattern. Across the room is a dresser with a digital clock, but nothing else.

In the corner is a small desk and an old computer monitor, also circa the early two thousands. Apart from a poster with a motivational phrase above the desk, the walls are bare. It doesn't look like much has changed in the last decade.

I wonder what young Miles was like. Was he studious? Did he have early-morning hockey practice on weekends? I glance at the bed again and because my mind is being a jerk, I picture the version of Miles I know lying on it in only his boxers.

When I speak, I sound like a squeaky toy. "This is great. Thanks."

He rubs the back of his neck. "I'm not sure when the sheets were changed last, so we can grab a fresh set from the linen closet if you'd like."

With the non-PG quality of my current thoughts, I don't think it's a good idea to be near a bed with Miles. "That's okay. I can manage. What time did you say your meeting at the home is?"

He glances at his watch. "Crap. In less than half an hour. I gotta run if I'm going to get there on time. I'll message later, though."

"Let me know how it goes."

"Sounds good." He turns his head and raises his arm, coughing once into his elbow, but his face is still covered by the mask.

"Oh no! Is it happening again? You need to get out of here!" Two allergic reactions back-to-back would be bad. I grab him by the free arm and drag him down the hall. Apparently I'm the biggest klutz in the history of the universe because I lose my footing on the stairs.

On the upside, instead of pulling Miles down along with me, he manages to snag me around the waist with his free arm. We land in a heap on our butts, me between his long legs.

"I'm so sorry!" I try to scramble to my feet, but his arm is still wrapped around my waist.

"I'm fine, Kitty. I'm not having another reaction. I just inhaled a hair or something, and it made me cough." For a moment, his arm tightens around me, and I swear I feel his nose in my hair, but then that could be because of the awkward position we're in.

"Oh. Wow. I turn everything into a medical crisis, don't I?" If my voice could turn colors, it would be red with embarrassment.

Miles releases me and I push to my feet, moving down a couple of steps so he has room to stand. "Well, to be fair, yesterday was freaky for both of us, so your concern is understandable. A repeat would not be welcome."

He follows me to the foyer, and I step outside onto the front porch with him.

He unhooks the medical mask from around his ears and tucks it into his pocket. His tongue runs along his bottom lip, commanding my attention. "Thanks again for everything, Kitty. And especially for staying the night. Here and at my place. I realize we probably got off on the wrong foot, and I kept sticking mine in my mouth. There's a good chance I'll still keep doing that, the foot-in-mouth thing, but it's not intentional."

I'm still staring at his lips, pondering their kissability, so it takes me several extra seconds to respond. "I could have been more empathetic to begin with. Not everyone is a natural cat lover. And I'm happy I could help last night and tonight."

"Me, too. I mean I'm happy too, about you helping."

We smile at each other for a few seconds.

"Good luck at the home. I hope it's the right fit for your mom." I don't know what to do with my hands, so I wrap them around me, like I'm giving myself a hug.

"Me, too." He pulls his keys out of his pocket and flips them around his finger. "I'd say have fun with Prince Francis, but considering how much damage he causes, I don't know that tonight is going to be all that awesome for you."

"I'm sure that when he realizes there's a lap to occupy, he'll be fine." I point to my crotch and realize too late that it's inappropriate. Talking to Miles was easier before my hormones took over and made me stupid.

He stutter-steps to the walkway and does a two-step thing on the way to his car, still flipping his keys between his fingers. I wait until he's pulling out of the driveway before I go inside.

I decide that the evening would best be spent on cat training. So I pull out my programmable buttons and get to work setting them up. The first button is the easiest one to inspire training: Treat. I settle cross-legged on the floor and shake my bag of treats. Prince Francis trots over and headbutts the bag of treats, which I tuck away in my pocket.

I press the button, and it says "Treat" in my voice. It gets his attention the way I want it to, and he sniffs the button, looking from me to it and back again.

For the next hour I sit with Prince Francis and teach him to press the button if he wants a treat. He gets the hang of it by the end.

Afterward, I make us both dinner, and then we settle in to watch a movie. Miles's mother has great satellite TV and access to loads of movies, so I put on *The Secret Life of Pets*, and Prince Francis makes himself comfortable in my lap.

After the movie, I change the sheets on Miles's childhood

bed and grab my pillow from the car. I've just changed into my jammies when my phone buzzes with a message from Miles.

Miles: *How is the demon child?*

I grin and send him a gif of a sphynx cat looking sinister, then another of a cat looking angelic.

Kitty: *He was on his best behavior.*

I follow it with a video of Prince Francis pressing the Treat button, then looking up at me expectantly.

I get a slew of shocked face gifs in response and then my phone rings.

"You taught him how to ask for treats? Can I get my dog to do that?" Miles asks by way of greeting.

"Oh yeah, Wilfred can definitely learn. You just need patience and time."

"You're amazing, Kitty."

"He's food motivated, and I took advantage of that. I'll add more buttons, but this is a good starting point." I glance at my reflection in the mirror. My nipples are peaked against the fabric of my nightshirt, and not because I'm cold. I'm glad this is a phone conversation and Miles can't see my face, or the rest of me. "How was the tour of the home?"

"It's a nice place. I'm going to bring my mother back to see it in a couple of days."

"That's wonderful news!"

"Yeah, they have a great staff and varying levels of care, which is exactly what my mom needs. Anyway, I just wanted to check on you and Prince Francis. Tomorrow night the team has a home game, but I'll be able to pop by the next day if that works for you. Can you text me in the morning, though, to let me know how it goes?"

"I can absolutely do that."

"Great. Thanks again, Kitty. You really are a lifesaver."

"It's really no problem. Have a good night, Miles."

"You, too, Kitty."

I end the call, turn off the light, and climb into bed. I haven't done an overnight cat-sit in a long time, and it's a welcome change in routine. It takes all of thirty seconds before Prince Francis hops up onto the bed. He makes himself at home on the pillow next to me, one paw covering the back of my hand.

I drift off to sleep with a smile on my face and visions of Miles in his boxer shorts playing behind my eyelids.

Extremely loud yowling startles me awake. I bolt upright in bed, confused as I take in my surroundings, because I'm not in my own bedroom, and I don't own a cat. For a moment, I'm thrust into the past, to the day my father passed away. Smokey had been yowling the same way, the sound forlorn and melancholic.

It takes me a good thirty seconds to get my bearings and

remember where I am, and that the cat isn't Smokey, but Prince Francis.

I throw the covers off and pad across the floor, a shiver runs down my spine when I hit a creaky spot. I flick on the hall light and wait for my eyes to adjust.

I spot Prince Francis, sitting in front of the closed door leading to one of the rooms.

"What's going on, buddy?" He doesn't look my way, just keeps up with the loud, melancholy yowls. He stretches out, his nails sliding down the wood, making a muted nails-on-chalkboard sound. I call his name a couple more times, but he continues to ignore me.

I pad down the hall, considering my options. I don't want to go snooping around, but there must be a reason Prince Francis is in full-on caterwauling mode. Maybe there's a mouse in there, or another rodent.

Before I open the door, I scoop Prince Francis up and tuck him under one arm so he can't go running in there before I've had a chance to make sure it's safe. He's like a squirmy baby, but I'm not taking chances, since Miles's mom is a semi-hoarder, and over the years I've learned that some people have rooms full of boxes that they keep hidden from the rest of the world.

I turn the knob and the door creaks open slowly, exactly as it would if we were in a horror movie. I flick on the light and am relieved when there's no masked man wielding a knife. It's not a hoarder lair; it's another bedroom. I set a wriggling Prince Francis on the floor, and he zooms across the room, jumps up on the bed, launches himself onto the dresser and then back onto the floor, yowling while I take in the space.

It's a child's bedroom. Not an infant, but a young boy maybe. There's a twin bed in one corner decorated with a dark comforter with a Spider-Man theme. The whole room looks like an homage to superheroes. Miles said he was an only child, so I have no idea what to make of this room.

Prince Francis stops zooming and plunks his butt in front of the wall. And he starts back up with the melancholy meowing, but this time it's directed at nothing. And when I try to pick him up, he hisses and follows with an admonishing swat.

Enticing him with treats doesn't work. At a loss, I leave him where he is, certain he'll stop eventually. Half an hour later Prince Francis is still yelling at the wall, and I'm convinced the house is haunted.

chapter eleven

THE PIECES OF WHO WE ARE

Miles

I check my phone for messages on my way to the bathroom. In the past, I'd wait until my coffee was brewing before I touched my phone, but now that Prince Francis and Kitty are part of my life, I look forward to the regular updates.

Kitty often sends gifs and pictures of her and Prince Francis. This morning's picture was taken in my childhood bed, Kitty smiling sleepily at the camera and Prince Francis curled around the top of her head. Underneath is the caption: *like my new hat?*

But under that caption are several other messages, sent about an hour ago.

Kitty: *Question: is your mother's house haunted?*
Kitty: *Another Question: is there a child living here that I don't know about?*
Kitty: *Question three: is it possible that there are things hiding in this closet?*

Under the last question is a picture of the closet in my younger brother Toby's room.

Kitty: *Such as small critters and/or possibly a portal to another dimension through which the undead can make their way into our realm?*

I drag a hand down my face. I probably should have filled Kitty in on the whole story when it comes to my family, but talking about my younger brother isn't particularly pleasant. Also, I don't think my mother's house is haunted, but I haven't lived there in a lot of years, so I suppose anything is possible. I've never really put much stock into the idea of the undead coming back to creep people out. But I don't discount the possibility of alien life forms, so I suppose I can't exactly discount undead ones, either.

I decide I need a shower and a few minutes of mental preparation before I tackle the questions from Kitty.

Fifteen minutes later I'm standing in my kitchen as I hit Call on her contact. She answers on the second ring.

"Hey, hold on, I'm dealing with some bad behavior." The phone thumps on what must be a hard surface. "One more time, Chumble Buns, and you're getting the spray bottle. I'm serious. No more climbing the curtains. Your mom would be very, very disappointed in you if she could see you now."

I hear some more rustling around and then, "I told you, and you didn't listen."

It's followed by a hiss and loud meow, then feet pattering on the floor. A moment later Kitty heavy-breathes in my ear. "Do you mind if I call you back later? I need to make sure Chumble Buns isn't about to knock every last thing off the kitchen counter in a fit of cat rage."

"Sure. I'm taking my mother to see the home later. I could call after? I can even stop by." This is probably a better conversation in person, anyway. "Can I ask what happened last night, though? Even if it's the abridged version?"

"Yes to stopping by later. Just shoot me a message when you're on your way. And Prince Francis was basically screaming his head off wanting to get into that room with the closed door. So I let him in, and then he yelled at the wall for a couple of hours. I didn't know what to make of it and was kind of worried that there was a missing child somewhere because it looks like a kid's room?" That last sentence is phrased as a question.

"Like it belongs to a young boy?"

"Yeah, but from like two decades ago."

I blow out a breath. "I'll explain later."

"Okay. I gotta go!" And with that she ends the call.

The toast I was in the middle of making when I called Kitty no longer seems appealing. I slather it with butter, though, aware that this morning is team practice, and then team brunch, followed by my allergist appointment and then an early game. If I don't put something in my stomach, it'll be hard to focus on my job.

As it is, it's going to be tough not to let my mind wander.

I don't like talking about my younger brother.

It's all tied up in the reason my family fell apart. And I often feel like all that loss contributed to my mom's fragile mental state.

I stand at the counter, counting my breaths, willing the memories to stay on lockdown. Once my emotions are back under control, I get ready for work on autopilot and pick up Josh on the way to the arena.

"Hey, man, how's your girlfriend? When's she sleeping over again?" Josh needles me the second he's in my car.

I wait until he's buckled in before I pull away from the curb.

"What is this, middle school? Get off my jock." I'm clearly moody as fuck this morning.

I can feel Josh's frown without even looking his way.

"Who pissed in your cornflakes?"

"No one." I'm snippy and short. And on edge.

"Why are you lying? I've been your best friend since seventh grade. You can't bullshit me."

I sigh. "Kitty stayed at my mother's place last night so she could keep an eye on Prince Francis in hopes that he would become a less destructive asshole, and she found Toby's room."

"Okay." He waits for me to continue.

"It doesn't sound like it's changed at all since my parents split." I grip the wheel and try not to grind my teeth. I don't need an appointment to the dentist to round out this shit-tastic situation. I brake for the red light and glance at Josh.

His eyebrows always tell a story. One is arched up under his hair, the other is flat across the top of his left eye. "Do you mean it's still decorated for an eight-year-old?"

"Yeah. Seems that way."

"You've been there plenty of times. How didn't you know this?"

"My mom always kept the door closed, and I never had the impulse to look," I admit. And maybe I was burying my head in the sand about how much my mother continued to struggle with what happened.

It's Josh's turn to sigh. "Man, that's . . . rough. Are you okay? Do you need to grab a beer or something after the game today? We could have drinks, lots of them. Get good and shitfaced if you want." Josh was around for the aftermath of the split, but not what happened leading up to it. Still, he knows how hard it all was for me back then. And still seems to be, despite it being nearly twenty years ago.

"I can't. I'm taking my mother to the home so she can check it out. And then I need to explain it to Kitty, since apparently Prince Francis was being a loud asshole last night, standing outside Toby's door and making all kinds of noise. Anyway, I'll take a rain check on the drinks. Let's change the subject. I need to focus on something else." I tap on the steering wheel, wishing I could erase the thoughts in my head and the history attached to them.

"Okay, I'll drop it for now, but we need a guys' night soon."

I nod my agreement and switch conversation gears. "I've been analyzing Parker's performance the last couple of games, and I think I've figured out a pattern in his plays." I feel like I should have made these connections sooner, but with everything else that's been happening, my focus has been split, which isn't great at the beginning of the season when the first games can set the tone for the season.

Josh rolls with it. "Okay. Lay it out for me."

"Sixty-seven percent of the time he passes to the right wing instead of the left wing players. It seems like Montreal figured that out, so they kept putting their strongest players on the right during the last game."

Josh is silent for a moment before he mutters, "Damn. You're right. Why didn't we see that last game?"

Because my head is all over the place, and I didn't put it together until I watched the replays and made notes on Parker, but I keep that part to myself. "There were a lot of chippy play distractions. But when Parker relies on the left wing for passing, he's fifty percent more likely to make a shot on net. Especially if he's on the same line as Mason. If we can make Parker aware of the pattern, we can start to use it to the team's advantage."

"Okay, this is good stuff, Miles. We can talk to Coach Davis about this and make a plan to tackle it with Parker."

Parker is young, and very, very good on the ice. But he's also a Gen Z kid, and his entire life he's been told he's amazing by his parents. It's like they showered him in fucking confetti every time he wiped his ass. He's always looking for praise, and constructive criticism needs to be layered carefully with a kid like him; otherwise, we can shoot his game to shit.

We meet with Coach Davis before practice to review the analytics from the last game and pull up the video footage, fast-forwarding to the goal Parker scored. Which happens to be when he passed to Mason on the left.

"If we can get Parker to make a few adjustments, it'll go a long way in helping this team get off to a solid start this season."

Coach Davis claps me on the shoulder. "This is good stuff, Thorn."

"Thanks." I bite back the grin, happy to have a win amid the chaos that is currently my life. Would it have been better if I'd made the connection before last game? Absolutely, but it's a step in the right direction and proving myself an asset to the team.

Davis pulls Parker aside and gives him some pointers, and it works, which elevates the positive energy on the ice. It's a good headspace for the players to be in when they're heading into a game this evening.

After team brunch, I have my allergist appointment.

I'm nervous, especially since it's sandwiched in the middle of my workday, but if I'm stopping at my mom's later, I'd like to know how bad this allergy is so I can plan accordingly.

"You sure you want to go on your own?" Josh asks. "I don't mind tagging along, in case you need a ride to the hospital again. Or do you want to call Nurse Kitty?"

I shoot him a look. "You're going to razz me forever over that, aren't you?"

"I can't believe she slept at your house and nothing happened."

"I already told you, I wasn't in any condition to try to make a move." Also, our mutual lack of appreciation for each other only shifted after the hospital fiasco. "I gotta roll. I'll be back in time for the game."

He goes back to watching a replay of the team's last game against Boston, and I head to my allergist appointment. I'm a bit anxious when they do the scratch test with cat dander. I almost expect my arm to swell to twice its size.

While it's clear I have a cat allergy, it's not the kind that should cause my throat to close and parts of my body to swell. I leave the office with an itchy arm and the knowledge that I can be in my mother's house without asphyxiating. Unfortunately, I still need additional tests to find out what caused the extreme reaction.

Parker plays like a dream in the game against Boston, which means I get more positive feedback from Coach. It's the boost I need before I head to the hospital to pick up my mother.

My mom has been moved from a regular hospital room into one of their on-site short-term care wings. It's a middle ground between a hospital and a home. Her insurance covers it, and while it's not quite like an apartment, it's also not as sterile as a hospital room, either.

My mom is sitting in front of the window, staring out at the parking lot. She's dressed in a pair of jeans and a sweater, her hair pulled back in a low ponytail. She used to braid it a lot when we were young, but I'm learning that with this disease things that were once rote become difficult, and sometimes impossible.

She looks normal today, and I cross my fingers that all the good of this day continues with our visit to the home. "Hey, Mom. How's it going?"

Her eyes light up, and for a second I think maybe it's a lucid day. "Toby! I'm so glad you're here."

Disappointment is a crushing weight I don't expect and don't know how to handle. I plaster on what I hope is a semi-genuine smile. "It's Miles, Mom."

"Miles? Oh. Yes." Her expression shifts, confusion pulling her brows together as she looks past me. "Why don't you ever bring your brother along? Doesn't he want to visit, too? How much longer am I going to have to stay here? Is that why he won't visit? Because I'm here?"

I avoid the questions about my brother, because they tend to cause me more headaches and her more stress. Instead, I focus on the stuff I can answer. "We're going to look at an apartment tonight, so hopefully you'll like it there."

"An apartment? But I have a house."

I don't understand how she can know she has a house but half the time thinks I'm my brother. I explain, like I do every time I see her, that the house is a lot to take care of, and that the apartment will have programs and activities and people to help manage.

"But I like my garden. And so does Prince Francis. How is my boy? I miss him. Will I be able to bring him with me?" She fiddles with the heart necklace she wears all the time. It was a Mother's Day gift from my dad when our family was still intact.

"He's good, Mom. I have a friend named Kitty who's helping

me take care of Prince Francis," I remind her. Sometimes she remembers who Kitty is, and sometimes she doesn't. Today it's apparently the latter.

"A friend? Is she your girlfriend? Why don't you bring her by, and we can have dinner together?" She threads her arm through mine. "Does Miles have a girlfriend yet? He was a bit of a late bloomer."

I remind myself it's not my mother's fault that her brain is failing her and she forgets our conversation from a minute ago. Instead of correcting her, I roll with it. It's easier for both of us this way, even if it makes me feel like shit. "Miles doesn't have a girlfriend."

My mother tsks. "He's already thirty. What in the world is he waiting for?"

"Probably the right girl to come along."

Once we're signed out of the hospital, I help my mother into my car and make the short trip to Regency Village, the retirement complex with varying levels of care. It's like a small, self-contained town with bungalow row houses for independent living. There are also four low-rise apartment buildings with increasing levels of care, including full-time nursing. My mother's current situation requires daily monitoring and a support worker.

We're greeted by a kind woman who looks to be in her early forties. She gives us a tour of the facilities, and then we're shown an apartment like the one my mother will have if we decide this is the right fit.

"There's only one bedroom. Where will you sleep, Toby?" My mother looks up at me, her expression reflecting her concern.

She's only in her mid-sixties. How could this be happening? The more time I spend with her, the guiltier I feel for not seeing this sooner.

"I have my own place in the city, Mom."

"Oh. Hmm. Do you work in the city?" she asks for the umpteenth time.

"Yeah. I'm a data analyst for the NHL."

"Oh. That's good. I always knew you'd do great things." She pats my hand and wanders around the apartment. She opens the fridge door and frowns. "I need to go grocery shopping. There's nothing to eat. I wanted to make you a sandwich."

Any small remaining hope I had that maybe she could handle living on her own disappears. And so does the hope that she isn't going to need as much support as the hospital staff warned. "You're not at home, Mom. We're here looking at an apartment." Every day feels like Groundhog Day. I can't imagine what this must be like for her. It would be terrifying to lose who you are most of the time. To not know where you are or why.

The receptionist gives me a sympathetic smile. "Would you like a minute?"

"Please." This is hard enough without an audience, and the emotions are clawing at me, making it even more challenging.

My mom wrings her hands. "Why can't I just go back to my house? I don't understand why we're looking at apartments when I have a place to live already."

I go with blunt honesty, which is probably the worst thing I can do under the circumstances, but my frustration wins out over my empathy. "Because you were wandering around the street in your pajamas, and you didn't know where you were."

She frowns and crosses her arms over her chest. "What a horrible thing to make up, Toby. I would never leave the house in my pajamas!"

"You have early-onset dementia, Mom. I'm not Toby. He's been dead for twenty years. I'm Miles, your other son. Most of the time you don't know who I am, and you probably won't remember this conversation tomorrow. Or even an hour from now." The truth doesn't feel good as it rolls off my tongue; it feels cruel and hurtful and like the last thing I should say, but it's already out and too late to take it back.

"You're trying to confuse me! Why are you putting me in a home? What did I do to deserve this?" She pushes by me and heads for the door, and I follow, wishing I'd thought this through better. Wishing that my dad didn't live on the other side of the country and my brother was here to help me with this.

My mom is so agitated that she starts yelling, and the nurses intervene. They call the hospital and get permission to give her a sedative to calm her down. It's my fault she's reacting like this, because I couldn't hold my frustration in, and I pushed too much truth on her.

One of the nurses gives my shoulder a squeeze. "It's not her fault, and it's not yours either. I know it's hard, but this is the best and safest place for your mother."

I don't know that I agree about it not being my fault, but she's right about my mom needing to be somewhere safe. "I'll come back tomorrow and sign the paperwork."

By the time I drop my mother off at the hospital I'm exhausted, but I still need to head back to her house and see how Kitty is making out. And explain what the heck is going on with the room she found. I don't know why I haven't been up front with her in the first place, other than I feel kind of like a jerk for not seeing the signs until it was too late.

Part of me wishes that my dad had handled things differently. That he had tried harder to help her after Toby died. That he hadn't moved so far away and left me to deal with this on my own.

I call him on the short drive from the hospital to my mom's house. "Hey, Miles, I saw the game this afternoon. That was a great win."

"Thanks. Parker's really getting his feet under him this season." I start with the easy stuff, although the win this afternoon feels like it happened a million years ago.

"That your doing? I noticed he's changed things up since the last game against Ottawa." My dad was the one who always took Toby and me to hockey games.

"Mm. I just assess the data and give those findings to the coach; management and the players do the rest."

"I think you probably had more to do with it than that, but it's good you're settling in with the team. With you on their side, they should have a banner season."

"We'll see." I drum on the wheel, not sure how to say what really needs to be said.

"How's Tabitha? Are things better?"

I could lie, but there isn't much of a point. "I took her to see an apartment tonight, and it was tough on her."

"How is it on you?" His voice is laced with concern.

"She's having trouble staying in the present. She's going to need care, more than I realized," I admit.

"How much care? Is she going to need financial help? Are you?"

"Her insurance should cover it," I assure him. "Most of the time she thinks I'm Toby."

He's quiet for a few moments before he says. "I'm sorry, Miles. I didn't realize it was this bad. I could take some time off, come visit, and help while you're getting her settled."

I consider that: my dad coming out here, potentially staying with me, helping clear out the house he hasn't stepped foot in since they got divorced when I was a teen. As much as it would be nice to have support, I'm not sure it's better for any of us. "I've got it handled, Dad."

"Are you sure? You've got a lot on your plate with this new job and now your mom needing all this support. It's okay to ask for some help if you need it."

"Honestly, it's okay." I don't know if that's true, but based on her reaction to the home, I can't see her dealing well with seeing my dad. "Once she's in the assisted living facility, it'll be fine. It's just getting her there. And I have a network here, so you don't need to worry about me. I gotta go, though. I'm checking in with the cat sitter."

"You're a good son. It's times like these I wish I lived closer. I'm sorry you're dealing with this on your own."

"It's all right, Dad. I'll be on the west coast soon enough. Thanks for listening."

"Any time, Miles. Whatever you need, I'm here for you."

I end the call with a promise to talk later in the week with an update. Would it be good to have my dad to lean on? Maybe. But he's spent a lot of years separating himself from the past, and for him it's better if it stays that way. And, more selfishly, it's probably better for me, because I don't know that my mom can handle more of the past haunting her.

chapter twelve

COMFORT IN CONNECTION

Miles

It's already well after eight by the time I arrive at my mother's place, and I still haven't had dinner. I should have stopped to grab takeout on the way over. And asked Kitty if she wanted anything, although I assume she's already eaten by this hour.

I knock on the door before I let myself in, so I don't scare the crap out of her. Especially since she's worried about ghosts.

"Hello!" I call out. "It's Miles!"

"I'm in the living room!" Kitty replies.

I round the corner and find Kitty in my mom's lounger, Prince Francis curled up in her lap. I'm envious of the little gremlin. "I hope I come back as a cat or a lap dog in my next life."

"It's the life, isn't it? Being eternally cute, snoozing when you feel like it, never having to make your own meals." She scratches behind Prince Francis's ear, and he tips his chin up and headbutts her hand, telling her he's not done with pets. "How was the home? Did your mother like it?"

I shrug, uncertain if I want to get into this with her or not. "Eh, she doesn't really understand why she can't come back here."

Her expression shifts from hopeful to sympathetic. "Oh no. I'm so sorry, Miles. Does that mean it didn't go well?"

"It's going to take her some time to get used to the idea, but once she's in there and living the retirement life, I'm sure she'll be okay." Maybe if I keep telling myself that, I'll will it to be true.

"I can imagine it's been a lot for her, being in the hospital, not ⸺ally understanding where she is or how long she'll be there." Kitty's empathy is soothing, but it also reinforces all the worries I'm still not sure what to do with.

"Yeah. This whole thing is a lot to get my head around, so I can only fathom what it's like for her." I don't know when Kitty got so easy to talk to, but this is a lot nicer than the earlier bickering matches.

"Change is scary."

"It is, isn't it? Anyway." I wave a hand around in the air, not wanting to drag Kitty's mood into the dumps along with mine. "You had some issues last night. I probably should have filled you in before now, but, uh—I honestly didn't realize that room hadn't changed since my parents' divorce." Which sounds doubly horrible since Kitty lost her dad and stuck by her mom all these years. Hell, she still lives with her so she can help with the house.

"I thought the room I'm sleeping in used to be yours." She scratches Prince Francis under the chin.

"It is. It was. The other room belonged to my brother."

"Oh. I thought you said you were an only child." She absently scratches between Prince Francis's ears. "Does he live far away or something?"

I shake my head and rub the back of my neck, too over-whelmed with everything to soften the revelation. "He died when I was eleven."

"Oh my gosh. I'm so sorry." She stops petting Prince Francis and carefully lifts him from her lap, setting him on the lounger. It's then that I notice the cat is wearing a tiny sweatshirt. "I didn't realize," she says softly.

"I probably should have told you sooner. I don't really like to talk about it. Basically, when that happened, my family fell apart."

She gives me a soft, sad smile. "I get it. Or sympathize, at least, about not wanting to talk about it. But maybe we could look at the room and make sure there isn't anything living in there that shouldn't be?" She clasps her hands. "I didn't want to go snooping around while you weren't here."

"I should have given the go-ahead to look around."

"Eh, I sort of wanted backup, in case there really is a portal to another dimension behind the closet door." She gives me a hesitant smile, and I return it with one of my own.

"Let's have a look." I incline my head toward the stairs.

She follows me down the hall to my brother's bedroom. My palms dampen as I approach the closed door, and I remind myself that it's just a room. As a math and logic person, I've never put a lot of stock in the idea of haunted houses. There's always an explanation. So there really isn't a reason for the heart palpitations, or the sudden roll in my stomach, apart from the memories I can't let go of.

I turn the knob and push the door open. The blinds are closed, the room dark. I reach around the corner for the light switch, then skim down, because it's been years since I've been in this room, and the switch is a lot lower now that I'm a good foot taller.

I exhale in a whoosh as I take in the space. "Maybe the whole room is a portal to another dimension," I mutter. "Nothing has changed. It looks the same as it did the day he died."

I run a hand through my hair and grip the back of my neck. All the should-haves and what-ifs are surfacing. I should have known about this. I should have been there for my mom instead of letting her push us all away.

Kitty's palm settles between my shoulder blades. "Are you okay?"

"I don't know what I expected, but it wasn't this." I clear my throat before I continue. "It's like a time capsule. A snapshot of our life right before it changed forever."

"I'm here to listen if you want, or if you need a minute on your own, just let me know."

She drops her hand, and I reach behind me and find the sleeve of her shirt. "If you aren't just being nice and you mean that, I want you to stay."

"I'm not just being nice. Tell me what you need, Miles." She squeezes my forearm gently.

"My mom always kept this door closed whenever I visited, and I never checked his room before now," I admit. "It brings up a lot of painful memories."

"I imagine it does. How old was your brother when he passed?"

"He was eight."

"Was he sick?" Her voice is soft and warm, like a blanket I want to be wrapped in.

I shake my head. "No. He got hit by a car."

She gasps and her fingers wrap around mine, squeezing once before she releases my hand. "Oh, Miles. That's awful."

I nod slowly, not wanting to step back in time with the memories I've tried so hard to shove in a box and bury, but the lid pops off and the past surfaces all the same. "He'd just gotten a brand-new bike. I was playing video games in the living room, and he asked if I could go outside with him because he wasn't allowed to ride without supervision. My mom was in the backyard in the garden, picking tomatoes. Those are the small details I remember. I found the tomatoes later, scattered all over the patio. She must have dropped them when she heard..." I shake my head, wanting to stop the words, but needing to get them out more. "She'd asked me to keep an eye on Toby. My dad was out playing golf with a client. I told Toby I just needed to beat this level, and then I'd come out and watch him. I must have taken too long." I cross over to the dresser, where a stack of books sits. A thin layer of dust coats the top, enough to tell me that my mom must clean his room fairly regularly.

"His helmet wasn't on properly, and it was close to dinnertime. One of our neighbors ordered pizza, and the driver took the corner too fast. Toby didn't suffer, at least."

"That must have been so horrible for you." Kitty's voice trembles with the same emotions that swirl in my gut. It's an odd comfort, knowing your pain is shared with someone.

"I felt responsible. Still do, I guess. Beating that level was such a trivial thing. Sometimes I wish I would have pressed Pause. Then Toby would still be here. And maybe our family wouldn't have fallen apart, and my mom wouldn't be so lost in the past."

Kitty's hand settles on my shoulder. "You were a kid, Miles. It's not your fault. But the what-ifs are the hardest to let go of."

I clear my throat again. I don't know how to respond to that, because in a lot of ways I feel like a different choice may have changed everything. "Seeing this...maybe she wanted to stay in the past, where she still had a family."

"Where the good memories were?" Kitty asks.

"Yeah. It sort of seems like that could be possible. I wish she would have let me help more. I wish I'd known she was struggling like this."

"Sometimes we keep our pain to ourselves because it's too hard to share," Kitty says softly.

I've shied away from the reality of our family's loss, because there's so much guilt tied to it. "That's remarkably true."

Prince Francis weaves between our feet and heads straight for the closet door. He plunks his naked butt on the carpet and meows loudly, then looks over his shoulder at us and meows again, unaware of the conversation he's interrupting.

"Do you want me to open the closet door?" Kitty asks.

"Probably a good idea." It also prevents me from using Kitty as a therapist.

Kitty crosses the room and slowly opens the door. The inside looks like any other closet that belonged to an eight-year-old boy. There's a Nerf gun on the floor, clothes on hangers, an outfit tossed in a laundry basket.

Prince Francis disappears inside and returns less than thirty seconds later with a toy mouse in his mouth. He trots out of the room and down the hall, toward the living room.

"Well at least we can confirm that there is no portal to another dimension in the closet," Kitty says, then grimaces. "Sorry, I shouldn't be making jokes."

"The levity is appreciated."

"Well, that mystery is solved, I guess. I feel kind of silly that I immediately jumped to the whole ghost-portal to another dimension scenario, but to be fair, I've been reading some weird paranormal books lately." Kitty pushes her glasses up her nose and opens her mouth to say something else.

Which is the exact moment my stomach rumbles like there's a beast living inside it.

Her eyes go wide. "Was that your stomach?"

"Either that or I've swallowed a demi-gorgon."

"Have you eaten dinner yet? Or maybe you just have an extremely high metabolism? My sister is a string bean, and she eats every two hours and can consume more food than most grown men without putting on an ounce. I clearly didn't get the same genes." She pats her curvy hip.

"I happen to like your genes, and I don't mean the ones made out of denim." I would like to summon a portal or maybe let the demi-gorgon in my stomach banish me to another realm until Kitty smiles.

Kitty narrows her eyes. "Are you making a joke, or is that a compliment?"

"Can it be both, but with a strong lean toward a compliment since the joke part is kind of cheesy?" I quirk a brow and give her a chagrined smile.

She bites her lip for a second, her grin widening. "Speaking of cheesy, I made bacon mac and cheese for dinner. There are lots of leftovers if you or the demi-gorgon living in your stomach is interested."

My stomach rumbles again, but quieter this time. "My stomach likes the sound of that."

"Come on, then. Let's feed your beast."

I follow Kitty to the kitchen. She pulls a huge casserole dish out of the fridge and scoops a generous amount onto a plate, then puts it in the microwave to reheat it. It's a bit strange to watch her move around the kitchen with ease and surety, but she's spent a lot more time here than I have recently, so it makes sense.

I hunt around in the cabinets for a glass. I find them next to the fridge. The same plastic ones my brother and I used when we were little are still on the lowest shelf. The adult glasses came from a garage sale, when gas stations carried Olympics glassware in the eighties and every time you filled your tank you got a new one. I pull two from the cupboard and check the fridge, but the only thing in there that's drinkable is coffee cream and orange juice. Juice and mac and cheese don't go well together, so I pour myself a glass of water instead and do the same for Kitty. "The only meals I've eaten here over the past decade have been around the holidays."

"Being here with all the memories you left behind can't be easy, especially with your mom in the hospital." The microwave dings, and she removes the plate. She holds it out to me. "Normally I stick my finger in the middle to see if it's hot all the way through, but I don't think you want me fingering your food."

I cough-choke on my water. I don't think she means it the way my brain has interpreted it.

Kitty's eyes go wide and she slaps a palm over her mouth. "Oh my gosh. That came out *so* wrong."

I set the glass on the table and smack my chest a couple of times to get the water out of my windpipe. When the coughing subsides, I cross the kitchen, where Kitty is still standing with the plate in one hand and the other in front of her mouth. "I'm sure your hands are clean, but I can finger my own food."

Her hand falls to her side and she gives me a look, but it's clear she's fighting a smile. "I meant that you didn't want my fingers in your food."

"I know, but I like that we're both channeling our inner

teenage boys." I stick my finger in the center of the mac and cheese casserole. "It needs a couple more minutes." I suck the cheese off the end of my finger and Kitty's cheeks flush a deeper shade of pink. I like this banter better than the therapy session.

She uses a fork to stir the food before she covers it again and puts it back in the microwave.

Kitty leans against the counter. "You said your parents are divorced? Where does your dad live?"

"He's on the west coast. He moved out there when I went to college in the city. There wasn't much of a reason for him to stay, and he has siblings out that way." I tuck my hands in my pockets.

"Weren't you a reason to stay?" she asks softly, then shakes her head. "Sorry. I'm prying, and it's rude."

"No. It's okay." As hard as these memories are to talk about, burying them doesn't seem to be an effective strategy for moving forward. "My dad would leave early for work to commute to the city, so my mom got me off to school. But after Toby died, she rarely got out of bed, she stopped cooking, and it was up to me to handle all the household stuff my dad couldn't manage with his hours." I fall back into the past, into the months and years that followed my brother's death. "It was clear to all of us that my mom wasn't dealing well. My dad did everything he could—therapy, family therapy, adjusting his hours at work. I remember there being medication, and her being flat for a long while...numb, I guess? Then things shifted. We weren't allowed to go in Toby's bedroom, and she refused to clean it out. After a while, she started sleeping in his room. I think that's when things with my parents really started to erode."

"That must have been hard for your dad. Grieving the loss of his son and watching his wife fall apart," Kitty says softly.

"It was, harder than I realized at the time maybe. I think I saw him cry once when Toby died, and then he just sort of shut off? Put on a strong front for my mom's sake, because she was struggling. I can't really imagine what it was like for them, losing a child." I rub my chin. "But my mom, she wasn't moving forward. My dad really tried, but then the fights started. And they got worse until they finally separated. She was the one who asked for a divorce. So my dad ended up moving to the city where his job was, and I went with him. It was messy and hard, and I visited here every other weekend. I think my mom was hurt that I chose to live with Dad, but I had hockey all the time and a schedule she couldn't manage."

I swallow down the guilt. "It wasn't that I didn't want to be there for her. She just wouldn't let us help her. Sort of shut us out. And I couldn't stay in that house with all the memories of what happened, and the fighting. I went to high school in the city, and you know what it's like being a teenager, friends over everything. I always had sports on the weekend, so those visits got fewer and further between. I feel shitty about it now, because she essentially lost everything. I wish I could have seen outside myself more back then."

"You were young, and the loss was yours too. You can feel

empathy, but it sounds like moving in with your dad was probably the best thing for your mental health."

"Yeah, but I still wish it would have gone differently."

The microwave beeps again. This time the plate is steaming, and Kitty needs to use oven mitts to take it out. I offer to do it, but she waves me away and tells me she's got it. She sets it on the table, then drops into the chair to the left of me. "When we look at the past through an adult lens, it's easy to beat ourselves up over the things we could have or maybe should have done differently. But at thirteen you didn't have the life experience to be able to make those kinds of informed choices, and you were a kid who lost his brother."

So many times, I came home from school and found her crying in Toby's bedroom. It made me feel powerless, and in some ways irrelevant. I understood the pain of the loss, but I needed a mother, and she couldn't be that. Not then. "It felt like it was my fault that he was gone."

Kitty reaches across the table and squeezes my forearm. "Oh, Miles. This was a tragedy and not yours to own."

"I was supposed to be watching him, though."

"That's a big responsibility for a child, and he was impatient, as kids sometimes are. You are not to blame for what happened. The person who hit him was. Like you said before, it's easy to get caught up in the what-ifs, and your mother's grief over-shadowed her ability to be a good parent, but that's not your fault either."

I nod once, but that memory is a deep wound I don't know

how to heal. "I see her struggle through different eyes now. And when I think back to my coming to visit while I was in college...and her sometimes calling me Toby...I feel like I missed a lot of signs, that I was too wrapped up in myself to see what was happening to her."

Kitty's smile is full of sadness and empathy. "The best and the worst thing about hindsight is that it's always twenty-twenty."

"That is absolutely the truth." I dig my fork into the mac and cheese, finally taking a bite.

It's delicious and comforting and exactly what I need.

"I can't pretend to know what it's like to lose a sibling the way you did, or the way you also lost your mother, but I do know what it's like to lose a parent. Moving forward can be tough. Sometimes we get stuck in the loop and don't know how to get out of it," Kitty says.

"It's hard not to make it mine, you know?" I take another bite.

"I do. I often wonder what would have happened if I'd found my dad sooner."

"You found him?" My stomach sinks, and my heart seems to skip a couple of beats.

"He'd been up in the attic by himself. He was supposed to bring the Christmas tree down. I assumed he'd found old albums or something and got caught up in whatever else was up there. He did that pretty much every year, would go up to get the tree and end up finding a treasure. It was my night to make dinner, and I was so focused on what I was doing that I didn't realize how long he'd been gone. By the time I went to check on him, it was too late to save him." She folds a paper towel into smaller and smaller squares. "All this to say, while I can't relate completely, I can empathize."

I reach over and cover her hand with mine. "I'm sorry for what happened to your family."

"And I'm sorry for what happened to yours."

Our eyes meet and lock, and I feel this connection we share in more than just the physical contact. Under her sunshine are some dark clouds, and it's a reminder that we all have struggles.

A bolt of lightning followed by a boom of thunder makes the house shake, and Prince Francis comes bounding into the room. He launches himself onto the kitchen table and scampers over to Kitty, then promptly tries to crawl inside her shirt.

She pulls her hand out from under mine and gives Prince Francis a reassuring pet. "It's okay, buddy, just a little thunder."

Another bolt of lightning shoots across the sky, lighting up the night, and rain patters the roof.

We continue to talk, sharing stories, talking about what it was like to grow up without a parent, while the storm rages on outside. I'm exhausted from the day and enjoying Kitty's company and the comfort she brings, so I call my neighbors to see if they can keep Wilfred for a sleepover. I feel bad, but Wilfred and their dog, Herman, are besties, and they're more than happy to dog sit, allowing me to stay the night with Kitty. She offers to set up her cot in the living room, but I tell her it's fine—I'll sleep in my mother's bedroom, and she can stay in mine.

We have an awkward moment in the hall when we're both

heading for our respective rooms, neither of us sure what to do. But eventually Kitty steps up and gives me a hug. "I'm glad the storm gave us an opportunity to get to know each other better."

I wrap my arms around her. "Me, too."

Of all the curveballs life has thrown at me lately, I'm grateful for the ray of sunshine named Kitty.

chapter thirteen

SUCH A BOOB

Kitty

I wake up to a wet nose nudging my cheek and the sound of purring. My eyes flip open, and I'm face-to-face with Prince Francis. He licks the end of my nose, his terrible kitty breath making me turn my head. He gives me a headbutt and meows in my ear.

"Is it breakfast time?" I scratch behind his ear, and he basically throws his entire body against my face.

"Some kitty is frisky this morning." I roll out of bed and slide my feet into my slippers. It's barely six, but Prince Francis is proving to be an early riser. And eternally hungry.

I open a fresh can of food, serve Prince Francis his stinky breakfast, and set a pot of coffee to brew. My stomach growls as I check the fridge. While I didn't stock the fridge like I'm moving in, I brought the makings of a solid breakfast. I pull out eggs, along with cheese slices, ham, and English muffins. I love a good egg sandwich in the morning, but I always make it with scrambled eggs instead of over easy, because I don't love the taste or the mouth feel of runny egg yolks.

While I crack eggs into a bowl and transfer them one at a time into a measuring cup, Prince Francis, already finished with his breakfast, meows at me.

"Don't worry, I'll give you a bit once it's cooked." I pick up the second egg as he jumps onto the counter, just out of reach of my elbow.

"Can I have one too?"

The deep male voice scares the living daylights out of me and I shriek, dropping the egg on the floor in the process.

Prince Francis hisses and launches himself at Miles, who is standing in the doorway, wearing a pair of plaid pajama pants that are about six inches too short. He's also shirtless. Gloriously shirtless.

He has a smattering of dark hair on his chest and, as I suspected, he also has defined abs. They're not as chiseled as the ones often on the covers of my romance novels. It always makes me sad to think that those very well-defined men might miss out on delicious things like carbs and cake in order to look that way, but I'm also curious as to how much Photoshop is used to create all the contours.

Miles has nice abs, the kind I imagine are achieved by exercise. Maybe playing hockey?

I realize I'm ogling him while he struggles with Prince Francis, who has managed to land on his shoulder and bite his ear and is now scaling down the front of him like a barkless tree. Miles's chest and shoulders are now covered with angry scratch marks, and a few on his shoulder are welling with blood.

"Oh no! I'm so sorry!" I tear a ream of paper towels and quickly run them under water, but Prince Francis is heading for the broken egg. The last thing I want is a sick kitty.

I thrust a handful of dry paper towels at Miles. "Can you cover the egg, and I'll handle Prince Francis?"

"Yeah. For sure." Miles takes the paper towels and waits until I've picked up an annoyed Prince Francis before he quickly swipes them over the broken egg and follows with the wet paper towels to get the rest of the mess.

While he dumps them in the garbage, I wash my hands, then grab new paper towels and wet those, too. I turn to face Miles.

"I didn't mean to scare you." His voice is gruff and raspy.

It's also sexy.

Parts of my body that haven't been getting a lot of attention recently react to the sound of his sleepy voice and the sight of his bare chest.

I move to stand in front of him. "Are you okay? Do we need to get your EpiPen in case?"

"My cat allergy isn't that severe," he assures me.

"Still. We need to disinfect those, since Prince Francis walks around in the same box he poops in." I dab at the places on his shoulder that are bleeding with damp paper towel. There are several spots on his chest.

He exhales in a whoosh when I accidentally skim his nipple. His warm hand wraps around my wrist, and he basically yells, despite only being inches from my face, "Uh, I need to...uh...I'll be right back!"

He spins around and rushes out of the kitchen.

"Make sure you disinfect those!" I call after him. Great, and now I've succeeded in making things unnecessarily uncomfortable without even trying.

Prince Francis rubs against my leg. And it isn't until I look down that I realize I'm wearing a pair of leopard print sleep pants and a pale pink tank with leopard print lace details along the edge of the bodice. And my nipples were just saluting his nipples.

"Why do you have to make everything so awkward?" I'm not sure if I'm angry at my nipples or myself for making breakfast in my pajamas.

I leave the makings of breakfast on the counter and head upstairs, arms barred across my chest so I don't embarrass myself or Miles more than I already have.

I'm relieved to find the hall empty, so I run back to my temporary bedroom and change into real people clothes, including a bra. I return to the kitchen before Miles. I decide my best plan is to continue making breakfast and pretend nothing happened.

Unfortunately, as soon as he appears again my mouth works before my brain. "I'm so sorry I wasn't wearing a bra and my nipples were eyeing your nipples." I drop my head and sigh. "Why did I have to lead with that? I'm so embarrassed."

Miles leans against the doorjamb, one hand in his pocket. He's wearing dress pants, a button-down, and a hockey-themed tie. His hair is neatly styled, and he looks far more edible than my cheesy eggs. He also appears to be fighting a smile. "Nipples aren't all that concerned about who sees them; it's just their owners who are, and it was cold in here."

I crack an eyelid. "It's mortifying."

Miles points to his chest. "This guy tackled you to the floor over a water gun."

"That was pretty bad."

"It wasn't my finest moment. I'm still sorry about that." He comes closer, warm eyes moving over my face.

The way he looks at me sends a thrill through me and makes my nipples peak. Again. Thankfully, this time they're covered by layers of padding. Man, I must really be in need of some physical release if him looking at me has this kind of impact.

"Can I help you with anything?"

I'm grateful for the subject change. "You could toast the English muffins?"

"Sure thing." Miles pops two into the toaster and grabs coffee mugs from the cupboard. "Normally I pour myself a bowl of cereal and feel pretty accomplished. I hope you're not going to all this trouble for me."

"Oh no, I always make breakfast. It's my favorite meal. I would eat breakfast for dinner pretty much every day of the week if I could." I pour the eggs into the frying pan. "Omelets are my number one because you can change it up by adding different things. And of course, waffles are delicious."

"My stomach approves of all of this." Miles grabs plates from the cupboard.

When the English muffins are ready, I pass him a slice of cheese for each muffin and fold a piece of ham between the egg before I slide those on as well.

We take our breakfast to the table, and because Prince Francis is clearly a fan of eggs, ham, and cheese, he keeps trying to join us, interrupting every attempt at conversation. Eventually I grab the water gun from the living room and set it beside my plate as a warning.

He plunks his butt down on the floor and glares up at me, obviously not impressed by my lack of sharing.

I cut off a chunk of cheesy egg and ham and drop it on the floor next to my foot. He gobbles it up and rubs himself on my leg, purring and happy again, meowing his gratitude.

"So fickle." Miles chuckles and swallows his bite of egg sandwich. "He's basically like a dog, isn't he?"

"Why, because he's begging for food?"

He motions to Prince Francis. "It's exactly what my dog does whenever I have something he wants, which is all the time."

"Wilfred is adorable," I tell him. And huge. He's the size of a small horse, but he has the temperament of a bunny.

"He's a giant suck. And he really loves bacon. More than anything else. Except maybe the cookies from Woof It Bakery. He becomes a drool fest when I bring those home."

"Is that like a dog café?"

"Yup, it's down the block from my place. They have a dog park right next door, and they serve dog treats and coffee and drinks for owners. It's his favorite place to go," Miles tells me.

"You said your neighbors are taking care of him right now?"

"Yeah, Mark and Joe. They have a teacup poodle named Herman, and those two are the best of friends. Whenever I take Wilfred for a walk, I usually take Herman too. They're like two little old men hanging out." He pulls out his phone and shows me Wilfred's social media account. Wilfred the Dane and his best friend the teacup poodle have countless pictures together. "He's got more followers than I do by a significant margin."

"Maybe if you posted more shirtless photos you'd have a bigger following," I say, then take a huge bite out of my egg sandwich so I can't say anything else embarrassing.

"Eh, I'm not really built for shirtless photos." Miles runs his hand down the front of his shirt.

"Says who?" I arch a brow. I'd happily look at his shirtless chest all day long.

"I'm kind of wiry."

"Who are you comparing yourself to? And there are lots of women who are fans of lean men. Personally, I'm not all that keen on guys who look like they could be the Hulk's less green brother."

"Oh no? You're more a fan of the spaghetti arms?"

"You don't have spaghetti arms. And I've seen you shirtless now, so I know exactly how nice they look." I reach across and give his biceps a poke. "Maybe spending all that time around guys who work out for a living has skewed your view of what's normal."

"Most hockey players are tanks." Miles's lips twist to the side, and he drops his eyes, his cheeks flushing. I like that compliments have the same effect on him as they do on me.

"A tank is necessary when you're headed for rough terrain, but I prefer sleek."

"That's good to know." Miles grins.

And I realize I've spent the last few minutes telling him that I find him attractive.

"Anyway." I wave a hand around in the air, as if that will erase this conversation. "With the next little while being a bit hectic for you with moving your mom, I wondered if you wanted me to switch you to my monthly plan instead? I know I sent you my schedule of fees in the beginning, but that was for short-term care, and maybe that's changed a bit? If you want, I can put Prince Francis on a regular rotation, and it'll be a bit more cost effective for you and your mom."

It takes him a moment to switch topic gears. "That would be great. I'm not sure whether she'll be able to bring him with her at all. But I'd like to get her moved and settled before I tackle that problem. And then I'll have to figure out what we're going to do with this place."

"It's a lot of big decisions. Let me know if there's anything else I can do to help." It seems like this place doesn't hold the same kind of fond memories for Miles that my family home does. Which is maybe part of the reason leaving it behind isn't something I've wanted to entertain much.

He smiles warmly. "You're already doing more than enough, and making me breakfast definitely isn't part of the Prince Francis care package."

"Consider it a bonus service." I wink and then wish I could

take that part back. My flirt seems to be turned up to full blast around Miles.

"I was wondering if—" Miles's phone dings, and he glances at the screen. "Oh crap. I didn't realize what time it was." He jams the last of his egg sandwich into his mouth and pushes back his chair.

"You need to get to work?"

He nods and raises a hand in front of his face, his words slightly garbled since he's speaking with a mouth full of food. "I have a meeting in an hour."

I leave the last two bites of my sandwich and follow him to the front door. His suit jacket hangs on the newel post. He shrugs into it, then slips his feet into his shoes and grabs his messenger bag, slinging it over his shoulder.

"Thanks again, Kitty. I uh...I appreciate you. Maybe I can return all the feeding favors by taking you out for dinner one of these days." He sneezes once, and then again. "Seems like my antihistamines might be wearing off. I'll touch base later."

"Sure, sounds good."

"Great. Have a good day!"

And with that he's off.

Prince Francis comes trotting into the front foyer. He rubs himself on my leg.

"Do you think when he mentioned dinner he was asking me on a date or just trying to thank me?" Either could be possible. Or maybe I'm reading into things.

Prince Francis meows and flops over on his side, batting at

something under the narrow table to my right. Whatever it is, he can't seem to reach it, and he keeps meowing, his cries growing louder. I drop to my knees and close one eye, trying to see what it is that has him so riled. It's a stuffed mouse toy. Possibly the one that was in Miles's brother's room.

As soon as I knock it out from under the table Prince Francis takes it in his mouth, meowing excitedly as he trots off to the living room, presumably to play.

With Miles gone and Prince Francis fed and cared for, it's time to start the rest of my day.

chapter fourteen

THE UNSTUCK

Kitty

I make my morning rounds, then stop at Kat's to work on invoices and create some content posts for Kat's Cat Café, something I was supposed to do a few days ago, but my schedule has made that a challenge.

"How are things? You're busier than usual these days," Kat says as we set up a new toy for the cats to play with.

"I'm sorry I couldn't stop by earlier in the week. I'll make up for it on the weekend."

Tux rushes over and immediately starts playing with the toy, purring happily and then rolling on his back and kicking at his face, as excited cats do. Kat takes photos while I take video footage.

"It's okay. I just miss your face around here, that's all."

"We really need to plan a girls' night catch-up." I keep saying this and then something always seems to come up. "What about tomorrow night?"

Kat bites the corner of her lip. "I have a date."

"Oh! Is this date number two?"

Her eyes light up. "Nope. This is three."

"Really? What did I miss?"

"We went for coffee yesterday. Tomorrow we're going for dinner."

"That's awesome. I need to hear about this. And we really need to plan something so I can get a full rundown of Friday night." I feel bad that I haven't been around as much as I should. Kat is one of my closest friends, and that I missed the second date excitement means I'm slacking on friend duty. I skip lunch in order to get a recap of date two with Brad, and we make a tentative plan to have lunch on the weekend.

I leave to manage my afternoon clients and pick up a few things for dinner on the way home. I find my mom in the living room, leafing through an old photo album. She usually only does this when it's approaching a birthday. "Hey, Mom, everything okay?"

Her eyes are glassy when she lifts her gaze, as if she's on the verge of tears. She sets the album on the coffee table and struggles to get the footrest down on the lounger. It's been giving her more trouble lately, which makes me nervous. I don't know how she'll handle it if my dad's old lounger stops working. I can't see her being okay with getting rid of it.

"Oh yes, everything's fine." The footrest finally goes down with a grinding metallic squeal and a clunk. "I was giving the shelves a dust and I pulled an album down and well..." She motions to the stack on the floor. "You know how that goes."

"I could give you a hand with that after dinner," I suggest.

"I can finish it up tomorrow since it's my day off. Let me help put the groceries away."

She follows me to the kitchen, and we unload the bags together.

"You've been gone a lot lately," she muses as she transfers the oranges to the fruit bowl.

"I've been helping out a new client with his cat," I explain.

"Which client is this? I get them confused since you have so many." She sets the canned tomatoes on the counter, along with the tomato paste. Tonight we're having lasagna soup for dinner.

I fill my mother in on Prince Francis, who I've mentioned before, and she hums and nods, but I'm not sure she's paying attention.

"His mother is going into a home soon, and he's not sure if she'll be able to take the cat with her. I'm hoping she can, or else Miles will have to find a new home for Prince Francis." I grab two onions and the cutting board, then move around the kitchen, pulling out ingredients for the soup while we chat.

"What kind of cat is it again? Hopefully not one that will be hard to find a home for," Mom asks absently.

"A sphynx. They're usually in high demand, so I doubt finding him a new human will be too difficult, but he can be destructive."

"You'll fix that, though."

"I'm working on it."

"Smokey was such a well-trained cat. I remember when your sister was a baby, and he would lie under her crib and then come get me in the morning when she was ready to be fed." Mom smiles wistfully. "I miss those days sometimes."

"Yeah, me too. He was a great cat." I swallow down the sadness that comes with thinking about Smokey. All the great memories I had of him as a child are tainted by a single event that changed our entire family. Normally, the second he started pulling on the screen, I would let him in. Except that one time.

Still, I wander down memory lane. "He used to follow Dad around like a shadow after dinner, waiting for him to sit in his recliner so he could take up residence in his lap."

"He was your dad's cat, that's for sure," Mom muses.

She's right, he was, and a few months after he passed, Smokey ran away. One day I let him out for his morning frolic in the back-yard, and he never came home. I feel as though I'm experiencing the sadness I associated with these memories through a window, a protective barrier from the pain.

Hattie messages to say she's going to be home later and not to wait on her for dinner.

"Are you here tonight? Maybe we can play a game of Farkle after we watch *Jeopardy*." Mom asks.

I hate to say no to my mom, but I need to get the situation with Prince Francis under control. "I'm going back to my client's house for the night. I'm trying to extinguish some bad behaviors, and Prince Francis isn't used to being alone all the time. But maybe tomorrow night?"

"That would be lovely, dear. I think it's wonderful that you're so dedicated to your job."

"I really do love it." But as I sit here, eating dinner at the table set for three, my dad's spot empty, though full of the weight of his memory, I realize that staying at Miles's mother's house has felt like a mini vacation. And that's saying something considering the emotional ghosts that live there.

I mull that over while I help clean up the dinner dishes. How Miles's house is full of memories he's trying to escape, while I'm trying to hold on to mine. It's almost like I've put my life on pause every time I walk through the door and stay that teenage girl. Any time my mom suggests redecorating, I've been the one to say I love it the way it is. But maybe I just love the memories. Even if the most pervasive one is a black cloud hanging. Like Toby's bedroom, mine hasn't changed much since I was sixteen. I see the parallels: his is a shrine to a life none of his family live anymore. And mine is a shrine to the days before I lost my dad.

I'm packing an overnight bag when there's a knock on my bedroom door. "Come in!" I call out as I stuff in a pair of pajamas.

Hattie pops her head in. "There's a pile of photo albums on the living room floor. Please tell me you didn't have to sit with Mom and listen to a story that went with every single photo."

"Uh no. I redirected us to the kitchen to make dinner before that could happen."

She closes the door behind her and drops into my computer chair. "Oh phew. I thought you'd gotten sucked in and I wasn't here to save you, and then I would have felt bad. Are you going somewhere?"

I don't mind going through old photo albums. In fact, it's more likely to be me pulling them off the shelves, but I leave that thought alone and explain that I'm staying another night at a client's house.

"Is this the client with the hottie owner?"

"The hottie son, yes."

"Is he staying over, too?"

"No, he's not." At least not that I'm aware. My heart leaps around in my chest at the possibility, though. So silly. I'm clearly holding on to his offhand comment about dinner too tightly.

"I'm going for drinks with some friends from school tonight. You can come with if you want." Hattie grabs one of my cat stress balls and tosses it from one hand to the other.

"I need to do some training with Prince Francis tonight, but thanks for the invitation." I add an outfit for tomorrow to my bag, and my mini handheld steamer.

Hattie spins around once in my chair. "Can I say something?"

"Sure?" I drag out the word, uncertain of her tone.

"I know you love your job, Kitty, but sometimes I wonder if maybe you love it too much."

I stop what I'm doing and give her my full attention. "How do you mean?"

She taps on the arm of the chair. "You're blowing me off to hang out with a cat."

"I'm being paid to take care of someone's pet." There's a difference. Also, I seem to have a crush on the son of the owner.

"Which I understand, but you can't have one quick drink with me and some friends? Do something social? Go out and see other human beings close to your own age and not someone's grandmother who basically wants your help, so they have someone to talk to for a couple of hours?" She raises a hand when I start to protest. "I'm not saying you shouldn't take your job seriously, or that there isn't merit in you being a friendly face for elderly cat owners, but sometimes I think, particularly in situations such as these, your job is kind of a convenient excuse *not* to come out."

"I'm not the biggest fan of crowds." I'm making another excuse, and I'm not sure why. I feel safest online, being the Kitty Whisperer with followers who post heart eyes. In real life, there are conversations, and while I love what I do, not everyone thinks cat sitting is a real job. So when someone dismisses me or thinks what I do is "cute," I'm compelled to defend my career. And that often leads to feeling insecure. The last time I went out with Hattie was to some house party. I ended up in a group of people I didn't know, and when I told them what I did for a living, they thought it was a joke. They weren't my sister's actual friends, but it still wasn't my favorite night, and I would like to avoid a repeat.

"It's a small group at a pub. You've met most of them before. I'm not saying you have to come tonight, but you're allowed to have a social life. I know groups can make you nervous, but sometimes it's good to step outside of our comfort zone, don't you think?"

I bite the inside of my cheek. Today I'd already been thinking about how my life is on pause. Maybe she's right. Maybe this is a good way to hit the Play button. And if I've already met these people, it's not too far outside my comfort zone. "Okay. I'll come for a drink."

"Yay! I promise you won't regret it!" She pushes out of the chair and wraps her arms around me. "Let's pick an outfit!"

I run my hands over my hips. "What's wrong with what I'm wearing?"

Hattie gives me a look. "This is fine for old people with vision problems. Not so much for the pub."

Half an hour later I'm sandwiched between my sister and one of her classmates. Everyone is familiar except the guy I'm sitting next to, Hattie's classmate named Bryce. His hair has a perfect swoop that reminds me of boy bands and ski jumps. It's also very blond, and so are his eyebrows. He looks sort of like a cross between a Disney character and a cartoon superhero. He's also very, very chatty.

And braggy. And he burps a lot. I have a feeling he ate either Caesar salad or garlic bread for dinner, because every so often a garlic and beer–scented burp wafts my way. It's a challenge not to grimace every time it happens. Instead, I plaster on a smile and try to follow the conversation, but it isn't easy with all the hot garlic wind.

"Are you still in college, too? I've never seen you on campus. I'm in the final year of my PhD."

"Oh wow. That's a lot of education. And dedication. What are you studying?" I ask. This is good. If I can keep him talking, then I don't have to answer questions. When I'm with old people or cats, I don't have to worry about making an ass out of myself.

"I'm taking alien studies."

I blink a few times, waiting for a punchline, but one apparently isn't coming. I wonder if my expression is the same as other people's when I tell them I cat sit and train them. "Oh, that's really...interesting. What kind of job would you get with that? Would you work for NASA?"

"Oh no. NASA is only looking for rocket scientists and people with engineering degrees. Or at least that's what all my rocket scientist friends are saying." He waves a hand around in the air. "I fell in love with aliens when I watched *E.T.* as a kid. Have you seen that movie? The one from the eighties?"

"Oh wow. Yeah. I've seen it. He's obsessed with Reese's Pieces, isn't he? The E.T. character?" This is an exceptionally odd conversation.

"Oh yeah, totally obsessed." Bryce nods exuberantly and burps again.

"If you're not in college, what do you do?" he asks.

"I'm a professional cat sitter."

He blinks once, twice, a third time, and then throws his head back and guffaws. It draws the attention of the surrounding tables, which in turn makes my face feel hot. When I don't join in, his expression sobers and his eyes round with shock. "You're serious?"

This coming from a guy who went into alien studies because of a Reese's Pieces–loving Hollywood-created extraterrestrial. "Yup. I own my own business."

He frowns. "You can make a living off of that?"

This isn't an uncommon reaction to my job, but it is frustrating. "There's a woman who makes six figures from farting in jars. Why can't cat sitting be lucrative enough to pay the bills?"

"Cats are kind of assholes, though. Like, dog sitting I get. They need to be let out and taken for walks. Cats are just doorstops that crap in a box," Bryce says.

"They're just as affectionate as dogs, and they need just as much love and care," I argue.

My phone buzzes in my pocket, which is a relief because I'm getting heated. More than just in my face. I check the message, half hoping it's an emergency. It's not urgent, but it is Miles. Listening to Bryce crap all over my job isn't my idea of a good time. But if Miles were here...On a whim made out of panic and kneejerk reactions, I invite him to the pub. It isn't until after I hit the Send button that I realize it probably isn't the best idea to invite the guy I have a crush on to a pub with my sister and her friends.

"Everything okay?" Bryce asks, seemingly oblivious to how much he's offended me.

"Yup. Everything's fine."

I proceed to panic-chug the rest of my drink and order another while Bryce tells me about the time he was abducted by an alien. It's better than him insulting my job, but not by much.

"I was only eight years old when it happened. It was the middle of the night, and I had a feeling, you know? I looked out my window and there was a UFO in the sky. I opened my window to get a better look, and then a huge spotlight shone down on the side of my house and boom." He snaps his fingers. "I was beamed up to the mothership."

"Wow. That must have been surreal." I need to ask my sister where the hell she met this guy, and why she stuck me beside him. Unfortunately, asking her right now would be rude, as she's currently flirting with a guy who looks a lot like Chris Evans's younger brother.

"I was prepared for the worst," he says solemnly.

"Like being anally probed?" I joke, sort of.

"That's actually a myth. Aliens don't do that." He stretches his arm across the back of the seat and leans in close, as if he's about to tell me a secret.

Which is the exact moment I spot Miles walking through the bar. He's wearing a suit and his glasses, and he looks so good. Like a sexy, nerdy, suit-wearing smart guy who crunches numbers like gym junkies crunch their abs. I raise my hand in the air and wave it around to catch his attention. For a moment his face lights up when he sees me. It makes my stomach somersault. And then his gaze shifts to my right, where Bryce is close talking in my ear. I consider how it must look to Miles. Here I am, inviting him to the pub while some random weirdo chats me up. About aliens.

"Can you excuse me for a second? My friend just arrived."

"Huh?" Bryce asks.

"I need to get out."

"Oh. Right. Okay." Bryce seems confused.

So does Miles.

But Bryce slides over, and I hop out of the booth, moving across the room to where Miles stands, looking uncertain and maybe like he's trying to shoot lasers at Bryce with his eyeballs. I rush over to him, and because I'm still in panic mode and thinking with only my hormones and none of my brain cells, I do something absurdly mortifying.

"I'm so glad you're here, and I'm so sorry for what I'm about to do. Please go with it. That guy sitting beside me is certifiable, and I need him to get a clue." I grab the lapels of his suit jacket and push up on my toes. Then I mash my lips against his.

chapter fifteen

WELL, THAT WAS UNEXPECTED

Miles

To say I'm confused would be an understatement. Kitty's lips are currently pressed against mine. And that dude she was sitting beside, who looks like one of the cartoon elves from that Claymation Christmas movie with the abominable snowman, is glaring daggers at me. There's also a woman staring at us with her mouth agape.

I stop focusing on the gawkers and focus instead on Kitty, whose lips are still on mine. They're soft and warm.

I'm not sure what's going on, but I'm not one to look a gift horse in the mouth, either. I wrap my arm around her waist and pull her against me. She makes a noise of surprise and parts her lips. I take the opportunity for what it is and brush my tongue against hers. Her mouth tastes fruity and sweet.

Kitty makes a noise of surprise and releases one of my lapels. Her hand curves around the back of my neck, and she tips her head, her tongue tangling with mine. What starts as an innocent kiss quickly escalates into a very public battle of the tongues. Eventually I have to stop because I'm at risk of getting a hard-on if I keep it up. It wouldn't be so bad if we had some privacy, but we're in the middle of a pub with a substantial audience.

I pull back far enough so that I can see her face. Her eyes are still closed, and her lips are parted.

"Hi." The word comes out about two octaves lower than usual.

Her eyes pop open and her mouth forms an *O*. She blinks at me a few times before she says, "I just attacked you with my lips. I'm so sorry."

"Um. I'm not?" I rub the back of my neck. There are little indents from where her nails pressed into the skin.

"You're not sorry I attacked you with my lips?" She seems perplexed. God, she's adorable. And gorgeous. And she has great lips.

I shake my head. "Not even a little sorry. You're welcome to attack me with your lips whenever you feel like it." *Wherever you feel like attacking me with them.*

"Except maybe when my mouth is full of food. That would not be great." She squeezes her eyes shut and grimaces. "Why can't I ever just stop when I'm ahead?"

"One of the things I like most about you is the way you don't stop when you're ahead." I incline my head marginally toward the table. "What's with the boy band member?"

"He's a friend of my sister's. I'm still sorry about the lip attack. This really wasn't how I envisioned our first kiss." She slaps her hand over her mouth. "I wish I could pluck that last sentence out of your ears and shove it back into my word hole."

I smile down at her. "If I'm going to be totally honest, that wasn't how I envisioned our first kiss going either, but I still very much enjoyed it and look forward to a potential repeat. Hopefully soon."

She rapid-blinks a few times. "You've thought about kissing me?"

"Many times," I admit.

"Me too. I even had dreams about it back when I thought you were a cat hater. That was frustrating, by the way, the whole finding you attractive while also being annoyed by you."

"I can imagine." I nod stoically, then incline my head toward the table. "Maybe I need to thank the boy band dude for being so clueless."

"I wouldn't go that far." She thumbs over her shoulder. "Do you want to sit down and have a drink? I can introduce you to my sister and her friends."

"That'd be great." I let her lead me to the table.

Boy band dude, whose name is Bryce, grudgingly gives up his seat so I can sit next to Kitty. She introduces me as her friend and blushes sixteen different shades of red when her sister says she's heard all about me and that she's happy to finally meet me. Based on Hattie's smirk and Kitty's pink-tinged cheeks, I'm thinking whatever she's heard has been good things. The whole laying a kiss on me is also a tipoff.

Hattie's friends are interesting, and I feel a smidge bad for

Bryce the boy band wannabe, since it's clear he's interested in Kitty and I came in and stole his thunder without even trying.

We stay for one drink before Kitty starts covering her mouth to hide her yawns. She pays for both of our drinks, despite my telling her it's not necessary.

Kitty hugs Hattie, who must whisper something in her ear that she finds embarrassing, because her face turns bright red again. We leave the pub together. "Are you staying in town tonight, or do you have to go back to the city?"

"The team has practice early tomorrow, so I have to head home tonight."

She adjusts the strap of her purse and nods a few times. "That makes sense. I didn't even think to ask what you were doing in town in the first place."

"I had to sign paperwork for my mother. We'll be able to move her into the home this weekend. And they've agreed to let me bring Prince Francis by for a visit, which is great because she's been asking about him a lot."

"I bet she misses him."

"When she remembers she has a cat, yes."

Kitty's expression turns sad. "Is there anything I can do to help?"

"You've done more than enough. I'll be by the house tomorrow sometime so I can do some packing." I shove a hand in my pocket and figure now is as good a time as any to ask her out. "I was wondering if you'd like to go for dinner, maybe next weekend? With me?" I don't know why I add the last part. Obviously, I'm not going to ask her to go out with someone else.

"You mean as a thank-you?" Kitty's bottom lip slides through her teeth.

"I mean, it could be a thank-you, but I'm more inclined to classify this as a date. I've been meaning to ask you, but I didn't want you to say yes out of obligation. However, since the lip attack happened, I feel a bit more confident that you might say yes because you want to and not because you don't want to hurt my feelings."

Kitty smiles and ducks her head. "I would definitely like to go on a date with you."

"Okay. Well, that's great." It's started to rain a little. Tiny drops land on my glasses, obscuring parts of Kitty's face. "I guess we can plan that tomorrow. I'll message when I'll be at the house?"

"Perfect. I'm going there now, so Prince Francis has a head to curl his body around tonight."

"I can honestly say I'm jealous of Prince Francis."

We smile and stare at each other's mouths for several seconds before we both take a step closer. Her hand slides over my chest and around the back of my neck while I wrap an arm around her waist. We both tip our heads to the left and she lifts her chin while I drop mine.

When our lips connect it feels like a whole truck full of fireworks have just gone off. In my pants.

I'm not sure how long we kiss for, but the rain picks up to the point that we're both going to be soaked to the bone if we keep it up much longer. I'd suggest we continue in either of our cars, but I worry that I won't have the ability to put a pin in it before it escalates to a potential indecent exposure charge.

"I'm sort of glad I attacked you with my lips tonight."

"Me too. And I'm hopeful that from now on it's going to be a regular occurrence." I open her car door and usher her in, then wave at her through the window before I rush to my own vehicle. The urge to follow her back to my mother's house is strong, but I remind myself that it would be a lot better to wait until I've had the opportunity to take her on a date, and hopefully end up back at my place, rather than in my childhood bedroom.

chapter sixteen

LITTLE PIECES

Kitty

The next week is filled with emergencies, which means I don't see Miles or Kat. Every time I think I'm about to get in time with either of them, I'm called away to another catastrophe. It also means all the effort I've put into upping my makeup game has been a complete waste.

It's mid-afternoon on Thursday, and Miles's mother is moving into the home this weekend. Miles has been here the past few days packing up things. I was supposed to stop by last night, but Mr. O'Toole called very upset because Bumbles had gotten stuck in the wall again. I was certain he was just trapped in the food cupboard and that it would only take ten minutes and I'd be on my way to Miles's mother's place, but when I arrived, I was shocked to discover this time he really *had* gotten stuck in the wall. How he got there remains a mystery, but we cut a hole in the drywall to get him out.

It was one of many emergency situations over the past few

days. I attribute it to the full moon. They always make cats and their humans a little squirrely.

Today I arrive at Miles's mother's house ready to spend quality time with Prince Francis. Now that he seems to have calmed down, I've been rotating nights, spending one at home and one with Prince Francis. He's stopped knocking things off shelves and dressers, so I'm considering it a win. Once Miles's mother is settled in the home, I'm crossing my fingers they'll allow him to live with her.

I expect Prince Francis to greet me as soon as I walk through the door, but he doesn't. I assume he's either mad at me for not staying over last night, or he's in nap mode.

I leave my purse on the table at the front entrance and toe off my shoes, no longer worried about broken trinkets since most have been packed or disposed of at this point. I'm on my way to the kitchen to grab his treats when I hear a female voice.

"Prince Francis! Come out from under the bed!"

I halt and listen, my heart suddenly in my throat. Miles's car isn't in the driveway, and I'm sure he would have let me know if someone was supposed to stop by.

"Come out, Prince Francis! I have treats for you!"

Maybe it's a neighbor? I consider leaving and coming back later, but what if it's not? I follow the voice up the stairs. I don't want to scare anyone, but if there's a catnapper in the house, I also don't want to alert them to my presence. I pick up a ceramic figurine on my way down the hall and cringe at the squeak in the floorboards.

The first door on the second floor is wide open. Toby's room. I peek in and find a woman crouched on all fours, with her cheek pressed to the floor. Her back is to me. Her long hair is pulled up in a ponytail and threaded through with gray. She makes a tutting sound and pleads with Prince Francis. "You know you're not allowed in Toby's room when he's at school. Come on out, Prince Francis, and I'll give you a big treat. I have cans of tuna in the cupboard. If you're a good boy, I'll share it with you."

My heart skips another beat; this must be Miles's mother. I have no idea how she managed to get here if Miles isn't with her.

I clear my throat and knock on the door, addressing her formally. "Excuse me, Ms. Thorn?"

She startles and pushes up onto her knees, twisting to face me. Her brows pull together in a furrow. I can see pieces of Miles in her face. They have the same eyes and nose, and the same lanky, lean build. "Hello. Are you Toby's tutor? He isn't home from school yet."

I give her a small smile, unsure how to proceed. "I'm a friend of Miles. I've been taking care of Prince Francis while you've been away."

That earns me another looks of confusion. "A friend of Miles?"

"My name is Kitty Hart. I'm a professional cat sitter." I figure facts are the best way to go. If she still thinks Toby is alive, Miles would only be eleven and not likely to have women friends in their midtwenties.

"Kitty Hart? Professional cat sitter?" She tips her head. Her mouth opens in an *O*, and her hands flutter around in the air. "Oh! Oh! Kitty Hart! I know you! I follow you on Instagram and TikTok! I love your posts!" She pushes up off the floor and wipes her hands on her hips. She takes one of my hands in both of hers and pumps it vigorously. "I told my son about you. I had to go away for a while." Her eyebrows try to touch each other. "I don't know why." Her expression shifts again, eyes suddenly murky and distant. "My youngest boy should be home from school soon. I should make him a snack."

I swallow down a pang of sadness as she pats me on the shoulder and heads for the door. "Come along, sweetheart, I'll make you a snack, too. Kitty Hart in my house. What a day."

I follow her to the kitchen, leaving Prince Francis in Toby's bedroom. He'll come down when he hears the treat bag being opened. I make a stop at the front door and grab my phone from my purse so I can message Miles. I have a feeling his mother showing up here isn't a surprise to only me.

She stops when she reaches the living room. "Oh my goodness! My knickknacks! Did someone steal them?"

"Prince Francis was knocking them off the shelves, so we boxed them up," I explain.

I quickly fire off a message to Miles to let him know that his mother is here, at her house, and that I'm trying to find out information but I'm not sure how successful I'll be, and that he should probably call the care facility and let them know.

He messages back right away to tell me he just got a call from the night nurse and that he's relieved that she's with me and not wandering the streets. He asks me to keep her talking and says that he'll be here as soon as he can.

Miles's mother—Tabitha—stands in front of the open fridge peering at the contents. "I can't remember what I'm looking for."

"You were going to make a snack," I remind her.

"Oh yes. A snack is a good idea. We can have tea and cookies."

"That sounds perfect." I open the cupboard where Prince Francis's treats are stored and shake the container. He comes trotting into the kitchen a few seconds later, meowing loudly.

"Oh! There's my boy! I missed you, Prince Francis!" Tabitha crouches and I pass her the treats so she can feed him. He rubs himself on her legs and purrs.

"He missed you too, very much."

"I feel like I've been away for a long time, but I'm not sure why." She gives me a small smile. "That happens a lot. I forget things."

"Do you know how you got here today?" I ask.

She purses her lips and rubs under Prince Francis's chin. "I must have walked?" She blinks a few times, as if she's searching her memory. "I came from the hospital, maybe?"

Based on what Miles has told me, the wing where she's staying is a bit less secure than the rest of the hospital. "Do you remember why you were there?"

She shakes her head and picks Prince Francis up, holding him like a baby. "Do you know?"

"Why don't you sit down and cuddle with Prince Francis. I can

explain what I know and see if it helps jog your memory at all."
Hearing about Miles's mother is a lot different from witnessing
it firsthand.

She nods and sinks into one of the chairs at the kitchen
table. I put the kettle on and drop teabags into mugs, then set
the milk and sugar on the table and take a seat across from her.
"You remember being in the hospital?" I'm not sure how quickly
her memories surface and fade, and I have no experience with
dementia. I've worked with other clients who have parents who
suffer the same affliction, but I've never met or talked to someone whose memory has started to fail them in the way it seems
Tabitha's has.

"Yes. But I don't feel sick."

I smile gently. "You're not sick physically. When Miles called
me to ask if I could help him look after Prince Francis, it was
because you'd left the house in the middle of the night and ended
up downtown, unsure how you got there or why you were there.
You'd forgotten."

She nods slowly. "I forget things." Prince Francis settles in her
lap, and she strokes along his back, gaze drifting across the room.
"Sometimes I'm not sure if I'm living in the past or the present.
This house does that to me."

My heart clenches, and I swallow past the lump in my throat.
"You have a lot of memories here."

She hums her agreement. "Not all of them good, though."
She drops her head. "I lost my youngest son when he was
just a boy."

It must be heartbreaking to live inside a mind that tricks you constantly, making you believe the things you've lost are still there one minute, and then taking them away again the next. "Miles's younger brother, Toby. Miles told me you lost him when he was only eight."

"It was such a tragedy. I couldn't get over the loss. And then I lost Miles and his father because I couldn't let go of Toby." She lifts her shaking fingers to her lips.

"That must have broken your heart." Losing my father, and feeling the weight of responsibility, was crushing, but to lose a child and then have your family fall apart, too, that would be soul shattering. Maybe mind breaking.

"It was my fault. I shouldn't have left Miles in charge of Toby. He'd just gotten a brand-new two-wheeler. I should have left the gardens alone and gone out with him for half an hour, but I was too caught up in picking the tomatoes before the squirrels got to them. Toby came outside and asked if he could ride his bike, and I told him to ask Miles to watch him. Miles was playing his video game—he had half an hour after school to play, and he was so good about sticking to that timeline. But it was a new game, and hockey, which he's very fond of." She smiles faintly, but it dissolves into sadness once again. "I guess he took too long to finish his level, and Toby went outside without him and we lost him."

Hearing the story from Tabitha sheds a different light on it. And I can see that Miles isn't the only one who feels culpability. "I'm so sorry. What a terrible tragedy for you and your family."

"Toby and Miles were so close, even though Miles was a few years older. They still did everything together. And then he was just gone. I wasn't a good mother for Miles after that, and I think he blamed himself for what happened to Toby, even though it was my fault."

The pieces of the puzzle fall into place, and I appreciate even more how difficult this must be for Miles. To be back in this house where his family fell apart. To see his mother's mind failing her, to have her slipping in and out of the present and back into the past from one moment to the next, with no understanding of what triggers it or how and when it got so bad.

I want to offer comfort, to give her some peace. I empathize with her on so many levels. And for Tabitha, she not only lost her son, but her entire family. And now she only remembers them in short blips of time. It seems as though there hasn't been closure for anyone in this family. They've been suspended in their grief, holding on to it, letting it grow. And the weeds of sorrow have spread out and blanketed them. Covered over the good memories, leaving behind only choking vines of pain.

I'm beginning to wonder if I've unwittingly done the same.

I cover her hand with mine and squeeze. But before I can say anything else, the front door opens. "Kitty? Mom?" Miles calls out.

"We're in the kitchen," I reply.

Tabitha's head lifts, and the clarity I saw in her eyes a moment ago is no longer there. Instead, it's replaced with a fog, as if those vines of memories have choked out reality again and replaced it with the past. "Oh! Toby's home from school! I'm so glad you get to meet him." She smiles as Miles appears in the doorway.

He looks frazzled, and his usually neatly styled hair is in disarray, as if his fingers have been in it. Or he got caught in a freak tornado that was only big enough to tousle his hair.

His gaze bounces between his mother, me, and the cups of tea on the table. "Hey, how's it going?"

"It's so good that you're home. And just in time to meet Miles's friend. Her name is Kitty. Is your brother with you, or does he have after-school activities today?"

Miles's smile falters fractionally, and his throat bobs with a heavy swallow. His voice is unsteady when he says, "I'm Miles, Mom."

"Oh. Yes. Of course. You always look so much alike." Her brow furrows. "Where's Toby?"

"He's not here."

"Did he go to a friend's house?"

Miles bites the inside of his lip, maybe debating whether he should be honest. "Yeah, he did."

"Oh, okay. I don't remember him telling me that before he went to school." She strokes Prince Francis, her lips pursed.

Eventually, Miles convinces her that they need to go for a drive. I can tell he's struggling with the lies, but that the truth could upset her.

"I can come along if you'd like," I offer quietly as Tabitha gets ready to leave.

He hesitates and clears his throat before he says, "You don't need to do that."

I put a hand on his arm. "I'd like to, if you'd like me to."

His jaw works for a few seconds before he nods once. "Yeah. Please. That would be great."

chapter seventeen

KITTY COMFORT

Miles

Kitty sits in the back seat while my mother sits in the front. She insisted that we bring Prince Francis along. I've never had him in a car before, so I pop an antihistamine to counteract any potential issues being in such a confined space with a cat may cause. On the upside, if I end up having a reaction, I have an EpiPen and there are lots of medical professionals where we're going.

When my mom realizes we're at the hospital again, she becomes agitated, and it takes a team of staff to get her out of the car and back to her room. All the while, she yells at me, telling me I'm taking her away from her home and that I'm only doing it because I blame her for what happened to Toby.

Kitty stays in the car with Prince Francis, which is preferable to having her witness more of my mom's meltdown once they get her through the doors. And even though I know it isn't her fault that she reacts this way, it's painful to watch.

Eventually they manage to calm her down. I return to the car and find Kitty has moved to the front. Prince Francis is in one of his favorite places: draped across her shoulders.

I drop into the driver's seat. "I'm sorry about this."

She squeezes my arm. "You don't need to be sorry. Would you like me to drive?"

"I'm okay." I feel the opposite of okay.

"You don't need to put on a brave face for me, Miles. I wouldn't be okay if I was in your shoes, so whatever you need from me right now, I'm here, whether it's just to be present, or drive, or listen."

I feel like a deflated balloon. "Do you mind driving?"

"Not at all." She unbuckles her seatbelt, unwraps Prince Francis from around her neck, sets him on the dashboard and exits the car, closing the door behind her, presumably so Prince Francis doesn't get any ideas about doing a runner.

I do the same and meet her at the hood.

It's cold today, the air puffing out in foggy bursts before disappearing.

She tips her head up, her expression full of compassion and sadness. She opens her arms. "You look like you could use a hug."

I don't even care that I'm so emotionally transparent. I wrap my arms around her, and hers wind around my waist. "Thank you." I lay my cheek on top of her head.

"No thanks needed. I'm sorry that was so tough." She squeezes.

"You make it better," I mutter.

And it's true. She does. I don't know how this happened, or

when we shifted from mutual disdain to like, but Kitty appeared in my life at exactly the right time. I send a thank-you to the powers that be and the internet for putting her on my screen and in my path.

I'm not sure how long we stand there, but eventually the muffled angry meows from inside the car force us apart. Kitty gets behind the wheel and Prince Francis immediately takes up residence on her shoulders again, grooming her hair, then shaking his head around when it gets stuck to his tongue. I attempt to relocate him to my lap, but he's determined to be an accessory.

"I'm so sorry you had to deal with that."

Kitty pulls out of the hospital parking lot and heads toward my mother's house. "It's really okay, Miles. She was actually quite pleasant but mostly confused. I understand there's a very different side to that, especially when she's confronted with reality."

I let my head fall back. "Yeah, that's been the biggest challenge. Telling her Toby is gone sets her off. It sucks to lie to her, but I don't want to send her over the edge all the time."

"There's no winning in a situation like that, for either of you. It hurts to see people you care about falling apart like that."

"I'm guessing you know this from experience, what with losing your dad when you were younger." I realize I need this kind of connection, someone who can relate to what I'm dealing with, even if it's not quite the same. Both of us have big holes in our lives created by the absence of people we love.

Kitty nods. "My mom really struggled when he passed away, which makes sense. They were best friends. They had the kind of love you see in Hallmark movies, and they made you believe in soul mates and forevers. He would literally do anything for her. The sun rose and set on my mother and my sister and me. Was it the same for you with your family?"

I think about that for a minute. What life was like growing up, how suddenly everything shifted. "Toby and I were close. He was more athletic than I was, better at sports, more of a natural, where I had to work hard. He played hockey like I did. And we always played together in the driveway. My mom would keep her car in the garage so we didn't put dents in it."

Kitty makes a face. "Did she learn that by trial and error?"

I chuckle. "Oh yeah. Toby hit the driver's side door and put a solid dent in it, but I didn't want him to get in trouble, because he was always the more mischievous of the two of us. So I said I'd been the one to do it. I don't think our mom believed us, but after that she parked the car in the garage."

"It sounds like you had a great relationship with her."

"I did. We all did. Obviously, our family wasn't perfect, but we were good. And then we lost Toby, and all those good memories were overshadowed by all the bad things that happened afterward. My mother fell apart. And my dad...he was devastated." I shake my head, thinking back to that day. "They blocked off the entire street when Toby got hit. Our neighbors were the first ones on the scene because it happened in front of their house. I heard it from inside the house, and when I went outside Toby was...his helmet hadn't been on properly. Sometimes he'd loosen it because he hated the chin strap." I pause, choking on emotions. "It was clear he was gone, but I still wanted to believe he was okay. My next-door neighbor stopped me from running across the street to get to him, and someone else went and got my mother in the backyard. By the time my dad got home, there were police cars everywhere and an ambulance. I think my mother broke that day. It was probably the same for my dad, but he had to keep it together when my mother couldn't. When Toby died, so did our family."

"My heart hurts for all of you." Kitty reaches over and gives my hand a gentle squeeze before she puts it back on the wheel and signals left into my mother's subdivision. "Your mom told me a bit about what happened that day."

The flashes of memory are hard to handle, and I swallow down the pain.

"She remembered that Toby was gone?"

"For a few minutes she seemed...clear? Like she knew what was real and what was the past. She admitted that she forgot things a lot, and she remembered losing Toby and how hard it was on you." She pulls into my mother's driveway and shifts the car into park, cutting the engine. "From my own experience, and from hearing more than one side of yours, it's easy to get caught in the fantasy of what if things had been different and live there."

I nod, absorbing her words. "That's it exactly. I want to go back and change the past, but I can't. And the way my family imploded after that was more than I could handle. I believed I was the reason it happened. And no matter how hard I try, it's difficult not to feel that way still." And in that moment, I see the truth in that statement. That my ignoring my brother and my mom's request to watch him is the reason we lost him.

"Tragedy can tear people apart, inside and out," Kitty says softly. "You just have to find a way to let it go so you can heal from it."

Prince Francis stretches out and settles a paw on my shoulder, headbutting my face and licking my ear while meowing plaintively.

I chuckle, glad for the levity, and give his head a brief scratch.

"Do you have to go back to the city, or do you want to come inside?" Kitty inclines her head toward the house. "Or does it hold too many sad memories tonight?"

"I can handle the memories." I don't want to leave now, not when it feels like Kitty and I are closer than ever.

I gather up Prince Francis, who surprisingly doesn't try to jump out of my arms, and we head inside.

"Should I make us some tea?" Kitty asks once we're standing in the mostly packed living room.

"Maybe we can see if there's something stronger hanging around?"

"Oh sure. I think I remember seeing brandy in the pantry. Let's check." I follow Kitty to the kitchen, and she opens the pantry door and pulls on the string dangling from the ceiling, the bare bulb lighting up the small space.

There are plenty of canned goods and cat treats. Prince Francis winds between our legs, meowing insistently. I spot a bottle of brandy and another of vodka, both on the top shelf, covered in a thin layer of dust. I pluck them from the shelf and Kitty grabs the dry food.

"I'm not sure what we have to mix this stuff with," I admit as I set them on the counter and open the fridge. "Ah! There's grapefruit juice and—" I frown and pull an old-school clear Tupperware jug that I remember from my childhood and hold it up for Kitty to see. "This looks suspiciously like Tang."

Kitty's cheeks flush and she ducks her head. "That's because it is Tang. Don't judge me. It's a guilty pleasure."

"I'm not knocking your Tang love. I'm the guy who orders the orange drink from McDonald's on purpose." I motion to the selection on the counter and pull two glasses from the cupboard. "What juice and booze combo would you prefer?"

"Tang and brandy?" It's more question than a definitive answer.

"How about I make one of each, and you can taste them both before you decide?"

"Sure. Sounds good."

Prince Francis yowls at her from the floor, his brow furrowed in displeasure because his wet food dish is empty. Kitty opens a new can of wet food, spoons half of it on his plate, and puts the rest in the fridge.

Once I've made two very stiff drinks, Kitty tastes them both and chooses the Tang and brandy combination, I down my Tang and vodka and make myself a second one before we head to the living room.

I purposely sit between two cushions, and Kitty drops down beside me, folding her legs under her so her feet rest against the side of my leg. "I didn't understand how bad things were with your mother until today," she admits.

"Neither did I. It's sort of been triage up to this point. I was struggling with the decision of putting her in a home, but after today I know it's the right move," I admit.

"She'll be safe there. Did you find out what happened that she managed to get out undetected?"

"Apparently she timed her departure with shift change and walked right out the front doors. By the time they realized she was gone, she was already on her way here."

"Wow. That's...impressive? She must have had a moment of real clarity."

I nod. "Either that or she got lucky? I guess she'd been asking about Prince Francis and when someone was bringing him to her. I told her I'd arranged for a visit. It's possible it got stuck in her head and she ended up here. After this, I doubt they'll let her keep him at the home. I worry that she'd lose him, or forget to feed him, or go in the opposite direction and overfeed him." I run a hand through my hair. "Maybe I should take him back to my place. I'm not sure how Wilfred would feel about having a cat in the house, but I don't see a lot of other options."

"I could take him. He could live with me." As if he knows we're talking about him, Prince Francis jumps up on the back of the couch, headbutts me in the cheek, then continues on, putting his butt right in my face as he rubs his cheek against Kitty's. He then sniffs her drink and hops down to perch on the arm of the couch.

"I can't ask you to do that."

"You're not asking. I'm offering. I see how much your mother loves Prince Francis, and if he lives with me, we can arrange for regular visits. He travels well in a car, and I'd be happy to take him." She reaches behind her and scratches his head. "It's been a long time since we've had a cat in the house, and he'd be the perfect addition to my family. And if things change and your mother ends up being able to take care of a cat, we can transition him back to her."

"Would you be okay with that? Keeping him temporarily?"

"We used to foster cats all the time when I was a kid. Smokey was our full-time kitty, but we would keep other cats for a few weeks at a time. We even had a few that stayed with us for close to six months."

"Wasn't it hard to let them go?" I can't imagine giving up Wilfred. Although with everything going on with my mother and my work schedule, it's been tough. Joe and Mark have been great about taking care of him while I'm dealing with this.

Kitty lifts a shoulder and lets it fall. "Sometimes. But we knew they were going to good homes, with humans who would love them and take care of them, so it helped ease the sting."

"Why did you stop fostering?" I ask.

Kitty takes a long sip of her drink. "Smokey was my dad's cat, always sat on his lap when he was watching TV. Basically followed him around like a puppy. He'd even go for walks with my dad. He ran away a few months after my dad passed and I just couldn't fathom getting a new cat. It was too hard. My heart couldn't take any more bruises. We were struggling to keep our heads above water as a family. So we put fostering on pause and never really took it off. Until now." She gives me a small smile.

"Are you sure you're going to be okay with that? Should you talk to your family first?"

"My mom has mentioned getting another pet, but I've often been the one to shoot down the idea. I'll run it by her first, but I think both she and Hattie will be on board. Although I have a feeling Hattie will be out of the house as soon as she graduates from college."

"Why do you say that?" I met her sister at the pub the other night, but I didn't get a chance to really talk to her.

"She's ready to move on with her life." Kitty props her cheek on her fist. "Our house is a lot like your brother's room."

"How do you mean?"

"Nothing has changed since my dad passed away ten years ago. Everything is the same, from the paint on the walls to the furniture in the living room. The only space that's shifted is Hattie's room. It's grown and changed with her." Kitty's lip slides between her teeth. "My mom still sets a place for my dad at the table."

My heart clenches, and I set my mostly empty glass on the coffee table so I can take Kitty's hand in mine, giving it a gentle squeeze. "Is that okay for you?"

Kitty sighs and looks up to the ceiling. "At first it was one of those things my mom did out of habit, and we've all accepted it as normal, I guess."

"Just like my mom never changed Toby's room."

Kitty nods. "I think in a lot of ways the situation with your mom mirrors my own. I'm starting to see that by not doing anything to really change the way we do things, I'm helping keep things...stuck. If I give in to change, I'm letting go, and I've had a hard time doing that."

"But you're not the one who sets the place setting for your dad every day."

"There have been times when I assumed my mom forgot, so I went ahead and did it for her. But maybe she hadn't forgotten, maybe it was intentional, and me setting the place anyway makes me part of the problem, not the solution." She laces her fingers with mine. "When your mom said that she thinks you blame yourself for what happened to Toby, it really hit home. Because in a lot of ways, I blame myself for what happened to my dad. If I'd been paying attention, I would have realized that Smokey wanted me to go upstairs for a reason. Maybe I would have gotten to him in time. But I didn't. So I've trapped myself in this loop of guilt and fear. I haven't been sure how to move forward, maybe because I feel a lot like I don't necessarily deserve to."

"Do you ever feel like maybe we were meant to come into each other's lives at exactly this time? Like destiny had a plan," I ask.

"And it involved a hairless cat." Kitty smiles softly and nods.

"And a trip to the ER."

We both grin.

"And being tackled to the floor over a water gun."

I cringe. "I'm never going to live that one down."

"I didn't mind being tackled by you." Her smile turns coy. "Sort of like you didn't mind being attacked by my lips."

"I loved being attacked by your lips." My gaze darts down as her bottom one slides between her teeth.

When I meet her gaze again, I see my own desire reflected back at me. We lean in at the same time, tipping our heads, eyes falling closed as our lips connect. Not an attack this time, but a gentle press. Soft, but sure.

I slide my hand under her hair and curl my fingers around the back of her delicate neck, parting my lips as she does the same. Every movement is a mirror, synchronized. We both hum and shift, and suddenly Kitty's no longer beside me on the couch, she's straddling my lap. She runs her hands over my shoulders and up the sides of my neck, fingers dragging along my scalp as she presses her chest to mine.

She's all soft curves as I trail my fingers down her side and let my hand come to rest on her hip. I want to pull her closer, touch more of her, get lost in the feel of her, forget about today.

Our glasses clink and mine push against my cheek as we deepen the kiss. We both pull back at the same time.

"Stupid glasses," Kitty mutters and takes hers off, folding in the arms and tossing them aside.

I do the same, and then we're back to making out.

Eventually her hands start to roam, leaving my hair to trail over my shoulders and down my arms. She gives my biceps a squeeze and makes a noise, somewhere between a hum and a sigh, and goes lower, until she reaches my belt buckle. I'm still wearing a dress shirt and tie, having come directly from a team meeting. She tugs the shirt free from my pants and shimmies back on my lap to give her enough space to start unbuttoning. I don't know exactly how far this is going to go tonight, but I'm unbelievably grateful that Josh tossed a box of condoms into my glovebox after I told him I'd asked Kitty out on a date. I'm also extra grateful that he took it upon himself to put one in my wallet, even though I assured him we weren't at the getting naked stage. It looks as though I might be wrong about that.

Kitty works her way through the buttons, but because I'm still wearing a tie, when she gets close to the top, she breaks the kiss and leans back. She makes the same face she did when she attacked me with her lips in the bar. "Here I am trying to take your clothes off without even asking if it's okay."

"I would have said something if I wasn't on board with the shirt removal, but I appreciate you making sure." I tug on my tie, loosening it enough that I can pull it over my head. "Would you like to finish the job, or would you prefer to go back to making out?"

She taps her bottom lip. "Both, to be quite honest, but I feel like the last two buttons will be a challenge if our lips are locked. So first we lose the shirt, then we go back to making out?"

"I'm absolutely willing to delay gratification for ease of shirt removal."

We both smile, and she unfastens the last two buttons. I tip my chin up for her when she reaches the collar, and her fingers slide between the fabric and the hollow of my throat. When she's done, she kisses the bottom of my chin.

I'm about to come back in for another kiss, but she covers my lips with two fingers. "If it's okay with you, I'd like to delay gratification for a few more seconds and take a moment to appreciate how sexy you are without a shirt on. The last time you were shirtless, I was trying to make sure you weren't going to bleed out from Prince Francis's nails."

"I'm more than happy to be the recipient of your appreciation." Being around guys who are built like brick shit houses means sometimes I get self-conscious about my lack of beefiness. But Kitty somehow makes me feel like Adonis.

She runs her hands down my chest and back up. "Oh! We should be even, shouldn't we?" Before I have a chance to unpack what that means, she pulls on the sleeve of her cardigan and tugs it free from her arm, then does a half wave with the other one, dropping it to the floor. She grabs the hem of her Kitty Whisperer T-shirt and yanks it over her head.

Under that shirt is a very sexy bra. It's pink and gray cheetah print—which should not be a surprise at all—with pink lace trim. And the cleavage. Good God the cleavage. Kitty has an incredible body. And I want to put my hands and mouth on every inch of her.

"Miles?" Her voice is soft and uncertain.

"Huh?" I drag my gaze away from her chest and up to her face. On the way, I notice that her neck and chest have turned a slightly blotchy red color.

"Should I put my shirt back on?"

"What? No. Hell no. Why would you suggest such a thing?"

"You looked like a deer in headlights. And not in a good way."

"Shit. Sorry." I give my head a shake. "I got lost in how sexy you are and how much I'm looking forward to ogling your nipples the way they ogled me the last time I was shirtless."

Kitty grins. "Oh, that's good. They'd actually be doing that right now if they weren't hidden behind layers of fabric and padding."

"Should we set them free and give them what they want?" I arch a brow. "And what I want, too, obviously."

Kitty nods and her hands move to her chest, which is when I realize it's a front clasp bra.

"I could do it. If you're okay with that."

"I am. It's a bit tricky, though." Her cheeks flush pink.

"If my struggle becomes embarrassingly long, you can help me out?"

"Okay." She nods once and rolls her shoulders back, jutting her chest toward my face.

As much as I want to dive right in and flick that clasp open, I slow things down. This is an experience I want to savor, a slow unveiling. I skim along her sides and wrap my hands around her waist, thumbs sweeping along the underside of her bra. I lean in and kiss her collarbone, then dip down and drag my lips along the lace edge before I sit back and follow the same path with my fingers until they meet at the clasp.

"Fold it out toward you, then one side goes up and the other goes down," Kitty whispers.

"Thanks for the tutorial." I slip a single finger under the clasp and do exactly what she says. At first, I go in the wrong direction, but it only takes me a second to realize it opens the other way. The two sides separate, and I grip them in my fingers, holding them together.

I lift my gaze to Kitty's. Her chest rises and falls with anticipation.

"This feels a lot like unwrapping a Christmas present," I tell her.

"It's my favorite holiday, aside from Halloween, which really isn't a holiday but should be," Kitty replies.

"I agree." I release the cups and the bra slides over Kitty's shoulders and drops onto the floor at my feet. If my brain were a gif, it would be the single word *boobs* flashing with balloons being dropped on my face in a torrent. "Can I touch them?" I ask her chest.

"We would like that," she whispers.

"Awesome." I cup one full swell in each palm. "Hello, ladies."

Kitty laughs, and I smile as I lean in and press a kiss to each swell, then circle a nipple with my tongue before I cover it with my mouth. I devote the same attention to the other breast—no one likes to be left out—and Kitty's hands slide into my hair, gripping the strands tightly as she arches.

Eventually she pulls my head back and claims my mouth with hers again. Unlike the soft, easy kisses pre-shirtlessness, this one is full of passion and desire. Our teeth clash and our tongues tangle. Kitty's chest presses against mine, skin to skin, and we wrap our arms around each other, like we're trying to fuse our bodies.

Our hands roam over bare skin, touching, groping, caressing. When we break the kiss, we're both panting.

Kitty's hands drop to my belt. "We should—" Her words are cut short when she screams and bars an arm across her chest. Her eyes are wide and her cheeks are flushed pink. "Oh my God!" She brings the other hand up to cover her eyes.

I look down at myself, wondering if I'm the problem, but all I see are my own nipples and my semi-abs and my hard-on pressing excitedly against my fly. I glance over my shoulder and shout profanity.

Sitting on the back of the couch, directly over my left shoulder, is Prince Francis. And he's glaring at us like he's been possessed by some demon.

"What the hell, buddy? Hasn't anyone ever told you it's rude to stare?"

His eyes flick over to me and then back to Kitty. He puts a paw on my shoulder and tries to bite my ear.

I bat him away, but instead of leaping off the couch, he drops to the cushion beside me, extends a leg, and starts licking his parts.

"Maybe we should take this to the bedroom?" I suggest.

Kitty makes the Vulcan sign with her fingers and peeks between the space. "That would probably be a good plan."

My childhood bedroom is not the most ideal location for hot sex; however, my mother's couch with a cat staring at us or alternately licking his own balls is less ideal. I grab my shirt and drape it over Kitty's shoulders, putting a hand on her waist to steady her as she shimmies off my lap. I push to a stand in the narrow space between the couch and the coffee table. My hard-on bumps into her stomach through my pants.

Kitty looks down and it's as if her hand has a magnet attached to it, because it rises and cups me. I groan and she hums. Prince Francis's head appears beside my leg.

"Okay. This is getting creepy, let's go." I grab her hand—the one currently cupping my junk—and pull her toward the stairs.

We rush up them, Prince Francis trotting along behind us, and I push her into my bedroom and follow her inside. Prince Francis tries to slip in the narrow gap, but I snatch him up. "Sorry, buddy, this is for adults only. No cats allowed." I toss him back out into the hall. He lands on the floor with a soft thud. I close the door and turn around. "Now where were we?"

Kitty lets my shirt fall to the floor. "I was about to take your pants off."

chapter eighteen

SEXY TIMES

Kitty

Miles crosses the room and takes my face in his hands. He slants his mouth over mine in a searing kiss I feel from the tips of my toes all the way to the top of my head. I clutch his shoulders and lean into him, the prominent bulge behind his fly pressing against my stomach. It's like there's a magnetic force at work, drawing our bottom halves toward each other.

I allow my hands to drift down his arms, squeezing his biceps on the way. When I reach his waist, I skim along his beltline. It takes real willpower to make room between our business parts, but the only way to get to the goods is to get him out of his pants.

I flick open the clasp of his belt, then pop the button and drag down his zipper. Miles groans when I slip a finger inside his boxer shorts.

His hands are still cupping my face. He backs up enough that his face is no longer blurry. "Should we move to the bed?"

"We could get each other naked first?" It's sort of a question.

"Unless you think it would be better to get naked after we're on the bed."

"All the way naked?" he asks.

"That's usually the best way to be if we're going to have sex. Unless that's not the plan?" I wish I could stop my mouth from saying things that could embarrass me, especially at times like this. "It doesn't have to be the plan. Maybe I'm getting ahead of myself. Or moving too fast."

"You're not. Moving too fast. I just... didn't want to make assumptions, because you know how that goes. It makes an ass out of you and me. I'm more than happy to get totally naked with you, right here or on the bed. Either way. I'm in." Miles pulls his wallet out of his back pocket and tosses it across the room. It lands on the comforter with a soft thud. "We'll need that, though."

"Good call." I push his pants over his hips, and they slide down his legs, pooling at his feet. Miles bends to get them off the rest of the way and removes his socks as well, which I appreciate because socks and sex aren't a great combination.

While he hops around on one foot, trying to free his left leg of his pants and lose his other sock, I shuck my pants and take off my socks too. And then we're both in our underwear. Miles's has a team print on them. Mine match the bra that's still on the floor in the living room. I don't know what possessed me to wear a sexy bra and underwear set today, but when I woke up this morning, I bypassed all my cotton comfort and went straight for my good stuff.

I'm grateful to the sex gods for that decision. Miles's gaze skims over my curves. "You are sexy times a million, Kitty."

I feel it. Especially with the way he's looking at me.

Miles closes the gap between us and drops his head, kissing me softly. "Wanna make out with me before we lose the underwear?"

"Yes, please."

He laces his fingers with mine and guides me to the bed, then rushes to move his wallet to the nightstand and pulls the covers back. I climb up onto the bed and he follows. We lie down next to each other, and I hook a leg over his hip, pulling him closer. And we do exactly what he suggested. We kiss and touch, an unhurried, gentle exploration.

I pull him on top of me and wrap my legs around his waist so we can grind against each other. His lips move along my neck and over my collarbones. And then he starts to go lower. He stops at my breasts, teasing my nipples with tongue and teeth, before he goes lower, pressing a kiss above my navel.

The fingers of his free hand trail down my side and over my hip. He follows the edge of my panties down to the junction of my thigh. He slips one finger under the fabric skimming my sex and at the same time he kisses my inner thigh. I suck in a breath when he brushes over sensitive skin.

He lifts his head, eyes hooded with lust. "I want to put my mouth on you, Kitty."

"I would really, really love that."

One side of his mouth curves up in a devilish smile as he

shifts so he's kneeling between my thighs, fingers hooked into the waistband of my panties at either hip.

I lift my butt, making it easier for him, and he drags them down my legs, tossing them over the edge of the bed.

And then he settles between my thighs and drops his head, teasing me with his lips and tongue. Every time I moan or gasp or sigh, it's met with a lamenting meow on the other side of the door, followed by the horrid sound of nails dragging down the wood surface.

Miles lifts his head and calls out. "Dude, you are killing the mood here!"

"Maybe we should put on some music? Drown him out?" I suggest.

"Good call. My phone is in my pants." Miles hops off the bed and grabs his pants, shaking them until his phone drops onto the floor. He quickly cues up a playlist, turns the volume up as high as it will go, and sets it on the nightstand.

I meet him at the edge of the bed and rise on my knees so we're eye to eye, and I can kiss him. I run my hand down his chest and slip my hand down the front of his boxers. Miles groans into my mouth as I wrap my fingers around his length and stroke him a few times. I reach across the comforter and find his wallet, which I fold his hand around.

"I want you," I tell him between kisses.

"I'm right there with you."

We rid him of his boxers, and he climbs back up on the bed with me. He dumps the contents of his wallet on the comforter in his search for the condom. There are several free coffee coupons from a local café, a couple of business cards, some cash, and a single condom. I pluck it from the mess and tear it open, make sure I have it the right way around, and then roll it down his length.

I wrap my hand around the back of his neck and pull him down on top of me. His erection glides along sensitive skin and nudges my entrance. Miles lifts his head, and our eyes meet as his hips sink down and I tip mine up. We both exhale on a groan and say, "You feel so good," at the same time.

Our smiles mirror each other. Then we chuckle and sigh as the laughter makes all my parts below the waist clench and his erection kicks inside of me. He lowers his mouth to mine, and I wrap my arms and legs around him. And then we start to move, finding a rhythm, learning each other in a new way.

His phone blares from the nightstand beside us, "We Are the Champions" crooning loudly as Miles moves over me.

"Oh shit, this is my workout playlist," he pants.

"It's very motivating." Not exactly romantic, but then I'm not sure it would be effective if the songs were slower and quieter. In the pause between songs, Prince Francis can be heard yowling on the other side of the door. But as soon as the next song starts, it drowns him out. My moans and words of encouragement are also helpful in drowning out Prince Francis's lamenting.

Despite the distractions, I still manage to keep most of my attention on Miles. It's not that difficult. His gorgeous face is a mask of desire, and he keeps whispering hot things against my lips, that he loves the way I taste and can't wait to put his mouth on me again, that he can't get enough of my moans, and that he thinks I'm the sexiest woman on the face of the earth.

When we can no longer keep our lips connected, he pushes up on one arm and his eyes lock on mine. "I'd really like to make you come."

"That would be amazing, but uh, I've never actually had an orgasm during sex before, so I'm not sure it's possible." If my cheeks weren't already flushed with exertion and desire, they would be flushed with embarrassment. "Now was probably not the best time to admit that."

He holds himself above me. It's impressive the way he can keep rolling his hips while having yet another semi-awkward conversation, this time in the middle of sex. "Never?"

I shake my head. I've been close before, but my previous partners reached the end before I could.

He makes a sound, sort of like a *huh* and a *hmm*, and then folds back on his knees. "How flexible are you?" His hands are on my waist now, and he's still thrusting, slower now, though. One hand moves between my thighs and his thumb brushes over my bingo button. I bow up off the bed, not expecting the direct contact or the intense zing below the waist.

"Oh my God. Can you do that again?" I groan.

"Of course." And he does.

And again I bow up off the bed.

"Fairly. I'm fairly flexible. I go to yoga with my sister, but only when she drags me and there are promises of a greasy breakfast afterward."

He does that thing with his thumb again at the same time as he thrusts and my eyes roll up. "I'm going to try something. Just let me know if it's not working for you, okay?"

"Okay?" It's a question more than anything, but I'm halfway to an orgasm at this point, and if he can make the impossible happen, I might just want to keep him forever. That part stays in my head thankfully.

He unhooks my feet from around his waist and lifts my legs so my heels are resting on his shoulders. He rises so he's on his knees, then grips my thighs and starts to lift and lower me, not a lot, but it's enough that he hits that spot inside with every careful shift.

And then he drops back down and leans forward. My knees hit my chest, and there is literally nothing I can do to help now, since I'm basically folded in half under him.

"Is this okay?" he asks.

"It feels better than okay," I tell him. "Way better, like, on a scale of not good to unbelievable it's an unbelievable times at least ten, maybe more."

The corner of his mouth curves up in a delicious smirk. "Good. It's supposed to." He starts to move again, and I don't know what it is about this position, but it absolutely does the trick. One second I'm moaning about how good it feels and how he's hitting the spot and then I'm gripping his forearms and screaming his name as an orgasm rolls through me. And not just any kind of orgasm, but one that steals my vision and makes the world turn black and white and starry before color returns in a vibrant burst.

He's wearing the sexiest victory grin as he unpretzels me and folds back on his knees, lifting me right along with him so I'm sitting on his thighs. I grip his shoulders as he bounces me in his lap. It's all I can do since I'm orgasm boneless and incapable of helping him. His expression is fierce and a bead of sweat runs down his temple.

"So fucking good," he groans, pulling me down one last time as his eyes fall closed and his jaw clenches. He shudders and his hips jerk and then he falls backward on the mattress, taking me with him.

We lie there for a minute, panting and sated. "The Eye of the Tiger" blasts from his phone on the nightstand. It ends and Prince Francis's meows fill the silence until the next song starts.

"Should I open the door now?" My cheek is still resting on his chest, and his heart is beating hard and heavy.

His fingers trail up and down my spine. "I think we have to if we want him to stop, but I'm not inclined to move."

"Me either," I admit. "But you're right about him being a mood killer and this not being the best sex playlist." I lift my head and prop my chin on his chest. I can see his nipple out of the corner of my eye. Miles's chin is a few inches away, and I note a small scar. I reach up and drag my finger along the pale line. "Hockey accident?"

He smiles. "Nope. I fell into the coffee table when I was three. I tripped over one of my own toys. Never left my crap on the floor after that since I needed seven stitches."

"Do you remember getting them?"

"Vaguely. I remember how much it bled more."

"That makes sense."

Prince Francis drags his nails across the door and starts up with the yowling again. The song blasting from Miles's phone seems like it might be appropriate for cooldown.

I push up off his chest. "I need the noise to stop. Give me a second."

Miles tries to keep me from rolling off him, but he seems just as boneless as me. My feet hit the floor, and I smile when he whistles and says, "You are effortlessly sexy, Kitty."

I throw open the bedroom door. Prince Francis has one paw raised in the air, mouth wide open as if he's about to yowl. He brings his paw to his mouth and licks between his toes. "Can I help you?" I ask.

He makes a noise like a harrumph and then trots off down the hall, tail flicking irritably. When I turn around, I notice that the music has stopped.

I leave the door ajar and consider beelining it across the room and jumping right back into bed, but Miles turns around and now we're facing each other. Still naked. I don't know what to do with my hands, or the rest of me.

Luckily, Miles seems to know how to manage himself when he's buck naked after sex. He crosses the room and wraps his arm around my waist, pulling me against him. I tip my head up and he bends until our lips connect. It's a brief kiss, soft, gentle.

"Hey." He brushes the end of his nose against mine.

"Hey."

"Wanna cuddle now that all the noise has stopped?" He inclines his head to the bed.

"Sure. Okay. Yes."

He keeps his arm around me, and we stutter-step our way back to the bed, Miles dropping kisses along my shoulder and up the side of my neck as we go. When we reach the bed, he dives onto it and stretches out an arm, patting the pillow beside him. I lie next to him, and he pulls the covers over us, then turns on his side, and I do the same. He runs a hand down my side and shimmies closer, pulling my leg over his hip.

"That's better," he murmurs. His hand disappears from my hip and then strokes gently from my temple to my chin while grinning.

"What's this about?" I poke the dimple in his cheek.

"I gave you an orgasm."

I blush. "You did. And I was very loud about letting you know how much I appreciated it."

His grin widens. "I appreciate your appreciation."

"You're pretty proud of yourself, aren't you?"

He lifts a shoulder and holds his fingers an inch apart. "Maybe a little."

I splay his hand out and press my palm to his. "Or a lot." I lace my fingers with his. "That was my first ever sex-gasm. It's worth being proud of. Hopefully it wasn't a one-time thing. I mean...unless this was just a tonight thing. I don't have expectations." But even as I say it, I'm not sure it's entirely true. We're supposed to go on a date, and now I've already messed it up by having sex with him before we've had a civilized dinner together. And he was vulnerable tonight and emotional. "Oh my God!" I slap a palm over my mouth.

Miles's brow pulls together in a furrow. "What's wrong?"

"I just took advantage of you."

"What?"

I sit up and unintentionally flash him my boobs, then pull my knees up to my chin along with the covers. "You were vulnerable and emotional after today, which totally makes sense considering everything that's going on, and instead of just being there for you, I took advantage of the situation and you." I flail a hand in his direction and almost lose my hold on the covers. "It's bad enough that I invited you to the bar as a shield for the alien studies weirdo and then attacked you with my lips. Now I've attacked you with my vagina too!" This is just so mortifying.

"I already asked you on a date, Kitty. And you weren't taking advantage of me. I told you before, you can attack me with your lips whenever you want. And I'm the one who turned you into a human pretzel and then tried to pound a hole through the mattress. There was no taking advantage of anyone."

"How'd you get so good at the pretzel move?" I cover my eyes with my palm again. "I'm sorry. You don't need to answer that. I think maybe I lost a few brain cells with that orgasm. Everything went black and white and starry for a second. Maybe I lost consciousness? Why can't I stop talking?"

"Hey." Miles's hand covers mine, and he gently pulls it away from my face.

My eyes are still closed, though.

He tucks a finger under my chin. "Kitty."

His lips touch mine. Brief. Soft.

"Can you open your eyes for me?"

I crack one lid.

He's close, close enough that I can feel his breath against my lips. "I love it when your thoughts come out of your head unfiltered. And I read about the pretzel move in a magazine back when I was in college. It was a real game changer. I'm totally happy to try it again and make sure it works more than once."

"Does that mean you're staying here tonight?"

"I'd like to, if you'd like me to."

"I would like that. And I would love to see if the pretzel move works more than once."

Miles grins. "That's not my only move."

"You have more?"

"I do." His smile turns salacious. "You want me to show you another one?"

chapter nineteen

ONE PAW AT A TIME

Kitty

It turns out Miles has a lot of moves. And we try out several of them. It also means we stay up ridiculously late.

Needless to say, this morning I'm not particularly rested, but I am definitely feeling good. Better than good. I'm on cloud nine, skipping down post-orgasm high road. Miles and I go out for breakfast to my favorite greasy spoon. He gets a giant stack of pancakes, and I order the eggs benny.

"There's no way you're going to be able to eat all of that." I point to the mountainous pile of pancakes. They're layered like a cake, with strawberries and whipped cream between each one.

"You gave me quite the workout last night, and this morning, Kitty, you'd be surprised at how much damage I can do." He winks and I blush.

"Do you want some help packing up your mom's place? Do you have a plan for what you're going to do with the house?" I pop a bite of eggs benny into my mouth. I'm trying not to shovel it in my face at warp speed, but now that I have food in front of me, I too realize how famished I am. Instead of eating dinner last night, we devoured each other.

"I might need to put it on the market, unless I can find a long-term renter. There's no mortgage left on it, thankfully, but my mom's pension from her job isn't going to cover the full cost of her care because she took early retirement. Selling the house would help, but obviously it would be better to rent it so we can keep the capital where it is until she absolutely needs it."

"It would be a good home for a family with small children, or a retired couple," I muse.

Miles nods. "Part of me just wants to get rid of it because of all the memories that were tied up in that house, but now . . . I don't know. I'm starting to see it a bit differently." His grin turns sly. "And recently I've made some pretty good new memories in there."

I smile and duck my head. "I'm glad there's some good in all of this for you."

"Me too."

We finish breakfast and head back to the house. I pack up Prince Francis and all his belongings and we load them into my car. It's better for him if we're not trying to pack the house while he's still in it. I haven't talked to my mom yet about keeping him, but I figure I can spin it as a temporary thing and then ask forgiveness later if it becomes permanent.

Miles has afternoon meetings, and there's a game tonight, so he walks me out to my car and kisses me goodbye. "I'll text you later." He dips down and kisses me again.

I run my hands over his chest. "Okay. Sounds good."

"If there wasn't a game tonight, I'd come back here," he says.

"That's okay. I know it's not practical for you to drive out here all the time."

"You could come to my place, though. The game should be done by nine. I can be home by nine thirty." His face lights up, like it's the best idea he's ever had.

His eagerness to spend more time with me is great for my ego. I pat his chest. "I wish I could, but I should get Prince Francis settled at my place. Dropping him off and leaving him isn't going to win me any prizes with him or my family. I'll come over here tomorrow night, though, and we can pack up all the things your mom will need at the new home. We can even go there early and decorate for her, so it feels like her space when she arrives. Bring some familiar furniture and the things she loves."

He smiles down at me. "That's a great idea. You're amazing, you know that?"

"So are you." Prince Francis yowls from inside my car. "I should go before he gets angry and rage poops on my seat."

"Probably smart." Miles kisses me one last time, then carefully opens the car door, but only enough that I can slip inside, and Prince Francis doesn't have time to make a break for it. As soon as I'm behind the wheel, Prince Francis hops up on the back of the seat and stands on my shoulders, his tail whipping me in the cheek as he scratches at the window and meows at Miles.

I buckle in and turn the engine over, then give him a chin scratch. "We're going to have a sleepover at my place tonight."

I back out of the driveway, waving one last time at Miles before I head home with Prince Francis draped over my shoulders. I'm in an amazing mood when I pull into the driveway. Both my mom's and my sister's cars are here.

I don't try to put Prince Francis in his cage, opting for a football carry. His little legs flail, like he's air running. "Just a few seconds and you'll be able to explore, I promise." I open the front door—it's unlocked—and call out as I close it behind me. "Mom! Hattie! I have a surprise visitor!"

My sister comes bounding down the stairs. "Did you bring your boyfriend home with you?" she shouts, skidding down the last few steps. She grabs the newel post and manages to avoid falling on her butt.

"Kitty has a boyfriend?" Mom appears in the foyer.

I give Hattie an unimpressed look. "That would have made things really awkward if I wasn't alone."

"Not more awkward than the two of you making out in the middle of the bar for half an hour."

"It wasn't that long." At least I don't think it was. It didn't feel that long. Maybe a minute or two.

"What's this about a boyfriend?" My mom's face lights up like fireworks on the May long weekend.

"Kitty has a boyfriend. I met him last week when he showed up at the pub. His name is Miles," Hattie tells my mom, then turns back to me. "Bryce was hella disappointed, FYI. He thinks you're intergalactically hot." She makes air quotes around *intergalactically hot*.

"I'm never going to forgive you for seating me beside him. He thinks E.T. is real."

"How do you know he isn't?" Hattie quirks a brow.

"If aliens exist, they'll be way more aerodynamic than E.T. His legs are three inches long. And why the heck does his finger light up? It's like he's a distant relative of Rudolph."

"What is happening right now? Why are you talking about E.T.? And who are Bryce and Miles?" Mom interrupts.

"I went out with Hattie last week. I ended up sitting beside an alien studies major named Bryce, and then Miles showed up. He's my friend, though, not my boyfriend." Who I've slept with. So *friend* probably isn't the right term either, but we haven't put a label on it. Up until last night we were two people who had kissed and were planning to go on a date. Now we've upgraded to being naked together, and my private parts have hugged his private parts.

"He's definitely more than a friend, considering the way you two were playing dueling tongues." Hattie smirks at me.

"Dueling tongues?" Mom asks.

I give Hattie another look, and she arches one brow and then the other before they both drop down, like an elevator suddenly losing a floor. And then they jump up again.

I look away, feeling very, very exposed. "She's exaggerating. And he's taking me on a date next week. Or weekend. I'm not sure. I've been sitting for his mother's cat. Which brings me back to our new houseguest." I look around for Prince Francis, but he's disappeared. "Shoot. I don't know where he went."

"Where who went? Not the alien?"

"No Mom, there are no aliens."

"You don't know that for sure," Hattie replies.

"I mean in the house. I didn't bring one home with me. I brought Prince Francis."

"I thought your boyfriend's name was Miles. Or was that Bryce? I don't think it's a great idea to date three different people at the same time. It sends the wrong message, even if one of them is royalty. Especially if one of them is royalty." Mom crosses her arms.

"Prince Francis is a cat, not an actual prince. Hold on. I need to find him." I whistle and reach into my pocket, but I don't have the baggie of treats I normally carry with me. I rush back out to the car to grab his litter box and my supply of treats, shaking the container and calling Prince Francis's name. A few moments later he comes trotting out of the kitchen.

"Oh my cuteness!" Hattie drops to the floor, crosses her legs, and pats her knees enthusiastically. "Give me the treats. I want him to love me. How long is he staying? Please say forever." She holds a hand out palm up, and I set the container in it. She nearly drops it, but recovers before it hits the floor. She places a treat on her knee, waiting for Prince Francis to sniff her out and take the bait. "He looks like a little pink gremlin. Or one of the adorable house elves from Harry Potter."

My mom has yet to say anything, and I worry that bringing Prince Francis home without clearing it with her first might have been a bad idea. But when I look over at her, she's smiling, her attention on Hattie and Prince Francis, who has very quickly surmised that this high-pitched and very excited human has food and is willing to give him lots of it.

I explain that Miles's mother has dementia, he's moving her into a home this weekend, and we didn't want to stress Prince Francis out with all the packing.

"Oh, that must be so difficult. Does he have siblings? How is his father handling this?"

"Uh, his dad lives in BC, his parents divorced when he was a teen. They lost his brother when he was only eight."

"Oh my goodness. That's so sad." Mom's fingers flutter to her lips.

"It is. That family has been through a lot."

"It's so good that you've found each other then, isn't it? You both know what it's like to lose people you love dearly." She smiles softly, and her eyes mist over.

"It really is. He's a great guy." And he seems to have come into my life at exactly the right time.

"You'll have to invite him over for dinner so I can meet him."

"Yeah. Definitely." I nod vigorously, but it's one thing for me to tell him that there's still a place set for my dad at the dinner table every night, and another to witness it. I'm starting to see how narrow I've made my world, and how I don't want to be the reason none of us are able to move forward. Bringing Prince Francis home, even if it's only temporary, seems like a small but good step in the right direction.

Prince Francis climbs into Hattie's lap and tries to hug the package of treats. She picks him up and cradles him like a baby—it seems to be everyone's go-to move with him. "He needs a sweater to keep him warm in the colder months. Oh! Can we go shopping for clothes for him? Unless he already has sweaters."

"I found a couple of shirts, but it doesn't hurt to have more."

"You can never have too many shirts. We don't want our naked kitty to be chilly, do we?" Hattie rubs his belly, and he snuggles into her arms. "He's just so weirdly adorable."

"He is, isn't he? And he's full of personality. We'll have to keep an eye on your knickknacks though, Mom. When he's feeling neglected, he likes to tell us by knocking things on the floor."

Mom's grin widens. "Just like Smokey used to do. I think it's going to be wonderful having a cat in the house again. It's been too long. Does he like tuna? Let me see if I have any cans in the cupboard."

As soon as Mom is out of earshot Hattie tosses a treat at me and hits me in the knee. Prince Francis jumps out of her lap and rushes over to gobble it up. Hattie makes some kind of mime circle motion around her face. "What the hell is going on?"

"What do you mean?" I try to maintain eye contact, but it's as if my eyeballs have turned into pendulums and they dart back and forth.

"You're all shifty-eyed and your face has gone blotchy. Did you stay at Prince Francis's house last night?"

"You know I've been watching him because he's having a hard time adjusting to being alone." I scoop him up, using him as an adorable kitty shield.

Hattie hops to her feet and gazelle leaps across the room. Before I can react, she shoves her nose in my hair.

"What are you doing?" I push her away.

"You smell like men's cologne!"

"Shh!" I poke her in the shoulder. "Can you keep it down, please? I don't think the neighbors down the street heard you."

She grabs me by the shoulders, and Prince Francis hops out of my arms, abandoning me in my time of need.

"Look at me, Kitty," Hattie orders.

I force my eyes to meet hers, but again they dart away a split second later.

"Oh my God."

I purse my lips.

"Oh my God. Did you and Miles bone?"

I make a face. "Really, Hattie?"

"Did you let him pound your—" She motions to her crotch.

"Why do you have to be so crass?"

"Oh my God, you totally did! We are going shopping this afternoon for cat sweaters and you are going to tell me all about it. Was it good? I bet it was. You two have crazy chemistry. You looked like you wanted to climb him like a tree at the pub, and he got so territorial over you with the arm around your shoulder and the glaring at Bryce. This is so exciting."

"What's so exciting?" Mom returns with a can of tuna and a dish.

"Hattie's happy about having a cat again. Even if it's temporary," I practically shout.

"Oh, well yes, I can totally understand that." Mom smiles when Prince Francis trots over and winds himself around her legs, meows, and flops over on his side, showing her his belly. "What a flirt you are." She crouches and gives him a chin rub before she sets a small dessert cup in front of him containing flaked tuna.

The three of us watch as he gobbles it up. I bring the rest of his gear into the house and set his litter box up in the basement. The cat door from when we had Smokey still works, so I show Prince Francis how to use it and let him sniff around, checking out his new surroundings room by room.

Eventually I take him upstairs to my bedroom, where he explores for a few seconds before trotting off down the hall. Hattie steps into my room, wearing a ridiculous grin.

"Why are you so excited about this?" I can feel my face flushing. I wish my embarrassment could stay in my head and not be so obvious.

"You have a boyfriend, and based on how much you're blushing, he's not a disappointment in the sack, and now we have a cat to take care of! This is like a day made of awesome! Let's go shopping for cat sweaters."

I grab my purse and Hattie grabs hers, and we head downstairs. Mom is sitting in the living room with Prince Francis curled up in her lap, looking like she won the lottery.

"What does Miles do for a living again? Does he have his own place?" Hattie asks as we drive toward the strip mall on the other side of town.

"He's a data analyst for the NHL, and yes, he has his own

place. He lives in an apartment in the city, which is good, because I obviously can't bring him home for the night unless I want it to be all kinds of awkward in the morning." The thought of having Miles stay the night in my bedroom, which hasn't changed much since high school, is mortifying. "I need to redecorate my room."

"Or you could move out? Get an apartment? Unless the cat care business isn't cutting it for you moneywise?" Hattie asks.

"It's not that. I mean, obviously I'm not going to get rich taking care of other people's pets, but it pays the bills. Plus I have a few sponsors now, so that keeps costs down and raises my bottom line. And I have some money saved." A good chunk actually.

"You just don't want to spend the money on rent?" Hattie presses. "That's why I went to college close to home instead of living in the city. I want to avoid debt as much as possible."

"Living at home might not be a party, but it's financially responsible." I did the same thing.

"Exactly." Hattie gives me a small, uncertain smile. "And I know that you've stuck around to help Mom with the finances, but the house is paid for, and my college is paid for. You don't have to keep putting your life on hold to make sure everyone else is okay indefinitely, Kitty."

Our parents put money aside for our education. Not quite enough to cover tuition fully, especially after Dad died, but with part-time jobs, grants, and scholarships, both Hattie and I were able to walk out of college mostly debt-free, which is huge. And one of the reasons I stayed in the house, even after I graduated.

My mom didn't want us to walk out of school and into life with loans hanging over our heads.

It means that everything that hasn't gone into my business start-up has gone in the bank. I have a decent amount of money set aside. It would be tight, but I could probably carry a mortgage on my own. My own place would mean being able to expand my business. "I just...I know the internship you have next semester is in the city. And I'm sure it will turn into a job offer."

"What does that have to do with your own plans?"

"I don't want to leave Mom on her own."

Hattie pulls into the strip mall parking lot and finds a spot near the Pet Emporium. They sell everything from food to litter, and they also have an adorable boutique shop with specialty treats and pet apparel. She shifts the car into park and looks at me, still gripping the steering wheel. "Can I say something?"

"I have a feeling I already know what you want to say." I clutch my purse, which happens to have a cat face on it.

"Want me to say it anyway?"

"Sure."

"Is it really about not wanting to leave Mom on her own, or about you being afraid to leave?"

"Probably a bit of both, with a stronger lean toward being afraid." I sigh. "I've been thinking about this a lot lately. Ever since I started sitting for Prince Francis. I look at Miles's mom's house and see parallels with ours. His brother has been gone for almost two decades, and his room has never changed. It's the same as it was when he died. Just like our house is the same. And for a while it felt comfortable, like if nothing changed, then maybe it would be easier to stay close to Dad, even though he's gone. But now . . . I don't know. Instead of preserving his memory, I'm stuck in the past and too afraid of the future to live in the present."

Hattie reaches over and squeezes my hand. "Well, I think bringing Prince Francis home was a small, cute step in the right direction. It's a little change, but it's still a change, Kitty."

"Do you think by my not moving out or moving forward with my life, I've made it impossible for Mom to move on with hers, too?" I ask.

She's quiet for a while. "No. You can only make your own choices, not other people's. If anything, it's symbiotic, and no one's fault. But I do think that you've put yourself on hold for the sake of our family. You and Mom have a bit of a codependency thing going on. And when you're comfortable with the way things are, it's hard to see how change can be good. I'm not saying you need to up and walk away, but maybe it's time for you to focus on your life, so you can both stand on your own a little more."

"I've created this bubble of safety, and now I'm starting to feel trapped inside it."

"Maybe it's time to pop it, then." Hattie gives my hand a squeeze. "You're an amazing, selfless older sister, Kitty. You've been Mom's helper since you were a kid. And we're all used to you being that. It's okay if you want to try on some new hats and see which ones fit better."

chapter twenty

RIGHT MEOW

Kitty

Despite me telling Miles I can meet him at his mother's place in the morning, he insists on picking me up. But he gives me a window of time, between seven-forty-two and seven-fifty-five. Which is oddly specific.

Despite this, when the doorbells rings, I'm still struggling my way into my shirt—it's a new one that Hattie picked out for me yesterday on our shopping expedition—as I rush down the hall to the stairs.

"That's for me! I can get it!" I shout. But I'm stuck in my shirt, my head apparently in a sleeve and my arm through the neck hole. I slam into the wall and fall on my butt with an oomph.

"I've got it!" Mom calls from the main floor.

My voice is muffled by my shirt, and I'm still trying to figure out how to right this wrong when I hear my mother's high-pitched greeting and Miles's deep voice filter up the stairs. I finally get my head out of the sleeve and my arm out of the neck hole, replacing one with the other. I smooth out my shirt and hop to my feet.

But I don't take into account where I've ended up, which is at the top of the stairs. It also happens to be directly in line with the front door. And that means Miles has had a clear view of me struggling with my shirt. I'm about to take a step down, but Prince Francis appears between my legs, setting me off balance once again. He meows and launches himself down the steps. My heel hits the lip of the top stair. They're polished hardwood and I'm wearing slippery socks, which means my heel slips out from under me and I don't have time to grab the railing before I land on my ass and slide-bump my way down the entire flight. I land on the floor in a heap.

"Oh my gosh, are you okay?" Miles rushes over to help me.

"She's just excited to see you!" my mom offers.

"I'm fine," I mutter, accepting Miles's extended hand. "Only my dignity is bruised. And maybe my butt."

"I can check that later for you," Miles whispers in my ear.

I blink a few times, not sure if I heard that correctly. When I meet his gaze, I can tell that I did, because his cheeks are turning pink.

"Why don't you come in, Miles? It's so lovely to finally meet you. Kitty's told us all about you, but she didn't mention how handsome you are."

I want to tell my mom to tone it down, but I can't do that without embarrassing her. And I think that my embarrassment plus Miles's embarrassment is enough to fill this entire room.

And then my sister appears at the top of the stairs. "What's all the racket about?" She's wearing a pair of sleep shorts and a T-shirt with a smiling donut on it. Her hair is pulled up in a messy bun, and she has sleep lines on her face. Even half asleep, wearing jammies, my sister is runway ready.

"Kitty's boyfriend is here!" Mom shouts joyously.

And the embarrassment keeps piling on.

I don't even look at Miles, not wanting to see his expression right now.

Hattie's eyes go wide, and she makes her oh-shit face, as her eyes dart from me to Miles and back to Mom. She must realize that she's not dressed appropriately and shouts that she'll be right back. I'm hoping we'll be gone before that happens, so I can limit the amount of foot in mouth Miles is exposed to where my mother is concerned.

"We should probably go. Miles and I are going to set up his mother's new apartment today so it's ready when she moves in." I try to get to the door, but my mother is standing directly in front of it.

"You could stay for coffee. You haven't even had breakfast yet. I could make you something. Maybe some scrambled eggs? That would be nice, wouldn't it? And maybe Miles wants a tour of the house and to see how Prince Francis is settling in." She looks so excited about the prospect. And as much as I want to avoid any further embarrassment, I don't want to wipe the smile off my mother's face. It's a real conundrum.

"Scrambled eggs would be great, thanks so much, Ms. Hart."

"Oh, you can just call me Lucile, and it's my pleasure. It's just so nice to meet you." She beams up at Miles. "I'll get started on the eggs, and Kitty can show you around."

She leaves us in the front foyer.

"I'm so sorry," I mumble.

"Don't be." He winks. "Why don't you give me that tour?"

I point to the stairs. "That's where all the bedrooms are."

He arches a brow. "You're not going to show me yours?"

"Do you want to see it?" I haven't even made my bed.

"Yes."

I haven't had a guy in my bedroom since high school. Anyone I've dated over the past few years, however brief, has had his own place, so we'd always go there. And maybe that's a problem, because it's made it easy for me to stay where I am. I haven't had a long-term anything since college.

I lead the way, my stomach filling with butterflies and my mouth growing drier with every step. Maybe because of the conversation Hattie and I had last night. Maybe because the last time I was in a bedroom with Miles I was naked. Or because my mother called him my boyfriend and my bedroom will contain just the two of us, where he could potentially say something about that.

"That's my mother's room, and the linen closet, and that's my sister's room." Hattie's door has a chalkboard sign on it with her daily schedule and a "studying in progress/sleeping in progress" door hanger. "That's the bathroom we share, and this is my room." I push open the door and step inside.

I don't have a chance to apologize for the mess, or the very cat-tastic decor, because Miles closes the door behind him and flips the lock. He closes the gap between us and takes my face between his palms. He tips my head back and covers my mouth with his.

I let out a shocked gasp, and he strokes his tongue inside on a low groan. One hand leaves my face and wraps around my waist, pulling me to him. I feel him, hard and insistent against my stomach, as he deepens the kiss.

We're interrupted by a low meow.

Miles breaks the kiss for half a second, then decides he doesn't care and fuses our mouths again.

Something crashes to the floor by my dresser.

This time when he breaks the kiss, he doesn't come back for another one.

We both turn toward the dresser where Prince Francis sits, glaring in annoyance. My alarm clock is on the floor. His tail bats back and forth a few times and he knocks over my jewelry tree, which scares the crap out of him and sends him skittering under the bed.

"Why is he such a cockblocker?" Miles grumbles.

"He doesn't like to share."

"That makes two of us." He brushes his lips over mine. "I like your bedroom."

"It's a mess, and you haven't even looked at it."

"It smells like you, and that triggers all kinds of positive memory associations for me." He sucks my bottom lip between his, then releases it.

"I'm sorry my mom called you my boyfriend. Hattie used the

word yesterday, and I know we haven't had any kind of discussion about it. But I don't want you to think that just because I've hugged your penis with my vagina that I automatically assume you want to be my boyfriend. I tried to say we were seeing each other, but my mom really latched on to the term *boyfriend*, apparently."

Miles grins. "I don't mind."

"I'll try to reiterate the whole being in the 'seeing each other' phase again when you're not here, but I couldn't call her out on it in front of you. No one needed to be more embarrassed than we already were. And there was the whole falling down the stairs piece." I really wish I could stop drawing more attention to the embarrassing episodes.

"Do you want me to check for bruises?" He drags his tongue along his bottom lip, and his eyes darken.

I swallow thickly, thinking about the panties I'm currently wearing. "Maybe later."

"Probably a good idea. Then I can do a very thorough examination."

"That would be great." I bite my bottom lip.

"We should probably leave your room before I try to get you out of your clothes and ruin your mother's good impression of me."

"That's probably a smart idea. She really seems to like you."

"And we definitely want to keep it that way." He dips down to kiss me one last time, then rearranges himself in his pants before he unlocks the door. He stops abruptly, which means I bump into his back, and he has to grip the doorjamb so he doesn't stumble forward.

"Oh hi, Hattie." Miles's voice is slightly pitchy as he lifts his hand in a wave, then turns sideways and motions for me to go ahead of him. "Ladies first."

Hattie grins widely and I silently plead with my eyes for her not to mortify me more than my own mouth and Mom already have. "Miles. It's nice to see you again."

"I'm just giving him a tour of the house."

"Uh-huh."

"Mom's making scrambled eggs."

Hattie's eyes widen and dart between me and Miles. "You should leave now unless you want to get sucked into staying for breakfast."

"We already agreed to the eggs," Miles says from behind me.

Hattie's expression says more than I want it to. "Do you want to fake a cat emergency?"

Miles's fingers rest on my hip. "We don't need to do that. Do we?"

I glance over my shoulder. He looks like he's trying to figure out whether Hattie is being dramatic or not.

I shrug. "I can make something up if the awkward level gets too high."

"I'll jump in if I need to," Hattie offers.

Miles looks like he has a lot of questions. He and I follow Hattie downstairs, and my palms start to sweat as we approach the kitchen. I can't remember the last time we had someone over for a meal. And now I'm worried about the empty spot where my dad used to sit being set.

When we reach the kitchen, I'm relieved to see four places set. Not five. The toaster pops, and Hattie steps in to butter the toast. I grab the orange juice, and Miles takes it from me, giving it a shake before he pours it into glasses. I add salt and pepper and ketchup to the table. My mom asks me to slice tomatoes, and again, Miles steps in to help.

I expect breakfast to be awkward. But when the food is ready, we all sit down, Miles taking the seat that's usually empty.

My mom smiles and shakes her napkin open. "It's lovely to have a full table."

And of course, because Prince Francis doesn't like to be left out of anything, he tries to jump up and join us. My mom's arm shoots out to thwart his landing. His legs splay and his mouth opens wide when he realizes there's a barricade. He does a flip midair and lands on his feet with a quiet thud. "No cats on the table, Prince Francis."

"That was impressive." Miles claps in appreciation.

"Our old cat Smokey used to try that move all the time. Usually, we'd keep a spray bottle nearby, and that would be enough to keep him on the floor, but it's been a while since we've had a four-legged friend around." My mom pushes away from the table and grabs a fluted dessert dish, the kind we usually use during holiday dinners for ice cream. She spoons a small portion of scrambled egg into the dish and sets it on the floor next to her seat, then takes her place at the table again.

Breakfast is...normal. Miles is adorably charming, and it's clear that my mom is a fan. She must tell him half a dozen times how nice it is to meet him. And that she hopes he'll come for dinner sometime soon.

My phone pings with a message, and I use it as an excuse for us to get going.

Once we're in his car I apologize again.

"When I picked you up, I knew I was going to meet your mother. I didn't expect it to be a one-minute introduction," he assures me.

"She really likes you."

"Good, because I really like you, and having your mom's seal of approval seems like it could be beneficial. Plus she makes great scrambled eggs."

"I really need to think about moving out soon. My sister and I talked about it yesterday. When Hattie finishes school, she'll probably move to the city, though, and then my mom will be alone in that house. It's a lot for one person to take care of." I voice some of the concerns I've been mulling over recently. Ironically, they coincide with meeting Miles.

"I'm sure she must realize you're going to want to move out, too, at some point," Miles says.

"Yeah. Probably. We've never talked about it." I fiddle with the whiskers on the front of my purse. "I think...I feel like I owe it to her to stay."

Miles glances my way and then refocuses on the road. "Why would you owe it to her to stay? I mean, I can understand wanting to stick around because you're a pseudo second parent to your sister. And financially it would make sense. But owing her?"

I swallow down the lump in my throat. If anyone could understand, it's Miles. "You know how I told you I found my dad?"

"Yeah, that must have been so hard for you. I can't even imagine."

I nod. "That's not the whole story. My cat knew something was wrong, and he was trying to warn me, but I ignored him. When I finally gave in and followed him to the attic it was too late. I was too preoccupied with what I was doing to pay attention to the signs, and I lost my dad because of it."

Miles pulls into his mother's driveway and puts the car in park. "That's a lot of responsibility to carry around with you. Does your mom know you feel this way?"

"No, but you see now why I stay. I'm the reason my mom is without my dad, so leaving her feels wrong." I sigh and motion to his house. "All of this, what you're going through with your mom, the way you feel about all of it, the guilt over something that wasn't your fault; I relate better than I realized. Because even though logically I know it isn't my fault that my dad died, it's still hard not to own it."

Miles stretches his arm across the back of the seat, his fingers sliding under my hair, and his thumb strokes along the back of my neck. "I'm so sorry, Kitty. I know how I feel about coming back here, but to face it every day . . . Living in that house where all that tragedy took place seems like a punishment you don't deserve." He gives his head a small shake. "Grant yourself some grace, Kitty—you do it for everyone else." He leans over and kisses me, just a soft press, but I feel it in my heart, spreading like a balm.

chapter twenty-one

LITTLE STEPS

Miles

Kitty and I barely make it through the door before our mouths are fused and she's trying to pull my shirt over my head. It's impossible to do both at the same time, so we disengage for a few seconds so we can make shirt removal happen, and then we're back at it.

I'm very glad I restocked my wallet with condoms, otherwise I'd have to take a pause to run out to my car to get them. Kitty ends up sitting on the entry table, the mail from the past week scattered on the floor. And the drywall behind the table isn't in the best shape when we're done. But we're both orgasm sated, and Kitty no longer looks sad, so all good things.

The stress relief seems to be an energizer as we tackle boxing up the things my mom will need for her new apartment. Once we have everything on the front porch I call Josh, who offered his truck to help with the move.

What I don't expect is the second truck, containing Parker and

Austin, another player from the team. "I brought reinforcements," Josh says as he walks up the front steps.

Kitty is inside, packing pantry items.

"Great, that will definitely make things move faster." And it will. Both Parker and Austin are great guys, and they play on the same line. It might give me a chance to talk to them about the recent data I pulled for the upcoming game with New York in a more relaxed environment. Parker has shown huge improvement over the past week and a half, and he's been coming to me more often, asking to look at numbers objectively and letting me explain what they mean and how that can help improve his game.

My only issue is that he's a relentless flirt. And I would really like it if he didn't flirt with Kitty.

"Pantry items are packed!"

I turn to find Kitty walking toward the front door, only her eyes peeking out over the top of the box. "Here, let me get that for you."

"I'm good. It's awkward, but light. I'll just set it next to your car, so it doesn't end up with all the other boxes." Her eyebrows pop when she spots Josh next to me. "Oh, hey, Josh. I didn't realize you were coming to help." She sets the box on the porch and holds out her fist for a bump. "Sorry, my hands are dirty, and sweaty. It's nice to see you again."

Josh bumps it back and gives her his customary panty-melting smile. "It's nice to see you again too, and it's cool that you're helping Miles today."

Most women, from infant to grandmother, have the same

reaction to Josh and his smile, and that's to giggle. Except Kitty doesn't giggle. Or blush. Or duck her head. She just smiles and slides her gaze my way. "I don't mind."

Parker and Austin amble up the driveway. Parker is about as subtle as a flashing neon sign with his team hat and shirt. Austin is dressed in regular clothes.

As soon as Parker sees Kitty, his eyes light up. She's wearing a pair of jeans and a non–Kitty Whisperer shirt. Most of those are loose, but today her shirt is fitted. And it has a V neck.

Kitty is usually a modest dresser. But that V shows off a hint of cleavage. Barely anything, but it was the first thing I noticed when I picked her up. Well, that's untrue. The first thing I noticed was her pale blue leopard print bra because she was struggling to get into her shirt at the top of the stairs. But the cleavage V was a close second.

And Parker, being an almost-nineteen-year-old walking hor-mone, can't seem to control his eyeballs or where they go as he approaches, because they are firmly locked on her chest. He raises his own palm to his beefy pec and stumbles back a step. "I can't even. I'm in the presence of a celebrity. Kitty Hart? The Kitty Whisperer."

Kitty glances from Parker to me and back again, questions in her eyes. "Um yes, that's me, but I'm hardly a celebrity."

"Parker O'Toole." He climbs the steps and takes one of her hands between his. "You take care of my great-grandad's cat, Bumbles. He's in love with you, by the way. Both my great-grandad and his cat. And I can completely understand why. I'm halfway in love with you already, and I've just met you." He starts to raise her hand to his lips.

Kitty's eyes are wide. She tries to jerk her hand free, but Parker can bench two hundred and fifty pounds and shoots a puck at over a hundred miles an hour.

"I wouldn't do that. I just cleaned a litter box, and I haven't washed my hands yet. You can get worms!" she practically shouts.

Josh coughs to cover a laugh.

"We need you on the ice tomorrow night, not in the ER pumped full of penicillin. And the headline on that would not be great. 'NHL player hospitalized for ingesting cat feces,'" I add, hoping he'll get the hint.

He does. He drops her hand and shoves his in his pocket, pulling out a travel-sized bottle of hand sanitizer. "Thanks for the warning, and the horrible mental image." He squirts a dime-sized amount in his massive palm and holds it out to Kitty, who accepts the sanitizer.

"I'm on the team Miles nerds out over numbers and stats for." He thumbs over to me and Josh. "And this is Austin. He plays right wing, and I play center. Do you watch hockey? You should come to a game."

"I don't have a lot of time for TV," Kitty says honestly. "But my dad was an avid hockey watcher."

"No time like the present to start. And the live games are the best. I can totally get you tickets." Parker winks, completely oblivious that he's making Kitty uncomfortable and that I want to punch him in the face.

"Oh uh, that's really nice of you—" Her eyes dart my way, and she takes a slight step in my direction.

"Can we get a selfie? You're a big deal in the cats of Instagram world. I follow you on social media."

"Way to be creepy," Josh mutters.

Parker is too busy putting his arm around Kitty's shoulder and yanking her into his side to catch the dig. And Kitty, being Kitty, is far too nice to say no.

Parker makes a face that reminds me of Derek Zoolander or basically any guy in the history of cocky jocks who believe that every single person in the world would be honored to have a selfie taken with him. To her credit, Kitty knows how to pose for a photo. She angles her body, rolls her shoulders back, adjusts her glasses, and smiles.

Parker takes eleven million pictures in five seconds. As soon as he lowers the phone, Kitty slips out from under his beefy arm and takes one large sidestep toward me and hugs my wiry one. It presses her boob against my biceps, which I appreciate, apart from the fact that other parts of my body are also appreciative, and those parts need to chill out until we're alone. Hopefully later tonight.

"Miles?"

"Huh?" Clearly I've missed something.

"Do you want to check to make sure we've got everything before we start loading up?" She tips her head up and bats her lashes at me.

"Oh yeah. Probably a good idea."

"We can get started with this stuff?" Austin motions to the boxes and furniture on the porch.

"That'd be awesome."

"I'll put this box on your hood, so it doesn't accidentally get put in the truck." Kitty nods to the box near the steps.

"I can do that." Parker's eyes dart between me and Kitty.

"I'll give the pantry one more pass, then," Kitty offers.

"Sure. I'll be right inside to help you."

She pushes up on her tiptoes and presses her lips to the edge of my jaw. Then she parts her lips and follows it with a gentle bite.

I glance at her out of the corner of my eye, and she gives me a saucy wink before she disappears inside.

Parker watches her disappear around the corner before he punches me in the shoulder. I stumble back half a step, not because I don't expect it, but because even his playful punches are hard. "Dude. Are you boning the Kitty Whisperer?" He thrusts his hips a couple of times.

Austin punches him in the arm, not playfully. "Asshole, we're standing in the middle of a subdivision, and you're basically a walking advertisement for our freaking team. You can't make obscene gestures in public. And there are kids playing." He inclines his head.

Three doors down there's a woman standing on her lawn, while her toddler does circles on his tricycle on the driveway. She's very clearly watching us. I raise a hand in a wave, and she waves back.

"Shit. Sorry." Parker also waves. "But seriously, the Kitty Whisperer. Man, she's even hotter in person than she is on IG. I bet she's feisty in bed." He waggles his brows.

I rub the back of my neck and fight with my lips not to move toward the sky, because she is, indeed, feisty in bed. "This isn't the locker room, Parker, and while you might be okay with talking about your sexual exploits with everyone you know, I don't kiss and tell."

"So you *are* hitting that." He smirks and nods knowingly.

"Can you stop being a frat boy for five minutes?" Josh grumbles.

"Can we get the trucks loaded?" I motion to the stuff on the porch. "And can you not flirt with Kitty," I say to Parker. "You're making her uncomfortable, and she's too nice to put you in your place. And if you touch her or make any further inappropriate comments, I exercise the right to punch you." I hold up a finger to stop him from interrupting. "And I won't give you the low-down on New York's defense, which is what we had trouble with the last time we played them."

He holds up his hands. "Shit, sorry. I didn't realize you two were an actual thing. I won't flirt with her. Just don't leave me hanging for tomorrow's game. We're having a solid run."

I leave them on the porch and check on Kitty. Who I find in the pantry, filling another box. "Hey. Sorry about Parker."

She sets a bag of fusilli inside the box. "He looks like he's still in high school. Does he even know how to use a razor?"

I laugh. "He's eighteen. He doesn't know how to do much other than run his mouth."

She chuckles.

"I told him to cut it on the flirting." I lean against the door-jamb. "And if you don't want him to post one of those selfies, I can tell him that, too."

"I don't care about the selfies, unless you do." She tips her head, her expression questioning.

"I'm fine with it if you're fine with it."

She pushes up on her tiptoes, trying to reach a box of cookies on the top shelf.

I grab it and pass it to her. "And if you want tickets to a game, I can get them for you, no problem. Maybe you want to bring your sister or something. If she watches hockey. But no pressure."

She steps closer and runs a hand up my chest. "I'd love to see what you do."

"My job isn't very exciting. The game is where all the action is."

"I don't know if I agree with that, but it would be fun all the same." She wraps her hand around the back of my neck and pulls my mouth to hers.

I get caught up in the kiss until one of the guys comes looking for me. "Let's put a pin in this until we're alone again."

We finish moving my mother's belongings into the home early in the afternoon. I thank the guys and Kitty for their help by taking them out for lunch, and then Kitty and I head back to the home to finish unpacking.

The next day I move my mother into the home. We decided that it would be best to wait until she settled in before we brought Prince Francis over for a visit; otherwise, it could be confusing.

I carry my mother's bag as we walk down the hall. She's in one of the highly monitored wings of the home, with individuals who suffer from similar ailments. The staff assured me that she would have people her age to mingle with, and that while the first few weeks are usually the most challenging, she'll adjust.

I unlock the door for her and usher her inside, the nurse aide following.

My mother walks down the short hall and steps into the small living room area. The whole space is less than a third of the size of her house, but it should be much more manageable for her. She crosses the room and stops in front of the bookshelf. It's next to the lounger. She trails her fingers along the trinkets—the ones we were able to save from Prince Francis's twitchy paw.

She picks up one of the framed photos. It's of her, me, and Toby, taken probably a year before he died and things fell apart. She looked happy. We all did.

She stands there for a moment, just staring at the picture, and I worry that I shouldn't have put it there. That it's the thing that's going to tip her over the edge. That she'll get angry and have a meltdown.

She turns to me and gives me a small smile, her eyes soft and watery. "Did you do all of this, Miles?"

I slip a hand in my pocket and nod, trying to hide my

surprise that she remembers I'm me. "I had some help from a few friends."

"It looks...familiar." She sets the picture back on the shelf and crosses the room. Her eyes are clear, like she's here with me in this moment and not floating in the past. She gives me a tremulous smile. "Thank you. I know I'm lost in my head a lot of the time and that I forget so many things, but I want you to know that I love you, Miles. And I'm sorry I forgot how to be a mother when you needed me the most. I didn't know how to deal with the hole I created in our family." She wraps her arms around me, and I swallow down the emotions, folding her into a hug.

"We all lost ourselves for a while when we lost Toby. I'm sorry I didn't go outside with him when I should have," I tell her.

"It was never your fault, Miles. It was my job to be watching, not yours. I'm sorry I'm going to forget this. I wish my mind was still mine."

"It's okay, Mom. It's not your fault. And I love you, too. And I'll keep telling you, no matter how many times you forget."

chapter twenty-two

CAT-TASTIC PARTY

Kitty

So I know this is probably last minute, and it isn't the dinner date I keep promising I'm going to take you on, but uh...one of the guys on the team decided to throw a Halloween party, and I wondered if maybe you'd be interested in coming. It's okay if that's not your thing, and you can say no, but I figured I'd throw it out there. No pressure." Miles sounds nervous, and I bet that if I could see him, I'd see him fidgeting with something. Probably a pen.

I'm currently standing on the screened-in back porch, trying to get Prince Francis to stop impersonating Spider-Man. He's splayed out on the window screen, desperate to get to the squirrel sitting on a tree branch less than fifty feet away. The squirrel is clearly taunting Prince Francis, and while it's somewhat hilarious, I don't want to replace any more screens.

It's a real conundrum, because Prince Francis loves it out here on the porch, but that squirrel has been playing hide-and-seek with him since he moved in last week.

"A Halloween party?"

Hattie, who is sitting in one of the chairs, sipping coffee and reading for one of her courses, looks up from her textbook and starts mouthing things at me.

I ignore her.

"Yeah. It's a costume party. I guess it's mandatory to dress up. Apparently, last year anyone who didn't got slimed."

"Slimed?"

"Well, it wasn't actual slime, but it was neon foam. And it stained people's skin until they showered. Or maybe it took a few days for the green to wear off. I'm sure there are pictures on social media about it. I'm not really doing a very good job of selling this, am I?"

"But if I wear a costume, I don't have to worry about the whole neon foam slime situation?"

"No. Not if you wear a costume. Does this mean you're interested in coming?"

"Sure. I think it sounds fun." And I'd like to see Miles with his colleagues. His friend Josh is nice, and while Parker has more energy and ego than I'm used to, Austin was down to earth.

"Great. Okay. That's awesome. I'll pick you up at eight on Saturday."

"Should we coordinate our costumes?" I ask.

"Hmm. Maybe. I hadn't thought of that. Do you have any suggestions?"

Hattie starts waving her hands around in the air.

"Let me think about it, and I'll get back to you? Or maybe you have an idea?"

"I'm not sure, but last year Josh went as a high schooler, and they tossed him in the pool because he didn't put in enough effort. Granted, he just threw on old track pants and a too-small shirt and borrowed his niece's kindergarten backpack. So... it should probably be better than that."

This is starting to sound a bit like a raucous party. "Hmm. Okay. Well, let's think about it and toss out some ideas and see if we can't find something that works."

I end the call, and Hattie claps her hands excitedly. "I know exactly what you should be!"

"I don't know about this."

"You look awesome. Now hold still so I can finish your eyes. This is the tricky part."

When my sister suggested that I dress up as Catwoman for Halloween, I immediately thought it was an awesome idea. I mean, how much more perfect could it get? Kitty, the Kitty Whisperer, dressed up as Catwoman. It seemed like a no-brainer. And obviously perfect. But that was before she poured me into a non-breathable, skin-tight zippered bodysuit.

"There's a lot of cleavage happening."

"You're a woman with boobs. And you're Catwoman. You

need cleavage. Miles is going to love this," Hattie assures me. "You're a smoke show."

"Have you seen some of those hockey players' wives? They look like models. Some of them even *are* models." I don't know why I'm suddenly self-conscious.

"Those are social media posts. They smooth everything out and make them look perfect. They're humans just like you and me."

"You look like a supermodel, too," I gripe.

Hattie keeps up with the eyeliner. "Just wait until Miles sees you. Then you'll forget all about being self-conscious. I promise."

"I'll have to take your word for it," I mutter, then go back to sitting still so Hattie can finish my eye makeup.

When she gets to the lipstick portion, I try to push her away. "Ow! It feels like you're putting cayenne pepper on my lips! What is this?"

"Can you stop, please? It's a lip stain. You don't have to worry about reapplying once it's set, but if you keep moving around, I'll have to start over."

I stop moving and let her do her thing because I don't want more lip torture than necessary. When I try to pop my lips, they get stuck together. "What is it? Some kind of glue?"

"No. Like I said, it's a lip stain. Keep them parted. I'm not done yet." She swipes over them with some clear gel stuff. I hope it's not like a finish coat for nails, otherwise this is going to be a seriously uncomfortable night for my lips.

A few minutes and a couple of plucked eyebrow hairs later,

she lets me look in a mirror for the first time since I sat in her computer chair. "Ta-da! What do you think?" She props her fists on her hips and smiles widely, clearly impressed with herself.

I have to admit, I'm equally impressed. I pucker my lips. They're bright red. They look full and pouty and kissable. "I look like me with a filter."

"You look like you, but with makeup," Hattie replies. She hands me the clear tube of lip gloss. After she put it on my lips they felt fine. Like my lips, not painted fingernails.

"I guess no making out in the car before the party," I muse.

"Oh you can totally make out. That's the whole point of a lip stain. You just have to remember to reapply the gloss regularly and that stuff will stay put all night long, even with make-out sessions."

"Seriously?"

"Super seriously. It'll make it through an entire blow job. Try to wipe it off," Hattie says.

I rub my fingers over my lips and glance down at them. There's nothing on them but gloss. The color is still on my lips. "What is this stuff?"

"It's magic. That's all you need to know. Now put your shoes on so I can take some pictures before Miles gets here. He's supposed to pick you up in fifteen, but that guy has no chill when it comes to you, so he'll probably be early."

I gather my bag, which of course is cat themed. And I make sure my cat ear headband isn't askew as I zip up my boots. They have three-inch heels, which I'm not accustomed to wearing, but they complete the outfit and wearing flats with a shiny pleather full-body suit would be a terrible fashion statement and ruin this costume, according to Hattie. It's hard to argue when my legs look like they go on for days.

She poses me and takes a ton of photos, airdropping them to me immediately. "You need to post on your Kitty Whisperer account. It's too perfect a costume."

I bite my lip, grateful for the lip stain and its ability to stay put. "I don't know if I should. It's not really business related."

"You're Catwoman on Halloween. How is that not business related?"

"Parker O'Toole, one of the guys on the team, took some photos when we were moving his mom's stuff, and I guess he made a reel out of them, or maybe he has a social media person who does that. Anyway, he tagged me, so I posted it to my reels because he added a clip of Bumbles to it, but there were some comments on it about staying in my lane and posting authentic content."

Hattie rolls her eyes. "There are always going to be haters, Kitty. You can't let them dictate what you post and when."

"They just don't usually comment on my posts like that."

"Your following is growing. It was one post, and it's Halloween. Grab Prince Francis and we'll post one about you and your sidekick, how about that?"

She takes a few pictures and a short video of Prince Francis doing what he does best, pretending he's my scarf while biting my ear. I post that one with a happy Halloween message and head downstairs to wait for Miles.

He arrives four minutes early. He's dressed as Batman, obviously. It's a bit ironic, considering our beginning, when I'd pegged him for a cat-hating jerk. I smile as I take in his costume. The torso is made to look like rippling abs. His smile slides off his face like an egg off a greasy pan. "Holy fu—" He doesn't finish the curse as his gaze lifts over my shoulder and his voice rises two octaves. "Oh, hello, Lucile and Hattie. It's nice to see you again."

I glance over my shoulder. My mother and sister are peeking around the door frame. They look like part of some cartoon comedy sketch with the way my sister's chin rests on top of my mother's head. "Seriously? Can you please have some chill?"

"We need a picture! You two look perfect together!" My mother rushes down the hall to the living room while Hattie pulls her phone out of her back pocket.

"You don't need a picture," I tell Hattie.

"I wouldn't mind some photographic evidence of this," Miles replies.

I arch a brow.

He lifts one padded, cape-covered shoulder. "You look amazing, and I definitely need a new screensaver."

I wrap my arm around his waist, and he slings his over my shoulder.

"This feels a lot like prom. Or what I think prom would have felt like if I'd gone."

"You didn't go to prom?" Miles asks.

"Stop making weird faces and smile, Kitty!" Hattie takes a few pictures, and then my mom comes out with a Polaroid camera and her phone and takes a bunch of her own. Finally, I'm allowed to grab my purse and escape. I'm grateful that my mom and sister do not stand on the front steps and wave as we pull out of the driveway. Instead, they stand in the kitchen, faux leaning against the counter, pretending they're making tea when they're really watching us leave.

"I need to know more about this. You didn't go to prom? Why not?"

"I skipped it. Me and my friend Kat went out for ice cream sundaes and then hung out at the local cat shelter instead. Prom wasn't my scene, and it wasn't Kat's either." I answer the unasked question I know is coming. "Was there a little FOMO? Sure. But we stopped by one of the after parties to see what the fuss was all about on our way home from the shelter."

"And? Did you regret the decision?"

"Nope. Half the girls were either crying or barfing, and all the guys were sloppy drunk. We decided we'd made the right choice and went home feeling satisfied with our decision."

"I feel like this is the glossed-over version of the story."

I give him the side-eye. It's the abridged version, but the rest isn't important, and the embarrassing parts don't need airtime. "Did you go to prom?"

"I did. I took my girlfriend at the time. At the end of the night, she was one of the barfing and crying girls, and since I was the designated driver, I got to watch all my friends get sloppy drunk and then pray no one would hurl in the car on the way home."

"Sounds like a bust."

Miles shrugs. "It wasn't the most ideal scenario, but Josh was there, and after everyone passed out, we went swimming in his parents' pool and ate his older brother's edibles, which made up for all the crying and puking I'd dealt with earlier."

"If you'd skipped out on prom you could have gone directly to the fun stuff, though."

"My story wouldn't be quite so interesting, or nostalgic." He arches a brow. "Who is this Kat person anyway? And is it coincidence or purposeful that you're Kitty and you have a friend named Kat? And how often did people call you Kitty Kat when you were together?" Miles asks.

I chuckle. "People called us that all the time. The coincidence of our names was the icebreaker in our grade nine drama class. After that, we were basically an extension of each other through high school."

"And you're still friends now?"

"Oh yeah. She owns Kat's Cat Café. I have an office in there that I use for paperwork and scheduling, and in exchange I help Kat with her social media posts. Which I need to remember to do this weekend. Anyway, the café is exactly what it sounds like: a coffee shop full of cats you can hang out with while you drink tea or coffee. It's pretty popular."

"We have a dog café close to the park, and I think maybe there's a cat café close by, but I haven't really paid attention since I only have Wilfred." Miles taps the steering wheel.

"I wouldn't be surprised if there is one. Doggy treat bakeries have been popular for a while, but cat cafés are starting to gain traction. If you weren't at risk of exploding by going in one, I'd offer to take you."

"I've only had that one reaction, and I have more tests coming up in a few weeks since my allergy to cats isn't bad enough to put me in the hospital."

"So they still haven't figured out what you're allergic to?" That makes me nervous, because it means it could happen again.

"Not yet, no. I've got the EpiPen with me until we figure it out."

I tap my lips. "Hmm. I wonder what you reacted to."

Miles shrugs. "Dunno. They told me to track my diet to see if it could be food related, but all I've deduced so far is that I eat a lot of salt and vinegar chips. And fries. Lots of fries."

I poke him in the side. "It doesn't show."

"One of these days it'll catch up with me, and my two-pack will become a zero-pack."

I laugh. "You have at least a four-pack."

"Tonight, I have a full eight-pack though." He pats the foam abs that cover his torso, then turns right into a subdivision.

It's in an estate subdivision outside of the city. The houses here are on huge lots, set back from the road, giving them ample room to decorate for Halloween. And decorate they do. "Oh wow, this is amazing. These houses are incredible!"

We've lived in the same house since I was born. It's a quaint two-story, three-bedroom house in a quiet neighborhood in a small town about forty-five minutes outside of the city—without traffic, anyway. And there's always traffic. It suits the three of us just fine, but this is a whole different level of house.

These are designed to be beautiful and to wow people with their long, winding driveways covered in interlocking stone, manicured lawns and gardens, and grand front doors. And every house on the street is decorated for Halloween. I don't just mean there are a couple of fake RIP headstones stuck in the lawn with a skeleton trying to claw its way out of the earth.

One lawn has a carriage drawn by skeleton horses, driven by a skeleton wearing a suit and a top hat. Another has a group of witches in front of a cauldron that's somehow lit up from the inside, casting a ghastly green glow over the witch faces.

"A bunch of the guys on the team live here, and they go all out for the holidays. There are a lot of families with kids, so they make it exciting for them."

"I can see that." I can only imagine what the collective income would be in a neighborhood like this.

Less than a minute later we pull into a circular driveway lined with cars. Like all the others, this one is also decorated for the holiday, but instead of being ghastly and full of scary things and skeletons, it's whimsical and cute. There's a girl skeleton with a bow in her hair walking a skeleton dog. Friendly ghosts hang from the trees, and spiderwebs with adorable spiders span the front porch.

My nerves kick in as Miles parks the car and hops out. His cape flares impressively as he rushes around the hood to open the passenger door for me. And my hormones flare when he holds out his hand and helps me out. He doesn't let go of my hand. Instead, he pulls me closer, and I tip my chin up.

"I'm pretty sure I've said this already, but you look amazing. Not that you don't always look amazing, because you do. But I'm going to be totally honest. As a teen I had a serious crush on Catwoman, like posters on my walls beside my bed kind of crush, so this is like a fantasy come to life."

"Batman was always my favorite superhero." I run my hand over his foam pecs.

"Oh really?"

"I loved that he was a regular guy who wanted to make the world a better place and was a total badass doing it." Miles is wearing the Batman mask, so only the bottom half of his face is visible. It draws attention to his strong chin and his full, very kissable lips.

His gaze darts down.

"I'd really like to kiss you, but I don't want to mess up your lipstick."

"It doesn't come off, so you can absolutely kiss me without us both looking like clowns gone wrong."

"Really?"

"Really, really." I press my lips to the back of my hand and show him.

"What is this sorcery?" He dips down and presses his lips gently to mine, then pulls back and rubs his thumb over his lips. It comes away with nothing but gloss residue. He comes back in for another kiss, this time with tongue, but again it doesn't last. He backs up enough to check the state of my mouth before he claims it again. This time I end up pressed against the side of the car. His thigh finds its way between my legs, so I part them and hook one around his and loop my arms around his neck.

I don't know how long we stand there, grinding on each other, but the only reason we break apart is because the flash of headlights coming down the driveway tells us we're not alone. Miles does some rearranging in his spandex pants, and he grumbles about being glad he has a cape to cover his issue, and that maybe we should make a brief appearance so we can go back to his place and pick this up where we left off.

I'm not opposed to that plan. I prefer small, intimate gatherings where I know most of the people over big parties. And if there's an animal in the house, I can often be found sitting with the four-legged creatures, since they're always riveted by my conversation skills.

The other car pulls in behind Miles and cuts the lights. A guy gets out of the front seat, and a woman unfurls from the passenger side. Her hair is long and dark, and she looks like she just stepped out of the pages of a magazine. She's clearly Belle in her huge yellow dress. It's so elaborate she reminds me of a cake topper. Which means the huge, burly man is supposed to be Prince Adam. He's wearing a suit, and his longish hair is slicked back.

The man looks between me and Miles, his brows pulling together as his eyes drop to the license plate on the car. His brows pop. "Thorn?"

"Hey, Beavin. Hi, Teresa, you two look great." Miles tries to tuck a hand in his pocket as they approach, but he doesn't have any pockets, so he props it on his hip for a second before he drops it to his side.

I'm still trying to figure out if Beavin is a nickname or a real name or a last name.

Beavin claps Miles on the shoulder, then pats his foam chest. "You been working out, man?"

"Nah, temporary ab implants." He runs a hand over them, then puts his arm around my shoulder. "Kitty, this is Mark Beavin. He plays defense. And this is his wife, Teresa. She runs a not-for-profit company that pairs children with support dogs."

"Oh wow. That's amazing! It's so nice to meet you both." I try to wipe my hand on my hip, but my outfit is pleather, so it doesn't absorb the sweat at all.

She doesn't say anything about my slightly damp palm as she shakes my hand and tells me it's great to meet me. "You two are so cute! Have you and Miles been dating long? Why haven't I seen you at a game?" Teresa hooks her arm with mine and guides me toward the house, leaving the guys trailing behind us.

"We've only been seeing each other for a few weeks," I explain.

"Well, we definitely need to get you out to a game. It's so much fun. And we have a box, and seats on the ice, so you can pick where you want to watch the action from."

"That sounds amazing."

The second we're in the doors, a group of women converges on Teresa. It sounds a bit like a flock of chickens clucking at each other. And not in a bad way, just in an excited to see each other way. It's clear that they spend a lot of time together and that they're good friends. I wonder what that must be like, to have a husband or boyfriend who travels half the year. I imagine it could get lonely, and that part of the reason they're all so close is because they need the support of their friends to manage those away-game stretches.

One of the women hands me a drink, and Teresa introduces me to the wives and girlfriends, all dressed up as princesses. I feel like I missed the memo in my Catwoman costume. And I stand out more than I'd like to.

Another group arrives. These guys look younger, and none of them have brought dates. They stop to say hi to the women surrounding me, complimenting them on their costumes. Again, I'm struck by how close the team is, and how they include Miles like he's one of them. There's a family-like bond.

Hattie played team sports, but I hadn't been good at them, so I stuck to clubs where getting hit by balls and potentially disappointing teammates wasn't a problem.

Parker inserts himself into the group. He's dressed up as . . . I'm not sure, but he's shirtless and wearing a kilt. Maybe he's a highland romance novel cover model. He gives me a once-over, his gaze lingering for a moment on my cleavage. "And who's this?"

Teresa, who is standing beside me, links her arm with mine. "This is Kitty, Miles's girlfriend."

His eyebrows shoot up. "Kitty? Oh shit. I didn't recognize you. Maybe I should have, though. Bomb-ass costume, girl. Kitty, the Kitty Whisperer, dressed up as Catwoman." He gives me a lopsided grin while nodding his appreciation.

"Wait a second. You're Kitty, the Kitty Whisperer." Teresa's hold on my arm tightens.

And suddenly I'm bombarded with questions. Half the women in the circle apparently follow me on social media. And that picture Parker posted when we were moving Miles's mother's stuff got a lot of traction. My follower count has gone up by a good ten thousand or more since then, and I've gotten a couple new sponsorship opportunities. At first, I was shocked by the sheer volume of new followers, and of course there were a number of messages from guys making lewd comments. Which I expected, because I'm aware the name of my cat-sitting company is a euphemism. I didn't make the connection until after the fact, and by then I was already established, and it was too late to change it.

Over the years I've gotten used to combing my posts for the juvenile kitty comments and deleting them, or responding with a polite redirect, letting them know that I'm not *that* kind of kitty whisperer and asking if they talk to their mothers with that mouth. That's usually enough to shut them up. But I didn't expect the mean ones about playing the game and elevating my social status with NHL players a decade younger than me. Maybe I should have, though. People jumped to conclusions that because Parker had his arm around me that I'd automatically jumped into bed with him. The women commenting were the worst, and extra catty.

There's a sudden flurry of excitement as the women surround me for a group selfie. And of course, because I seem to be a divining rod for all four-legged animals, an adorable, chonky pug lumbers over to introduce himself. He jumps up, his paws on my thighs, and sniffs my crotch while we're in the midst of another round of photos.

"Barnaby! Where are your manners! You know better than to do that!" Sadie, the host of the party, scolds him, while pulling him away. "I'm so sorry."

"It's okay. It's how they say hello." Big dogs jumping up on me can be a bit much, but this guy is too small to knock me over.

A black-and-white tuxedo cat comes trotting down the stairs, almost the same size as the pug, probably because he heard his four-legged housemate getting scolded and wants to watch the show. He plunks himself down beside Barnaby, who's busy looking very guilty for his behavior.

"And who is this little guy?"

"That's Cleveland. These two are best friends or total enemies, depending on the time of day," she informs me.

I'm asked all sorts of questions about my cat-sitting business, how I got started, how I've managed to make it a full-time job. I discover that a lot of them are involved with volunteer and charity organizations, many of them animal related. All of a sudden I'm being offered introductions and new opportunities I never could have imagined. And all for agreeing to come to a party. I try not to let the comments on that post Parker put up bother me, but I worry there will be more if I accept some of these generous offers. Although the potential benefit of being able to take care of more kitties in need probably outweighs the negative comments.

Miles sidles up next to me and apologizes for taking so long.

I smile up at him. "It's okay. I'm having fun."

Parker pops his head between ours and holds out his phone, snapping a quick selfie.

"Hey, careful what you post, okay?" Miles tells him.

"Sir, yes sir." Parker salutes him and moves on to the next couple to do the same thing.

I frown, and he drops his head so his lips are at my ear. "Everyone thought he was dating you after that last post, and he's getting himself a reputation for being a ladies' man," Miles explains. "I just don't want any more negative attention for you."

I turn into him and tip my chin up. "I can handle a little negative attention."

His smile turns wry, and his hand settles on my hip. "I know you *can*, but it doesn't mean you should have to."

I push up on my toes and kiss the bottom of his chin. "I need to use the ladies room."

"Can I get you anything?" Miles asks.

"A water would be good." That last drink was strong, and I'm feeling the effects. "I'll be back in a minute."

He dips down to kiss me, the hard plastic of his nose poking me in the cheek.

Someone snaps a photo, cooing about how cute we are.

I'm accustomed to being called cute. I'm not particularly tall, and most of the time I wear cat cartoon–inspired shirts.

I excuse myself from the group and disappear down the hall in search of the bathroom. On the way back to the living room

I notice Barnaby and Cleveland sitting by the sliding glass door, looking like they want to be on the other side of it.

I check with Sadie to see if they're allowed outside.

"Oh yes. Give me a minute, I'll take them out. It's getting close to Barnaby's bedtime, and we always give him one last run around the yard," she says.

"I can do it for you. I really don't mind." As fun as this party is, I could use a few minutes before I dive back into being social.

Her gaze shifts from me to her pets and their swishing tails. "You're our guest. I can't ask you to do that."

"Honestly, I would love to," I assure her.

Her husband, Matt, pops his head in the kitchen and asks where he can find lemon slices. "Give me a second and I'll cut up another one." She bites her lip, then says to me, "You're sure you don't mind?"

"Totally paws-itive." I wink. "You take care of your guests, and I'll take care of the fur babies."

She squeezes my arm. "You're amazing, Kitty. Thank you."

"My pleasure."

I leave her in the kitchen and grab a poop bag from the roll by the door, tuck it into my sleeve since this costume has no pockets, and let Barnaby and Cleveland outside. Barnaby runs across the deck into the expansive yard, which lights up as he trots across it, tongue lolling happily. Cleveland flops down on the deck and starts grooming his stomach.

A few seconds later Barnaby comes bounding back toward the deck, a Frisbee twice the size of his head in his mouth. He skids to a stop in front of me, tail and butt wagging with his excitement.

"Do you want to have a little play?" I ask.

He drops the Frisbee at my feet and barks once, butt still shimmying back and forth on the deck. Cleveland pauses in his grooming to give him a disdainful look, then returns to his task.

I pick up the Frisbee, which Barnaby playfully tries to grab from me, but when I manage to free it from his teeth, he prances around a couple of times and then plunks his butt on the deck.

I throw the Frisbee, and he rushes across the lawn, jumping into the air to catch it before it hits the ground. I know I shouldn't be gone long, or Miles will wonder where I've disappeared to. I'm not used to huge crowds, or this many people knowing who I am. Sure, I have a lot of followers on social media, and people in my town know who I am, but this is a different level of attention. It makes me wonder how intense it must be for the players, since they have so many fans who would recognize their faces.

I toss the Frisbee again and wait for Barnaby to bring it back. Cleveland jumps up on the railing and slinks across it, his focus on the tree that hangs over the edge of the deck.

I hear the taunting chatter of an animal, and Cleveland's tail flicks back and forth. Barnaby drops the Frisbee on the deck and trots over to Cleveland, who is still as a statue, apart from his swishing tail. Barnaby whimpers, and Cleveland lets out a low growl.

I decide it's time to take them inside. The last thing I need is Cleveland trying to scale a tree or Barnaby chasing down a poor animal and using it as a chew toy. Not that he could do a lot of damage, but no one likes to round out a party with a dead squirrel.

I open the sliding door and call both of their names, but they either ignore me or can't hear me over the chatter of voices inside the house. I whistle to draw their attention, but Cleveland's back arches and his tail puffs up.

"Crap." Whatever is in the tree has them totally entranced.

The sound of an animal scrambling in the tree is followed by the rustle of branches, and then something lands on the railing and skitters onto the deck. Cleveland yowls and hisses, and Barnaby barks, which scares the bejesus out of the animal— and me.

As the critter bumbles toward me, I realize it's a raccoon. And not just any raccoon, but a baby one. Disoriented, it runs toward the sliding door. I dive for it, but I'm wearing heels, and I trip over my own feet, landing on the deck in a heap. Cleveland is the second four-legged creature through the door. I manage to snag Barnaby's collar before he can launch himself after them.

His bark gets cut off abruptly and he jerks back. I feel bad, but a murder scene in their very lovely, very light gray and navy living room would certainly get me uninvited to future events.

Shouts and screams can be heard from inside the house. And despite how small he is, I'm struggling to keep my hold on Barnaby.

"Can I get a hand?" I shout, but I'm not sure I can be heard over the ruckus inside the house. Parker notices me struggling with the dog and comes to my aid.

"Can you hold him? There's a raccoon loose in the house!"

"Holy shit. Yeah."

He picks up the squirming dog, and I slip inside, closing the door to keep them outside so Barnaby can't join the hunting party. I glance around the room. There are women in dresses screaming and guys with their arms held wide. Someone has a laundry basket, and Austin has a pool cue.

I head for the fray.

But the chase isn't on the floor anymore.

The baby raccoon has scaled the curtains and is sitting on top of the rod, and Cleveland has jumped onto the sideboard. It's clear his plan is to get to the raccoon however possible.

I push my way through the crowd, assessing how best to corral the raccoon while doing the least potential damage to their beautiful, very expensively decorated house.

Miles, who is at the edge of the group, comes rushing over. "What are you doing? That raccoon could be rabid!"

"I can handle this. I'll be fine." I glance at the terrified raccoon, hissing down at Cleveland, who hisses rights back. He's scared, but not dangerous. Still, I don't want to deal with a raccoon bite or any potential diseases.

I search the room for the guy with the laundry basket and the one with the pool cue. I need to act quickly, before this already bad situation gets worse.

"You! Laundry basket guy and Austin, I need your help." I feel bad that I can't remember Laundry Basket Guy's name, but there's a lot of pressure, so hopefully he's not offended. I turn back to Miles. "And I need your cape and a boost."

"What's your plan?"

"Just trust me." I pull the tie on his cape, then grab onto his shoulders. "I need a lift."

He doesn't question me, maybe realizing there isn't much time before Cleveland goes after the masked intruder.

Laundry Basket Guy and Austin converge on us. "Miles is going to give me a boost. When I'm up, you poke the raccoon with the cue, Austin, and you"—I point to Laundry Basket Guy—"hold the basket under me. I'm going to use Miles's cape to get him safely in the basket."

"What if it doesn't work?" Austin asks.

"Trust me, it will," I say with conviction I don't feel, but at least I sound confident. If it doesn't work, I'm probably never going to be able to attend another party with Miles's team again. But if it does work, no one will need a rabies shot after this, and it will make one hell of a story.

I grab Miles by the shoulders, and he makes a bridge with his hands. I set one foot into his palms and grip his shoulders while he hoists me up. The plastic nose of his mask pokes me in the crotch. I don't have time to focus on the fact that my lady business is in his face, because the moment I'm in the air, I release his shoulders and get the cape ready. Austin gets into position, and Laundry Basket Guy does the same.

"Poke him!" I call out.

Austin follows the order, and when the raccoon jumps, I cover him with the cape, wrapping it around his tiny, flailing body. Miles must not expect the sudden movement, because it sets him off balance. I drop the cape-wrapped raccoon in the laundry basket, which someone else promptly covers with a pillow before Miles and I go tumbling to the floor.

His nose stabs me in the crotch, and I roll to the side, curling into a ball and cupping my girl parts, as Cleveland hurtles over me. There's a flurry of activity and a lot of yelling to use the side door and not the sliding one as Laundry Basket Guy rushes across the room with a hissing, angry, and terrified raccoon bumping around in there.

"Kitty? Are you okay?" Miles's face appears. He's crouched on the floor beside me, his cheek against the hardwood, just like mine.

"Your nose stabbed me in the crotch." I accept his offered hand and stop protectively cupping myself since there's still a huge group of partygoers standing around us in a semicircle.

"I'm sorry. I'd offer to kiss it better right now, but that would be awkward with all of these people watching."

I chuckle and blush.

"Rain check, though?"

"Absolutely."

I let him pull me to my feet, and his teammates break into a round of applause and whistling. I brush it off as no big deal. I'm not sure most of them realize it was me who let the raccoon into the house in the first place.

We stay for a while longer, but once the adrenaline starts to leave my body, the fatigue that comes with this much socializing, plus the raccoon drama, sets in. I'm envious of the way Cleveland and Barnaby are curled up together in his dog bed in the living room, oblivious to the party.

Miles and I say our goodbyes, and we get in his car and head to his apartment.

"I'm sorry about your cape." It ended up in the trash since the raccoon peed and pooped all over it.

"Don't apologize. It was worth losing a cape to see you be such a badass. You totally saved the day." He kisses my knuckle. "I can't wait to get you back to my place and out of your Catwoman suit."

"Or maybe we should leave them on," I suggest, sort of joking, sort of not.

"Maybe we should," he agrees.

We make it back to his place in record time.

chapter twenty-three

PAWS-ITIVELY PURRFECT

Kitty

After the Halloween party, my social media accounts see another spike in new followers. Being tagged by a bunch of professional hockey players and their significant others is incredible free marketing. It doesn't hurt that someone took a video of me saving the raccoon. Thankfully, they cut the video before I took Miles to the floor. And the angle didn't show his face mashed into my crotch.

There always seems to be a counter action to the positivity, though. Along with the new followers comes a barrage of private messages and comments—some of them disparaging. I get called some nasty names, and of course there are horrible jokes about me offering up my personal kitty services to hockey players now. It's disgusting and mortifying.

It's the Wednesday after the party. I meant to visit Kat on Monday, but my schedule was so hectic, with cat visits and managing/

deleting/monitoring the social media stuff, that I couldn't make it work. I bring a load of old blankets and towels with me to Kat's Cat Café, and a bunch of sponsor items as an apology. I need to go over my calendar for the month and place a supply order. Kat and I usually do this together, because we get a better discount that way.

"Hey, hey, my famous friend! I was starting to wonder if I was ever going to see you again." Kat's tone and expression tell me she's hurt.

"I'm sorry. Things kind of exploded after the Halloween party in a way I didn't expect, and I've been trying to juggle all the balls and put out fires." We've messaged since the raccoon video came out. The more attention I get these days, the more I see the other, less friendly side of social media. Aside from the nasty comments about hockey players, several people questioned what happened to the baby raccoon. I assured my followers that he was returned to the outdoors and his family. I'm trying to stay focused on the positives.

Kat wrinkles her nose. "I saw some of those comments about playing with balls."

I roll my eyes. "They don't even make sense. Hockey has pucks, not balls."

"Is this some kind of new strategy to build your business that I don't know about?" Kat picks up Tux, who keeps bumping his head against her shin.

"What do you mean?"

She shrugs. "I don't know. You're taking care of that one

player's cat, and now you're always with that Miles guy who works for the team."

"I'm taking care of Parker's great-grandfather's cat, and Miles's mom's cat. It's a happy coincidence that they're affiliated with the same team."

Kat bites her lip. "I'm not saying it's a bad thing. Just be careful, okay? You tend to focus on the positive, and that's great, but remember where you started and what your goal is. Being internet famous because you love cats and named your business the Kitty Whisperer is a lot different from being internet famous for hanging out with hockey players."

I purse my lips. "You sound like you're drinking the comments Kool-Aid."

She holds up a hand. "I'm sorry. That came out wrong. I just don't want you to get hurt. You're used to cat lovers following you, but this is a whole different breed of people. I just want you to stay true to your vision. Gaining new followers is amazing. You just want them to be your followers for the right reasons."

"I get what you mean, and I'll be careful." I don't want her to be angry with me or to focus on all the negatives right now. I hold up the bag. "I brought some supplies, all freshly washed. Should I put them in the stockroom?"

"Yeah, sounds good." Kat sets Tux on the floor. "Now tell me all about the party and exactly what happened with that baby raccoon."

I fill Kat in on the party, and we make a plan to have dinner the following evening. Miles is away with the team for the next few days, and while I miss him, it's not all bad. It means I can dedicate some time to my friends and my family, who haven't been getting the attention they deserve lately.

Although I've noticed that my mom's been making plans with friends more often and not sticking to the routine that we've followed for the past decade. Instead of watching the same old TV shows, I'll put on the game in the evening while I tackle emails. And if my mom comes home in the middle of a period, she'll join me.

They're small things and little changes, but it gives me hope that if she can move forward with her life, I'll be able to do the same.

It's Saturday evening, a week after the Halloween party, and I'm staying the night at Miles's place. It's the first time I've seen him since he returned from the away games, and we're ordering in because I don't want to have to wait to climb him like a tree.

As soon as I'm in the door we're on each other. He's still wearing his suit, and I'm dressed in a pair of leggings and a comfy oversized sweater. I manage to get him out of his shirt without popping any buttons off. It's a lot easier to get me naked.

We don't make it past the living room couch. Wilfred disappears down the hall, likely into Miles's bedroom, embarrassed by our nudity.

Forty-five minutes and a couple of orgasms later, we're sitting on the couch, eating Chinese takeout straight from the box. Wilfred is standing close by, giving us sad eyes, clearly hopeful that we'll miss our mouths at some point.

"You know what might be good for your social?" Miles has been scrolling through the recent posts.

Since the party, I've gained even more followers, which is mostly great. My sister checks the comments now, so I don't have to see the hurtful things people like to say. Even though I'm back to posting my normal cat videos, a few icky responses inevitably show up on my posts and reels.

"What's that?" I'm wary about his response. Miles is very pragmatic about social media and considers it a tool, and sometimes a necessary evil.

"Video Q&As."

"Answering questions about the kinds of services I offer to hockey players doesn't sound like a good idea."

Miles sets his takeout container on the coffee table and stretches his arm across the back of the couch. "I want to punch every douchebag who's made a comment about that. What I mean is, there are a lot of people asking valid questions, like how you knew what to do with the raccoon."

Every time I think about that, I imagine all the ways it could have gone very wrong. "I was flying by the seat of my pants. I just didn't want the little guy to destroy their house. And it was my fault he got in in the first place."

"You couldn't have known that was going to happen. It was wildly unpredictable. And you were super badass. Maybe you were winging it, but there was intuition at work there. You had some idea what would be effective. You need to cut out the noise, Kitty."

"How do you mean?"

Miles taps the back of the couch. "It's like when Parker has a kick-ass game, the fans cheer him on, in the arena and on social media. But if he misses one? Everyone has an opinion, and social media is where they share it. When it's good, it's great, but when it's bad . . . it can really mess with your head."

I poke at my noodles. "But the jerks will keep commenting no matter what."

"You're right. They will. So when I say cut out the noise, Kitty, I just mean cut out the stuff that doesn't matter, and that's the negativity and the douchebags. When Parker has a bad game, we post videos of him working out, or at practice, or even at home, making a meal or hanging with his great-grandpa and that freaking cat with the buttons. It makes him a person, not just a player who's at the whim of the fans. Combat the bullshit by doing what you do best, sharing your love of animals and how to care for them."

I blow out a breath, feeling a tightness in my chest. He's right. I need to be proactive. "Just be me."

"Exactly. You don't need to be anything but yourself. And you're allowed to hang out with hockey players. They're the most laid-back sports professionals out there; at least that's how I feel. Your true followers adore you, so if you started a segment where you answered *their* questions and allowed for interaction,

I think you'll have less of the other noise. Don't feed into it. I know you already have some sponsors who send you products, but with the way you're growing, I bet there's going to be even more interest."

"I had to turn away a few people this week because I can't take on more clients," I admit. "I think I'm going to have to look at hiring someone to help me. But that means I'll need to find time to interview and train people. And then I'd be managing them, and I'll still have my daily check-ins with clients. It's a lot to think about." Adding to my already full plate will take away from my new social life, and I don't want that, either. It's a tough balance.

"I know this seems daunting, but when growth happens this quickly, it forces us into action. If you hire even one person to start part-time, then you won't be running everything on your own."

"I'll talk to Kat. She might know someone who needs a part-time cat-sitting gig."

"That would be a great start. And we can make a few of those videos tonight if you want. See if they can give you back some of the warm fuzzies you get from your followers."

Over the next few weeks, I start posting regular Q&A videos. At first the nasty commenters show up, but over time they dwindle. Apparently the gossip over my affiliation with Parker and the rest of the NHL team is no longer exciting enough to hold people's attention.

And Kat, being the awesome friend she is, helps me through the first few weeks by taking part in the Q&A videos so I don't have to do it on my own. What begins as a way to support each other turns into a weekly segment for Kat's Cat Café, where we showcase one of the cats up for adoption.

I'm lucky to have a friend like her, who stood by me even when I was being self-absorbed. Our weekly segments not only shine a bright light on her café, but also give us a chance to spend more time together. And smooth out some of the rough edges that have come with me trying to balance a new relationship, our friendship, and my growing business.

Since Kat has appeared in the Q&A sessions, more than half the cats up for adoption at the café have new homes—a lot of them to NHL players—and she's been offered her own sponsorship opportunities. I also start interviewing for a part-time helper, because Miles is right, I can't do it on my own anymore.

Pet product companies have been sending me everything from cat brushes to toys to treats. I barely have time to keep up with my daily routines and home visits, let alone make sure the samples are produced ethically. It's only after that that I'll make videos of the cats enjoying them. And now I have one of the bigger pet product companies offering me brand sponsorships. It's amazing, if somewhat overwhelming.

On the upside, I've been able to stop buying food and toys almost entirely because so many sponsorships are coming my way.

I'm very conscious that my followers are big on the fact that I engage with them on a regular basis, so I make sure the videos aren't about shoving new products down people's throats. And it seems to be drowning out the noise.

A few weeks after Miles's mom moves into the home, we bring Prince Francis for a visit. I put him in his carrier, even though he would happily ride on my shoulders and isn't likely to try to run away. But it's the home's rule, and I don't want to take any risks.

I haven't seen Tabitha since we moved her into the home, but it's clear it's been a positive environment for her. She looks good, like she's being well taken care of. Her gaze moves from me to Miles, her eyes lighting up when she sees the cage in his hand.

She glances to the right, where a whiteboard has the daily activities written on it, along with a special message in a different-colored dry erase marker:

Miles (oldest son) and Kitty (girlfriend) are coming to visit and bringing Prince Francis.

"Prince Francis! How is my sweet boy? Come in." She steps back and motions us inside.

I give Miles's hand a squeeze and let it go so we can walk down the short, narrow hall. Tabitha reads the whiteboard one more time before she follows us.

He sets the cat carrier on the couch and turns to his mom. "I'm Miles, your son."

"My oldest." She says it like she's reciting facts.

"That's right. And this is Kitty, my girlfriend. Prince Francis has been staying with her since you moved."

Her attention shifts to me. "Thank you for taking care of him for me. Prince Francis and Miles."

For some reason those words choke me up. Maybe it's her sad smile, or the soft knowing in her eyes as she looks between us.

"It's absolutely my pleasure. But I like to think we all take care of each other."

"That's how love should be." Tabitha opens the cage, and Prince Francis pokes his head out, peeking around before he deems it safe to come out. "Isn't this a cute sweater!" It has MOMMA'S BOY written across the back. She picks him up and nuzzles him, and he rubs his face on her cheek, then licks the edge of her jaw.

"I missed you too, my sweet, sweet boy. I hope you're not giving Miss Kitty any trouble."

"He's been great. He's very interested in the squirrels in our backyard. Spends a lot of his day on the windowsill, wishing he could join them, or use them as toys."

Tabitha chuckles. "Can I get either of you something to drink? I can make tea and put out some cookies."

"Why don't you let me do that, and you and Miles can sit and chat?" I suggest.

"That would be great. Thank you." Miles kisses my temple, and I set about putting the kettle on while they get comfortable in the living room.

Prince Francis settles in her lap immediately, and she strokes his back and rubs under his chin while she and Miles talk. She shows him her schedule and how she marks every task when it's done. And that there are a lot of people who have the same problem she does, so they understand what it's like to be forgetful. "We put our contact information in each other's phones with our room numbers and a picture so when I'm having trouble remembering someone, it's easier to find the information."

She shows Miles her phone and he scrolls through her contacts. "This is great. Who's Allen, and why does he have a gold star beside his name?"

Tabitha scrolls through his information, reading it to Miles. "He's a friend. He's older and a widower. He lost his son in a car accident." There's a pause and I look over my shoulder. I can see that she's squinting at the screen. "I lost my son too. Toby."

"That's right, Mom. When he was eight."

"And you're Miles. My oldest."

"I am."

My chest tightens at his sad smile, and I have to fight with my emotions to keep them in check. He's so patient with her, repeating the same thing when she loses her train of thought. I stay busy in the kitchen, taking my time with the tea. Eventually I join them in the living room, setting tea and biscuits on the coffee table. I take the spot beside Miles and adjust the pillows, which is when I notice the crocheted cat beside it. I pick it up and turn it over. It looks exactly like Prince Francis. "Who made this little guy?"

Tabitha keeps petting Prince Francis. "They have all kinds of classes here. One of my friends made it for me." She pauses, maybe searching for a name, but shakes her head and continues. "I used to crochet when I was younger, but I can't remember how anymore. She knows I've been missing Prince Francis, so she made me one."

"I'll have to bring him by for visits more often." I feel bad that I haven't been able to make it here sooner. Miles has been visiting regularly, though.

"That would be great." She scratches behind his ear. "I miss his company."

After we finish our tea, Tabitha offers to take us on a tour and introduce us to all her friends.

"Should we leave Prince Francis here?" Miles asks.

"I have his harness, if it's okay with the staff."

"Harness?" Miles's brow quirks up.

"Yup, I have a harness and leash for him. I started training as soon as he moved in with me," I tell him.

"You mean a harness and a leash? Like a dog?"

"Basically, yes." I'm unsurprised by his surprise.

Most cats have the same reaction to a harness at first. They fall over and lie there dejectedly until someone takes it off. But over time they get used to it, and Prince Francis has been great about wearing his when I take him into the yard to run around. We have a cat run set up between the trees so he can frolic around and chase after the annoyed squirrels and birds.

"Why don't you let me check with the staff."

Miles calls the front desk and gets a thumbs-up, so I get Prince Francis ready. And just like a dog would, he trots beside us to the common room, where we meet Tabitha's friends. Prince Francis steals the show, though, climbing into laps and spreading his kitty love.

With all the things put in place to help Tabitha, she's doing much better, and it gives Miles some assurance that he made the right decision. Change is never easy, but without it we can't move forward.

chapter twenty-four

AN ABSOLUTE CAT-ASTROPHE

Kitty

Over the weeks that follow, Miles and I finish cleaning out his mother's house. More than once we drop everything and vacate the house because Miles has a reaction. They haven't been as severe as the first one, but that might be because as soon as he sneezes or gets a tickle in his throat, we're out the door. He's been for more tests, and they've ruled out a lot of things, but they still haven't gotten to the root of the cause. So he has yet another scratch test appointment in a couple of weeks.

And last week I hired a part-time helper. It was hard at first to bring on someone new, change being something I don't usually invite. I've been a lone cat for the past three years, running everything on my own, but Miles and Kat are right: I needed an extra set of hands to make it easier to juggle my schedule and my personal life.

So I hire Fancy Summers, a vet tech student at the local college. She has years of shelter volunteer experience, and her family has a farm with half a dozen barn cats, three goats, two dogs, and an owl. I have her trained in no time. And she's incredibly organized, which has been amazing. It also means that on weekends, which is when I stack her hours, I can stay at Miles's place without worrying about having to get back to town the following morning.

It's Saturday, and Miles had to duck out early to meet up with Parker and Austin before practice. His team has a game tomorrow night, so they're going to go through the other team's recent stats. The stress he was feeling at the beginning of the season has begun to wane, particularly since he's organically become a bit of a mentor for Parker and Austin.

When my dad was alive, I would sometimes sit and watch hockey with him. Usually I'd be reading a book at the same time, or doing mindless homework that didn't require a lot of attention. Now I find myself enthralled, listening intently as Miles nerds out about player and team stats. When he's done, I'll attack him with my lips, and other body parts.

This morning he left a note on his pillow—which Wilfred drooled on—letting me know that he'll be home between ten and eleven. I roll out of bed at eight and pad to the kitchen, Wilfred and Prince Francis trotting after me.

Two weeks ago, I brought Prince Francis with me for a sleepover. We wanted to see if he and Wilfred could be friends. And also make sure he wouldn't send Miles back to the hospital. I was nervous that Wilfred might want to use Prince Francis as a chew toy, but it turns out all my worry was for nothing.

Wilfred didn't even bark once. All it took was fifteen minutes and one nose swat for them to decide they would be better friends than enemies. Since then, they've become the best of friends. Unless Wilfred tries to eat Prince Francis's food—then he gets a bop on the nose to remind him that he's not the king of the castle when Prince Francis is around.

I feed them and make myself toast and coffee. They sit side by side at my right, Wilfred's tail wagging while he rests his chin on my leg and gives me his puppy-dog eyes. Prince Francis licks between his toe beans.

When Wilfred realizes I don't plan to share my toast, he trots off and returns a minute later with his leash. He drops it at my feet.

"Would you two like to go for a walk in the park?"

Wilfred barks once and does a quick spin. Then he picks up the leash again and drops it in my lap. I laugh and scratch behind his ear. "That's a yes then, huh, Wilfred? Let me get ready and we'll go."

Winter is closing in, bringing with it cooler temperatures, so I dress Prince Francis in a thick sweater before I put on his harness. It's not his favorite clothing combination, but he loves the walks in the park, so he'll suffer through it. I put on my winter jacket, clip Wilfred's leash to his collar, snap a quick pic of the two of them, and post it on social media, and then we're off to the elevators.

We stop a few times on the descent. One woman does a double take when she sees Prince Francis, then whispers something I don't catch to her boyfriend. They giggle. I ignore them. I'm used to the curious looks and whispers I get when people realize that I'm walking not only a dog but also a cat.

We grab a cookie from the Woofable Treats Café for Wilfred so he can say hello to his friends there. Prince Francis takes up residence on my shoulders while we're at the doggy café, feeling safer from a high perch until we're back on the street. Next we stop at the Cat-tastic Café for Prince Francis. Wilfred waits outside, staring dejectedly through the window while his new best buddy mingles with his feline friends.

We don't stay for long, and then we're on our way to the park. As usual, I get a few curious looks. I smile and ignore the people who don't get it, cutting out the noise like Miles always tells me to.

We pass regular parkgoers, who stop and say hello, giving both Wilfred and Prince Francis pets and greetings. Wilfred sniffs everything he passes, stopping occasionally to lift his leg and leave a reminder that he was here, too. Whenever this happens, Prince Francis will plunk his butt down near my foot and groom himself.

I spot a group of teenage boys skateboarding along the path, doing jumps and spins, weaving in and out of dog walkers, scaring some of the smaller dogs. Before I have a chance to move off the path and get a better grip on Wilfred's leash, they whirl toward us. At the same time, a gaggle of geese, who have presumably also been frightened by the skateboarders, come weeble-wobble running across the park about twenty-five feet away.

It's the perfect storm.

The skateboarders pass by, only inches from us, causing Prince Francis to jump and scale my leg, his sharp nails digging into my skin. The shock of pain makes me lose my hold on Wilfred, who lunges at the skateboarders. I grab for him but trip over an uneven crack in the sidewalk. Instead of hugging him around the chest, I fall on top of poor Wilfred. My hand connects with the side of his head, and at the same time, I'm pretty sure I elbow Prince Francis.

The combination of the skateboarders, the geese, and the surprise of me falling on him has Wilfred yelping in what sounds like shock and pain. I push up and try to roll to the side while blindly searching for his leash. He headbutts me in the face as I grab his collar, which sends my glasses flying. Prince Francis, who is still clinging to my side, hurtles himself off me and lands on Wilfred's back. Someone yells at me to stop hurting my dog. I'm too busy trying to get my feet back under me and keep my hold on Wilfred and Prince Francis to bother responding.

Wilfred yelps again and lurches forward, making a horrible gagging sound because I'm gripping his collar. He drags us into the middle of the gaggle of angry geese. They hiss and snap, and Prince Francis arches and hisses in return, swatting at the livid geese, who have surrounded us. Wilfred tries to buck Prince Francis off while I attempt to shoo the angry geese away. In the process, I lose my hold on Wilfred's collar. All without my glasses. Which is the moment one of the geese nips Wilfred's tail. And then he's off, barking as he busts through the gaggle and races through the grass.

Prince Francis holds on until they run by a tree, and then he flies through the air like he's channeling his inner Spider-Man and lands on the trunk of the tree. He scales the side and perches on a branch, sending a few squirrels down on the way. They chatter their displeasure and bounce off.

"Wilfred! Stop!" I shout, chasing after him as he continues to run, nearly knocking over a toddler bumbling between his parents. I'm thankful he didn't try to use one of the geese as a chew toy. Eventually Wilfred must notice that he no longer has a passenger, at which point he runs in circles, barking anxiously, looking for his four-legged bestie.

I finally manage to get him to listen, and he returns to me, head down and eyes all sad, because he thinks he's in trouble.

"It's okay, Wilfred. It wasn't your fault." I grab his leash and give him a scratch behind the ear, thankful he's no longer running around the park like a menace, scaring small children. I check his tail and make sure he's not injured before I gently tug him in the direction of the tree. "Come on, let's get Prince Francis."

As we approach the tree, I realize I've garnered a lot of attention and that the skateboarders are no longer weaving through the dog walkers and morning strollers. Instead, they're gathered with their phones in their hands. I shoot them a look and then go back to ignoring them.

I want to get out of here, but first I need to retrieve Prince Francis. I catch a few comments about not taking your pet out in public if you can't control them. Another woman makes a comment about bad pet owners. I hear someone mention the Kitty Whisperer, and I want to hurl.

I try to maintain my composure while I attempt to lure Prince Francis down with treats, and Wilfred tries to appeal to him by barking and whining. But Prince Francis refuses to budge from his safe perch more than fifteen feet above us. There's no way for me to get to him. And the longer I stand here, trying to cajole him out of the tree, the more people stop to watch. A few attempt to help, but it's proving futile, and I have a feeling the crowd is making Prince Francis less likely to make the descent. I politely ask if they can give us some space, and a few people comply, but it doesn't seem to make a difference.

Eventually I give up and call the fire department. Which gains even more attention. My mortification levels are at an all-time high. Falling up the stairs on the first day of high school has nothing on the enormous group of people gathered around the tree while three firefighters approach, carrying a ladder. They're dressed in full firefighter gear, and the truck sits directly in front of the park entrance, lights flashing away.

I still haven't been able to recover my glasses, and I'm almost grateful that anyone more than twenty feet away has a blurry face. I'm dressed in a winter coat and a hat with cat ears. I didn't bother with makeup, assuming this would be a quick stroll around the park, where Wilfred would watch the squirrels and Prince Francis would wish for wings so he could catch birds.

As soon as the firefighter reaches me, I apologize. "I'm so sorry.

I didn't want to call you. I know you have much better things to do with your time, like fighting actual fires and saving people, but my cat is stuck in that tree, and I think this horde of humans is giving him climbing fright, like the cat equivalent of stage fright." I point to the branch where Prince Francis is lounging.

He's repositioned himself. He's now lying on the branch, his legs hanging on either side of it. He does not look the least bit stressed by the audience.

"Is that cat wearing a leash?" the firefighter asks.

I clasp my hands so I won't fidget. "He is. Cats are very trainable. And they love walks if you can get them comfortable with the leash and harness."

"Bernick, you want to do the honors?" One of the other firefighters claps a hand on his teammate's shoulder. He gives me a curt nod and turns to Bernick, but then his gaze slides back to me. "Holy crap. You're Kitty, the Kitty Whisperer. Dude—" He nudges Bernick with his elbow and repeats. "This is Kitty, the Kitty Whisperer."

Bernick gives him a questioning look, then mutters, "Don't advertise your porn watching habits in a public park with a hundred people standing around, Hopkins."

Hopkins rolls his eyes. "She's a cat whisperer, you dirtbag. She trains *cats*. Sorry, ma'am. My partner here lives in a gutter apparently."

"It's okay. I get that a lot. I should have taken it into account when I named my business, but it didn't occur to me until after I started getting inappropriate messages, and by that time I already had an established following." No one needed that explanation, but apparently I haven't sustained enough embarrassment today, so I added to it myself.

He nods a couple of times. The third firefighter sets the ladder against the tree. "One of you want to stop with the flirting and hold the ladder?"

"We'll be right back, Miss Kitty." Bernick touches the brim of his fire hat and inclines his head.

"Wait! Here!" I pull a baggie of treats out of my pocket and pass it to him. "These might help."

I wait with Wilfred while the third firefighter holds the ladder for Bernick. Prince Francis is clearly wary, and he hisses and swats at Bernick until he pulls out the treats. It's too much of an enticement, and Prince Francis finally relents. As soon as he's in my arms, he climbs onto my shoulders and burrows his way under my hair, then settles into his living stole position, most of him hidden under my curtain of hair.

I want to leave as soon as I have Prince Francis, but Bernick asks for a picture, and my autograph, which is a little weird, especially when he has me sign his son's second grade wallet photo.

Finally, we can leave. I don't make any stops on the way back to Miles's apartment. I keep my head down, but I swear people are whispering and glaring as I pass. I convince myself that I'm being paranoid.

But when I get back to Miles's place, I make the fatal mistake of checking my messages. I have one from Miles telling me he's on his way home. Based on the time it was sent, he should be arriving any minute. I also have messages from Kat and my sister. On top of that, I have countless tags and notifications on all my social media accounts. While it's not uncommon for me to have a lot of notifications, the number is exceptionally high, and every few seconds my phone lights up with more notifications. I'm afraid of what this means. It's clear people were filming and taking pictures of what happened at the park.

I don't have a chance to check the messages from my sister and Kat, because Miles walks through the door. "Hello, beautiful girlfriend! Would you like to get naked first and then go for breakfast, or would you like to fuel up and then get naked?"

He finds me sitting on the couch. "Maybe we should make breakfast here," I suggest.

I don't have much of an appetite, and I'm not all that interested in going out in public. I may never be again.

"Is everything okay?" Miles grabs the back of the couch and bends to press a kiss to my cheek.

"I guess it depends on your definition of okay."

He rounds the arm of the couch, moves Prince Francis from the cushion beside me to my lap, and sits down beside me. "What's going on?"

I explain what happened this morning while I was taking our four-legged friends on what was supposed to be a nice, uneventful walk.

"Oh, Kitty, I'm so sorry. That must have been awful. But it's fine now."

"I don't know if it is, though. Can you check my social media

account and tell me if there are fires I need to put out?" I pass
him my phone, too nervous to do it myself.

"I'll check Instagram first, okay?"

I nod and pet Prince Francis, hoping that I'm being paranoid
and everything is going to be okay. But Miles's expression tells me
a lot of things. Like my self-reassurances are potentially incorrect.
His eyebrows do several bounces up and down. His lips flatten in
a line. Sound blares out of the phone. It's my voice, me calling
out *stop*, followed by a high-pitched yelp. It must be a recording
of when I fell on Wilfred. Miles turns off the volume.

"It's bad, isn't it?"

"It'll be fine."

"The way your eyeballs keep darting around like you're following a light laser tells me that is a complete lie."

Miles sets the phone facedown on the table. "There are a couple
of videos that are being taken out of context. And some gifs."

"A video? Some gifs?" I echo.

He swallows thickly. "And a trending hashtag."

"Oh my gosh." I sink into the cushion, wishing the couch
would open like a mouth and swallow me whole.

"It'll be fine, Kitty. Once people understand that you weren't
trying to hurt Wilfred."

"People think I was trying to hurt him?" My voice is shrill.
"What kind of video is it?"

Miles tugs on his bottom lip with his teeth a couple of times.
"This stuff changes by the hour. By tomorrow everyone will have
forgotten about it."

"I think I need to see the video."

Miles blows out a breath and reluctantly hands me my phone once the video is cued up. It's not long, maybe ten seconds, but it looks like I'm tackling Wilfred, and the angle also makes it look like I punched him in the side of the face. And that I put him in a choke hold. The video on its own is bad enough, but it's the comments that make my stomach roll.

"Oh my God, Miles. People are calling me an animal abuser." I cover my mouth with my hand as my eyes well with tears. And I scroll through the videos and gifs, all with me tackling Wilfred, some of them with text on them calling on people to cancel me. "The things people are saying."

"It's out of context. We'll fix this. You can put up a video explaining what happened and dispel the rumors. Come here." He opens his arms. If the couch won't swallow me, I guess a Miles hug will have to do.

Prince Francis hops off my lap as I slide over and allow Miles to wrap me in his arms. I want him to be right, that we'll be able to fix this, but there's an uneasy feeling in my gut that tells me he might be wrong.

chapter twenty-five

THE CAT'S OUT OF THE BAG

Miles

My team has a game on Sunday night, and while Kitty has an open invitation to attend, she makes up an excuse about needing to be home. I don't call her out on it. I know she's upset about what happened at the park.

I accompany her and Prince Francis to the parking garage. On the way down, three people avoid getting on the elevator, saying they'll wait for the next one, and someone else asks if she's the one who punched a goose at the park. Apparently, the story has morphed quite spectacularly since yesterday afternoon.

It gets worse when we reach her car. Someone has spray painted a huge X across the side of her car.

"Oh my gosh, Miles." Kitty, who was already looking like a deflated balloon after the elevator incident, seems to shrink even further. If she were a cartoon, she would be a puddle on the ground with a very sad face. "Why is this happening? How am I going to fix this?" She motions to the red spray paint.

I wrap my arm around her shoulder. "Why don't you take my car? I know a guy who can get this taken care of like that." I snap my fingers and Prince Francis, who is wrapped around her shoulders, tries to bite them.

"I can't take your car. Then you have to drive this." She motions to her defaced vehicle.

"I'll be fine. Take the Tesla. I'll get this handled so you don't have to worry about it." I take the keys to the Cat-mobile and pass her the ones to my car.

"You're sure?"

"Paws-itively positive." I stroke her cheek, and she gives me a weak smile.

"Thank you." Her chin trembles, a sign she's on the verge of tears again.

"Anything for you." I kiss her and pull her in for a hug, wishing I could erase the videos and find a way to help her drown out the noise.

Josh gets out of his sports car, his expression slack with disbelief. "Dude. Why are you driving the cat car?" He gets a load of the graffiti on the passenger side. "Oh shit."

"Yeah. Oh shit is right." I got a lot more than just looks from people. Someone threw what was likely an expensive latte at the car, several people flipped me the bird, and someone else tossed a burrito on the windshield. I put the wipers on and ended up smearing guac all over the place; I had to pull over because I couldn't see. There's still a chunk of tomato stuck under the wiper blade.

"Is this because of that video?" Josh rubs the back of his neck.

"Yeah. I told Kitty I could get the car fixed. I'm hoping one of the guys can refer me to someone who can make a not-liar out of me."

"You must really be into her if you're willing to drive around in this thing. I'm guessing that means she has your Tesla."

"You're right on both counts. I feel horrible for her. There are so many freaking people just gobbling this shit up." I run a hand through my hair and sigh. I hate that I'm very, very wrong about everyone forgetting the video. #kittywhispereranimalabuser is the number one trending hashtag today.

"One of the guys will know someone." He claps me on the shoulder. "And maybe we can find a way to make something good out of this shit situation."

"You didn't see her this morning. She looks like someone ripped the head off her favorite stuffed animal. She's been such a huge source of support for me while I've been figuring out all the stuff with my mom. I really hate to see her like this. I just want to make it better, but I don't know how." Kitty has been taking Prince Francis to visit my mom at least once a week, if not twice. I've been trying to do the same. It's not a conventional relationship, but some days she has periods of lucidity and we talk about my childhood and Toby. It might be helping her remember I'm me more often. Or maybe that's wishful thinking on my part. Either way, it's good for us.

But now Kitty is hurting, and I don't know what I can do to help make it better.

We head into the arena to meet with Coach Davis and the players. And of course, because a lot of those guys are completely dialed into social media, almost everyone knows about what happened at the park yesterday.

I explain how it went down, and that she tripped and didn't mean to tackle Wilfred or hit him.

"People are assholes." Parker shakes his head as he scrolls through the memes—those are new—gifs, and videos that have flooded the internet.

"Don't I know it," I grumble.

"Hold on. Have you seen this?" Parker holds his phone two inches from my face.

I push his hand back until the image comes into focus. Then grab it out of his hand. "Holy hell. Is that Brit Sheers? The actress?"

"It sure is. And it looks like she's defending Kitty."

I turn the volume up on the video.

"Anyone who follows Kitty Hart knows she has a legitimate heart of gold and wouldn't hurt a fly. I don't care what it looks like. That video clip is taken out of context. I dare the person who posted it to put up the whole thing instead of the piece that turns a person who pours her whole heart into taking care of animals into an abuser."

Brit Sheers often makes somewhat controversial and political statements. But she's also very involved in several charity organizations and is particularly passionate about animals and speaking out about animal cruelty. She's the founder of A Home for Honey, a not-for-profit animal shelter that focuses on rehoming abused or neglected pets, or animals with high needs.

Sitting in her lap is Honey, a blond tabby that Brit found in a garbage can on her morning run two years ago. Honey has a rare congenital birth defect that makes it difficult for her to get around and also makes her look like she ran into a wall. She's adorable, and her social media following is unreal.

"You should reach out to her," Parker suggests. "Maybe she can give Kitty some positive press and help bury all this other crap."

"Yeah, maybe I should." I don't know what I'll say, or whether a message from me will get seen by her, but it's worth a shot. Anything to help right this wrong.

I send her a private message, introducing myself as the boyfriend of the Kitty Whisperer, asking if she'd be interested in meeting Kitty in person. And then I wait.

Over the days that follow, Kitty seems to fold in on herself. It gets worse when she loses a couple of new clients who tell her they can't risk leaving their animals in the care of someone who abuses animals.

I manage to get the giant red X removed from the passenger side door, but she's still mortified by what happened, and no matter how many new videos she posts to explain what happened in the park, the backlash and the negativity bury any-thing positive she puts out there. She nearly has a panic attack every time she leaves the house, and there have been a few times when people have yelled at her and called her names. She's taken to wearing sunglasses and an oversized hat to hide her identity. And she refuses to drive her car.

It's the middle of the week and we're at my place, snuggled on the couch watching hockey. Kitty is dressed in a pair of jeans and one of my sweatshirts. "I don't know how those guys do it." She flings a hand toward the TV, then lets it drop to her lap.

"Do what?"

"Handle all the opinions people love to share. I could deal with the jokes and the occasional poking fun at me for what I do, and because I named my company the Kitty Whisperer. I could laugh it off then, because there was balance, and most of the time my followers would come to my defense, but this isn't the same. It's just crap piled on top of crap. Every time someone tries to defend me, they become a target. It's awful. I can't escape it. I've never been embarrassed to be called a cat lady, but this is so different. People aren't even willing to listen. They just attack. And then to see all these people who were once on my side defecting over this one video, and it isn't even accurate." Tears spill over, and she pulls a tissue out of the sleeve of the hoodie to dab at her eyes.

I put my arm around her and kiss her temple, at a loss for what to say. I got a response from Brit's social media, but it was a stock reply thanking me for the message and saying Brit appreciates my love and support and to keep smiling. I sent an email and got another canned reply. I even commented on a few of her recent posts, citing who I was and that I'd messaged her privately. Those messages got a lot of attention from her fans, most of it positive, but some of it just as negative as the stuff Kitty is dealing with.

"I'm sorry this is so hard, Kitty. I wish I could scrub the internet for you. I could tell you to ignore the haters and shut out the noise, but I know it's impossible because they're in your face. The people who truly know you support you."

"I'm losing business over this. I can't go anywhere without being recognized. I think I need to trade in my car."

"You can keep driving mine until this all dies down," I tell her.

She gives me a small smile, but her eyes brim with tears. "I appreciate the offer, but I know you must be getting heckled for driving it. I can sell it as is and get something used."

Up until Saturday, Kitty's business had been growing steadily, and now the opposite is happening. "Maybe give it another week before you make any final decisions about that, okay?"

She sighs. "Okay. I can wait a week. But I don't think anything is going to change how I feel."

I tip her chin up and kiss her softly. When she doesn't pull away, I deepen it. If I can't fix her problems, I can at least take her mind off them.

The next night I'm sitting in the arena, Josh on my right, both of us following the players on the ice. I keep an eye on the opposition, looking for patterns so we can gain the advantage and keep possession of the puck.

The seat to my right is empty and often reserved for the family members of the players who come to watch them play. A few minutes before the end of the first period Teresa, Beavin's wife, drops into the chair beside mine.

"Hey." I tip my chin up and focus my gaze back on the ice.

"They're doing good tonight," she observes.

"They are." Parker has really blossomed this season, and so has Austin. Parker is a naturally gifted player and only at the beginning of his career. Once something is pointed out, he's quick to use it to his advantage. It's been good to see positive results and to have Coach Davis and the GM backing my role with the team.

Teresa knows that my job is to watch the game and assess the plays and the players, so she waits until the period is over before she says anything else. I've been met with a lot of chagrin and pity over the past week. That's not what I get with Teresa, though.

"How are you, and how is Kitty?" She crosses one leg over the other.

"I'm okay. Kitty is . . . struggling."

She nods knowingly. "Public opinion can be tough to handle. Did the videos she posted explaining what really happened make any difference?"

I shake my head. "There's just so much negativity, and it's sucking the joy out of her."

"I get it. People love to take things out of context and make them into something they're not. It's annoyingly scandalous for a woman who is a cat lover to punch a dog." She shakes her head. "It's frustrating that there isn't a video out there that shows the entire thing so she can dispel the rumors."

"I know. I've been scouring the sites, but I haven't been able to find anything to balance out the crappy stuff. And then I just get angry about the things people are saying."

She pats me on the shoulder. "People are assholes. They love to tear people down. And there's a weird belief that public figures don't have feelings, or that their feelings are made of Teflon and that they can handle ridicule and being put under a microscope better than the average person."

"This is very true," I agree. I see it all the time with players. They're held to a different standard. And when they make a mistake, on or off the ice, everyone has something to say about it. "I don't think Kitty sees herself as a public figure, but I guess she is, isn't she?"

I'm often in the background of team pictures and videos, but no one ever singles me out. My dog has more followers than I do.

"Oh yeah, she's totally a public figure now, and a celebrity in the cat-osphere. Brit Sheers has been talking about it for the past week."

"I tried to reach out to her, thinking maybe if Kitty got a message from her or something that it might boost her morale, but I don't think she manages her own social media."

"I have her number. I can reach out if you want," Teresa offers.

"Seriously? Even if she just got a message or an email, or anything really. That would be fantastic. I don't know how to make this better, and it's killing me seeing Kitty so down. She's always a ray of sunshine, you know? It's like a huge black cloud is hanging over her head."

"I totally get it. I've messaged Kitty a few times asking if she wants to get together with me and the girls, but she said she's busy. I didn't want to push," Teresa says sympathetically. "I'll message Brit now. She usually records her episodes in the afternoon, so hopefully I'll hear back from her before the end of the game."

Period two begins, so I focus my attention on the ice. Halfway through, Teresa gets up to take a phone call. She comes back as the period ends, wearing a huge smile.

"I talked to Brit. She wants to know if Kitty would be open to doing a live interview. She's a huge fan."

"Seriously?"

"Super seriously. She's outraged by what's happening to her. I gave her your contact information. She's supposed to be flying out this way next week to visit a shelter, and she thinks this would be a great way to help smooth things over for Kitty and give her the positive press she deserves."

And just like that, the sun peeks through the clouds.

chapter twenty-six

PURRFECTLY PAWSITIVE PEOPLE

Kitty

W here's your car?" I stop in the middle of my driveway, noting the distinct absence of Miles's Tesla.

He stuffs his hand in his pocket and rocks back on his heels. "I left it at home."

"Why? How did you get here?"

"I Ubered. Do you have your keys, or do you need to go back in and get them?" He pulls on his tie. His eyes dart from me to my car and back again.

"I don't want to drive that thing." I sneer at my car as if it's the reason for all my problems, not a stupid viral video.

"Then I can drive."

"Let me rephrase that. I don't want to be seen in that car, regardless of what seat I'm in." I haven't driven it since the park fiasco. I'm too mortified. Before, I wasn't bothered by the sometimes questioning looks I got. But it's shifted into outright verbal assault. On one hand, I appreciate the animal rights activists' passion, but being on the receiving end of their wrath unfairly has shown me a very ugly side of humanity.

Miles settles a hand on my shoulder. I stare at his chest. If I look at his handsome face, there's a chance I'll get emotional. It's been like that recently. Spontaneous tears. Questioning my purpose.

"Kitty, look at me."

I drag my reluctant gaze to his empathetic one.

His expression is soft, but he also looks determined. "I know this has been really hard on you, and that you're struggling to figure things out, but this"—he motions to the car—"is part of who you are. It makes you distinctly you. And you are loved by a lot of people. Sometimes when we fall, we need to take the hand that's been offered to us, get back on our feet, dust ourselves off, and keep going."

I sigh. "I don't want my car to get vandalized again."

"I know. It won't."

Since the park incident, I've been borrowing my sister's car a lot. And Miles has been good about lending me his. We're just driving to his place, and after the side of my car was spray painted, they've increased the underground parking security. His apartment had footage of the person who did it, but they were wearing a ski mask and nondescript all-black clothes.

"I'll grab my keys."

"That's my girl." He dips down and presses his lips to mine.

Instead of heading for the highway, Miles goes in the opposite direction, toward downtown.

"Where are we going?"

"I need to make one stop," Miles informs me.

"What? Why?" I'm suddenly on high alert. Stops were not on the menu. It's supposed to be a straight shot from my mom's house to his apartment.

The only places I've gone to willingly lately have been Kat's Cat Café and the grocery store. And only when it's necessary and I have access to my sister's car. I also often sneak in the back door, so I don't have to face anyone but Kat. And I've taken to shopping at the grocery store on the edge of town, where fewer people will recognize me and ask me questions.

"It won't take long," Miles reassures me.

I don't know what's going on, but he's being…sketchy, maybe? He's more fidgety than usual, but it's possible my anxiety is rubbing off on him.

A few minutes later Miles parks across the street from Kat's.

"Why are we here?"

"I have to pick something up."

"Why didn't you ask me to pick whatever it is up? I have a key and an office here."

"I knew you weren't going to have time to stop here earlier because your schedule was full."

He's not wrong, and like all my other clients, he has access to my daily and weekly calendar. Despite the horrible things people are saying about me, most of my clients have been supportive. Only a few of the newer ones jumped ship.

"I promise it'll be quick, and there are multiple orgasms waiting for you at my place."

"Okay." I sigh, wishing the promise of multiples could alleviate my anxiety. I expect the people passing us on the street to yell mean things when I exit the vehicle. No one does, but a couple walking their dog give me a dirty look and crosses to the other side of the street.

"Just ignore the assholes." Miles settles his palm against my lower back and guides me toward the front door. As we approach the café a woman stops me. I brace for more hate, but she tells me she doesn't believe what everyone is saying, and she hopes I can get this mess cleared up soon. Then she hugs me, and I almost burst into tears.

"See? You've got people on your side."

"I just miss the days when I had more people on my side than not," I murmur, swallowing down the emotions.

It's hard not to let the hurtfulness seep in and taint the good parts. When we reach the entrance, I pull on the door, but the closed sign is hanging in the window. "That's weird. It's usually open until nine. Let me get my key."

Miles knocks on the glass door while I rummage around in my purse.

"Where the heck is it? I was holding my keys a second ago." I peer inside. People are moving around. "Maybe they had a bathroom accident or something." It's happened before. Usually it only takes a few minutes to clean up.

Merlin, one of the baristas, opens the door for us. "Oh great! You're here. Perfect! Come on in." He opens the door so Miles and I can squeeze through, then locks it again.

"What's going on?" I mutter. This seems like we're getting ready for an illegal cat fight or something.

I move to the right so I'm standing beside Miles instead of behind him. I suck in a shocked breath. When I was here earlier in the week everything was normal. But today the tables have been moved around so the center of the café is open. And in their place is a single table with two plush chairs. Surrounding those chairs are lights, microphones, and a video camera.

But it's not the setup that has my heart palpitating. It's the woman sitting in one of the chairs. "Oh my gosh. Is that Brit Sheers?" I grab Miles's arm because I suddenly feel light-headed.

"It is."

"What is she doing here? She's my unicorn. I think I'm going to hyperventilate. Where is Kat? What's going on? Does she know about this?"

Brit pushes out of the chair, her wide, perfect, white-toothed smile glinting in the camera lights. She's even more beautiful in real life than she is on camera, and that's saying something.

"Kitty Hart! It's so wonderful to finally meet you!" She extends a hand.

"You're real, and you're talking to me," I mumble.

Black spots and white dots swim in the edges of my vision, slowly washing over her face like the tide coming in. I don't have a chance to hold out my own hand, because suddenly the world goes dark.

"Kitty? Babe?" There's a hand on my cheek, tapping gently.

I blink.

"I think she's coming around." Miles's face appears, the wave of black slow to recede. "Hey, you okay?"

"I . . . have no idea." I'm completely disoriented.

Kat is hovering over his shoulder, her fingers at her lips. "I told you the surprise would freak her out."

Miles helps me into a sitting position. "Take it slow."

My gaze shifts from Miles to Kat, who is wringing her hands, but also smiling ear to ear. I realize that Brit Sheers wasn't a strange dream. I'm really sitting on the floor of Kat's Cat Café, and Brit's really here.

"Oh my gosh, did I just faint?"

"You did. I'm sorry. I probably should have told you what I was planning, but I didn't want to give you the chance to back out, and I know how much you love Brit. I thought maybe she would reach out and send you a message, but she wants to interview you, so here we are," Miles word-vomits those two very long sentences in under ten seconds.

It takes me six times as long to process them because I'm still hazy after my fainting spell.

Brit Sheers hands me a glass of orange juice. "Here, drink this. It'll help."

"I can't believe you're real and you're handing me orange juice. I also can't believe I fainted." I take the glass, then tack on a "thank you."

I take several sips, wait a couple minutes for the sugar to work its magic, and then allow Miles and Kat to help me to my feet.

I'm lucky that it's winter and I'm wearing a dress and leggings, and that I didn't flash anyone my underwear.

I wobble my way to the chair opposite Brit. "I'm confused about what's happening here," I admit.

A trio of people stand off to the side with what looks like a toolbox. Brit holds up her hand. "Give us a minute, then you can work your makeup magic."

They shuffle off, muttering apologies.

Brit's attention returns to me. Miles is standing by the treat display with Kat. I would love it if he was holding my hand, but I realize that would be super awkward.

"Miles reached out after what happened on social media, and I saw a great opportunity to showcase you and your business. I've been a fan of yours for a long time, and I want more people to know about the woman behind that video and give you a chance to share the true story."

"That video has been the worst thing to happen to me," I mutter.

"That video was totally taken out of context. And I know exactly what it's like to be in your shoes." Her smile is full of empathy. "I'm hoping we can clear up the misunderstanding with today's interview."

"I'm not sure how you'll do that when there's no proof that I didn't intentionally tackle my boyfriend's dog," I admit.

"I'll be able to help with that. I want the world to see the authentic you, the same you that I fell in love with when you started your cat-sitting business four years ago. It'll be like having a conversation at the dinner table. Casual and informal. Just be you."

"I can do that. Just be me."

Her makeup team swoops in and takes care of my face and hair before they touch her up. And then the camera crew is counting down from five. I glance over at Miles, who gives me a thumbs-up.

As if on cue, Tux comes padding across the room and jumps into my lap as we go live. One of the crew members steps up, as if he's going to remove the kitty, but Miles stops him.

Tux nudges my chin with his nose, then kneads my legs to make himself comfortable, despite the camera crew and all the lights shining directly on us.

"Hello, fans! I'm on location just outside of Toronto in the quaint town of Terra Cotta, at Kat's Cat Café and Rescue Shelter with the one and only Kitty Hart, owner of the famous cat-sitting and training company, the Kitty Whisperer. Kitty, it's a pleasure to have you with us today," Brit says brightly.

Tux headbutts my face again, so I give him a few pets, then push on his butt. He takes the hint and settles in my lap. "It's a real pleasure to be here today, Brit, but I have to be honest, I'm really hoping I don't do anything embarrassing that's going to result in another meme." I really wish I'd stopped before the sentence became a run-on. Like I need to give anyone ideas about making more memes. There's currently one of poor Wilfred with wild eyes and me on his back with the line "get off me, crazy cat lady" on it.

Brit chuckles. "You know you're in the big leagues when you're a meme! I remember my first meme. I got caught yawning at the Emmys. I'd been so nervous the night before the event I hadn't slept a wink, and of course someone caught me mid-yawn." She holds up an iPad with the meme on it. "Such a flattering picture, isn't it?" She chuckles and rolls her eyes, then gives her attention back to me. "Jokes aside, can you tell me what the last week has been like for you? I can imagine this hasn't been easy on you."

I take a deep breath an exhale some of my anxiety. "I can handle the memes, and I'm used to people poking fun at my car, but the worst part has been how someone took something and twisted it to make it look like I was intentionally harming an animal. I won't even kill spiders, and I certainly wouldn't purposely tackle Wilfred." I pause and clear my throat, the topic making me both emotional and frustrated.

"I've been following you for years, Kitty, and while we don't know each other personally, I can say, with confidence, that I believe you didn't intentionally set out to hurt your boyfriend's dog."

"Thanks. Now I just need to convince the rest of the world."

"I might be able to help with that." She nods to the camera-man, who brings over a laptop and sets it on the table between us. On the screen is a social media account of what appears to be a college student. "We were able to track down the origin of the video and the person who posted it. For the sake of protecting that person's identity, we're not disclosing his name, but he has something he wants to say to you, Kitty, if you're interested in hearing him out."

"If he's going to say nasty things, I'll pass," I tell her.

She throws her head back and laughs. "This is why I love you, Kitty. No mincing words."

I blush and shrug. "It's been a rough week. I don't need anyone, especially not the person who made it so hard, giving me the gears."

"No, you certainly don't," Brit agrees. "And this young man would like to apologize for the problems he's caused you, if you're interested."

I can't see Brit bringing this guy on her show if all it was going to do was make things worse, so I nod my agreement.

A video feed comes through, and a second later I'm staring at a college-aged kid. He's wearing glasses and a manga T-shirt. He looks nervous.

I look to Brit. "Will everyone be able to see his face?" I ask.

She shakes her head. "To be clear, only we will know the identity of the young man who posted the video."

I nod again. "Okay. People make mistakes, and I would not want the same thing that's happened to me this week to happen to someone else. Even the person responsible for it."

"I love that even though this week has been a nightmare for you and you're seconds away from finding out who that person is, you still don't want to throw them under the bus. What I'm offering today is proof that the video that's been making your life a nightmare isn't even remotely accurate." Brit turns her attention to the laptop. "I think you have something you'd like to say to Kitty?"

The young man runs his hands over his jean-covered thighs. "I shouldn't have posted that clip. I didn't think about how it would impact anyone, and I didn't think it would go viral the way it did. And I'm sorry for that. I saw you trip. And I knew you didn't mean to hurt your dog, and it was wrong of me to edit it and make you look bad."

"You have the full video?" I glance from him to Brit.

"He's already sent it to me, and we'll be airing it."

"Oh. Oh wow." I turn back to the young man. "Thank you for apologizing. And for sending Brit the full video."

He chews on his bottom lip and nods vigorously. "I'm really sorry, Kitty. I wish I could take it back. My mom is a huge fan of yours, and we have two cats. I would never have posted it if I knew the damage it was going to do."

I swallow down the lump in my throat. "Thank you for being brave enough to come forward and help set the record straight."

Brit thanks him and runs the full, unedited clip. It's not particularly flattering, but it does capture the boys who skateboarded far too close to us and the flustered flock of geese. It's a comedy of errors with the way Prince Francis attaches himself to my hip, and I trip over an uneven crack in the sidewalk, causing me to fall on top of poor Wilfred and accidentally smack him in the nose as I try to wrap my arms around his neck and keep him from lunging or bolting, and it feeds out to everyone watching the live interview.

Once the clip has finished running, Brit's attention returns to me. "It's amazing how different that looks when it hasn't been edited down, isn't it?"

"You know, before we had the complete video, it was one of those situations where you need to be there to believe it could happen. It was literally the perfect storm for poor Wilfred. And Canada geese, while cute, are aggressive. It's like Canada channeled all their meanness into that one animal!"

That earns me another laugh from Brit, and then she shifts gears, steering the conversation away from what happened in the park to ask me about the Kitty Whisperer and how it all started.

It's a great interview, and when it's over, the outpouring of positive messages helps dull the sting of the negativity that came with the original video that went viral. It's as though someone has switched the lens I'm looking through, and now all I see is the good that can come from something bad.

As soon as we're in the door to Miles's place, I fuse my mouth to his, breaking the kiss only long enough to say, "I can't believe you did that for me."

"I had some help."

Wilfred's nose nudges against our hips. I put making out on pause while Miles takes him outside for a bathroom break and I fill Wilfred's bowl. I'm quicker than Miles, so I strip out of most of my clothes, apart from my bra and panties, and wait for them to return.

Wilfred goes straight to his bowl, Miles following down the hall. "Where were w——" His eyes go wide, and he drops Wilfred's leash on the floor. "Damn. I missed the striptease." His gaze moves over me on a hot sweep.

I arch a brow. "Have you ever had a striptease?" Jealousy tints the question. I don't know why I'm asking this right now, apart from slightly morbid curiosity.

Miles arches a brow in return as he crosses the room. "No. But if it were you unwrapping yourself like a gift for me, I'd be willing to change that."

"I'll keep that in mind."

He cups my face between his palms and tips my chin up, eyes heavy with emotion. "You were so brave today, Kitty." His lips brush over mine. "I love watching you shine like that."

"Thank you for making it possible." I suck his bottom lip and let it slide through my teeth. At the same time I start flicking open the buttons on his shirt.

"Thank you for trusting me." He lifts me on the counter and steps between my parted thighs.

My fingers tremble as I make my way through his buttons and push his shirt over his shoulders. I run my hands over his chest, pausing to press my palm over his heart as our lips meld and our tongues tangle. Tonight feels different, emotions heightened.

I slide his belt through the loop and free the clasp, then pop the button and drag the zipper down. He covers my hand with his before I can slip it inside his boxers. "Let me take care of you first," he murmurs against my lips, his free hand flicking the clasp of my bra open.

The straps slide down my shoulders, exposing my breasts, and he kisses a path over my collarbones. Going lower, his mouth covers a nipple, his free hand cupping my other breast. He drops to his knees and rids me of my panties, then brings me to orgasm with his soft tongue and his gentle teeth.

I'm boneless and desperate by the time his mouth returns to mine, tasting of my desire. I grip his hair and wrap my legs around his waist, keeping him close. "I need you inside me." I ease a hand between us and free him from his boxers.

He sheaths himself with a condom and then he's filling me, gaze locked on mine. We both shudder and sigh as our bodies join. Everything slows. I stroke his cheek, and his thumb brushes along the column of my throat. No longer in a rush, we shift and move together, sweet and tender.

"I love you so much," I whisper.

He smiles, nose brushing my cheek as he speaks against my lips. "I love you, too."

We stay like that, wrapped in each other, bringing each other to the edge over and over until we tip into bliss.

chapter twenty-seven

MOVING FORWARD

Kitty

Life shifts after the interview with Brit. My ideals shift along with it. I love what I do, and I love my authentic fans, but I need separation from the social media onslaught. So Fancy takes over posting on my socials, which means I can focus on taking care of my clients. I still interact with my followers, but I don't want that part of my job to influence the way I feel about myself, or what I do, so I try to let go of some of the responsibility. I take on what I need to and give myself space from the rest.

A few weeks after the interview, I help move my sister into her new apartment in the city with the assistance of Miles and Josh. It's a busy day full of lifting boxes and unpacking, but it's totally worth it to see my sister so excited for her future.

Once we're finished, Miles and I head back to his place, which is only a few blocks away. Prince Francis and Wilfred appear at the end of the hall as Miles ushers me inside the front door. They come in for pets and love, then head for the kitchen. I've taken to bringing Prince Francis along when I stay at Miles's place, since he and Wilfred get along so well. We've found that adding Herman to the dynamic isn't as seamless, since Prince Francis gets jealous. But it's a relationship work in progress.

I follow Miles down the hall, and we feed our fur babies before he grabs a beer for himself and glass of wine for me. We should probably shower, but a drink on the couch seems like a good way to decompress.

"How do you think your mom is going to handle Hattie's move?" Miles asks as he takes the cushion beside mine.

"She had friends over when we called to give her a virtual tour of the apartment, and that feels like a big step in the right direction." I sip my wine, considering how different things have been over the past few months. How my mom's social life has flourished recently. "I think...I've been using my mom as a crutch."

"How do you mean?" Miles stretches his arm along the back of the couch and fingers the end of my ponytail.

"My mom isn't the one who had a problem moving on. It's been me. I didn't want things to change, or maybe I made it difficult for her to feel like she could change, so nothing did. But over the past few months she's started to live again. She's spending more time with friends. Doing different things, developing new hobbies. I feel like I've been holding her back this whole time." And recently she stopped setting a place for Dad at the table. The first time it happened I was shocked, thinking maybe she just forgot. I didn't set the place, though. And then it happened the next time we sat down for a meal, and the next, and the next.

Miles strokes my cheek with a single finger. "It's not fair for you to shoulder the blame for that. Or for you to take responsibility for your mother's lack of action until now. Maybe the changes in *your* life have inspired her to make changes in her own. From what I've seen, you're a very tight family, and it seems a lot more likely that it wasn't one-sided. You were all holding each other up, and sometimes when people lean on each other too much, they can't step back and see how it's impacting them. But your career is taking off, and Hattie is starting hers, so I'm guessing your mom saw you taking steps forward and maybe realized she could do the same. You can only make your own choices, Kitty, and the ones you've been making since I met you have all been in line with supporting the people you love, and learning how to give yourself permission to live your own life."

"How do you always know exactly what to say?"

"I don't. I just know what I see in you, and that's an amazing, caring, selfless woman who has spent a lot of time putting her family's needs ahead of her own. I get that some of that was based on guilt over what happened to your dad. But you were a teenager who was trying to make dinner and not step on your family pet. If you'd had any idea your dad was in trouble, you would have dropped everything." He sweeps his thumbs under my eyes, wiping away tears.

"I don't know why I'm so emotional."

"Because things are changing, and it might be for the better for everyone, but it doesn't mean it stops being scary, or hard."

I cover his hand with mine. "I'm so glad you came into my life when you did. You're the one who made me see that sometimes change is exactly what we need."

"The feeling is completely mutual, in case you were wondering. And if you're interested in making any additional big changes, you're always welcome to take up the right side of my bed permanently." He gives me a lopsided, slightly uncertain smile.

"Are you inviting me to move in with you?" My stomach does a somersault, and my heart stutters.

"I'm extending an open invitation for whenever you're ready for more change." He cups my face between his palms. "In case you need reminding, I love you, Kitty. My favorite days are the ones where I wake up with you beside me."

"I love you, too. And I'd absolutely love to claim the right side of your bed permanently. I'll happily deal with a cat who gets jealous when we spoon and waking up to Wilfred breathing in my face."

He dips down and presses his lips to mine. I feel his love, not just in his words and his kiss, but right down to my soul.

chapter twenty-eight

HART TO HART

Kitty

O n Sunday afternoon I head back home. I definitely want to move in with Miles, but it means a lot of schedule changes and commuting out of the city to make my current client runs. It will take planning and possibly hiring another person. I can handle the bulk of the clients who are on the fringe of the city, and I have a handful I don't want to give up, but I'm sure I can make it work.

The other, bigger issue is telling my mom. Especially since I just moved Hattie yesterday, and I'm aware that having two adult children move out one right after the other is beyond monumental. So I'm fully prepared to make the transition slowly, over several months if necessary.

I don't want to abandon my mom, but I do want to start building a life of my own. One that includes Miles and Wilfred and Prince Francis. If I've learned anything since I met Miles, it's that the people who hold you up are the ones you need to hold on to the tightest.

When I arrive home, my mother is pulling a fresh pie out of the oven. She stopped by Hattie's yesterday to see the apartment. It's the first time she's driven into the city in years. Hattie invited me to come for lunch, and because her apartment is close to Miles's place, it was easy for me to join them.

"Oh! I didn't realize you were coming back tonight. I thought you'd be staying with Miles until the morning."

"I have a couple clients I need to check on this evening, and I have early stops in the morning," I explain.

"I was planning to have dinner with Marie." Her expression reflects uncertainty. "Should I cancel? Or maybe you'd like to join us?"

I don't want her to feel bad for having a life and living it. "That's okay. You don't need to change your plans on my account. It was a busy weekend, so I'll be in bed early."

"If you're sure you'll be okay on your own." She still seems ambivalent.

"I'll have Prince Francis to keep me company."

He comes trotting into the kitchen and plunks his butt by his food dish.

"Okay. He's definitely good company." Mom bends to give him a pet, then unties her apron and hangs it on the hook. "Hattie's new place looks great. I'm so glad she had you to help her."

"It is. And she's excited about this new job and living in the city. And it's nice that her apartment isn't too far from Miles."

"You've been spending a lot of time with him lately. It seems like it's getting pretty serious." I can tell she's fishing.

I decide to bite the bullet and tell her the truth. "He asked me to move in with him."

She props her hip against the counter and smiles knowingly. "I wondered when that was coming."

"You don't seem surprised."

"That boy is a smitten kitten. That was clear from the first time he came to pick you up. And you click. It reminds me of the way your dad and I were when we first met. You have the spark. Moving in together is the next logical step."

"Mmm. It is, but it's a big step."

"What worries you about it?"

"I've never lived anywhere but here, and with anyone but you and Hattie, and Dad...until he passed. I've never lived on my own. It's a big shift to go from living with family to living with a partner."

Mom nods in understanding. "Everyone's path is different, and ours hasn't necessarily been the easiest one to navigate. There's no right or wrong way to do this, Kitty. If you want to move into your own apartment first, then you can do that. But if you feel like this is the right time to move in with Miles, then that's what you should do."

"What about you, though? You'll be in this big house all by yourself." This is the part I'm having the hardest time with. "And Hattie just moved out, and now I'm dropping another potential move-out bomb on you."

Mom covers my hand with hers. "Oh, honey, it's not your responsibility to make sure I'm taken care of, and I realize that's a role you've taken on for a lot of years." She sighs. "After your dad passed, I felt...lost and broken. My heart was in pieces because my partner was gone, and it felt like my soul had been torn in half. And there you were, making sure dinner was on the table every night when I was struggling to keep it together. You made sure your sister got to school every day and that she didn't forget her lunch."

"We were all grieving, and it was hardest on you."

She smiles gently. "You don't need to make excuses for me. I wasn't a very present mother for a couple years. And I know you went to a local college so you could make sure Hattie and I were taken care of. You've spent so much time putting your own life on hold to make sure our family was okay. In a lot of ways you became both mother and father. And I've struggled to find a way to step back into those shoes. But I can do that now, for you. You've sacrificed more than enough for this family, Kitty. If moving in with your boyfriend is what you want to do, then you should, without worrying about anything but how you're going to feel about someone else's dirty socks being mixed in with yours."

"Will you be able to carry the house on your own?" The mortgage is paid off, but the cost of running a house on a single income might be more than is reasonable. I don't want my mom to lose this tie to Dad, and I don't want her to have to work more hours to make ends meet.

Mom nods. "I have things covered. And I have it on good authority that there's a unit in Marie's subdivision coming up for sale soon. I really love it there. With Hattie already in the city and you potentially moving in with Miles when you feel the time is right, it's probably a good time for me to consider downsizing. This is a great house for a family, but you're right that it's a lot for one person."

"Would you sell the house?" I've lived here my entire life. Every first took place inside these walls. And maybe that's another reason I haven't taken this step, because moving out would mean leaving behind so much of my history.

Mom taps her lip. "It's a hard balance to strike, isn't it, letting go of the things that hold so many important memories for us?" She takes my hands in hers. "For a long time, I needed the comfort of the memories, but I allowed them to take over. I see that now. And as much as I love this house and the memories we made here, they're all tucked safely inside our hearts." She squeezes my hands gently. "Sometimes, we have to let go of the past to make room for a brighter future."

She pulls me in for a hug, and I feel her love like a balm to my heart. We're all moving forward, leaving behind the hurts of the past so we can embrace what's coming next.

After we shed a few tears, I usher my mom out the door, telling her to enjoy her night with Marie. Once she leaves, I plop down on the couch with my laptop. Prince Francis joins me, so I move the laptop to the neighboring cushion. Prince Francis kneads his sharp claws into my legs until I'm tenderized and curls into a ball in my lap. He's wearing a sweatshirt that I'm pretty sure my mom made for him out of old baby clothes.

It's awkward to check my social media when my computer is sitting next to me. I only do this every couple of days now, but I'm grateful that it no longer scares me the way it did after the meme situation. People still love to share their feelings, and they don't always sugar-coat them, but I've learned to put what Miles calls my Lego armor on before I do that: a temporary shield that I can put on or take off when I need to. I remind myself that there are always going to be people who like to tear each other down, and when that happens, I'll take a break and let someone who doesn't have the same emotional connection to my audience deal with it. Sometimes an impartial observer is the best way to go.

I go through new tags first, thanking people and commenting on posts, before I switch to my email. I start at the oldest ones first, scheduling responses to go out first thing in the morning so I don't get replies in the middle of the night on a Sunday.

There are several new client emails. There's now an integrated form so people can provide details up front, including days and times they would be looking for cat-sitting services, whether it's long or short term, and the age and personality of their pet. That way, when we're looking to pair them with one of the Kitty Whisperer staff, we can assess who would be a good fit before we've even had a chance to meet.

As I'm working through my emails, one in particular catches my attention. It's from a prominent and well-known animal rescue association. I click on the email and read the contents:

Dear Ms. Hart,

As longtime fans of Brit Sheers and her heavy involvement in cat and animal rescue initiatives, we watched your segment on your cat-sitting and training service business, and we love what you're doing. We're currently in the process of developing a new initiative in Toronto that focuses on cat rehabilitation and pairing cats in need of special care with loving humans. With your knowledge and experience in the field, we feel you would make an incredible addition to our team. Your gentle approach would make you a fabulous leader for our carefully selected staff. We would love to meet with you to discuss this further at your earliest convenience. You can find out more about this pilot project HERE.

We look forward to hearing from you and hope that you'll consider joining the A Place for Paws Team.

Best,
Mary Jane Felt
CEO of A Place for Paws

I read the email over at least six times before I finally click on the link. And my heart melts. The proposed initiative is to create a training and adoption program for cats that have various exceptionalities with a focus on integration and regular visits from the staff at A Place for Paws while the adopted cats transition into their new homes.

It's essentially my dream job. And they want me to help lead the pilot project.

My stomach does a few flip-flops as I compose a response. I pause to scratch Prince Francis's head when he butts it against my thigh. "I feel like everything is falling into place. How much would you love to be the older brother to a whole bunch of kitties?" I give him a scratch under the chin, and he yawns widely. "I see how it is. You're playing it cool. What an amazing opportunity. I have to go for the interview."

Prince Francis meows his agreement.

I hit Send on the email.

chapter twenty-nine

PAWSITIVE CHANGES

Kitty

This is clearly fate telling us that you're supposed to move to the city and we're destined to live together." Miles kisses me on the temple, then trails several more along my cheek until he reaches my lips.

"Let me get the interview under my belt before you go dusting off your crystal ball." Any other thoughts I would like to put into words get lost in my head when he covers my mouth with his and kisses me breathless.

Half an hour and two orgasms later, Miles and I are sitting on the couch in his living room. Wilfred and Prince Francis are close by, snuggling in Wilfred's bed. Which is also now Prince Francis's bed. Those two are practically inseparable these days. And on the nights where we're not here at Miles's, Prince Francis is mopey, as though he misses his best four-legged friend.

"I can put a pin in making officially official plans for you and Prince Francis to move in with me and Wilfred until you've gone for the interview, but this job sounds perfect for you." Miles adjusts my legs so they lie across his lap.

"It really does." I called Miles last night to tell him the news, after which he went on a Google mission to find out everything he could about the company. Then he created a pros and cons spreadsheet about taking the job over continuing to grow the Kitty Whisperer. And he also created a third column, with the potential to continue to do both without burning myself out.

"If you want to do both, you can, and there's real potential for the Kitty Whisperer to continue expanding, if that's your goal. I bet they'd even be willing to partner with you if you brought that to the table. You're an invaluable resource, Kitty, and they clearly see that. Your face on their pilot project will go a long way to making it successful. Ask for what you want tomorrow, and tell them you don't want to give up what you've built. And if you like what they're offering you, then ask them to help you find a way to make it work."

"It's hard to believe a few days ago I was plugging along, doing my day to day, and now here I am, interviewing for a new job, potentially moving to the city. It's like my whole world has been turned upside down in the best way possible." After the initial panic, in which I questioned whether I could honestly and truly handle all the changes life was throwing at me, I called my sister.

She echoed what my mother said. And then she told me to go upstairs and stand in her bedroom and tell her what I saw. Nothing had changed in the days since she moved, but everything had changed. The things that had made it her room had gone with her to the apartment in the city. Sure, it was still a bedroom, but the life that had occupied it was missing. The little things that would trigger memories had disappeared.

Change happened regardless of whether we called on it. I could choose to embrace it or fight it, but it was coming for me, no matter what. So I embraced it. All of it. From the interview to moving in with Miles. And I started by bringing over a few outfits to keep in his closet.

The next morning Wilfred wakes us up with his stinky dog-breath alarm.

"Stay right where you are. I'll take care of these two, and then I'll take care of you." Miles rolls out of bed, and Prince Francis and Wilfred follow him to the bathroom. They sit in front of the door, tails wagging in unison while they wait for him to do his business and then continue to the kitchen to feed them.

I grab a fruity Mentos from the roll in the nightstand drawer and lose my nightshirt. We finally figured out what Miles is allergic to. Apparently, as a kid he used to have a strange reaction to anything minty. His tongue would get itchy and his mouth would peel, so he's avoided all minty things since. A few weeks ago, I kissed him after I had a mint hot chocolate, and his lips puffed up slightly, but an antihistamine later, they were back to their normal full kissableness.

The following week, I picked up a toy for Prince Francis that contained catnip. And Miles had a full-blown allergic reaction that required me to inject him with his EpiPen, a trip to the ER, and a formal mint allergy diagnosis. Catnip is part of the mint family. No more getting high for Prince Francis, and no more mint-mocha beverages for me.

A minute later, Miles returns and closes the door behind him, so we have some privacy. We've learned the hard way that leaving the door open, even a crack, is not a good idea when we're planning to have naked fun.

Prince Francis yowls when I moan too loudly, and Wilfred joins in with forlorn howling. Feeding them tends to keep them busy long enough that we can get in some private time without an unwanted chorus.

Miles joins me under the sheets, our legs tangling. "I can't wait to wake up to your beautiful face every single morning." He slants his mouth over mine, and we both sink into the kiss. We make slow, lazy love, enjoying the closeness and the comfort we find in each other before we leave the haven of his bed.

My interview isn't until ten this morning, and Miles doesn't have to be at the rink until eleven, so we take our time making breakfast, and we talk about the interview and the questions I should ask.

Miles walks me down to the parking garage at nine-thirty and gives me a long, lingering kiss. "I'd wish you luck, but you don't need it, since this is basically them trying to woo you."

"Cross your fingers for me that it goes well anyway."

I hop into my Cat-mobile and drive to A Place for Paws. It's only twenty minutes from Miles's apartment, which is another checkmark in the pro column.

I'm greeted by a young woman dressed in scrubs with a cat face pattern on them. "Kitty Hart! You're here." She extends a hand; her eyes are wide and she looks as nervous as I feel.

"Hi. And yes, I am."

She shakes her head and has a full-body reaction that reminds me of someone being shocked. By a live electrical wire. "I'm so sorry. My name is Annie. I'm one of the resident cat lovers. My job is to love the new kitties they bring in for us to rehabilitate. Mary Jane is just speaking with the vet, but she'll be out in a minute. Can I show you around while you're waiting?"

"Sure. That sounds great."

"Awesome. Fantastic." She claps her hands and grins. "I'm still kind of in shock that you're standing here. I'm a huge fan." She cringes. "I promised myself I'd keep my cool, but I'm failing so hard right now."

"I'm just a cat lover who happens to have gone viral with a video." I wink.

Her eyes go wide again. "I can't believe that happened. And I saw the whole video that Brit Sheers posted. And you were right about the geese. It is like we've channeled all our meanness into that one animal."

"I know! They're ridiculously surly creatures, aren't they?"

"They really are." Annie nods her agreement and leads me down the hall.

She opens a door to a large room. It's a cat's playground

paradise. There are cat trees spread throughout the room at various intervals, and stairs fixed to the walls leading to perches for cats to hang out on. Several kitties keep watch from the highest points in the room, guarding their territory. Other cats lounge in beds or zoom around the space, playing with toys or each other.

"This is incredible." It's exactly the kind of space I wanted to set up for the Kitty Whisperer in the future when I had my own house and could dedicate a space to my furry charges. Or when I had the capital to rent a space.

"It's my favorite room. This is where our healthy cats who enjoy the companionship of both humans and furry friends hang out during the day. We have a smaller room for the more skittish ones, and the ones who need social training," Annie tells me.

"This is perfect. Where do they sleep at night?"

"Come, I'll show you." Annie guides me down the hall to another room. This one has individual cages, but they're not like little cells. Instead, they're decorated with toys, and each one has a cat bed and a cat stuffie. "This is where we keep the kitties who sleep best on their own, but we have another room for communal sleeping."

She takes me next door, where there are a few cats curled up together, enjoying naptime. A tabby puts his paw over his eyes and rolls away from us, obviously not interested in being disturbed.

"Do you foster feral families sometimes?"

"We do. We have special rooms for them as well."

A woman peeks her head in. "I thought I might find you in here. I hope you're enjoying your tour."

"It's great. Annie is a fantastic guide."

The woman, who I recognize as the CEO of A Place for Paws, holds out a hand. "I'm Mary Jane. We spoke over email. Thank you so much for taking time out of your day to meet with us."

"It's honestly a pleasure. This place is fabulous."

She doesn't take me to a boardroom; instead we grab coffees (with takeout cup lids to avoid drinking cat fur) and sit in the kitty playground, where she tells me all about the pilot project.

We both end up with cats in our laps as she talks about how her vision is to take what I've built with the Kitty Whisperer and make it a full-service program, with a vet on staff and feline care support available for the adoptive families.

"We don't want to take you away from what you've already built, Kitty," Mary Jane explains. "We're hoping, if you're interested, that we could merge your business model with ours. That way you can keep doing what you love, while helping us start up this new program."

"This all sounds amazing. I'll need a few weeks to get things organized with my staff, though."

"You can take all the time you need. I don't want to get ahead of myself, but does this mean you're coming on board?"

I don't even have to think about it. I already know the answer. "I would love to be part of your team."

Over the next few weeks, I find myself busier than I've ever been. I approach Fancy, my vet tech student, about taking a more managerial role in the Kitty Whisperer, which she's more than happy to do. We agree that over the next two months my time will slowly shift from three days a week with the Kitty Whisperer down to two, and eventually down to one, where I'm just signing off on paperwork—we hire someone to take care of most of that—and reviewing client files. But I keep one day a week for visits, because my love of cats is the reason I started the Kitty Whisperer.

And as I transition, that's what I find myself doing. I not only spend time with my feline friends, but I also help find them new homes, and I work with people who love animals with the same soft heart I do.

While I'm making big life changes, so is my mom. She ends up buying a smaller, two-bedroom house in the same development as Marie and sells the house I grew up in. Hattie and I help her pack. There's catharsis in sorting through our history. And while we might shed some tears, there's also laughter and love, and the knowledge that our memories stay with us. Home doesn't have to be defined by a place, it's where we find our strongest emotional bonds. It's a shelter created from love.

HOLD THE A-CLAWS

Miles

One Year Later

I wake up to the feel of a sandpaper tongue on my cheek. I crack a lid and find two blue eyes staring back at me. "You look like an angry gargoyle." I roll over, but I'm greeted with dog breath. "Why don't they harass you in the morning?" I grumble.

"Because you're the one who gives in whenever they beg for food." Kitty's front presses against my back, and her arm comes around my waist.

I roll her way and press my lips to her temple.

Prince Francis takes the opportunity for what it is and plunks his butt down on my chest, continuing with his angry gargoyle impression. Kitty giggles and rubs under his chin. He flops over on his side and lands in the crack between our bodies. He struggles to right himself for a moment, then relocates to the pillows and wraps his body around Kitty's head.

Wilfred sets his chin on the edge of the mattress and gives me his sad eyes while whimpering.

"I feel like we're going to end up with really spoiled kids if these two are anything to go on." My eyes flare, and I look down at Kitty. "I mean one day, eventually, in the future. Probably the distant future. After we get married." I purse my lips and bite them to keep me from digging a bigger hole.

While a lot of things have changed in the past year, my ability to stick my foot in my mouth has not.

"Are you saying you want to marry me?" Kitty's smile is full of amusement.

"I'm kind of attached to you."

That beautiful smile of hers widens. "I'm kind of attached to you, too."

She tips her chin up and I tip mine down so our lips can connect.

"I love you more than Wilfred loves cookie treats." I slide my arm under her and pull her closer.

"And I love you more than Prince Francis loves licking his balls in front of company," Kitty replies.

We both snort-giggle, then go back to making out.

Wilfred paws at my arm and whimpers, while Prince Francis starts grooming our foreheads, forcing us to break apart.

"Maybe we should hit pause and feed them before this goes any further," I suggest.

Kitty sighs. "Probably a good idea. I'll feed Prince Francis, and you feed Wilfred?"

Two minutes later we're back in bed, the door to our room closed as we make morning love. It's my favorite way to start my day.

Forty-five minutes later we're sated, showered, and dressed. Kitty and I stand side by side in the kitchen, working around each other as I fry bacon and she toasts English muffins for our egg sandwiches.

Despite having just eaten their own breakfasts, Wilfred and Prince Francis are also seated side by side on the kitchen floor, their tails swinging in tandem, hopeful that we'll drop something delicious. We sit at the kitchen table and talk about our plans for the day.

"I'm heading to Terra Cotta this morning, and I'm taking Prince Francis and Wilfred by to see your mom while I'm there."

The pilot project with A Place for Paws has gone over incredibly well. It's been backed by several celebrities, including Brit Sheers, and they're developing a training program so other shelters can create something similar. And the Kitty Whisperer has grown exponentially, thanks to the support and help of A Place for Paws. We have a storefront now, with an office and staff, still based in Terra Cotta, where everything started. Kat's Cat Café has become part of the project, too, and cats who are good with people often end up there on their way to finding their forever home. It's been amazing to watch Kitty grow as a person and a businesswoman. She's an inspiration, and I'm lucky to have her sunshine in my life.

"That'll be great. She'll love that." The home has been great about allowing pet visits, and my mom is thriving in the social setting. "Will you stop and see your mom, too?"

"She's squeezing me in for a lunch date between all the other things she has going on."

"Sounds like someone else I know," I say teasingly.

Since her move, Lucile's social life has blossomed, and she's mentioned a "gentleman friend" that she's been out with a lot recently.

"The apple doesn't fall far from the tree, apparently," Kitty says with a sly grin.

We finish breakfast, clean up our dishes, and get ready to leave for work. Kitty and I dress Prince Francis and Wilfred in matching sweaters, since today is supposed to be on the chilly side.

"Don't forget that we have dinner plans tonight," I remind her after we load our fur-children into the back of her Cat-mobile.

"It's on my calendar. I'll be home before five so I can de-fur myself and make this pretty." She motions to her face.

"You're always pretty."

"And you're always handsome."

I drop a kiss on her lips and open the driver's side door for her. I allow her to pull out of her spot before I hop into my car.

I head to work in a great mood, but I'm distracted during practice, because my head is elsewhere. Thankfully, Josh is on the ball, and he picks up my slack. Parker has truly blossomed over the past two seasons. He's one of the top players in the league, with an impressive scoring record. The team renewed my contract for five years and I've been given a substantial raise. I feel like I've found my calling, and there's real satisfaction in knowing that I'm part of the reason why our team has been steadily improving since they brought me on board.

"Tonight's the night?" Josh asks as we leave the arena and head for our cars.

"Tonight's the night."

"You need any help setting things up?" He spins his keys around on his finger.

"Nope. But if all goes well, I'm going to need your help a lot over the coming months."

"I'm ready for it." He claps me on the shoulder. "Kitty's sister will probably be heavily involved, too, won't she?"

I give him the side-eye. "There's a very good chance of that, yeah."

He managed to get her number after he helped move her into her apartment, but I warned him not to get involved with her if she was just going to end up as a notch on his bedpost. I'm guessing he took the advice and backed off, because as far as I know, he never did call.

I'm grateful that my day ends early. It means I can pick up all the things I need for tonight, including a premade dinner from Kitty's favorite restaurant. That way all I have to do is heat it up and not make a mess of the kitchen. I arrive home at four in the afternoon. I preheat the oven and jump in the shower, then put on fresh dress pants and a button-down.

The moment Kitty walks in the door, she makes a beeline for the bathroom, telling me she needs to have a quick shower.

I call after her to take her time. I feed Prince Francis and Wilfred, because they'll follow me around and Prince Francis will yell at me until I give him food, which is distracting, and I don't need to be tripping over them when I'm rushing around.

I quickly set the table, light a couple of candles, and put dinner in the oven to warm. By this time, Prince Francis and Wilfred have finished scarfing down their dinners, so I dress them up in their new outfits. I pull the bottle of champagne from the fridge and set it on the table. I don't want to pop the cork preemptively. Just in case.

"Okay! I'm all set! I don't think I asked where we're going tonight. Oh!" Kitty comes to an abrupt halt when she sees the setup. "What's all this?" She bites her lip, gaze flitting from me to the table to Wilfred and Prince Francis. Wilfred is being his usual well-behaved self, sitting beside me, tail wagging happily. Prince Francis has one leg extended and is licking his toes.

"I thought we could have a romantic night in." I clasp my hands in front of me, then behind my back, suddenly nervous.

Kitty crosses the room and comes to a stop in front of me. She smooths her hands over my chest and links them behind my neck. "I love it. What's the occasion?"

I lift a shoulder and let it fall. "Not really an occasion, per se. I mean, I'd like it to become an occasion. But it isn't one yet."

Her brows pull together in a slight furrow. Probably because what I've just said is confusing.

"I love you," I blurt.

"I love you, too."

"And I want to love you for the rest of my life."

She smiles up at me. "That's good, because I want to do the same thing."

"Good. Okay. That's great. This sort of seems like the perfect segue."

I get another confused look. "Perfect segue for what?"

I unlink her hands from around my neck and jam my hand into my pocket. At the same time, I drop to one knee in front of her. Unfortunately, Prince Francis's tail swishes in my direction as I kneel, and his tail ends up under my knee.

He yowls loudly, hisses, and swats at me, managing to get the back of my hand. The one holding the small velvet box. Which I drop on the floor. It pops open and Wilfred lunges for it, probably thinking it's a toy.

"No, Wilfred!" I do the only thing I can, which is shoulder him out of the way and cover the box with my body. Wilfred clearly thinks this is a game, because he jumps on top of me and starts trying to nose his way under me, his dog breath and his tongue all over my face.

"Oh my gosh! Wilfred, off!" Kitty pulls him back. "Sit!" she orders. "That's a good boy." I roll over and sit up and covertly check the small box to make sure the contents are still inside. Thankfully it is.

"Are you okay? Your hand is bleeding."

"It's fine. I'm fine. It's just a scratch." I glance around the room for Prince Francis. He's now sitting on the arm of the couch, licking his tail, giving me his angry gargoyle face.

"I should check it out, and we should disinfect it." Kitty's expression reflects her concern.

"In a minute. You can let go of Wilfred." I grab one of his toys from the floor and toss it across the room, then resume my kneeling position and flip open the box.

Kitty's breath leaves her on a whoosh. "Oh."

"Kitty, you came into my life exactly when I needed you the most."

Prince Francis meows loudly from the arm of the couch as Wilfred rushes by and drops his toy at my feet.

"Let me amend that. You and Prince Francis came into my and Wilfred's life at exactly the right time."

Wilfred sets his chin on my outstretched arm. Kitty bends to pick up the toy and throws it again. "And you came into our lives at exactly the right time."

"I love you, and every moment of every day, that love grows. I want to spend the rest of my life waking up next to you and falling asleep beside you. I want to raise fur babies and real babies with you. I want you to be my wife. Will you marry me?"

"You are the most amazing man, Miles Thorn. And I can't imagine my life without you in it. I want all the same things, and I would absolutely love to be your wife."

I lift the ring from its velvet cushion and manage to get it on her finger before Wilfred comes back again with his toy. I try to nudge him out of the way, but he licks my face, completely oblivious to the moment he's ruining.

"Dude, read the room." I push up to a stand, which means Wilfred tries to stuff his nose in my crotch.

Kitty laughs, and I do too. And then I take her face in my hands, ignoring the scratches on the back of it, and press my lips to hers. "You're a sunrise in human form," I tell her. "And I'm lucky I get to see you shine every single day."

ACKNOWLEDGMENTS

As always, thank you to my husband and daughter, who inspire me endlessly and are my biggest and most amazing supporters.

Debra, you're the pepper to my salt and the Kat to my Kitty.

Kimberly, thank you so much for helping me mold and refine every tale I tell. You're amazing, and I appreciate all you do.

Sarah Pie, I'm forever grateful for your friendship. Thank you for being such a steadfast and amazing source of support all these years. Hustlers, you're fabulous, and I adore you.

Leah and my team at Forever, thank you making this book such a joy to write and refine. I'm so glad Kitty and Miles have a home with you.

My Beavers, thank you for your love of love stories and for sharing my excitement for every release! You're my favorite place to be when I'm not hanging out in my imagination with my characters.

To my book world friends Deb, Tijan, Trisha, Catherine, thank you for being such awesome people. I'm lucky to have you in my life.

Krystin and Marnie, thank you for always celebrating the

wins with me. You're incredible friends, and it's an honor to know you.

To my readers, bloggers, bookstagrammers, and booktokkers, thank you for loving love stories and for sharing that love. It's an honor to be part of this special community.

ABOUT THE AUTHOR

New York Times and *USA Today* bestselling author Helena Hunting lives outside of Toronto with her amazing family and her two awesome cats, who think the best place to sleep is her keyboard. She writes all things romance—contemporary, romantic comedy, sports, and angsty new adult. Helena loves to bake cupcakes, has been known to listen to a song on repeat 1,512 times while writing a book, and if she has to be away from her family, she prefers to be in warm weather with her friends.